Whatever it was between them, it couldn't be stopped.

She slid her hand down his chest, his heart beating beneath her fingers.

"I've been dead inside for so long. But now, with you, I feel..." Tucker paused, his gaze swallowing hers. "I feel alive. So for tonight, let's concentrate on what we have right here, right now. And tomorrow will take care of itself. Okay?"

"Absolutely," she whispered, getting lost in his eyes.

He crushed his lips to hers, their shared passion igniting into full flame. The kiss was as much a contest of wills as anything. Each of them trying to find control, and each knowing it was a losing battle.

He pushed her back onto the bed and she fell back against the pillows, pulling him with her, their lips still joined in an endless kiss that seemed to give and take and fill her all at once. For the first time in her life, Alexis let go, surrendering herself completely.

Raves for Dee Davis's A-Tac Series

DESPERATE DEEDS

"Delightful... The perfect weekend or vacation read. The fast-paced story takes you through an intriguing game of cat and mouse as protagonists solve the crime, save the world, and, of course, fall in love."

—*RT Book Reviews*

"Five Stars, Top Pick! This series is fast-paced and action-packed. This book is a keeper. I, for one, cannot wait to see what Ms. Davis will bring us next."

—NightOwlReviews.com

"Her books... hold my attention like a vise. I highly recommend this book."   —FreshFiction.com

"It is obvious that Ms. Davis has done her research to bring readers characters with knowledge and expertise... [A]n outstanding series."

—RomanceJunkiesReviews.com

"The characters were charming, the action fast-paced, and the romance hot. This is an author who knows how to pace a book and add conflict."

—Bookpleasures.com

DANGEROUS DESIRES

"Rich in dialogue [with] a strong heroine and intricate plot. Full of twists, turns, and near-death encounters, readers will consume this quickly and want more."
—*RT Book Reviews*

"Danger, deception, and desire are the main literary ingredients in Davis's high-adrenaline, highly addictive novel of romantic suspense." —*Chicago Tribune*

"Dee Davis never fails to write exciting, sensuous stories featuring a diversity of strong flawed characters you empathize with. *Dangerous Desires'* pace is perfect, the dialogue clever, and the plotlines are surprising, captivating, and brilliant." —ReadertoReader.com

"Five Stars, Top Pick! Exciting…It will grab your attention and keep a hold of it until the last page. I have put Ms. Davis on my auto buy list."
—NightOwlReviews.com

"Dee Davis is the reason I started reading romantic suspense…A definite page-turner that will have you clinging to the edge of your seat."
—Renees-Reads.blogspot.com

DARK DECEPTIONS

"High-stakes action and high-impact romance...Dee Davis leaves me breathless."
>—Roxanne St. Claire, *New York Times*
>bestselling author

"Dee Davis always keeps me on edge from start to finish! I read this book in one sitting...a keeper!"
>—FreshFiction.com

"Dee Davis sure knows how to nail a romantic suspense. Packed full of tension, action, and romance, this book is a page-turner from beginning to end."
>—BookPleasures.com

"5 Stars! Sparks fly between Annie and Nash...If you like a good romantic suspense story, you'll really enjoy this book."
>—JustShortofCrazy.com

"An exciting, fast-paced romantic suspense packed with action, adventure, and hot romantic chemistry."
>—FictionVixen.com

DEEP DISCLOSURE

DEE DAVIS

FOREVER

NEW YORK   BOSTON

Forever
Hachette Book Group
237 Park Avenue
New York, NY 10017

www.HachetteBookGroup.com

Forever is an imprint of Grand Central Publishing.
The Forever name and logo are trademarks of Hachette Book Group, Inc.

The publisher is not responsible for websites (or their content) that are not owned by the publisher.

Printed in the United States of America

First Edition: September 2011

10 9 8 7 6 5 4 3 2 1

ATTENTION CORPORATIONS AND ORGANIZATIONS:
Most HACHETTE BOOK GROUP books are available at quantity discounts with bulk purchase for educational, business, or sales promotional use. For information, please call or write:

Special Markets Department, Hachette Book Group
237 Park Avenue, New York, NY 10017
Telephone: 1-800-222-6747 Fax: 1-800-477-5925

*For the Whine Sisters—who keep me sane on
days when it doesn't seem possible!*

PROLOGUE

Walsenburg, Colorado

I 'm telling you, he likes you."

"Oh, please, there's no way." Lexie stopped at the corner under the streetlight and glared at her best friend. "He never even talks to me."

"That's because he likes you." Amanda smiled, shaking a finger to emphasize her point.

"Definitely circular logic," Lexie said, her heart beating just a little faster at the thought that Mike Kennedy might actually like *her*. Mike was the captain of the football team and practically the best-looking guy in town. Too high profile for her father, of course, but Lexie couldn't help thinking how it would feel to be Mike's girlfriend. She'd be the envy of all the girls, and, well, practically normal.

"But you want it to be true." Amanda's eyes sparkled in the lamplight.

"Yeah." Lexie grinned. "I guess I do. You really think there's a chance?"

"I'm sure of it." Amanda reached over to give her arm

a squeeze. "You're prettier than any of the other girls at school. And you're a heck of a lot more fun. All you really need to do is get out a bit more. I mean, in the six months since you moved here, this is the first time you've ever come with me to a basketball game."

"I'm not that into sports." Lexie felt the familiar weight of her guilt settle in her gut.

"Bull. I saw you at the game, remember? You were having a great time." Amanda frowned, her expression troubled. "Is there something wrong at home? Something maybe you should tell me?"

"No." Lexie shook her head, forcing a smile. "Everything's fine."

"So you'll come to the party on Friday night?"

"I don't know." Lexie sighed. "I'd like to, but I really don't think my dad will let me." Actually there was no question about it at all. Going to things like parties and basketball games were totally off limits. She'd only been able to go tonight because she'd lied to her mother and said she'd be at the library.

But there was no way she wanted to start making a habit of it. Her father's reasons were sound, and Lexie really didn't want to jeopardize everything by defying him. There'd be other nights when she could manage to slip out. But certainly not twice in one week.

"All right." It was Amanda's turn to sigh. "I won't push. But Mike Kennedy will be there."

"I know." Lexie chewed the side of her lip, thinking that maybe she could manage to sneak away. It was only a party, after all. No danger in that. "Maybe I can manage to go for a little while." She glanced down at her watch. "But only if I get home on time."

"Glad I don't have a curfew." Amanda's eyes were sympathetic. "Want me to walk with you?"

"No, I'm fine. I'll see you in school tomorrow." Lexie hugged her friend and then hurried down the street, breaking into a sprint as she headed for home. She was already a few minutes late, but in truth, her parents wouldn't be angry. They trusted her. Which made her feel all the worse for having lied. It seemed like she lied to everyone these days. To her friends about her life at home, and to her family about her life with her friends.

It was almost as if she were two people. One of them normal. One of them not.

She sighed, her thoughts turning to Mike Kennedy. It would be so amazing to be his girlfriend. But even as she had the thought she dismissed it. Some things were just beyond her reach. And no matter how much she might play at being a regular teenager, she wasn't one.

Lexie rounded the corner and skidded to a stop, her throat tightening as she tried to swallow her scream. At the end of the cul-de-sac, what was left of her house shown black against the fire-illuminated sky. Flames shot out of the roof, thrusting upward toward the heavens as if hell itself had found a portal from one world to the other.

Maybe it had.

Fire trucks and ambulances filled the street, neighbors standing barefooted on their lawns watching in horror. Lexie fought against the terror that held her frozen. She had to find her family, had to be sure that everyone was okay. She concentrated on her body, forcing her feet forward, one step at a time, moving faster and faster until she was running.

She tripped on a piece of fallen debris, the asphalt

from the street tearing her palms. Choking on bile and tears, she pushed herself to her feet and would have run again, except that someone was there, stopping her.

"Lexie, no. It's too late. There's nothing you can do."

She looked up into the face of her father's friend, trying to shake off his hands, to go to her father and mother. They struggled for a moment, and then she broke free, sprinting forward, only to hesitate at the sound of his voice behind her.

"You can't go. You're the only one left. If they get you then they win."

Lexie didn't want to hear his words, didn't want to face the reality of a world without her father, without her family. But she was her father's daughter, and the instinct for self-preservation was ingrained soul deep.

She sucked in a breath, her eyes still on the carnage in front of her. "You're sure they're all dead?"

"Positive." George's voice was as soft as his hand on her arm. "They're gone, Lexie."

"And the authorities? Do they think it was an accident?" She felt as if she'd aged a thousand years in a single moment, her childhood incinerated as completely as the house she'd called home.

"They're not saying anything. And I was afraid to ask." There was a note of apology in George's voice, but Lexie shook her head.

"It's all right. Daddy wouldn't want you to be caught either." There was a code among those in her community. Protect the right to anonymity at all costs. Some of the people she knew had done things, in the name of right, that if discovered would mean time in prison. Others, like her father, had simply been accused of things they'd never done.

But either way, the network would be secure only if they adhered to the rules.

Her gaze settled on the fiery tomb in front of her. Someone had obviously broken that trust. Betrayed her family. Betrayed her father.

And one thing Lexie was absolutely certain of—she wouldn't rest until the traitor paid.

CHAPTER 1

Redlands, California—Thirteen Years Later

Tucker Flynn was turning into his father. The old man had been nothing if not predictable. So much so that Tucker and his brother had always sworn to be just the opposite. And looking at recent history, he'd have to say they'd achieved their goal in spades.

Until now.

Tucker checked his watch as he stepped out of the car: exactly 10:30. Shit. It seemed he'd developed a routine. The coffee shop beckoned even as he considered hopping back into the Jeep and heading for the hills. Or at least somewhere that wasn't exactly the same as yesterday, and the day before that, and the day before that.

Hell.

He blew out a long breath and shook his head in disgust. After years in prison in San Mateo, he'd have thought routine would be the last thing he desired. And yet here he was, newspaper in hand with a hankering for a cup of coffee and the caramel rolls Weatherbees was famous for. After holding the door for an exiting man in a Dodgers hat, Tucker walked inside and took his customary place in the corner booth, partially from habit, but also a remnant of his espionage days. It was always better to keep your back to the wall and your eyes on the room.

Not that there was anything to see, really. Redlands was a sleepy little town with little to recommend it but a university, a backdrop of mountains and orange groves, and a handful of mansions left over from the railroad-baron days. Tucker's father had been a schoolteacher. His mother...well, *bitch* was the word that came to mind. She hadn't been able to deal with small-town America, even Southern California style. So she'd hit the road, leaving Tucker's dad with two little boys. He'd risen to the occasion but lost a part of himself in the process.

Maybe that's why all the routines.

Tucker nodded as the waitress brought him his coffee and roll. He never talked to any of them, but that didn't mean they didn't know who he was. There'd been a flurry of newspaper articles when he'd first come home. Native son, risen from the dead and all that. The official story was that he'd managed to escape the plane crash that killed the rest of his unit, but wound up in a hospital with no memory of what happened.

Of course the real truth—his escape from Colombia, his friend's betrayal, and Lena's death—none of that was public knowledge. Hell, the brass at Langley had buried it so damn deep Tucker doubted it would ever come to light. Which suited him just fine.

He sipped his coffee, his gaze moving slowly around the diner. The place was pretty empty, the morning crowd long gone and the lunchtime rush still an hour or so away.

A couple across the way was canoodling over lattes. A businessman one booth up was lost in the financial pages. And an older man in the far corner was fidgeting with his spoon as he gazed out the window, clearly waiting for something or someone.

Tucker dropped his gaze, trying to focus on the sports page. The Bulldogs had pulled out a walk-off win in the ninth. And in LA the Angels had beaten the Yankees. First game in the series. If Drake were still here, they'd probably be on their way to the stadium right now. But Drake was in New York, at Sunderland. Or maybe he was off on a mission. Hard to know for certain. Although his wife, Madeline, usually called when he left the country.

Maybe Tucker should have gone with them when they'd headed back to New York. Maybe he'd be better off working again. But that part of his life was over. Dead and buried. Pain, pointed and heavy, speared his gut. Lena. He closed his eyes, memories of her smile dancing just beyond his reach, her laughter echoing deep inside him.

Angry at his maudlin turn of thought, he took a sip of coffee, the hot, acrid beverage pulling him firmly back into the present. The older man was standing now, a smile of joy spreading across his face as a young woman strode through the doorway, arms extended.

"George," she cried, throwing herself into his arms. "It's been so long."

The two of them moved out of earshot as they walked back to his table, but even without words Tucker could feel her joy. Blonde in a way that only women in California seemed to be able to achieve, naturally or otherwise, she was tall and lithe, her body bronzed by the sun, a dimple in her left cheek making her seem even younger. Her eyes crinkled at the corners when she smiled, and her hands were in constant motion as she talked. The old man's face lit up in her presence, the years seeming to drop away.

Tucker idly wondered at their connection. Father, maybe. Although she'd called him by his first name. He rejected the notion that they were amorously connected. Neither of them seemed the May-December type. Old friends, then. That much was clear. He smiled, still watching the two of them, their hands joined together as their voices lowered and the tone of the conversation turned serious.

Tucker shook his head, wondering when his life had gotten so dull he'd started living vicariously through total strangers. Next he'd start adopting cats. He cut off a piece of the caramel roll and stuffed it into his mouth.

A burst of synthesized music signaled an incoming call, and he grabbed the cell phone, grateful for the interruption. "Flynn," he barked into the phone.

"Same here," came the answer, a thread of laughter lacing through his brother, Drake's, voice. "Thought I'd check in and see how you're doing."

"Bored out of my fucking mind," Tucker said, not making any effort to sugarcoat his words. "I'm at Weatherbees, and I think I'm turning into Dad."

"It could be worse," Drake replied. "You could be turning into our mother."

"Bite your tongue." Tucker shifted so he could better see the blonde. "Anyway, what's up? You don't usually call to chat." She was still waving her hands, but they clearly conveyed anger now. Seemed the joyous reunion had turned sour.

"Hey, can't a guy check in on his brother?" Drake asked, pulling Tucker's attention back to his conversation.

"A guy, yes. You, no. You're not the nurturing type."

"Well, I sure as hell better be," his brother mumbled. "Actually, that's why I'm calling. I've got news." There was a pause, and Tucker smiled. His brother was never at a lack for words. Except when it had to do with Madeline.

"So, what?" Tucker teased. "Your wife left you?"

"Give me a break," Drake said. "The woman adores me."

"That she does," Tucker admitted, still smiling. Madeline Reynard Flynn was the kind of woman who loved without reservation. Drake had been lucky to find her. And Tucker was happy to have played a part in it. "So what's the news?"

"Hang on," Drake said, fumbling with the phone. "There's another call. Avery. Be right back."

The line went dead as his brother took the call from his boss. Tucker felt a stab of envy. He'd sworn he wouldn't go back to the life, but that didn't mean he was immune to the pull of it. There was a rush involved with working black ops, an adrenaline surge you couldn't get anywhere else.

He leaned back, phone to his ear, waiting for his brother to return. The blonde was on her feet now, her hands cutting through the air as she argued with the old man. He was standing too, fists on the table as he tried to make her see reason. Good luck with that. Tucker recognized the set of her shoulders. She wasn't about to give in. Whatever had set her off, the old man wasn't anywhere close to assuaging her.

"Hey, Tucker, you still there?" Drake asked. "Sorry about that. Company business."

"So you off to somewhere exciting? Is that the news?" Tucker waited, half listening, as he watched the blonde.

With a final snap of her head, she pivoted and stalked from the coffee shop, the old man left standing there, a look of resigned acceptance coloring his face. Whatever they'd fought about, he hadn't come out on the winning side.

"No. Well, actually, maybe yes. But that's not why I called. Madeline just found out she's pregnant. I'm going to be a father."

Drake's words were slow to penetrate, but when they did, Tucker let out a whoop. "Holy shit. That makes me an uncle."

"Well, not yet. It takes time."

"Nine months, I believe," Tucker said. "Anyway, it's awesome news." Outside a motor roared to life and the blonde peeled out of the parking lot. The old man was still standing there, hands on the table, looking as if he'd lost his last hope. "How far along is she?" Tucker asked.

"Just under two months. We're actually supposed to wait until after the three-month mark to tell people. But I couldn't wait."

"A new generation of Flynns. Definitely something to celebrate." Across the room the old man sat back down and reached into his pocket. Tucker nodded as his brother talked, even though he couldn't actually see him. Despite the importance of his brother's news, something was tugging at his brain.

From force of habit he searched the diner, trying to figure out what was bugging him.

"Tucker, are you listening to me?" his brother's voice broke into his reverie and he shook his head, certain that he was overreacting. This was Redlands, for God's sake.

"I'm here. Sorry. Just got distracted for a moment." He shook his head, chagrined at himself and his voyeuristic tendencies. "You were talking about due dates."

"Yeah. I said we want to be sure you're here when the time comes. Hell, you know I want you up here permanently."

"What? And turn into a Yankees fan?" Tucker laughed, his eyes still on the old man as he struggled to find something. "Not fucking likely."

"Hey, I'm still Angels all the way. You can take a guy out of California…"

"…but you can't take California out of the guy," Tucker finished for him. It was a catchphrase their dad had always used. "Well, at least some things don't change."

The old man was reaching into his back pocket now, his hands shaking as he struggled to find whatever he was looking for. Tucker frowned and then blew out a slow breath as he finally figured out what the hell it was that had been bugging him. A backpack. Underneath the old man's table. He tried to remember if the blonde had brought it in. But, to be honest, he'd been too distracted by her honey-colored skin and golden hair to notice. From its positioning, though, he was fairly certain it didn't belong to the old man.

"Tucker, what's going on?" Drake asked, concern coloring his voice. "You're not pissed because I'm having a baby before you?"

"Yeah, right." He frowned, forcing himself to ignore his instincts and concentrate on his brother.

"I'm sorry. I shouldn't have said that. I mean, if Lena had…" Drake trailed off, clearly uncomfortable.

"Lived? Yeah, well, even so, neither of us was the childrearing kind. So no worries, little brother."

"I didn't mean to—" Drake started, and then stopped.

"I know. And it's okay. Besides, I'm serious. I'm not cut out to be a father. Hell, maybe not even a husband.

Especially not now. Anyway, I'll leave all that to you and Madeline, and I'll play the role of doting uncle. That I can do."

"Yeah, I shudder to think exactly what that'll mean."

"The perfect trifecta. Baseball, hot dogs, and beer." Tucker laughed as the old man finally located his phone and started to dial. Beneath him the corner of the backpack lit up, blinking red. "Fuck," Tucker said, his gaze moving to the other patrons in the diner. "Everybody get down. Now."

"Tucker?" He heard his brother's voice as he dove underneath the table, the world around him suddenly splintering into light and sound, the force of the blast tearing through brick, plaster, and plate glass.

It was over in a moment, the little restaurant suddenly eerily still, debris raining down, sounding almost like rain against the tabletop. Carefully, Tucker pushed aside the rubble and crawled out from under the table. Sirens wailed in the distance, a cloud of dust choking him as it descended with the debris. The couple across the way were bloodied, but alive, the boy's arm protectively around the girl, his eyes still wide with fear.

"You okay?" Tucker asked.

The boy opened his mouth to reply but nodded instead, words deserting him as he pulled his sobbing girlfriend closer.

The waitress emerged from behind the counter, her arm clutched to her chest, blood snaking down from her shoulder. Like the couple, her face was ashen. "Lou," she whispered, her eyes cutting to the floor. "He isn't breathing."

Tucker pushed through the rubble to where the businessman had been sitting. Lou. The man was curled in a fetal position on the floor, a piece of sheared glass bisecting his neck. Blood pooled beneath him. Tucker grabbed his wrist, feeling for a pulse, already knowing the answer. His eyes met the waitress's, and he shook his head.

"Oh God," she moaned.

"Get them out of here," Tucker said, motioning to the couple. "The rest of the building could come down at any minute. It's not safe."

The woman hesitated, her eyes still locked on the dead man.

"There's nothing else you can do for him," Tucker told her, his voice gentle. "You need to go. Now."

She acquiesced, and with the help of the boy, the three of them climbed over the broken tables out onto the street.

"Tucker?" Drake's frantic voice echoed amidst the rubble and Tucker realized he was still holding his cell phone.

"I'm here."

"Are you okay?" Drake asked.

"I'm fine," Tucker answered, his eyes on the spot where the old man had been sitting. There was nothing left but rubble. The booth was gone. Incinerated.

"What the hell happened?"

"Bomb." Tucker said, his mind going to the moment before the explosion—the backpack, the old man, and his cell phone. "Someone just blew the fuck out of Weatherbees."

CHAPTER 2

Alexis Markham stopped pacing long enough to glance out the hotel window. Clouds were gathering on the horizon, a storm descending from the mountains. On any other day she'd have stopped to drink in the beauty. She'd always loved the mountains. But these days, more than ever, they only reminded her of everything she'd lost.

And George was trying to take it all away. Again. He was the only family she had left. They might not share blood, but their bond was still a strong one. George had been there during the worst time of her life. He was the one who'd quite literally saved her—from the horror, the pain, and eventually even herself. He'd been her touchstone. Her anchor. Even when he was in prison, they'd found ways to stay in touch. But now—

She clenched her fists, turning her back on the mountains. Now he wanted nothing more to do with her. His words echoed in her head. "We can't do this anymore.

You've got to build a new life. One without me in it." She'd argued, fought back, pleaded even, but George had been resolute. So she'd walked out on him. It was modus operandi, even after all this time. Disappear first. Question later.

She crossed her arms over her chest as the canned laughter coming from the TV mocked her. Some sappy family show. Seemed appropriate. She sank down on the bed, fighting against tears. She hadn't cried in years. Hell, she hadn't even known she still could. Most of her heart had died with her family. Her mom and dad. Her brother. And now George wanted to destroy the only part that was left.

Angrily, she wiped away the tears. Maybe he was right. Maybe there was no place left in her life for him. After all, she'd made a place for herself in the world. A shadowy one, to be certain. But without George, her ties to the past were gone.

No one was looking for her, and, thanks to George, no one even knew she existed. Lexie Baker had died in an explosion with the rest of her family. Alexis Markham had taken her place. Thirteen years was a long time to carry such a burden. Maybe it was time to let it go. She frowned, sucking in a breath. There'd been something more to what George had been trying to tell her. He hadn't just wanted to sever ties; he'd wanted her to create a new identity.

And considering how carefully they'd laid the groundwork for her current existence, that didn't make sense. Unless someone else knew who she was. Suddenly nervous, she carefully checked out the room, and then, satisfied that she was safe, at least for the moment, she reached for her cell.

It wasn't really hers. Just a throwaway she'd bought for the trip. Never take chances. That was George's motto. And he'd drilled it into her head. Nothing that can be traced. Ever. In today's technology-driven world, it wasn't always easy. But so far, at least, she'd managed to stay off the radar. She closed her eyes, calling to mind the number George had given her. Another untraceable phone. Maybe she'd been too hasty in running out. After all, he'd been the one to suggest the meeting. And he'd looked genuinely happy when she'd walked into the diner.

She chewed on her lip, staring down at the phone. Part of her wanted to call. To hear George's voice. To get some kind of reassurance that everything was okay. But he'd wanted to cut her out of his life. That much had been perfectly clear. She hesitated, fingers on the keypad. Then, resolutely, she started to dial.

Across the room, the blaring notes announcing a news bulletin interrupted her concentration and she swung around, her attention on the screen. There'd been an explosion, the announcer said. Downtown. At least three casualties. The camera panned across the burning wreckage and Alexis's heart jumped to her throat as she recognized what was left of the diner.

The cell phone dropped to the floor, her mind on overdrive as she searched for some sign that George had left before anything happened. That the explosion wasn't related to her or to him. But the camera panned closer, zooming in on a smoldering crater marking the center of the explosion. The booth where they'd been sitting. There was nothing left except debris.

She choked as the camera moved closer still, a ragged piece of canvas and a braided leather band lodged beneath a pile of stones. She recognized the leather. It was a bracelet she'd made for George sixteen years ago. It was the only time she'd been allowed to go to summer camp. George had made it possible, so she'd made him the bracelet. He'd never taken it off.

Tears fell in earnest now, her mind going numb as pain cut through her. George was dead.

Dead.

Bile rose in her throat as she thought of their last conversation, her angry words. If only she'd been there—but then she'd have been dead too. Or worse. She fought for control and won, icy resolve overshadowing everything else. George hadn't wanted her dead. That much she was certain of. The report cut away from the carnage, reverting back to the artificial world of the sitcom. Alexis started throwing things into her suitcase, wiping down the room as she went, removing all traces of having ever been in the hotel.

The most important thing now was to escape. From what or whom she had no idea. But George was dead, and there was every possibility that someone had seen them together, that somehow they'd put two and two together. She had nothing to hide, but she'd learned long ago that innocence meant nothing.

She swung her bag over her shoulder and, using a handkerchief, pulled open the door. The cold, hard truth was that the good guys didn't always win. In fact, sometimes they were persecuted to death. It had been true with her father. And now, most likely, with George. And as much as she wanted to mourn him, she knew she couldn't. Instead, she'd do what she'd always done.

She'd run.

*   *   *

"I think you should be at home in bed," Drake said, his face twisted into a scowl. "You've just survived a bombing, for God's sake."

"Give me a break," Tucker protested as they stepped out of the car, the charred shell of Weatherbees still crawling with forensic specialists. "I've been through a hell of a lot worse and you know it. Besides, I checked out okay. The doc said there was nothing but a few scrapes."

"And three bruised ribs," Drake reminded him. "I didn't fly across the country to see you injure yourself after the fact."

"I'm fine. And you know you're as anxious to see what they've found as I am. If only so you can get back to that pregnant wife of yours. Sorry to have pulled you away at such a critical moment."

Drake smiled. "It's not like she's having the baby right this minute. And besides, Madeline was the one who bullied Avery into getting me here posthaste. In fact, it was only with Annie's intervention that I stopped her from coming herself."

"Annie can be pretty imposing when she puts her mind to it." Tucker agreed. Annie Brennon and her husband, Nash, were both part of the same CIA black-ops unit as Drake, the American Tactical Intelligence Command, A-Tac for short. Its members masquerading as college professors, A-Tac was based out of Sunderland, an Ivy League college in New York. Anyway, Annie and Nash had been quick to volunteer to help Drake rescue him from San Mateo. He owed them both a hell of a lot. "I'm still not sure I understand why A-Tac is here at all. Seems like something for the local police or, at most, maybe the FBI."

"Well, first off, you're my brother," Drake said. "Which makes you part of A-Tac whether you like it or not. And we take care of family."

"Hey"—Tucker held up his hands in apology—"I'm not complaining. Just curious. There's got to be something more than just me. Unless you guys have gone off book again?" The mission in Colombia hadn't been officially sanctioned. In fact, there was some evidence that certain parties within the CIA would have preferred that he stay in San Mateo indefinitely, the better to keep a major fuckup from going public.

"No way." Drake shook his head. "These days we can't take a piss without someone documenting it for the records." A-Tac had been infiltrated by a mole. A man they'd all trusted. A friend. Tucker understood the difficulty in dealing with something like that. He'd been betrayed too.

"So is it still really bad?" he asked.

"Things are quieting down a little. We've all been cleared again for duty. And everyone's back to work. Which is a good thing. But we're still dealing with the fallout. I keep expecting to see Jason or Emmett as I round every corner. The truth is, we all jumped at the opportunity to get the hell out of there for a little while."

"We?"

"Nash, Tyler, Hannah, and me. Harrison and Avery are holding down the fort. And Lara is still on leave." Lara Prescott's longtime partner, Jason, had been killed by the man who'd betrayed them. Tucker had met her only once, briefly, but he understood her pain.

"Well, I'm glad you're here," he said. "But I'd still like to know the rest of the reason A-Tac's on the job. Is it something to do with what happened in Colombia? You think di Silva was behind this?" Tucker asked, his eyes on the remains of Weatherbees.

"We can't rule it out completely, of course." Drake slowed to a stop as they reached the plastic canopy serving as temporary headquarters for the investigation. "His operations took a hell of a hit. "

"Glad to see you made it out in one piece," Nash said, looking up from a table spread with debris. "Can't say as much for the bastard sitting at ground zero." He nodded to a basket filled with evidence gathered from the site, including a well-worn leather bracelet.

Tucker closed his eyes, the image of the old man and the blonde filling his mind. He could see their clasped hands—see the bracelet on his wrist. "The bracelet belonged to the old man in the booth," Tucker said, opening his eyes on a sigh.

"George Atterley," Hannah Marshall confirmed, closing the computer she'd been working on, her spiky hair streaked blue. Hannah was A-Tac's intel expert. She'd also coordinated logistics for his escape from San Mateo, including a last-minute helicopter rescue.

"Good work," Tucker said. "I figured with only a first name to go on we were going to have problems. I mean, there sure as hell wasn't enough left of him for an ID."

"You'd be surprised." Tyler Hanson smiled, walking up to the table. Tyler was A-Tac's ordnance expert. Tucker didn't know her well, but he knew his brother thought the world of her. According to Drake, there wasn't much she couldn't do with a bomb—on either side of detonation. "But in this case it was a security camera. There wasn't a lot left of it, but thanks to Harrison's magic fingers, we managed to resurrect the video right before the explosion."

"And from there we managed to isolate a photo and use facial recognition to ID him," Hannah added.

"Who's Harrison?" Tucker asked, feeling like he'd been dropped into a secret clubhouse without the password.

"Harrison Blake. Our new computer dude," Drake replied. "I told you about him. He worked with us when we were trying to stop the nuclear explosion in Manhattan."

Tucker nodded. "Used to work for Cullen Pulaski. FBI. I remember. Is he here?" He glanced around the space, looking for someone he'd missed.

"No." Hannah smiled. "Well, at least not physically." She tapped her computer lovingly, then swung it around so Tucker could see the monitor. A tousled-headed guy with the rumpled look of a geek and the physique of an athlete stared out across the pixels.

"Glad to hear you're all right," Harrison said, his voice disembodied as it came from the speakers next to Hannah. "From what I hear, you're one lucky son of bitch."

"Thanks." Tucker grinned. "I think. So what have you got on this George Atterley?"

"Well, he's not known for coloring inside the lines," Hannah said. "He was just recently released from prison. Spent the past six years doing time for racketeering, among other things."

"He's low profile in the extreme," Harrison picked up, his virtual face turning somber. "Until he was apprehended, he was pretty damn good at staying off the grid, starting with a round of civil disobedience that ended in a campus bombing. There wasn't enough evidence to convict him at the time, and he fell off the radar shortly thereafter."

"So someone from his past wanted him dead? Couldn't they have accomplished that more easily while he was incarcerated?" Tucker was more than familiar with how easy it was to arrange for an accident in prison.

"Seems probable," Nash said, "unless whoever it was didn't have the contacts to pull something like that off."

"The girl," Tucker said, frowning as he remembered. "Did you get an ID on her?"

"No." Tyler shook her head. "Nothing yet. The pictures are grainy, and the shots of her are mostly from the back."

"But we're working on it," Hannah said, turning the computer around again, Harrison's image disappearing as well.

"We do have more information on George, though," Nash said. "He's been linked to a network of black market dealers."

"While he was in prison?" Drake asked.

"It wouldn't be the first time someone called the shots from the inside," Nash said. "Anyway, according to our intel Atterley was trying to sell technology for weaponizing biotoxins."

"A method of turning the toxin into an aerosol, which in turn renders it that much more lethal," Hannah added.

"On a grand scale," Drake agreed. "But I didn't think the technology actually existed."

"There's never been confirmation," Hannah said. "But it was linked to a weapon developed a few years back. There was an accident, and an entire town was wiped out."

"Only the people behind it tried to cover the whole thing up." Drake frowned.

"Yeah, it was a huge debacle—brought down two senators in the process. But if you believe the scuttle, the original technology was developed in the late seventies, early eighties. There's no verification, of course, because the project was unauthorized and supposedly shut down when politicos got wind of it."

"There were rumors that the formula was stolen," Nash added. "But there was nothing to substantiate the story."

"But you have intel connecting George Atterley to a similar weapon and now he's turned up dead." Tucker leaned back against the table, turning over this new information in his mind. "So you guys weren't already following him, right?"

"I doubt we'd have been apprised of any of this if you hadn't been involved," Nash said. "But now that we are on board, Avery wants us to make it a priority to figure out what really happened here."

"So assuming Atterley was really trying to sell the thing, do you have any idea who the buyer might be?" Tucker asked.

"There's some evidence that points at a group known as the Consortium," Hannah said.

"So can't you trace it backward through them?"

"Not a chance." Tyler shook her head. "These people are like ghosts: We suspect they were behind the nuclear bomb planted in Manhattan. But knowing it and proving it are two different things. If George Atterley was involved with them, they could be behind his death. We've already seen firsthand their preferred methodology for tying up loose ends. "

"I'm sorry about your father," Tucker said, belatedly remembering that Tyler's dad had been killed by the same shadowy organization. "I know how hard it is to lose someone you love. Particularly like that."

"Thanks." Tyler smiled but the gesture didn't reach her eyes. "I'm dealing. Anyway, if we're right, and this is the work of the Consortium, then that could mean they've already got the formula."

"Unless the girl's got it," Drake said. "Maybe the meet was a transfer. And then, mission accomplished, she offed the old man. Was she carrying the backpack when she came in?"

"I don't remember seeing it, but there's no way I can say for sure." Tucker shrugged, angry at himself for not being more alert. "What about the video? Anything there?"

"No. There was no sign of the backpack," Drake shook his head. "The only shot we've got of her was after she was already at the table. Everything before that was too degraded."

"Well, I think until we can determine otherwise, we have to assume she's involved," Tyler said.

"What about the bomb?" Tucker asked. "Was there a signature?"

"Nothing yet." Tyler shook her head, her blond ponytail shimmying with the movement. "But that doesn't mean we won't find something. It just takes time."

"Which we may not have," Hannah said with a frown.

"What do you mean?" Nash asked as they all turned to look at her.

"I mean our girl is on the move. I've been monitoring footage at the airport, and looks like she arrived about half an hour ago."

"Can you tell where she's headed?"

"New Orleans. I've pulled up the manifest. We'll run the names. But until we can ID her, seems like one of you should head for Louisiana to keep tabs on her."

"I'll do it," Tucker said, surprised to hear the sound of his voice.

"Bro, you're not on the payroll anymore, remember?" Drake raised his eyebrows in question. "And anyway, I thought you liked being retired."

"I lied. It sucks. And besides"—he tipped his head toward the photo—"tailing her will be a walk in the park."

"It'd be easy enough to set him up with a background she'll believe," Hannah said.

"As soon as we figure out who *she* is," Tyler added.

"That's just a matter of time," Hannah said, already back at the computer.

"We are kind of shorthanded with Lara on leave." Nash nodded, with a shrug.

"Then it's settled." Tucker ignored his brother's glare. "I'm off to the Big Easy."

CHAPTER 3

New Orleans, Louisiana

The bank, like the rest of the street, was shabby chic, New Orleans at its best: part French, part southern, with a little bit of sleaze thrown in for good measure. Nestled between a voodoo shop and a lawyer's office, the bank was small and nondescript, the perfect place to store her most valuable possessions.

Alexis pushed open the heavy door, the whine of the air conditioner cutting through the otherwise hushed lobby. There were still signs of the opulence that had died a half century or so ago—marble, mahogany, crystal, and wrought-iron fixtures—symbols of a more elegant time. She crossed the foyer and stepped into the quiet alcove that fronted the safe deposit vault. Just being here was breaking protocol. And even though her new name had never been connected to the old one, it was still a risk.

But then the things she kept in the bank were a hazard as well. Definitely forbidden in the world of subterfuge and underground existence. No pictures. No personal items. Nothing that could lead to identification. She'd always followed the rules. Always.

Except when it came to her backpack. The one she'd been carrying the night her family died. It wasn't smart. A ridiculous risk. She'd spent years hiding the purple-and-pink pack from George. But it was all she had left. A stupid collection of nothing and everything.

And ever since she'd been on her own she'd kept it here. At Security Bank and Trust. She nodded to the woman behind the desk and handed her an identification card. In short order, she'd signed in and been escorted to a room lined with boxes, her own laid out on a center table inlaid with teak. With a sigh she opened the box, knowing it was probably for the last time.

Her cover might still be intact, but there was no way to know for certain. With George dead, she had to assume the worst. Meaning the life she'd so carefully constructed would have to be left behind. It wasn't that she had anything that mattered, really. It was more that in the six years George had been away, she'd managed to put down roots of a sort. New Orleans was full of secrets, which meant hers had gone mostly unnoticed. There'd been a few moments across the years, but nothing that had made her feel the need to run.

Until now.

In all honesty, she wasn't even certain her existence mattered to anyone. It wasn't like she'd done anything wrong. But the sins of the father, even falsified ones, couldn't be ignored any more than her connection to George. And his sins were very real. She had to face the fact that, if someone wanted George dead, there was every conceivable reason to believe they'd be after her as well, if for no other reason than to tie up loose ends.

She lifted the lid of the box and pulled out the backpack. The colors were faded, but in her mind's eye, she still remembered the day she and her mother had bought it. At the time, purple had been her favorite color. And she'd been certain it would set her apart from all the other girls at John Mall High School. Of course, her father wouldn't have approved of the thought, but, thankfully, pink-and-purple backpacks didn't fall into his high-risk category.

She unzipped the pack and pulled out the contents. Not much, really. A favorite book that had belonged to her mother. Mary Stewart's *Airs Above the Ground*. A notebook Alexis had filled with poetry and quotes, typical adolescent angst. A turquoise ring George had given her after her father died. And a smooth black stone from the Rio Grande. Her brother had given it to her.

She palmed the rock and picked up a couple of photographs. One of her and George taken a few years back. She was supposed to have thrown it away. Photos were forbidden. But she'd kept it anyway. Just because they'd been so happy. A rarity in her life.

She picked up the other photo. This one of her family. It, too, was a dangerous keepsake, taken before her family had gone underground. She looked down at the black-and-white picture. Her brother was only a little baby tucked in her mother's arms, her dad standing off to one side, glasses crooked, looking bemused, as if he wasn't quite sure how he'd fallen into such domestic bliss.

Alexis hadn't even been born yet. She'd never known her family in normal times, and she'd spent a lot of her childhood resenting the fact. If only she'd had an inkling of what was coming, maybe she'd have fought her father

a little bit less. Spent more time with her brother. And
appreciated her mom. But she hadn't known. And now it
was too late; there was nothing left of their family but an
old piece of Kodak paper.

She tucked the photo back inside the pack with the
notebook and ring. Then she added the book and the stone,
leaving only the sweatshirt she'd been wearing the night
her life had, quite literally, exploded. The purple panther
was beginning to peel off the front, the jersey frayed from
age. It was a stupid keepsake, and yet somehow a marker
of everything she'd had. Everything she'd lost. That night
in Walsenburg, her childhood had ended. And some part
of her had never really gotten over the fact.

She swallowed the lump in her throat and shoved the
sweatshirt into the bag. Life wasn't a fairy tale. And there
wasn't much point in wishing for something different.
She was alive, and she was safe, at least for the time being.
And she had her memories. Besides, George always said
that the only thing that was important was the here and
now.

To that end, she checked the front compartment of the
bag. There were a couple of false IDs. And a stack of
hundred-dollar bills. Her back door. George had always
insisted. The door at the far end of the vault opened, and
a thin man in a black suit walked inside. Her hand moved
defensively to the backpack and her muscles tightened,
ready for flight.

"I'm sorry to intrude," the man said. Alexis breathed
in relief, shifting her hand away from the backpack as she
read his nametag. _ELI MUNRO_. An assistant manager with
the bank. She'd met him once ages ago. "I just wanted to let
you know that we had a little incident here a few days ago."

"An incident?" Alexis asked, her fear resurfacing. "I'm not sure what you mean."

"I mean that someone"—he paused, in that supercilious way of bankers, eyeing her over the top of his glasses—"other than you, tried to access your safe deposit box."

Alexis frowned, her stomach clenching as her fears became grounded. "When exactly was this?"

"Day before yesterday. Just after noon. We've had a new girl handling the boxes, and she wasn't clear on procedure. So she let him come back here."

"Him?" Alexis choked out, trying to hold on to her composure.

"Yes. A man. So, clearly, not you. But as I said, Lois was a new hire. Anyway, fortunately, I was apprised of the situation and intervened before any real harm was done."

"So he wasn't allowed inside my box?" she asked, her mind scrambling to make certain nothing had been missing.

"No. Absolutely not."

"Do you know who he was?" she asked, not certain she wanted to hear the answer.

"He said he was related to you. Your uncle, I believe."

"That's impossible." Her frown deepened as she tried to make this newest information make sense. "I don't have an uncle."

"Oh, dear," Mr. Munro said, blanching at her pronouncement. "I am so sorry. But at least I was right to turn him away."

"Yes. Absolutely." Alexis touched her throat, her pulse beating against her fingers. "Did he give his name?"

"No. He just said that you'd asked him to come. But, of

course, I couldn't take the chance. And when I offered to call you, he told me he'd handle it himself. Even verified where you live."

"You told him where I lived?"

"Absolutely not. It would be against policy." Munro held up his hands in denial. "But since he already knew, I confirmed it. I mean, at that point I thought he was your uncle. Obviously, I shouldn't have been so forthcoming. But I did leave you several messages."

"I'm sorry. I've been out of town," she said.

"I see." Mr. Munro nodded, clearly seeing nothing at all. "I would have called the police, but it's not illegal to inquire about a box."

"No, of course not." Alexis shook her head. "And I agree—there was nothing to report."

"If you're sure." It was clear that Mr. Munro was ready to wipe his hands of the whole thing.

"Absolutely. I mean, you're right—nothing actually happened. There's probably even a logical explanation."

"Yes, yes," Mr. Munro quickly agreed, clearly relieved, "that's what I thought. We can change your box if you want. Maybe to another location? Or, if you prefer, another bank."

"No." She forced a smile. "I'm quite happy here. Let's just leave it as is. But if he does come back"—she paused, raising her gaze to meet Munro's—"you'll contact me immediately?"

"Oh, of course." He nodded. "And I can't tell you again how sorry I am that it happened in the first place."

"No worries. There was no harm done." She forced a smile as she hitched the backpack over her shoulder and closed the box.

"But I thought you were keeping the box." He tilted his head with a frown.

"I am," she lied, still smiling. "I'm just taking some of my things. That's why I came in today in the first place."

"Oh, I see," he said on an exhale of breath.

"Seriously, it's all good," she said as they walked from the vault. "And I'm sure there won't be any further problems. But if there are…"

"I'll be sure to call you. Immediately." He stretched out his hand as they reached the front door of the bank. "And I can assure you that I'll be vigilant about making sure there are no further breaches in our security."

"Good. I'll count on it. Thank you, Mr. Munro," Alexis said, squeezing his hand for effect. Then, with another false smile, she turned and headed out into the sunlit street, stomach still churning as she faced the fact that New Orleans, in all of its languid beauty, no longer offered safe haven. Whatever had happened to George, it had followed her here. And until she could figure it out, she had to find a new place to hide, before the past had a chance to rise up and destroy her.

It took almost thirty minutes for Alexis to make her way from the bank to the Garden District and home. Mainly because she'd doubled back several times to make sure no one was following her. And even now, satisfied that she was on her own, she kept looking over her shoulder, waiting for the other shoe to drop, wishing she'd waited to hear George out. She was certain now that he'd been trying to warn her. But she'd been so angry at his perceived betrayal she hadn't been willing to listen.

Juggling the backpack and her duffel, she opened the gate leading to the front yard, the familiar sight of her garden instantly soothing her. There was something so wonderful about taking an empty patch of dirt and coaxing it to grow and thrive.

And now she'd have to leave it behind.

She moved up the pathway, stopping automatically to deadhead a couple of roses along the way. It was only when she stepped up onto the porch that she hesitated, something suddenly feeling off. Pushing the backpack higher on her shoulder, she edged forward, trying to figure out exactly what had set off her internal alarm.

The porch was exactly as she'd left it, the windows closed, the curtains drawn. The mailbox was empty, but that wasn't surprising. A person who didn't exist didn't get a lot of mail. Just a few bills to the fictional woman who paid them. The door was closed as well, but when she touched the handle, it creaked open. Frozen in place, she waited, heart hammering, but nothing moved. So, on a deep exhale, she stepped over the threshold and stood listening for some sign that she wasn't alone, but the house was quiet. Dumping both backpack and duffel, she rounded the corner into the parlor, her heart dropping to her stomach as she surveyed the wreckage there. Someone had quite literally torn the room apart.

The furniture had been upended, sofa cushions ripped, drawers emptied, and books tossed. Two vases lay shattered near the window, wilted rose petals spilling bloodlike across the floor. There was nothing left untouched—everything destroyed.

The kitchen was the same, with dishes smashed to the floor and the sour smell of milk filling her nostrils as she picked her way through the remnants of boxes and jars that had once occupied her refrigerator and pantry.

The dining room looked almost sedate by comparison. The chairs were overturned, but a large ceramic bowl filled with lemons still held court in the center of the table. A mirror had been shattered, but two floor lamps still stood sentry by the front windows, the heavy drapery shredded in places but still shuttering the house from the afternoon sun.

Tears filled her eyes as anger washed through her. Someone had been intent on destroying what little life she had left. Without stopping to think about the danger, she bounded up the stairs, skidding to a stop at the sight of the carnage there. The mattress had been torn open, stuffing spilling onto the floor where it had been upended to check the bottom. The bedside tables had been overturned and a bookshelf toppled into a corner, the books thrown into a pile, ripped pages littering the floor.

It was amazing, really, how much she'd managed to acquire in the six years she'd lived here, a false sense of security making her relax into what had, at least on the surface, appeared to be a regular life. She fought her pain as she surveyed the wreckage.

At least now it would be easier to walk away.

Somewhere behind her there was movement, a slight shuffle against the wooden floors snapping her out of her reverie. She spun around, eyes on the doorway, certain now that someone was still in the house. She quickly scanned the room for some sort of weapon, settling for an iron poker from the bedroom fireplace.

Another footstep, this one on the staircase. No effort at all for concealment. And then another.

She ran over to the window, jerking back the curtains, trying to calculate how far a jump it might be. But in her fear she'd forgotten the wrought-iron security bars she'd recently installed, a way to keep intruders out that now effectively held her prisoner.

The floor squeaked as the intruder rounded the corner into the hallway, his gait faster now. After a desperate look for another way out, Alexis lifted her chin and swung the poker up baseball bat–style, determined not to go down without a fight.

CHAPTER 4

It was hotter than hell. The air was heavy, the smell of flowers heady in the heat, as though the humidity was amplifying the scent somehow, the resulting perfume overwhelming the senses. Tucker had spent years in the humid rainforests of Colombia, but there had been a conspicuous absence of humanity. Here, mixed in with the smell of flora was the odor of sweat, beer, and urine: the excesses of New Orleans taking olfactory form.

The house was at the end of a block, just off the St. Charles trolley line. The homes here, while still echoing their grand history, were more run down, yards overgrown, paint peeling. Still, he could see the bones of what had once been a lovely house, New Orleans at its very best.

He pushed open the wrought-iron gate, careful to keep it from squeaking. He wasn't really sure what he expected to find, but it was always best to be careful. He had no way of knowing if the woman from the coffee shop would even be here. It was nothing short of a miracle that

Hannah had manipulated the information on the flight manifest to yield a name and an address. Clearly the lady preferred living off the grid. No charge accounts, no subscriptions. Just the basics. Shelter and food. And, apparently, flowers.

The roses brushed against him as he made his way up the walk, his senses moving to high alert as he noted the open door. Just inside on the floor was a duffel, and above it, lying on a credenza, a backpack. Pink with purple flowers. He frowned, wondering if the woman he'd seen in the coffee shop had a child. That would certainly complicate matters.

Above his head, something crashed to the floor. He spun around, pulling his gun, eyes on the stairs. For a moment silence reigned, then a woman's shriek was followed by something heavy slamming into a wall. Taking the stairs two at a time, Tucker hit the landing on a run, swinging into an open bedroom doorway in time to see a man in black with his arm locked around the struggling woman's neck.

Alexis Markham.

As if he'd said the name out loud, Alexis lifted her gaze to his, and with a flash of fierce resolution, jammed her elbow into her opponent's rib cage. With a muffled curse the man loosened his grip, and Alexis took the opportunity to break free, spinning out of the way to give Tucker a clear shot.

The intruder, however, rolled to the floor, exchanging fire with Tucker, the assailant's bullets barely missing Alexis as she dove behind a four-poster bed. Tucker hit the floor as well, taking cover behind a wing chair. The gunman shot again, the bullet cutting into the upholstery of the chair, sending a spray of feathers into the air.

Using the distraction to his advantage, Tucker popped up from behind the chair and shot again, this time hitting his target, the man clutching his chest as he fell to the floor. After kicking away the man's gun, Tucker bent to check his pulse.

"Is he dead?" Alexis asked.

"Yeah." Tucker swallowed a curse. "Although I'd have rather had him alive. Might have given me some idea of what he was doing here."

"I'd have thought that was obvious," she said. "He was trying to kill me."

"Actually, if he'd wanted you dead he'd have shot you. Looked to me like he was trying to subdue you."

"Yeah, well, that didn't work out too well, did it?"

He searched the man for identification, but there was nothing. Just some extra ammo. He pocketed it and started to push to his feet.

"Drop the gun or I'll shoot." Alexis's voice was low and throaty, the soft slur of her accent almost sultry, but there was also a steely note of determination that he couldn't ignore. He laid the gun on the floor, holding his hands out. "All right," she said, "now I want you to turn around slowly."

He pushed up from the floor, considering his alternatives. He could probably take her, but there was always the chance the gun would go off, and he didn't much relish the idea of being shot. Better to use words to defuse the situation. He turned around.

"Who the hell are you?" she asked, the intruder's gun in her hand. Her fingers were trembling, but her stance was strong and her eyes clear.

"Right now, a friend," he said. "I heard you scream and figured you could use some help."

"How do I know you're not part of all of this some-how?" She indicated the man on the floor and then the room summarily tossed, her belongings strewn everywhere. "This could all just be some kind of a ploy."

"Lady, I don't play games," Tucker said, letting frustration get the better of him. "I shot the bastard because he was trying to kill me."

"I thought you said he wasn't trying to kill anyone."

"I said he wasn't trying to kill *you*. He seemed rather intent on eliminating me. So I took him out. I had no choice."

"And you just happened to be walking by carrying a gun?" A vertical line formed between her eyebrows as she scowled at him.

"No." Tucker shook his head. "I came to see you. I said I was a friend."

"Not of mine." Her voice was resolute as she leveled the gun. "I've never seen you in my life."

"Yeah, well, I know George Atterley. Which makes me a friend of a friend. And since you were the last person to see him alive, I figured maybe you had some idea as to why someone would want to blow him away."

The words hung between them for a moment, and then, tired of the game, Tucker launched forward, grabbing Alexis's gun hand as they fell to the floor. Weapon secure, he pinned her hands above her head, using his body weight to hold her still.

"Let me go," she spat, smoky eyes full of venom. If the situation had been different he might have enjoyed the feel of her body beneath him. The swell of her breasts, the feel of her hips against his. But Tucker knew, given half a chance, she'd come up swinging.

"Not until you promise to listen," he said, his breath

stirring the tendrils of hair curling around her face. She glared up at him, clearly considering her options, and then, with a small jerky nod, acquiesced, her body going slack.

He released her wrists, but before he could push off of her she rammed a knee into his groin, thankfully missing the intended targets. Still, pain rocked through him and, anger surging, he slammed her back to the floor, securing her hands again. "That wasn't very ladylike," he hissed, satisfied to see a flash of fear flitter across her face.

"I wasn't feeling much like a lady," she whispered as their gazes locked. Clearly Alexis Markham could give as good as she got. Not that he gave a damn. In another place, another time, he might have allowed himself to get lost in the smoky gray of her eyes, but she was an assignment, nothing more. Although he had to give her kudos for bravery. Most women would have folded by now.

"Look, we can do this the easy way or the hard way," Tucker said. "Your call. But me, I'd prefer to have this conversation somewhere off premises. My guess is that our man over there isn't working alone. So unless you want a repeat performance..." he trailed off, waiting.

"Fine," she conceded with a curt nod, her eyes narrowing as she held his gaze. "I'll go with the easy way. So can we get up now?"

"You're not going to try to make a eunuch out of me?" His groin still throbbed, and he winced as she shifted beneath him.

"Not for the moment." She chewed on the side of her lip, still watching him.

"Not good enough." He tightened his hold on her wrist.

"Okay, I promise I won't try anything funny. Satisfied?"

He wasn't, not in the least. But there was a note of resolve in her voice, and for some reason, Tucker felt inclined to believe her. At least for now. He rolled off her and reached for the gun. No sense in letting her gain the upper hand again.

"So any idea who the dead guy is?" he asked as he pushed to his feet.

"No." Her eyes shot to the body lying on the floor. "I've never seen him before."

"Why the hell didn't you get out when you saw the place had been tossed?"

"I wasn't..." She looked down at her hands, for the first time seeming a little vulnerable. "I wasn't thinking. I just wanted to check the house. To see what they'd done."

"Is there something particular they were looking for?"

"No." She shook her head. "Nothing. At least not here."

He waited, watching her.

"I had a few things in a lockbox at a bank in the Quarter. But except for some money, none of it is worth someone trying to steal, either. Just some things from my past." The last was said with a hint of despondency, but almost before he'd identified it, she'd squared her shoulders, her face carefully neutral again.

"So you have no idea what he might have been after?"

"I thought you said it was me."

"I said he didn't want to kill you. Which isn't the same thing. And destroying your house isn't exactly a subtle way to lie in wait."

"So what?" she asked, arms crossed as she paced restlessly to the window and back. "You're saying he ransacked my house and then when he couldn't find what he wanted, he decided to take me?"

"It's possible," he murmured, bending down to search the dead man again. There were no identifying marks. No scars, no tattoos. He took out his phone and took a picture of the body. It was tempting to call Drake and have A-Tac check out the scene. His brother and Hannah were ensconced in a hotel nearby. Backup, as it were. But he didn't want to alarm Alexis. She was already skittish, her pacing signaling her reluctance to trust him. One wrong move, and Tucker had no doubt that she'd bolt.

"Why the picture?" She stopped, staring down at the dead man.

"Well, I figure you don't want to call the police. And since we can't risk staying here, a photograph might help if we get the chance to identify him."

"There is no 'we.'" She shook her head, arms still crossed, her eyes back to shooting daggers. "I appreciate the help, but I can handle it on my own now."

As if to belie the fact, the window glass shattered and Tucker dove to pull Alexis to the ground. "Son of a bitch," he said, rolling them behind the relative safety of the bed. Bullets slammed into the side of the mattress, causing more stuffing to spill onto the floor. "Can you shoot?" he asked, holding out the dead man's gun.

"No." Her obvious regret gave her words credence. "I was bluffing before. I hate violence."

"Well, you certainly seem to attract it," he said, popping up to shoot once through the window. There wasn't a chance in hell he'd hit anyone, but maybe it'd buy them a few minutes to regroup. "Is there a way out of here besides the front door?" He shot again, then ducked back to the floor as a new round of gunfire slammed through the room.

"There's a back door," she whispered, her eyes on the window. "But it's directly under this window."

"They've probably got the front door covered too, but it's worth a try," he said. "If there is only one of them and he thinks he's got us cornered, he won't want to abandon position."

"Okay, so what do we do?" Her voice was amazingly calm, all things considered, but he could see her hands shaking, her fingers intertwining as if trying to force each other to be still.

"On my count, head for the door into the hallway. I'll be right behind you."

She nodded, and he mouthed the countdown. One. Two. Three. *Go.*

She sprang forward, heading for the door as he followed, firing once at the window, keeping low to avoid the responding gunfire.

After the cacophony of the gunfight, the hallway seemed abnormally quiet. Alexis opened her mouth but Tucker shook his head, lifting a finger to his lips and nodding toward the staircase. For a moment he thought she might argue, but when a shot strafed the wallpaper behind her, she leaped into motion and he followed her to the top of the stairs.

"I'll go first," he whispered, pushing her behind him as he headed slowly down the stairs, gun leading. They made it to the lower landing just as a mirror across from the front door shattered. "Looks like there's more than one of them out there."

"We're trapped."

"You're awfully quick to give up."

"I just don't see another way out. They've got the doors

covered, and the windows all have wrought-iron grates. I thought they'd keep me safe." She stopped, her eyes filled with apology. "I'm sorry."

"Look, sweetheart," he said, "I learned a long time ago that it ain't over 'til it's over. So think. There's got to be another way out."

"There's a cellar. But there aren't any windows," she said.

"How old is the house?"

"Built in the 1850s," she said, frowning. "But I don't see what—"

"I'm guessing the original furnace used coal."

Her eyes widened as his point sank home. "The coal chute. I've seen it. I think it's nailed shut, but it's wooden and there aren't any bars."

"And they won't expect it. I say it's worth a shot."

Alexis nodded and started forward, reaching for the backpack on the credenza by the door. Moving on pure adrenaline, Tucker ran out into the foyer, just missing her arm as she grabbed the bag. A volley of bullets slammed into the wall above her head, and, with a muffled curse, he managed to jerk her back into the shadow of the stairwell as a second volley ricocheted around the foyer.

"What the hell do you think you were doing? You almost got us both killed."

"I'm sorry. But I couldn't leave without my backpack."

He glanced down at the purple-and-pink vinyl bag. "Seriously?"

"It's all I've got left." She lifted her chin, daring him to argue, and, although he was tempted, he knew there wasn't enough time.

"Fine. But we've got to move. Now. Your little sojourn cost us valuable time."

"I'm sorry," she whispered, eyes on the front door as she hitched the pack over her shoulder. "What next?"

"Where's the door to the cellar?" he asked.

"Straight down the hall behind the staircase." She tipped her head toward the hallway leading off the foyer. "It ought to give us a little protection."

"Yes, but only after we clear the door," Tucker said. "Look, you go first. Stay low, and I'll provide covering fire. Once you're clear of the front door, head for the cellar as fast as you can. No deviations. Got it?"

She nodded, dimple flashing as she gave him a tight smile.

Tucker lifted his hand, steadying the gun, and then signaled her to go. The sound of bullets flying was deafening as they ricocheted off the foyer's walls and floor, the shooter clearly having used the brief interval to close the distance. Following Alexis, Tucker continued to shoot until he was safely into the hallway behind the stairwell.

She was already at the cellar door, fighting to open it. "Damn humidity. It's swollen shut."

"Let me," he said, checking behind them for signs of activity. The hallway was quiet but he knew they had only minutes before one of their assailants made it into the house. As if to underscore the thought, a floorboard somewhere behind them squeaked as someone crossed the floor.

"Hurry," Alexis said, her voice rising with her fear as she moved so that he could better access the door. He turned the knob, and then, bracing himself against the adjacent wall, pushed for all he was worth. At first the door refused to budge, but then, with a final screech of protest, it swung open.

"Go," he whispered, shoving her through the opening and onto the stairs. He followed, taking time to pull the door closed behind him and jam a broken broom handle across the doorway. It wouldn't hold for long, but at least it would buy them a little time. At this point every second mattered.

The cellar was small, divided into one large room with two smaller ones opening off each end. The floor was damp and, in places, covered with moss, the sound of dripping water echoing off the bricks that lined the walls and floor.

"The coal chute is over here," Alexis said, motioning to the room to the right.

He followed her inside and stopped in front of the boarded-up chute. Beneath it sat a rotting wooden crate stained black from years of holding coal. "We're going to need something to get it open."

"Here," she said, holding out a rusted crowbar. "It's not perfect, but it ought to get the job done."

Tucker took the crowbar and reached for his weapon. "You take the gun and keep watch."

"I already told you, I don't—"

"This isn't the time to take a pacifist stance, Alexis. Just take the damn gun and if anything moves, shoot it."

She stared at him for a moment and then, with a grimace, took the gun and moved to the door, her eyes trained on the staircase.

"Women," he mumbled under his breath as he pulled off the half-rotting boards. Sunlight streamed through the opening, sparkling as it filtered through the dust whorls created by the falling two-by-fours.

"Someone's coming," she whispered, glancing back over her shoulder. "How much longer?"

"Now," he said, tossing the crowbar as he pulled off

the last of the boards. "Hurry." The stairs behind them groaned as someone descended. He took the gun and then boosted her up and through the opening. Behind him, someone opened fire, the bullets going wide as he pulled himself through the chute and slid out onto the lawn.

"Over here," Alexis called, already running across the grass toward a dilapidated garage. "I've got a car."

Tucker followed behind her, dodging as the second shooter found them and opened fire. The garage, like the cellar, smelled of age and damp. They rushed through an anteroom filled with castoffs and into the main part of the garage. A beat-up Chevy filled almost all the space, an Impala Super Sport the size of a tank and something over forty years old, judging by the chassis.

"What the hell?"

"It came with the house," she said, grabbing a key off a hook by the door. "It's more lively than it looks."

"I sure as hell hope so," he said, wrenching open the garage door and sliding inside the car, Alexis following suit. "I'll drive."

She nodded, tossing him the key just as a bullet shattered a rear side window.

"Get down," Tucker yelled as he jammed the key into the ignition, grateful when the old girl sprang to life. Alexis ducked, and he slammed the car into Reverse just as the shooter moved into the garage's doorway. The Chevy screeched, and its tires spun as he pushed the pedal to the floor, splitting his time between navigating the driveway and keeping an eye on the shooter.

Almost before the front tires hit the road he pushed the gearshift into Drive and held on as the car lurched forward, picking up speed with comparative ease. Behind them, he could see the gunman in the street, still firing even though the Chevy was out of range.

"We're in the clear," he said, returning his eyes to the road ahead of them.

"So what do we do now?" Alexis asked as she sat up, her gray eyes full of questions.

At least she'd used the word *we*. It was a start.

Tucker glanced sideways, noting again how fragile she looked, a definite contrast to the inner strength he'd already witnessed. Contradictions had always intrigued him. Anyway, whatever the hell was going on, it was clear she needed help. And he intended to use that need to extract information.

Someone had killed George Atterley. And now someone was after Alexis. It seemed fairly certain that there was a link. All he had to do was figure it out. And the first step toward doing that was to gain Alexis's trust.

He glanced over at her, hunched in the seat, clutching that damned bag, expression unreadable. She wouldn't be an easy sell.

But hell, he'd always enjoyed a challenge.

CHAPTER 5

S o you want to tell me who you are?" Alexis asked. They'd left New Orleans behind, heading northeast on Highway 90 toward Lake Borgne. So far there'd been no sign that anyone was following them, but Alexis couldn't shake the feeling that she'd somehow stepped from the frying pan into the fire.

"My name is Tucker." He kept his eyes on the road, and she allowed herself a moment to study his profile.

He was just this side of handsome, his nose strong and straight, a crescent-shaped scar just below his right ear. His dark hair was a little too long, a silver streak of gray cutting across the right side, almost as if someone had spray-painted it there. He didn't look old enough to be going gray, or punk enough to have designed it on purpose. Yet, somehow, it seemed to suit him. He was a big man, muscular and hard.

"Tucker," she repeated, trying it on for size. "It suits you."

His smile was slow, his eyes crinkling with the gesture. "It's a family name."

"And is it just Tucker?" she asked.

"That'll do for now."

They rode for a moment in silence, Alexis sorting through her cascading emotions. In less than forty-eight hours she'd lost George and almost been killed. Her house had been trashed and her carefully built life destroyed in one short afternoon. It was a lot to take in. And Tucker-with-no-last-name just added to the puzzle.

"So you said you knew George?"

"Yeah." He nodded, eyes on the road. "We go way back."

"You worked with him?" she asked.

"No. I met him in prison. We found we had mutual interests and from there formed a friendship of sorts."

"Of sorts?" she queried, frowning at the thought of Tucker as a criminal. Somehow she'd managed to categorize him as a good guy, and this newest information didn't seem to jibe—although she'd lived most of her life with the idea that being accused of something didn't always make a person guilty.

"Prison is like summer camp," he said. "Some people you meet, you're just as happy to forget once you're on the outside again. And others you know you'll be bound to for life. George fell in the latter category."

"And he told you about me?"

"Only that you meant a great deal to him. And that if anything happened to him, he wanted to be sure there was someone to look out for you. So when he turned up dead, I figured it was time to honor my part in our bargain."

"He promised you something?"

"No. He didn't have to. He'd already helped me get

some information I needed. To clear my name—" He broke off, and she realized he wasn't going to tell her anything else. But for some absurd reason, the idea that he was innocent of whatever the hell it was made her happy.

"How did you know he was dead?" she asked, forcing herself to keep her guard up. Something about Tucker made it all too easy to let down her defenses.

"I was there." The words hung between them, and Alexis's mind went into hyperdrive trying to remember if she'd seen him.

"At the diner?"

"Yes." He nodded. "I was in the back. In a booth. George was going to introduce us, but—"

"I didn't give him a chance." Guilt flooded through her. If she'd stayed...

Silence filled the car, the only sound the whisper of the tires against the road. She turned to look out the window—trees skimming by, their leaves turned fiery in the twilight.

"You couldn't have saved him," Tucker said, his voice soft. "I was twenty feet away, and there wasn't a goddamned thing I could have done. If you'd been there, you'd be dead too."

She jerked out of her reverie, turning back to face him. "You can't know that."

"Trust me when I say that I've seen more than my fair share of explosions," he said. "If you'd stayed in that booth, you wouldn't be here right now. There wasn't time to have made an escape."

"Maybe I'd have seen something," she said. "I just can't get the thought out of my mind. I deserted him. Left him there to die."

"But you didn't know that. And neither did I."

"Was it..." She paused, swiping tears from her eyes. "Was it quick? I mean, did he suffer?"

"No," Tucker said. "He would have died instantly. I doubt he even had time to realize what was happening."

"And you?"

"I was lucky," he said. "Just a few scratches and some bruises. But under the circumstances I figured it was time to make good on my promise."

"To watch out for me." She sighed. "I suppose I can't fault your timing."

"If that's your way of saying thank you, you're welcome."

She bristled at his tone, her positive feelings for the man evaporating as quickly as they'd come. "I could have taken care of myself."

"That would explain the man with his arm around your neck."

She ignored the sarcasm, her mind still on George. "If you're telling me the truth, George would have made sure you had something that would convince me."

"He was going to introduce us. So I don't think he'd considered the possibility that I'd be finding you on my own."

"Still, he must have told you something. Something that will make me believe you're telling the truth."

"Well, first off, I *am* telling the truth. I mean, what possible motive can I have for jumping into the middle of a gunfight with a relative stranger? As I told you earlier, the fact that they were shooting at me seems to negate the possibility that I was working with them. And then there's this." He reached in his pocket and produced the bracelet she'd made George all those years ago.

"But George didn't give that to you. I saw it," she said, frowning. "On the news when they showed the blast."

"I picked it up. I knew he always wore it. So I figured it might mean something to you."

"I gave it to him," she said, reaching out to take the beaded leather and slipping it onto her wrist. Memories swam to the surface. George cheering at her softball games, helping her mom do dishes after a party, helping her blow out the candles on her birthday. And now he was gone. She closed her fingers over the bracelet. "Thank you."

"No worries. I had George in my corner too, remember? I can only imagine how hard this is for you."

"He was everything," she whispered on a sigh. "That's why we argued. He wanted us to go our separate ways. He demanded it, actually. And I just couldn't understand why he'd do that to me."

"Well, it wasn't because he didn't care. More likely he knew something was coming down. Something that culminated in the bombing."

"And the men at my house." She closed her eyes, trying to control her emotions. She didn't know this man. And no matter how close he'd been with George or how comfortable he made her feel, she couldn't trust him. He might have saved her life, but that didn't mean she owed him her confidences.

"So when George asked you to look after me, he didn't tell you why?"

"No. He didn't." She opened her mouth to protest but he waved her silent. "And I didn't ask. George wasn't a spill-your-guts kind of guy. And I figured if he wanted me to know more, he'd tell me. To be honest, I didn't really think anything would ever come of it."

"Well, you were wrong about that." She slid her fingers across the bruised skin at her throat.

"Are you in pain?"

"Not the physical kind," she said, letting her hand fall back into her lap. The sun was sitting low on the horizon now, a bright orange globe sinking into the bayou.

His fingers tightened on the wheel. "Any idea why someone would be after you—or George?"

She shook her head, thinking there were a million reasons, none of which made any sense but all of which could possibly have brought this down on their heads. "I think he wanted to tell me, but I didn't give him the chance."

"Doesn't matter. It's like I told you before—if you'd stayed, you'd have been dead."

She shivered despite the fact that the night was warm. "Where are we going?"

"Someplace off the radar where we can regroup."

She wasn't certain whether she should protest or thank him. Maybe for the moment she'd just let it be. Let someone else be in charge. She'd been on her own so long she'd forgotten how nice it was to have someone on her side. She'd had George, of course, but he'd been in prison. And that meant she'd had to deal with life on her own, not daring to allow someone close enough to share the burden. Not that she was going to do that with Tucker. He was practically a stranger. And she knew better.

But surely it wouldn't hurt for one night.

The car swerved suddenly, slamming Alexis into the car door despite her seat belt. "What the hell?"

"There's someone on our tail," Tucker said, his eyes moving between the road ahead and the rearview mirror.

"Shit." The word came of its own accord. "How did they find us?"

"I'm guessing they tagged your car. I should have thought to look but we didn't exactly have time for a leisurely search."

"You're saying there's a bug in the car?"

"Unless it's on you." He turned slightly, his eyes meeting hers for a moment.

"No. It's not me. They couldn't have. I'm wearing clothes I had with me on the trip to California." She looked down at her tank and jeans.

"What about the backpack?"

Again she shook her head. "It was in the lockbox. I went there before coming to the house. So they definitely didn't get to it." She turned to look behind her. "Are you sure they're following us?"

"Positive," he said, speeding up slightly. Behind them a blue sedan followed suit. "They've been with us since we passed the cutoff to I-10."

"And you haven't felt the need to tell me until now?"

"I wasn't sure. And I didn't want to scare you."

"Well, so much for that idea." Alexis twisted so that she could watch the car behind them. "Any chance we can lose them?"

"I don't think we can outrun them, if that's what you're thinking. But I'm sure we can figure out something."

"Like a shoot-out on the highway?" She tried to smile but couldn't quite manage.

"It's an alternative," Tucker agreed. "But last ditch, okay?" His gaze met hers for an instant, and damned if she didn't feel better.

"Okay." She nodded. "So what do we do in the meantime?"

"Let's start by abandoning Plan A." Without another word, he yanked the wheel hard left, and the Chevy spun around, tires squealing in protest. A passing car swerved right onto the shoulder honking in annoyance, and the blue sedan skidded to the left as its driver slammed on the brakes.

Alexis reached out to brace herself on the dashboard, the ancient seat belt not promising much in the way of protection.

"You're used to driving this car, right?" Tucker asked as he finished the U-turn.

"Yeah. Enough."

"Not exactly a ringing endorsement, but we're just going to have to go with it."

"I'm not following."

"Unless you've given up your aversion to guns, we're going to need to switch places."

"You think they're going to open fire?" She glanced behind her. The blue car, a Honda, had made the turn and was closing fast.

"I don't think we can afford to take chances. So we're going to switch seats. You go up, I'll go down."

She nodded, already in motion, trying to ignore the tightening in her stomach as she squeezed across him. She grabbed the wheel as he pushed over into the passenger's seat, the old car groaning in protest as she pressed the accelerator back to the floor. The traffic had thinned to almost nothing, the sun almost below the horizon now. She flipped on the car lights, the scraggly trees lining the highway looking sinister in the shadows.

Beside her, Tucker had pulled his gun and swiveled around so he could watch the Honda. In a million years, despite the violence that had ended her family's lives, she'd never imagined she'd be here in a car trying to outrun men who were trying to either kill her or kidnap her. Whatever George had gotten her into, it was bad.

Unless this wasn't about George. Her father's voice echoed in her ears. "You have to understand, Lexie. We can't trust anyone. There are men looking for me. Bad men. And if they find me, I'm dead. And, honey, they won't stop there. They'll hurt us all." Alexis shuddered, the past slamming full force into the present.

"You okay?" Tucker's voice cut through the memories.

"I'm fine. Just trying to figure out why this is happening."

"We can work that out later," he said. "But right now you need to concentrate on driving. Think you can do that?"

"Yeah." She nodded. "I can."

"Okay, there's a road about a quarter mile up on the left," Tucker said. "I saw it when we passed it earlier. When we're almost there, I want you to turn."

"What if there's traffic?" Alexis asked, tossing a glance over her shoulder at the Honda, now only a couple of car lengths back.

"Figure out how to dodge it. But I'm betting there won't be any. And if there is, I'm sure you can handle it."

"Thanks for the vote of confidence, but I'm not sure it's valid. It's not like I've driven for NASCAR."

"Actually, you'll be more like Evel Knievel if this goes right."

"Who?" She frowned over at him.

"No worries," he said, his smile enigmatic. "You just concentrate on driving and follow my instructions."

She nodded, still frowning, her eyes back on the highway. Tucker was watching the road now, shooting the occasional glance at the Honda still close behind them.

"Okay, you're almost there," he said. "Make the turn and then gun the car. I don't want them to have any time to think."

She sucked in a breath, and, as they drew near the dirt road stretching back into the twilight, she swung the wheel to the left, crossing the other lane. Behind them, the Honda's wheels squealed as it followed suit, the honking of an oncoming car punctuating the sound.

"Gun it," Tucker said, his eyes locked on the road behind them. "Good—they made the turn too."

She pushed the pedal to the floor, praying that the old sedan had the heart to hit the high notes. As the speedometer pushed past eighty and the wheel began to shake, the chassis bounced down the road, shaking Alexis's teeth so hard she could actually hear them. "I'd have thought you'd have wanted them to miss the turn."

"Would have been too easy." Tucker shook his head. "This will be better. If it works they'll be stuck here a good long while, buying us the time we need to disappear."

"So what's the plan?" she asked, already certain she wasn't going to like the answer. He had the look of a mischievous little boy, and, considering the circumstances, that couldn't be a good thing.

"There's a bridge up ahead. Only, according to the sign I saw when we passed the turnoff before, it's out."

"What?" The word exploded from her mouth, her knuckles turning white as she gripped the wheel. "You want me to jump the bayou? Oh my God. *Evel Knievel.*" It took every ounce of courage she had to keep from slamming on the brakes. The lights of the Honda behind her swelled as it moved closer and, with a mumbled curse, she pressed harder on the accelerator.

"Relax," Tucker said, clearly enjoying this whole thing a tad too much. "You're not jumping anything. They are. When you're almost to the bayou, turn the car. Hard right. Full spin. If this works, they'll be ass deep in mud before they have time to register what we're up to. And we'll be halfway back to New Orleans."

"But won't they have seen the sign?"

"Not a chance. Going east it was almost covered by a tree branch. And coming this way there wasn't any kind of warning."

"What about when we get there? Surely there'll be something about the bridge being out."

"I'll just have to make sure they're otherwise occupied," he said. "You just keep your eyes on the road and make that turn."

If she had any doubts about what he'd meant by "occupied," they vanished when he rolled down the window, taking a shot at the car behind them. It swerved but kept coming, and then responded with a volley of bullets that shattered the back windshield.

"Shit." The word was swallowed by gunfire, the sentiment summing up the situation nicely.

Tucker fired again, and the Honda fell back just enough to be out of range. Alexis pushed harder on the accelerator, the speedometer now at almost ninety. "I'm not sure we're going to last much longer," she said. "The hot light's coming on. This car's too old for this."

"We've just got to hang on a little longer," Tucker said, his eyes back on the road ahead. "We're almost there."

The shadows had deepened, a thicket of trees growing along the bayou's edge shutting out the sky. "You ready?"

"As I'll ever be." She nodded, still gripping the steering wheel with all her strength.

"Okay," he said, his voice sounding absurdly calm. "In five, four…" The trees were thinning slightly now as they approached the water. In front of her, Alexis could see where the pavement ended. A slight rise—and then nothing. "Three, two, one…" Behind her the Honda had closed the distance slightly, matching the Chevy's speed. "Now."

Alexis sent a prayer heavenward and, using every ounce of strength she possessed, yanked the wheel to the right. The Chevy hesitated for a moment and then spun to the side of the road, its momentum carrying it a hundred and eighty degrees. The Honda sped past, its driver fighting for control and losing the battle as the smaller car hit the ramp and then went airborne, flying out into the bayou.

Alexis hit the accelerator again, wheels spinning, as the air behind them erupted with water and mud and the screech of a dying engine.

"Go," Tucker yelled, his eyes on the car in the bayou.

"I'm trying," Alexis said, pumping the accelerator, praying for the old car to find traction. With a lurch the tires found solid ground, and the car sprang forward as she guided it back onto the road. On an exhale of breath, she headed back the way they'd come. Behind them the evening descended into night. "Oh my God." She tipped her head back, the wind whipping through her hair as she drove, elation making her giddy. "I can't believe it. It worked."

"I told you it would. All you had to do was have a little faith." Tucker was smiling too.

"And nerves of steel." She blew out a long breath. "What about the Honda? Did you see what happened?"

"I saw them go off the ramp. And heard them hit the bayou. Which means at the very least, they aren't going anywhere anytime soon."

"And at the very worst?"

He shrugged. "They aren't going anywhere ever. Either way we win."

She nodded, but the idea was sobering. She'd already seen one dead man today and was, at least indirectly, responsible for his death. The idea that two more might be dead should have mortified her. But it didn't. Not if the bastards had been part of the plan to kill George. "So what do we do now?"

"We ditch this car and make our way back to New Orleans. One thing I learned a long time ago—it's always better to hide in plain sight."

CHAPTER 6

Montreal, Canada

I wasn't expecting to see you again in person," Alain DuBois said, careful to keep his tone even as he gestured to the chair across from his desk, city lights flickering to life as night descended. "I thought we'd agreed that you'd use the drop we arranged."

"I would have, but there's been a small setback." George Atterley, or whoever the hell he really was, took a seat in one of the chairs artfully arranged in front of Alain's desk.

Alain studied the man as he fought against a surge of anger. Several weeks ago a man claiming to be Atterley had approached an associate, trying to sell a formula for aerosolizing biotoxins. Because of the magnitude of the weapon, he'd needed a buyer with not only deep pockets, but also with the ability to keep the sale completely off the radar. The associate had brought the proposition to Alain. Who had then brought it to his bosses.

Despite the fact that the man was clearly lying about

his identity—the real George Atterley was in prison, or at least he had been—it had been decided that the prize was well worth the risk. The deal had been struck.

Alain sat back, steepling his fingers. Perhaps they'd acted a bit too hastily. "I'm not sure I heard you correctly," he said.

"I said, I don't have the formula," the other man repeated, his eyes darting around the office. "I'm having more trouble than anticipated retrieving it. I just need a little more time."

"Our deal was very specific, Mr. Atterley. The formula you claim to possess is very valuable, but it is also a liability. We live in a digital age, information pulsing around the world in nanoseconds. And your fumbling attempts to find a buyer cannot have gone unnoticed. Which means that the window for a safe exchange is closing quickly."

"I told you it's just a delay. Nothing to worry about." Atterley lifted his chin. "We had a deal."

"With time constraints attached. And, as you were no doubt aware when you accepted advance payment, my associates and I are not about to forgive a debt. You agreed to bring us the key to weaponizing biotoxins, and if you can't"—he waved a hand through the air to emphasize his point—"there will be consequences."

"I understand your position, but let me remind you, Mr. DuBois," Atterley said, his gaze turning hard and calculating, "that without me, you have no chance at all of getting your hands on the formula. And if something were to happen to me, I can assure you that the technology would suffer the same fate. Bottom line is that I hold the winning cards. Not you. And so if I say you have to wait—then you'll have to wait."

"There is certainly truth in what you're saying," Alain said, biting down his anger. There was no sense in antagonizing the man. Not when they were so close to obtaining the formula. "But please don't make the mistake of underestimating the people you're dealing with. If this is some kind of trick, then you'll be the one to pay. We've already spent a great deal of time and money on this project. But we're not willing to risk exposure because of your ineptitude. And if that means ultimately losing the formula"—he paused, waiting until the older man dropped his gaze—"so be it."

"Look, I came to you. And it's in both of our interests to conclude this deal as quickly and quietly as possible."

"You never did say why you wanted to sell now. After all this time."

"It's simple," the man said, his shrug pragmatic. "I need the money. I made some bad investments."

"Haven't we all," Alain said, hoping this wasn't one of them. "Anyway, whatever your personal problems, I assure you double-crossing us will make them seem like a walk in the proverbial park."

"I'm not double-crossing you, and I promise you that I have every intention of fulfilling my end of the bargain. It's just going to take a little more time than I anticipated. There are fail-safes. For both of our protection." Atterley stood up and offered a hand.

Pushing to his feet, Alain ignored it, signaling instead to a man standing a few feet away. "François will see you out."

Atterley stood for a moment, his gaze still locked on DuBois, and then, with a brief nod, he preceded François from the room.

"You heard everything?" Alain asked, his eyes dropping to the telephone on the credenza behind his desk.

"I did." Michael Brecht's voice filled the room even though it was only an amplification from the speaker phone.

"And your thoughts?" Brecht was his boss, so it was crucial that Alain stay on his good side.

"I think," Brecht said, "that, as you already alluded, Mr. Atterley is quickly becoming a liability. But the formula is important. It'll move us years ahead in the quest to achieve our ultimate goals."

"So you believe him when he says that this is only a delay?"

"My instinct tells me there's something more going on, but until we can sort it all out, better to let him believe that we've bought into his assurances. Things have just gotten more complicated, I'm afraid. I've just had word that A-Tac is sniffing around again."

"I'm afraid we opened a Pandora's box when we allowed their operative to be a part of the organization."

"Well, it's a box we're going to have to close."

"So what's set them off this time?"

"I'm assuming they picked up the chatter surrounding the surfacing of the formula."

"Because of Atterley." Alain nodded even though Brecht couldn't possibly see him. "So what do you want to do?"

"For now we wait. If we're lucky, before A-Tac can find anything concrete, Atterley will produce."

"And if that doesn't happen?"

"Then I'm afraid we'll have to throw Atterley under the proverbial bus, and if we play our cards right"—there was

a pause, and Alain could almost feel Brecht thinking—
"then maybe we can arrange it so that he takes A-Tac with
him."

New Orleans, Louisiana

"Hey, you're supposed to be watching Alexis." Drake
frowned as Tucker walked into her house. Drake and
Hannah were running the scene with the help of a couple
of co-opted forensic techs from the local FBI office.

"It's not a problem," Tucker reassured him with a
shake of his head. "She's back at the apartment. Last I
heard, headed for a shower and bed."

"Where does she think you are?" Drake asked.

"Here, actually. I told her I had to ditch the car we stole
and then check on things here. See if maybe I could find a
clue as to who's behind all of this. I'm assuming you guys
already took care of the car."

"Done," Hannah said, from her perch on the sofa, her
ever-present laptop in front of her on the coffee table. As
usual, her glasses and hair were at odds with one another,
the former a vibrant shade of purple and the latter streaked
turquoise blue. In any other town her look would have been
memorable. But not in New Orleans.

"So what have you got here?" he asked, tipping his
head at the tech who was kneeling at the foot of the stairs
taking a photo of something on the floor.

"Not much so far," Drake said. "Unfortunately, they
managed to get the body out before we got here, along
with casings and anything else that might have been use-
ful in identifying the shooters."

"What about the picture I sent?" He'd managed to text the photo just before all hell had broken loose.

"So far it hasn't matched anyone in our databases. But I've only just started looking," Hannah said. "So I'm still hopeful we'll be able to ID him."

"What about the bomb site?" Tucker asked. "Tyler have any luck there?"

"Nothing definitive yet." Drake reached for the pitcher of cream. "But she's put together a profile, and she's running it through the ATF registry to see if she gets a hit. Maybe we'll get lucky and find out this wasn't our bomber's first time around the block."

"And Alexis Markham? What have we got on her?" Tucker asked, dropping down into the chair adjacent to the sofa.

"Nothing condemning." Hannah shook her head. "She's definitely kept herself off the grid. Lives mainly off cash. Best I can tell, never been on the Internet. Or if she has, she's used an alias. She rents the house. Long term. Paid cash for the full term of the lease. No driver's license, at least in her name, and only one bank account."

"So where is she getting money? Does she have a job?"

"Nothing that's traceable. I'm guessing whatever she does, it's an off-the-books, cash-only kind of operation."

"Like arms sales." Tucker frowned, trying to reframe his view of Alexis.

"It's a possibility we can't ignore. George Atterley could have hooked her up with the right contacts. And she's certainly in a position to use his name," Hannah agreed. "But there are a lot of ways to make money without leaving a paper trail. Especially in a city like New Orleans."

"We pulled her fingerprints from the house," Drake

said, "and so far no hits. But we'll keep digging. And we've got DNA too. From dirty dishes in the kitchen. We'll run it against every database we've got access to. Maybe something will pop."

"And, in the meantime, I'll keep watching Alexis." It wasn't exactly a hardship assignment. The woman was easy on the eyes, and the truth was it beat the hell out of the life he'd been living in Redlands.

"Yeah," Drake agreed. "Avery wants to keep this within the unit. If we're right and Alexis, or someone she's associated with, is trying to sell the formula to the Consortium, then we need someone on the inside. And you've got the background to go to ground with her."

"What about my history? Alexis isn't stupid. She's going to check my story."

"Well, she won't find anything about Colombia," Hannah said. "Everything that happened there has been buried so deep it's unreachable."

"Yeah, well, if they'd just told the truth from the beginning, there wouldn't be anything to bury—at least stateside." There was bitterness underlying his brother's words.

"Hey," Tucker said, his eyes meeting Drake's. "I'm alive. And we're together. And we've got Madeline."

"*I've* got Madeline." His brother smiled, the expression chasing away the shadows. "And you've got us. Emphasis on 'us.'"

"Believe me, I know. I've seen the way she looks at you." Lena's face filled his mind, her dark eyes smiling. But he shook his head, pushing thoughts of the past aside. There was nothing to be gained by reliving his losses. "So," he said, lifting an eyebrow as he turned his attention back to Hannah, "I'm assuming you've got all the bases covered as far as the rest of my cover is concerned?"

"Yes. If anyone contacts the prison, they'll confirm that you were a prisoner there. And that you were on the same cell block as George Atterley. That'd put you in rotation with him in the yard and at mealtimes. It would have been easy enough for you to have been friends."

"And if someone digs a little further?"

"Got that covered too." Hannah smiled. "There's documented evidence of your conviction and incarceration, as well as your release. There's also proof that you were set up, and that a tip from George Atterley figured prominently in your name being cleared and the record expunged."

"You guys are good. So how did you keep the lid on George's death?"

"Avery pulled a favor with the local constabulary, an inside track for some federal funding they've been after in return for a new name for the bombing vic. A homeless man—predeceased George by about ten hours. His body was unclaimed at the morgue. So it was easy enough to change cause of death. Did you get a read on the shooters?" Drake asked.

"Wasn't a lot of time." Tucker shook his head. "But, based on the firepower, I'd say that the outside shooters, at least, were pros. There was coordination at a level you wouldn't expect with gangs or run-of-the-mill criminals."

"And the guy on the inside?"

"Definitely seemed more intent on taking Alexis than killing her. He was carrying a Walther. I've got it here." He passed a small bag containing the weapon across the table to his brother. "No serial number, which again could signify almost anything. He wasn't carrying ID, just some ammo."

"Do you think the shooters were working with the inside man?" Hannah asked.

"I hadn't considered any other possibility until now, to be honest. I suppose they could have been separate incidents. Especially if you consider that the second group of shooters didn't seem as interested in sparing Alexis."

"So basically we've got three incidents that may or may not be related," Drake mused, his eyes narrowed in thought. "The ransacking of Alexis's house. The attempted kidnapping. And the shooters at the house."

"Actually, if you want to quantify it that way, then there are the shooters in the car as well. Although if I had to call it, I'd say they were the same men shooting at us here. Did you find bodies in the bayou?"

Hannah shook her head. "No such luck. Just the car. We pulled it out of the muck and have forensics people going over it now. But so far nothing to identify the occupants. We tried to run the registration, but the VIN had been removed."

"Sorry I didn't manage to take them out. What about the Chevy being bugged? Did you find anything on the car?"

"That was a little more revealing." Drake nodded. "The bug was located in the wheel well. A very sophisticated piece of nanotechnology, not something just anyone would have access to. Follows with your take that the second set of shooters were pros."

"But that wasn't the most interesting part," Hannah said, her expression tightening. "The specific technology used is government issue. U.S. government."

"So you think this is some kind of inside job?" Tucker frowned, running his thumb along the ripped arm of the chair. "You'd know if it was CIA, right?"

"If it was sanctioned," Drake said with a shrug. "If not, well, hell, it could be anybody. FBI. NSA. Even a freelancer. Anyone with the connections to get hold of that kind of device. But it does signify a major player."

"At least it's something, I guess." Tucker shook his head, the motion negating his words. What they had were a hell of a lot of unanswered questions.

"Well, we know for certain that someone was trying to find something at Alexis's." Drake leaned forward, arms crossed. "And that they didn't find it. And by extrapolation, I think we can assume it was the formula."

"Yeah, but all we've got is chatter indicating that the formula might have surfaced," Hannah said. "And contextual evidence that the Consortium is involved somehow. But we've got nothing to verify any of it."

"Yet." The word hung in the air for a moment, and Tucker's gaze encompassed them both. "But we do have Alexis Markham."

"So maybe we should bring her in?" Hannah asked.

"No." He shook his head. "Whatever the hell is going on, she's been off the grid a long time. My guess is that she doesn't trust authority. Hell, I don't think she trusts anybody. We bring her in now, and it'll take extreme measures to get at what she knows."

"And you think you can do better?" Drake frowned.

"Maybe. But more importantly, I think if she's out there, she's still a target. So even if she doesn't spill her guts, there's every chance that we'll get another shot at the people who want her. And this time we'll be ready."

CHAPTER 7

The apartment was dark.

Tucker closed the door and reached for the light, then thought better of it. If Alexis was sleeping, he didn't want to disturb her. The french doors separating the living room from the bedroom were more ornamental than functional, making the two rooms, for all practical purposes, one.

Light from the city outside served to illuminate the apartment enough to make getting around possible. It wasn't too far above places that probably rented by the hour, but it was serviceable and suited his purposes.

For the most part, he'd stuck to the truth when talking with Alexis. Her questions hadn't been particularly probing, and it had been easy enough to mix his fictional life with his real one. There was safety in the truth—at least an edited version. Although he had no illusions that keeping her believing would be an easy task.

He crossed the silent living room and stopped by the

door to take a look into the bedroom. At first he thought she was huddled in the corner of the bed, but closer inspection sent his blood pressure rising. Throwing open the door, he crossed to the bed, only to find his suspicions confirmed. The covers were drawn over pillows stacked together in the shadows, the resulting shape taking human form.

Shaking his head at his own gullibility, he checked the bathroom and the balcony, with no better results. Alexis wasn't in the apartment. He felt like a fool. How quickly he'd forgotten everything he'd ever learned on the job. Trust no one. Always expect the worst. And never let your guard down.

He felt like a rookie operative just out of training. But even then he hadn't been this stupid. Blowing out a long breath, he tried to think where she might have gone. She'd seemed so genuine when she'd said she was going to retire for the night.

Fuck.

The curtains in the bedroom window fluttered in a sudden gust of wind, and he caught a glimpse of the fire escape as the gauzy material billowed. At least now he knew how she'd managed to get out.

Double fuck.

He crossed to the window and was in the process of straddling the sill when he heard a small gasp of surprise coming from his left.

She was curled into the corner of the fire escape, her long legs bare, the soft white cotton of her tank outlining her breasts with mouthwatering clarity. The light from the street below turned her hair almost silvery. Ethereal.

And he found himself short of breath. As if he'd entered into the presence of something truly special.

Ridiculous thought.

He shook his head, breaking the spell. At least she hadn't run.

"What are you doing out here?" The words came out sharper than he'd intended, relief making him sound harsh.

"Watching the stars," she whispered, lifting her face to the sky. "When I was little, we moved around a lot. And when I was sad about it—which was most of the time—my father would take me up on the rooftop wherever we were and show me the stars. He'd always say that they're the same no matter where you go. It was his way of reassuring me that some things never changed. That everything was going to be all right."

"And did it work?"

"Yeah," she said, pushing to her feet. "Sometimes. Anyway, I don't know what I was thinking. He's been gone a long time now. I guess I was just looking for some perspective. Stupid, I know."

"Not at all. I think everyone needs a compass. External or otherwise. And the stars have been guiding mankind for a hell of a long time. I'd say they're as good as anything else when it comes to figuring out where you stand. So did you find that perspective?"

"No." She shook her head, her long hair dancing in the light. "Not that easy, I guess. Just feels like I've been down this path before."

"I'm not following. Someone's tried to kidnap you before today?"

"No. But it seems like I've been running my whole

life. For one reason or another. This is just the latest in a long line."

Alexis crossed her arms and leaned against the railing, the movement pushing her breasts higher, and Tucker stepped farther back into shadow, not convinced he could control his body's reaction to hers. She was totally oblivious of the way she looked, unaware of the fact that she was stealing his breath away.

Again.

Maybe that was what was so damn compelling about her. He'd first seen it at Weatherbees, an almost lethal combination of innocence and sensuality. He'd never met a woman so completely unaware of her femininity and yet so completely embodying it.

Somewhere in the distance a saxophone wailed, almost as if someone had cued the music. Laughter drifted up from the street below, and the air was heavy with the scent of flowers and the imminent fall of rain.

"I brought some of your clothes," he said, waving through the window at the duffel he'd thrown on the bed. "No idea if I got what you wanted. But I figured you'd be happier with your own things."

Her smile was slow as she turned around. "That was really nice."

They stood for a minute, energy passing between them, the electric current almost physical. He took a step forward, then stopped himself, fists clenching as his body tightened.

She licked her lips, her gaze still locked with his. "What you did for me, today..." She trailed off.

"I was just in the right place at the right time." He shrugged, still trying to contain his rising attraction.

She took a step closer, her eyes shining in the starlight. "I'm not very good at saying thank you. Too much time on my own, I guess."

"You don't have to say anything."

She reached out, her hand inches from his face. "I know, but I just…if you hadn't…what I mean is…" Something indefinable crossed her face. Pain, maybe, or something more. All he knew was that he wanted to pull her into his arms. To make promises he knew damn well he couldn't keep.

Then, with a soft laugh, she shook her head, the moment broken. "I don't know what's gotten into me." She gave a little shrug, her eyes crinkling as she smiled. "I'm not usually so emotional. Or sentimental." She turned her back on the stars. "Why don't we go back inside and I'll get dressed and then we can talk?"

Tucker nodded, the tension between them dissipating as suddenly as it had come. "It might make it easier for me to concentrate. Not that I'm complaining about the view."

Her answering laugh was lost on a gust of wind as she climbed back through the window. Tucker stood for a moment watching the heat lightning in the distance, the bank of clouds black against the night sky as it moved toward the city, already beginning to obliterate the stars.

He'd never really spent a lot of time staring at the heavens. In Colombia, the trees had formed a canopy that blocked the sky. And in Redlands—hell, the truth was he'd never looked up. He wasn't the introspective type.

He grasped the railing, angry at himself for letting Alexis get to him. For all he knew, the woman was trying to sell plans for what could potentially lead to the world's most dangerous weapon.

He climbed back into the bedroom to find her standing by the french doors, dressed now in a pair of sweats and a second tank. The look was less revealing, but the woman was no less attractive. Maybe Hannah had been right. Maybe he wasn't ready for this. It was too soon and too much had happened.

"Why don't we go into the living room?" Tucker asked. "I could use a cup of coffee." In truth, he could use a cold shower, but that seemed a bit obvious.

"Sounds good," Alexis said, following him over to the peninsula that separated the tiny kitchen from the living area, thankfully unaware of his train of thought. "Did you find anything at the house?"

"No. Someone had been there before me. Cleared out the body along with any solid evidence." He measured coffee into the percolator and then filled it with water.

"What about the car? Did you make sure it couldn't be tracked back to us?"

"Yes. I left it in Metairie, near a dealership. And I wiped it down. As soon as it's discovered, it'll be returned to its owner. No harm. No foul."

"Good." She nodded, slipping onto one of the barstools in front of the counter. "I guess retrieving my car is out of the question?"

"Absolutely. Anyway, I thought technically it belonged with the house."

"It does. It's just that I've gotten kind of used to it after all this time. It's such a beast. I guess I'll kind of miss it."

"Well, maybe when this is over you can get it back." The coffee pot hissed as the last of the water dripped into the pot.

"When this is over"—she sighed, accepting the cup of coffee he offered—"we don't even know what *this* is."

"I was kind of hoping you could help me with that. Surely you've got some idea as to what's going on?"

"No, I don't." Alexis cupped her hands around the mug. "I told you, I walked out on George before he had the chance to tell me anything. And our conversations while he was in jail were limited. He didn't want me to come and see him, and they monitor all the mail. So I've got no idea what any of this is about."

"Any chance it could be about you? I mean you were there at the diner too. If you hadn't run off—"

"I'd be dead too? So you told me." A shadow crossed her face, but she shook her head.

"Look, I'm just trying to put this together. And you've got to admit you're up to your neck in something. Depending on your take, the men here were either trying to kidnap or kill you. Which makes it valid to ask if this is somehow about you."

"And I got George killed?" She shuddered, tipping back her head, eyes closed. "Don't you think I've thought about that? But I've been over it and over it. And I'm telling you there's nothing. I live a really quiet life."

"What about work?" he asked, thinking that she was definitely hiding something. It was there in the set of her shoulders, the tight lines around her mouth. But whatever it was, she wasn't ready to share it with him. He'd have to earn her trust first.

"I don't actually have a job." She opened her eyes, staring down at her hands, and then lifted her gaze to meet his. "I have money. Not a lot—but enough to get by. George made sure I'd be all right before he went away."

"He cared a lot about you," Tucker agreed, well aware that he was treading on sensitive ground. "How long have you known him? You said you gave him the bracelet." He tipped his head toward the beaded leather around her wrist. "I assume when you were a kid?"

"Yeah." She nodded. "I made it at camp. I couldn't wait to give it to him. He said he'd never take it off." She traced the line of the beading. "God, I can't believe he's dead. It just all seems so surreal."

"Don't you have any other family? You mentioned your dad was gone. But what about your mom? Or maybe siblings?"

She dipped her head again, her hair swinging forward, hiding her face. "There's no one. They're all dead."

"I'm sorry."

"Doesn't matter." She lifted her head, twisting her hair into a ponytail, the effort making her look suddenly older. "I'm used to it. Even with George. It's not like he's been around, you know?"

"Yes, but if he's all you had left, then that makes his death that much harder to take."

She tipped her head studying him with clear, gray eyes. "So you said you met George in prison. Why were you there?"

"Wrong place, wrong time. I was framed for something I didn't do. "

"And George helped you out." The shadow of a smile crossed her face. "He's always been like that. Helping other people, I mean. After my family"—she swallowed, pain cresting in her eyes—"he was...he was there for me. Holding me together, quite literally sometimes."

"That's pretty much the way it was with me. I lost

someone very important to me. And then wound up incarcerated for something I didn't do. I didn't think I'd ever be a free man again. But George believed me. And he called on some friends who ultimately dug up the information that set me free."

"So when did he mention me?" She took a sip from her mug, her gaze inquisitive.

"After we'd gotten to know each other. Trust each other. I told you prison is like camp. You make decisions about who to trust a lot more quickly on the inside. Who you ally yourself with can be the difference between living and dying in there."

He thought about Madeline and the bonds they'd formed in San Mateo. His brother's wife had quite literally saved his life. She was as much a part of his family as Drake. Had been even before he'd known that she'd fallen for his brother.

"You're smiling," Alexis said, pulling him from his reverie. "It must be a good memory."

"Just a fierce loyalty. One that's deserved." She, of course, thought he was talking about George Atterley, and he had no intention of disabusing her of the notion.

"George was lucky to have a friend like you."

"It went both ways. Anyway, he talked about you a lot. But only in generalities. So if you're worried that I know things I shouldn't, I don't."

"There's nothing to know," she said, her denial too quick, too practiced, to ring completely true. "So when exactly did he ask you to watch out for me?"

"It was after I got out of jail. Maybe a week before he was released. He said he needed a favor. That if anything happened to him, he needed for me to watch out for you.

That's it. I've told you everything I know. He asked me to meet him at the diner. Said that you'd be there and he'd introduce us. You know the rest."

"None of this makes any sense. I've never had anything to do with George's business dealings. He was really careful to keep me separated from all of that. So there's no reason for anyone to be after me."

"Except that they clearly are. And it's pretty clear from the way they left your place that they were looking for something."

"But I told you, I haven't got anything."

"Maybe it's something you don't realize you have. What about your lockbox? You mentioned it in the car. You said you kept your pack there."

"And some money. But there's nothing in the pack except a few remnants from my childhood. A book, some photos, a rock—you know, childhood keepsakes."

"I guess that explains the purple and pink."

"It was very chic when I was in high school." She laughed, the sound surprisingly melodious. "Or at least that's what I told myself. Anyway, it's just a bunch of stuff from when I was little. Nothing anyone would want to steal."

"So why keep it in a lockbox?"

"It's silly, really. But George insisted I have the box as an exit strategy. Some money, some papers, things I'd need if I ever had to make a quick getaway."

"I thought you said you had a boring life."

Her eyes sparked with anger. "I said quiet. Not boring. But it was never about *my* life." Her fingers tightened around the mug and again he had the sense that she was holding something back. "He just wanted me to be prepared."

"In case something went wrong."

"Look, you say you knew George. You met him in prison, for God's sake. So you have to know the kind of life he led. The possibility was always there that someone would try to get to him through me."

"Except that George is dead." He hadn't meant to sound so condemning, but he couldn't take the words back.

"And now you're thinking maybe I had something to do with it? Come on. You saw my house. Saw the man trying to kidnap me. You were there when the bullets started flying. Not exactly the kind of thing that makes me look like the one pulling the strings."

He held up a hand in protest. "I wasn't implying anything. I was just trying to examine what's happened from every possible angle. The best way to figure out what's going on is for us to be honest with each other."

Again the shadow of something chased across her face. "I'm trying. But you have to understand, I've spent my whole life staying off the radar. It was George's way, and he was all I had. So it isn't easy for me to put my faith in a man I barely know—no matter how many times he saves my life."

"Well, at least you're giving me some credit for being on your side."

"I don't doubt that you're on my side, Tucker." She lifted her gaze to meet his. "It's just the reasons behind your decision that I'm still a little hazy about. But for now, you're all I've got. And I definitely need help. So why don't we agree to at least trust for the moment?"

He had a feeling it was something she didn't offer lightly, so he nodded solemnly. "Agreed."

"Okay," she said, taking a deep breath. "Then I think I know what our first move should be."

He waited, sipping his coffee, his senses prickling.

"Someone tried to get into my safe deposit box while I was in California. I didn't want to stir up anything when I found out. I just wanted to get my things and get the hell out of Dodge. But before I had the chance, everything went crazy. Anyway, I'm betting there's security footage. And if we can figure out how to get our hands on it, maybe that'll give us something more to go on."

"Well, there's no way you can go back to the bank. There's sure to be someone watching. And if I go, I'll run into the same problems as the guy who tried before. But I have an idea where we can go for help."

"You want to call in someone from the outside?" She leaned back, crossing her arms, eyes narrowed. "How do I know this isn't a trick of some kind?"

Tucker shook his head in impatience. "Look, we've covered this ground before. If I was out to get you, I'd have done it already. I'm here to help, and I've got a friend—well, more a friend of a friend—who's a whiz with computers. A hacker, as it were."

"Actually, now that you mention it, I know one too. A good friend, actually. And he's right here in New Orleans."

"Was he a friend of George's?" Tucker asked, his mind racing to find the right words to dissuade her. His brother and Hannah couldn't stay in New Orleans indefinitely and even if they could, direct contact was a risk. He needed an inside man.

"Yeah, why?" Alexis asked, eyes narrowed.

"Because until we know what we're facing, we can't trust anyone with a connection to George."

"Milo would never hurt me."

"I'm not saying he would. I'm just saying with my man, we can be certain there aren't any conflicting interests." It wasn't exactly the truth, considering that Harrison Blake was A-Tac's tech guru and that his mission, like Tucker's, was to find the formula. But it was like Alexis had said—for the moment there was trust and their goals coincided. And for now, that would just have to be enough.

CHAPTER **8**

S o this guy just dropped everything to come here and help us?" Alexis asked as they walked across Jackson Square toward a small hotel at the corner of Chartres and St. Peter. She'd followed Tucker's instructions to the letter, donning sunglasses and tucking her hair under a hat, her tennis shoes and shorts making her look like every other tourist in the square. In the center, a statue of Andrew Jackson held court with the facade of St. Louis Cathedral in the background. On both sides, walkways lined with artists and small shops were crowded with people.

What was it Tucker had said? Better to hide in plain sight?

"He's always game for a round of Beat the Establishment. Especially when it involves computers." Tucker, like her, was dressed in tourist attire. Jeans and T-shirt, an Angels cap on his head. In truth, she thought he had little in common with the overfed, underdressed tourists they'd passed. He was a lion among lambs. Even the way he walked seemed predatory. "I've worked with him a couple of times when I needed information on the fly. And he owes me one."

"And you're calling in your marker for me?" They walked out of the park, past a couple having a caricature made. They looked so relaxed and happy—and nothing at all like the drawing emerging on the paper.

"I am," Tucker said. "I take my promises seriously."

"Right. George." She knew she shouldn't feel disappointed, but somehow she did. "You're doing this for him."

"Look," he said, shooting her a sideways glance, "I know you're used to doing things on your own, but everybody needs a little help now and then."

"Even you?" she queried, not sure exactly why she'd asked the question, but curious now to hear the answer.

"Especially me." A shadow crossed his face, the emotion there so powerful it made her want to cry. But just as quickly it was gone, his jaw hardening as he pushed away whatever it was that tormented him.

She'd heard him in the night, tossing and turning, locked deep in a dream. He'd called out for someone. She hadn't been able to catch the name, but his pain had been evident and she'd been tempted to go to him, but something told her he wasn't a man who easily accepted comfort.

"We're here," he announced, pulling her from her thoughts, his hand warm on her elbow. They walked across the lobby and over to the elevators, waiting with a foursome of midwesterners arguing about the virtues of Aunt Sally's Pralines versus the ones at Laura's until the doors slid open.

"What do you think?" one of the women asked Alexis. "Do you like your pralines thin and crisp or thick and chewy?"

"Thin," she answered with a smile. "Definitely thin."

"And you?" the woman continued, turning her attention to Tucker, her eyes taking in his lean hardness with appreciation. "What's your preference?"

"I'm not big on sweets," he answered with a shrug. "But if I had to pick, I'd take chewy."

"Figures," Alexis said as the elevator lurched upward.

"Honey," one of the woman's friends said, "it's the differences in life that make it worthwhile." There was a titter of laughter as all four women admired Tucker.

Alexis kept her eyes firmly on the ascending numbers, relieved when the doors opened and the women made their exit.

"Nice ladies," Tucker said, the corner of his mouth twitching with a smile.

"They certainly seemed taken with you." She reached up to pull off her hat, but stopped when Tucker shook his head, tipping his chin toward the tiny camera embedded in the wall above them.

They waited in silence as the elevator rose to the top floor. The doors slid open, and they stepped into the hall. It was a small hotel, the floor T-shaped. Tucker steered her to the right.

"So you think there's a chance someone is monitoring the hotel security feed?" she asked, glancing behind her at the closing elevator doors.

"Anything's possible, and I figure it never hurts to be careful."

"You've done this kind of thing before?" It came out

a question, but she was pretty sure she already knew the answer.

"Like you, I've lived my life in the shadows," Tucker said as they stopped in front of room 417. "And in my world, we don't ask questions. It's just better that way."

"I didn't mean to—" she started and then stopped. What the hell, she *had* meant to ask. She did want to know more about him. Although for the life of her, she wasn't sure if it was because she was trying to protect herself or because he intrigued her.

Tucker knocked on the door, and it was opened by a man with tousled brown hair and eyes that were both green and brown, as if they couldn't quite make up their mind what color they wanted to be. "Hey," Tucker said. "Thanks for coming."

"Couldn't pass on a chance to help a pretty lady," the man replied, his eyes full of speculation even as his smile held her with its boy-next-door charm. "I'm Harrison." He held out his hand.

"And I'm Alexis." Apparently, like Tucker, Harrison didn't believe in last names. She shook his hand and then followed him into the hotel room. It was nicer than the apartment where they'd been staying. A suite, with a living room that opened out onto a balcony overlooking the square. A hotel room on Chartres didn't come cheap.

"Sorry," he said, reading her mind, "I'm a sucker for good hotels. Especially with a view. Besides, I figured it was less likely someone would be watching for you here. Hiding—"

"—in plain sight," she finished for him. "I know. It's practically become a mantra."

"Well, sometimes a cliché is a cliché for a reason."

Harrison smiled, a hint of laughter in his oddly colored eyes. "So have a seat, and let's see if we can get into that bank of yours." He picked up a laptop and dropped down into a chair by the window.

"Have you had any luck with the man in the photo?" Tucker asked as he crossed to the window, looked out, then sat on the windowsill.

"Not yet, but I haven't given up. Might even have more for you while you're here." He nodded toward a second computer set up on the desk. It beeped and whirred almost as if it was part of the conversation. "I'm searching databases as we speak. Good thinking to take a picture. I'm assuming the body is MIA?"

"Got it in one," Tucker said. The conversation seemed absurdly normal considering the actual topic, and Alexis found herself wondering again how often Tucker, and for that matter Harrison, found themselves in this kind of situation. Clearly this wasn't the first time for either of them. "When I went back to the house, someone had sanitized the scene."

"I'm assuming from the conversation you've already told Harrison everything that happened?" Alexis interjected, taking a seat on the sofa.

"Yeah, when I called him last night. You said it was all right." His gaze met hers, his eyes questioning.

"Yes, of course." She nodded, with a curt smile.

"Okay," Harrison said. "It's Security Bank and Trust, right?"

"Yes," Alexis confirmed. "On Royal."

"Good I've already been working on their encryption. So when did the guy try to get into your safe deposit box?" Harrison asked, turning his attention to his laptop.

"According to the assistant manager, three days ago.

Around noon. He said it was a man on his own claiming to be my uncle. Except that I don't have an uncle. Anyway, he managed to intercept the guy before he could access my box."

"Shouldn't take too long," Harrison said, tapping on the keyboard. "I'm already over halfway there. And once we're in, it won't take much longer to find the right time stamp." He glanced up with a grin. "Trick is to do it without anyone realizing I'm in there."

"You were right." Alexis smiled at Tucker. "He does love the challenge. So how did you guys meet? You said it was the friend of a friend?" The minute the words were out, she wished them back. Tucker had warned her about asking questions. But Harrison seemed unconcerned.

"I did some virtual work for him. Referral through a friend. That went well, so he called me the next time he needed a little cyber snooping."

"Harrison is easy to work with," Tucker added. "Knows just when to keep his mouth shut."

Alexis ducked her head, anger and embarrassment washing through her.

"Don't mind him," Harrison said with a wave of his hand. "He's always Mr. Doom-and-Gloom. 'Watch your back.' 'Mind your words.' Caution personified."

"Well, he's right," Alexis said, surprised at her desire to defend Tucker. "It does pay to be careful. I mean, if I'd just turned and run the minute I realized my house had been broken into, maybe none of this would have happened."

"Or maybe it would have just played out somewhere else," Harrison said, his tone turning serious. "Somewhere without Tucker there to intervene."

"Believe me, I'm more than aware of how lucky I am."

She sighed, staring down at her hands, feeling not only inept but stupid as well.

"Hey, right place, right time," Tucker said. " If I hadn't been there, you'd have figured a way out."

She lifted her head, unable to stop her grateful smile. For a moment it was just the two of them, then Harrison cleared his throat.

"I think I've got it."

Tucker crossed over to stand behind Harrison's chair, motioning for Alexis to join him. Harrison tapped a couple of keys and the video became a still; another couple of keystrokes and he'd enlarged the image. Alexis could see Eli Munro standing with another man in the safe deposit vault. "That's the bank manager," she said, pointing out Munro.

"And the other man?" Tucker asked. "Do you recognize him?"

Alexis shook her head, disappointed. "No, I've never seen him before. I don't know what I expected. Maybe the guy from the house."

"It's possible they were working together," Tucker said. "Harrison, you've got a copy of the still, right?"

"Yes," Harrison answered. "Got the entire sequence as well. It crosses a couple of cameras but I can splice it together. You want to see it from the beginning?"

"Please." Alexis bent over to get a better view of the screen. Harrison opened a program and, in short order, had the sequence spliced.

"Here goes." He hit a key, and the bank's lobby came into view. A couple of seconds later, the unidentified man entered the bank. He stopped for a moment in the entrance, his gaze moving slowly around the lobby.

"Clearly checking the place out," Tucker observed.

"Right," Harrison said. "Now he's headed for the vault." There was a little blip, and the camera moved to the desk outside the safe deposit box vault. The man talked to the woman at the desk for a few seconds, and she buzzed him through to the vault. He disappeared from view, and the woman picked up the phone, presumably to call Mr. Munro. The screen switched again, this time to the camera inside the vault. The man stood in the center of the little room, drumming his fingers on the table as he waited.

Munro arrived, and the conversation was fairly short, the man waving his hands in anger as he realized that he wasn't going to be allowed access to the box. The two men talked a few minutes more, then Munro escorted the intruder from the room. Again the camera switched, this time to the lobby. The man emerged from the vault room and headed for the door, stopping once mid-lobby, then exited the bank.

"Hang on," Tucker said as Harrison paused the video. "Can you go back a few frames? To where the guy stops?" Harrison moved the video back to the point Tucker referenced. "Okay, now can you zoom in on the guy?"

"Sure." Harrison hit a key, and the man's face filled the screen.

"Okay now play forward."

This time Alexis could see the man shake his head, his attention on someone standing at the far corner of the lobby. "He's signaling to someone."

"Looks that way," Tucker agreed. "Any way we can zoom in on the corner?"

"Shouldn't be a problem," Harrison said, adjusting the screen so that the focus was now on a man standing near the teller windows. He was deep in shadow, and Harrison's first attempt to zoom in on his features yielded a grainy, unidentifiable image. "Wait a minute—let's see if I can clean this up." With a couple of keystrokes the man's face suddenly became clear.

"That's the man I killed," Tucker said.

"Which means we still have nothing." Alexis sighed. "Just faces without names."

Tucker moved back over to the window, checking outside again. Then, seemingly satisfied, he turned back to face them. "At least we know for certain that the two incidents were connected."

From across the room Harrison's second computer beeped, the sound making Alexis jump. "Does that mean we have an ID?"

"Yeah." Harrison leaned over the computer to study the screen. "And nothing particularly surprising, either. Jason Fogerty. A contract player."

"Contract player?" Alexis shook her head. "I don't understand."

"A hired gun," Tucker said. "Basically the man will do pretty much anything if the price is right."

"Looks like he made the NSA's most interesting people list." Harrison frowned down at the computer screen.

"So he's a terrorist?" Alexis felt her stomach revolting.

"No." Tucker shook his head. "Just someone they were watching. Mainly for his contacts, I suspect."

"You seem to know a lot about this sort of thing." She frowned over at Tucker. "I mean, what exactly was it you were doing before you landed in prison with George?"

"Let's just say I don't like playing by the rules either."

"So you're a contract player too?" she asked.

"I'm someone who likes to help the little guy even the odds. People like you who get caught up in things they shouldn't be caught up in."

"That's not much of an answer."

"I could ask you how you wound up with George—but I haven't. I could ask what happened to your family—but I haven't done that, either. And you know better than most why I haven't asked."

"Because it's part of the code."

"Okay," Harrison said, swiveling around to face them. "Now you've lost me. What code?"

"People who live off the grid don't ask each other questions," Alexis explained. "They form a loose network, a family if you will. But they don't ask for details. Everyone has a right to their secrets. And everyone has the right to choose whom they share those secrets with. So I was breaking the code when I asked Tucker about his life."

"Seems to me, in a situation like this one," Harrison said with a shrug, "honesty is the only thing that's going to keep you both alive. But then what the hell do I know? I'm just a lowly hacker."

"I've got the feeling there's nothing at all lowly about you or your work." Alexis laughed, grateful the tension had lifted.

"So what else do we have on this guy?" Tucker asked. "Anything that would connect him to Atterley?"

"Nothing specific. I'm running a more in-depth cross-check now, but a guy like Fogerty wouldn't have obvious connections to anyone," Harrison said, squinting at the screen as he scrolled through the file. "He's American. Ex-military. Had a couple of low-level jobs in government security before he turned to more lucrative endeavors.

He's pretty much kept to the shadows, but there's evidence linking him to arms dealers and drug runners out of Colombia."

Tucker and Harrison exchanged a look, an uncomfortable undercurrent suddenly filling the room. "What aren't you telling me?" Alexis asked. "That this is somehow related to drugs? To Colombia?"

"I've honestly got no idea," Tucker said. "But we know that George was involved with moving illegal goods. It isn't that far a leap to think this could be connected to trafficking."

"Look, I know George usually comes down on the wrong side of the law. But there's no way he was involved with drugs." Alexis crossed her arms, shaking her head. "He'd seen firsthand how it could affect people. He had a girlfriend in college who died of an overdose. That kind of thing stays with you."

"We're all just guessing here. Trying to connect dots that might turn out not to have any relation at all. It's possible Fogerty was exactly what we said—a hired gun," Tucker said. "What about the guy in the bank? Any chance we can get an ID on him?"

"Already ahead of you," Harrison replied, hitting a couple of keys on the computer. "I've been searching databases using the picture from the security footage. Let's see if the computer's found anything."

A new screen opened, the picture of the man in the bank on the left, a series of photographs flashing across the screen on the right. It only took a few moments, and the screen froze; a box flashing the word MATCH. Harrison clicked on the box and another window opened, this one with the picture of a younger version of the man.

"Well, this is odd," Harrison said, scrolling down through the accompanying information. "I got a hit. But it's not out of any of the criminal databases. It's from DOD. The guy's got a security clearance. Pretty damn high, in fact."

"So you're telling me the man is a suit at the Department of Defense?" Tucker moved so that he could see the screen.

"No." Harrison shook his head, still scrolling. "He was part of the security detail there. But he's been out now for a while."

"So he's retired?"

"Doesn't say here. Just shows that he's not at DOD anymore, and there's no record he's working for anyone else. Name's Peter Dryker. Ring any bells?" Harrison's gaze included them both, but Alexis knew the question was meant for her.

"No." Alexis's stomach clenched at the thought that DOD might be involved in all of this somehow. It didn't make any sense. Not after all this time, but she couldn't ignore the possibility. "I've never heard of him."

"You look like you've seen a ghost," Tucker said. "You sure you haven't heard his name before?"

"I'm positive." She knew her words were clipped, but she couldn't help it. She wasn't ready to tell Tucker about her father. "I'm just spooked by the idea that somehow this whole thing could be tied to the government. George was always certain they were after him. Even after all this time."

"But George is dead, so even if this started out being about him, there's got to be something that links this all to you."

"Maybe it's over," she said, wishing the words true. "Maybe they've realized I don't have what they want, and now they'll just leave me alone."

"No. I'm sorry to say it, but I don't think so. For one thing, Fogerty is dead. He's a bottom feeder, but there are still bound to be repercussions somewhere along the line. And if they were satisfied that you didn't have what they wanted, they wouldn't have tried to kidnap you. Or come after us in the car."

"So what do we do?"

"It'd help if we knew what they wanted." Tucker said. "Did you keep any letters George might have sent from prison? Any documents he might have stored with you?"

"No. I don't have papers or files or anything. All I have is the bracelet you gave me and a ring George gave me after my dad died."

"Well, keep thinking. There's got to be something." Tucker gave her a smile meant to reassure, but in truth she only felt more confused.

"So what do we do in the meantime?" she asked.

"We need to find a connection. Something that links Fogerty and Dryker to George," Tucker said. "I know Atterley was in prison for quite a while, but he had a life before that. Does he have a house somewhere?"

"No." Alexis shook her head. "He's always been somewhat of a wanderer. Used rentals. Never really put down roots."

"What about a storage facility?" Tucker moved back to the window, his expression calculating.

Alexis started to shake her head, then smiled instead, dimple flashing. "Wait. He had a cabin on the Rio Grande. I haven't been since I was a kid. I don't even know if he still owns it. It was near South Fork in Colorado. He and my father liked to fish. "

"Yeah, I'm on it," Harrison said, typing again on the laptop. "Nothing in the county property taxes that show George Atterley. Any other name he might have been using?"

"Actually, there were several. But his favorite was always Dick Charles." Alexis smiled, remembering. "He was a big Dickens fan."

Harrison nodded, still typing. "Got it. Or at least there is a Dick Charles who owns property. Had it since the eighties. That seem right?"

"South Fork is small. I can't imagine there'd be another Dick Charles. Although I suppose it's possible."

"Only way to know for certain is to go there and see for ourselves," Tucker said. "How do you guys feel about a road trip?"

CHAPTER 9

"Hey," Tucker said, stopping just inside the apartment building's lobby. "Wasn't expecting to hear from you so soon." He adjusted the phone as he stepped back into the shadows, his gaze moving across the room to make sure no one was listening. "I'm assuming you're back in New York?"

"Yeah, we got back a couple of hours ago," Drake responded. There'd been nothing more to do at the scene. So the decision had been made to leave Tucker and Harrison to handle Alexis, with the rest of the team coordinating things from Sunderland. "Sorry to interrupt. Hopefully I didn't put anything at risk."

"I was on my way to get takeout," Tucker said. "Alexis is upstairs. But you'd better make it quick. I'm assuming it's important?"

"Yeah. Maybe something you can use as leverage with Alexis. Actually, there are two things," his brother told him. "The first is that Tyler got a hit on the bomber's MO."

"The one that killed George."

"Right," Drake said, his tone grim. "It's a match right down to the way the bomb was constructed. Ignition, size, blast radius—all of it. The interesting part is that it dates back thirteen years."

"That's a hell of a long time to wait for the second act."

"Agreed. But the similarities can't be ignored. It happened in Walsenburg, Colorado. A house was destroyed along with everyone inside. A family of four. Guy taught at the local elementary school. His wife worked in a flower store. Case was cold almost before it started. No leads. No reasons anyone could find why this family was targeted. And with no one living, there was no one to push the case, so it was shelved unsolved. We're lucky it was even entered into the database."

"Is there any connection between the bombing and George Atterley?" Tucker asked. "Or Alexis?"

"Not directly, but there is if you connect the dots," Drake said. "Harrison told me about the house in South Fork. It's about a hundred and twenty miles from Walsenburg."

"Well, I think we can be fairly certain that Atterley didn't blow himself up."

"Agreed," his brother said. "But there's more. We did a little more digging into Alexis's past—and came up with nothing."

"Which is bad because..." Tucker swallowed his frustration, wondering why the hell it suddenly seemed to matter so much.

"Because when I say nothing," Drake said, "that's exactly what I mean. Nothing. We can trace her back in New Orleans for like six years. A little more. But before that there's no record of her anywhere."

"Well, she said she was off the grid with George for at least part of her childhood."

"That's just it, though. We—"

"And of course by 'we' you mean Hannah."

"Roger that." Drake laughed. "I honestly believe Hannah can produce intel from a pile of sand. Anyway, the point is *she* can't find any record of an Alexis Markham that fits the stats. There's no one. It's as if she sprang full blown into New Orleans without any kind of past at all."

"So Alexis is using an alias. Again, not that surprising based on what she's told me," Tucker said, leaning back against the wall, his eyes still on the empty lobby.

"Here's the really interesting part," Drake replied. "We ran her DNA and didn't get a match. Which wasn't all that surprising since she's clearly taken great care to stay off the radar. But then Hannah widened the perameters a little bit, just in case there was something we'd missed, and she got a hit. A partial match. Close enough that it could only come from a sibling or parent."

Tucker felt the hairs on his neck rise and knew he wasn't going to like what Drake had to say next.

"The hit was a man named Randolph Baker. A DOD employee. He was a high-clearance chemist who worked on several weapons development programs, including the Omega Project circa 1980."

"The one tasked with developing the formula for aerosolizing biotoxins." Tucker clenched a fist, waiting for the other shoe to fall.

"Theoretically," his brother said. "The project was shut down in 1982, and some claim it never existed. Certainly it was never for public consumption. Anyway, whatever the hell they were working on, Baker's partner,

Duncan Wallace, was found dead in his lab shortly before the program was dismantled, and not too long after that, Baker disappeared."

"He's the one who is supposed to have stolen the formula."

"DOD, quite understandably, denies that. But yes, that's the story that was circulating at the time. Bottom line, Baker just fell off the grid."

"So why was his DNA on record?"

"Apparently it was standard op for weapons development programs in the day, especially those requiring tight security."

"And you're certain that Alexis is related?"

"You can't fake DNA," Drake said. "And based on his age, I'd say he'd have to be her father."

"What do the records show? Did Baker have a family?"

"According to DOD insurance records, there was a wife and child—a son. But that's all we've got."

"Well, if Alexis was his daughter, she wouldn't have been born yet. So there wouldn't be a record then."

"And after that, if he was living underground," Drake said, "there wouldn't be a birth certificate. At least not in that name."

"According to Alexis, her father's dead. And I'm guessing from context that he's been gone awhile," Tucker said, gut churning as the facts suddenly fell into place. "You think it was Baker who died in the bombing in Walsenburg."

"It seems conceivable," Drake concurred. "And it explains a lot. Like why Alexis is living off the grid. And probably how she was acquainted with Atterley. He'd have been in the same situation and therefore moving in the same circles."

"She said her father and George used to go fishing. That's how she knew about the cabin in South Fork. But according to your intel, the entire family died in the explosion, right?"

"Yes," Drake agreed. "But it's possible she wasn't there that night. As I said, there wasn't a long-term investigation. The house was completely incinerated. If Alexis did survive, it would have been easy enough to simply let authorities think she died along with everyone else. And considering that someone murdered her family, I can certainly see the attraction of staying dead. Bottom line, if Randolph Baker did steal the formula, and if Alexis is in fact his daughter, then there's every possibility she's got it now."

"But she would have been just a kid when he died," Tucker protested.

"A teenager. And if her father trusted her, she may very well have known everything, and then sat on it until she was old enough to do something with it or felt like it had been long enough not to raise too many red flags."

"I don't know if I'm buying any of this."

"Maybe you just don't want to," Drake suggested.

"No. It's just that the further into this I get, the more I'm certain that she isn't trying to sell anything. And I definitely don't believe she killed George Atterley. The man was like a father."

"I think we've pretty well established the fact that she didn't kill George. First off, we've got the fact that Atterley's bombing was almost an exact match for the one in Walsenburg. And when you add in the father's partner's death..." Drake trailed off.

"Don't tell me," Tucker said. "It was an explosion."

"Officially an accident. But there were pyrotechnics involved and a severe fire. Not exactly the same MO. But it was enough to send Baker underground. And given the scenario we've come up with, I think it's highly likely Duncan Wallace's death is related to Baker's and Atterley's."

"We're just missing the connection."

"And for my money," Drake said, "innocent or not, Alexis Markham is the key to that connection."

"You're absolutely sure? Everything he told me is the truth?" Alexis glanced up from the phone toward the door of the apartment, almost as if she expected Tucker to materialize.

"Yes," Milo Alozono confirmed.

She'd agreed to using Tucker's friend, but that didn't mean she'd agreed not to contact Milo. Despite Tucker's warnings she trusted the man. Milo was a utility player, capable of handling most anything—for the right amount of money. He'd helped her set up her new ID when she'd moved to New Orleans. George had recommended him, and in truth, she'd liked his easygoing Cajun manner and over the years they'd developed a close friendship.

"All the details checked out," Milo continued. "Prison. His conviction being overturned. All of it. And I even found proof of George's involvement. I only had time to scratch the surface. But for what it's worth, the guy seems to be on the level."

Relief flooded through her, and she released a breath she hadn't even realized she'd been holding. "Thanks, Milo."

"I can do some more digging if you want me to," Milo

offered. "Or you can just talk with George. He's out of prison now, isn't he?"

"Yeah," Alexis said, forcing herself to sound cheerful. Tucker had insisted that she not tell anyone about George's death. All the better to keep his killers off balance. "I will. He's just out of pocket for the moment. I think he needed time on his own for a bit."

"Figure he's got some itches that need to be scratched," Milo's voice held a note of laughter.

"I'm sure," she said, choking up as the image of the explosion filled her mind. "Anyway, I knew you'd be able to verify the truth. And at least for now, I don't need anything further. Except maybe Tucker's last name?"

"Flynn." Milo said. "His name is Tucker Flynn."

The door to the apartment opened, and Alexis mumbled her thanks and punched the button on the phone to disconnect.

"Who were you talking to?" Tucker asked, his voice calm and not at all accusatory. But she felt guilty all the same. For a moment she considered lying, but something in his eyes reminded her that the man valued honesty. It was important to her too. Even living in a world that necessitated lying.

"My friend Milo. I was checking out your story, actually."

He didn't seem the least bit surprised. "And what did you find out?"

"That you've been telling me the truth. About prison and George helping you." She slid the phone into her pocket, chewing the side of her lip as she waited for him to say something.

"I'm surprised it took you this long," he said, the hint of a smile playing about his lips. "So, learn anything new?"

"Just that your last name is Flynn." There was something comforting in his calm acceptance of her doubt. "Nice Irish name."

"My dad would be happy to hear you say that. Even though he never set foot on the Emerald Isle, I think he liked to believe he had a bit of the blarney." The last was said with a soft, rolling lilt.

Alexis smiled, even more charmed than before. "I thought we weren't talking about personal things."

He sobered, his face tightening as he sat across from her on the arm of the sofa. "Actually, I think it's time we broached the subject. Most specifically, your past."

She flinched, the words like ice water, banishing whatever camaraderie they'd shared. "I don't know what you mean."

"Alexis, I've been doing some digging too. You should know that bombers are a bit like serial killers. They adopt an MO. A preferred methodology. And no matter how many times they act, or how long a period there is between these acts, there's usually something unique that identifies them. So several years ago, the ATF created a database. One that helps them track arson and bombing incidents based on past behaviors, and it turns out that the bomber who killed George has acted before."

Her hands were shaking, and she fought to maintain control, rage warring with sheer terror. "How the hell did you get access to an ATF database?"

"Harrison. You've already seen what he can do."

"But how would you have even known where to look?"

"I was in the military for a while. Worked with ordnance some. It really doesn't matter. What's important here is that the other bombing occurred thirteen years ago." He paused, his gaze locking on hers. "In Walsenburg, Colorado. It was a house. A family was killed."

The air rushed from her lungs, and she could literally feel the blood drain from her face. It had been so long since she'd even let herself think about that night. The fiery sky. George's hand closing around her arm. Her family gone. Her world destroyed.

"Look, it's not that hard to put together. Your dad and George were friends. And George had a place in Colorado. Alexis Markham just sprang into existence six years ago. And you told me your father was dead. I swear, I'm not trying to ambush you. But anything you tell me about that night...about why someone would want to kill your family..." He trailed off, waiting.

She fought for breath, pushing away her emotions. It wouldn't help anyone to lose it now. And she'd spent too many years erasing her past to let it swamp her now. As before, she considered lying to Tucker. But again she couldn't do it. Maybe she trusted him more than she should. Or maybe she was just being practical. After all, if this was about her father she needed help. And Tucker was the only one volunteering for the job.

"My family was on the run," she whispered, lacing her fingers together to stop the shaking. "I never knew any other way. I'd had three names by the time I was thirteen. My father said moving would keep us safe. That and keeping to ourselves, staying off the radar. That's how we first met George. He worked with us when we moved to Colorado. Secured the necessary paperwork and IDs. Helped my parents find jobs and a home."

"And then something happened?"

"Yes." She nodded, her mind forced back to the past

and the memories of that horrible night. "Someone blew up our house. Someone who wanted my father dead. And my mother and my brother got caught in the crossfire."

"And you?" Tucker asked, his voice unusually gentle.

"I'd snuck out to go to a basketball game. I told my mom I was going to the library. And she let me go. My dad hadn't come home yet. He was really strict about us appearing in public places—even the library—but my mom understood that I needed my freedom. But she wouldn't have agreed to me going to the game. I've always wondered if it was me..." She trailed off, tears choking away the words.

"It couldn't have been you, Alexis. There wasn't time. The bomb was premeditated. It would have to have been set up in advance. Your going to the basketball game had nothing to do with the bombing. Although it saved your life."

"The police just assumed I was dead. And George thought it was better if I just disappeared."

"But surely if this was about your father, it wouldn't have had any further impact on you."

"You're kidding, right?" She couldn't believe he'd even had this thought. "It changed everything. My life was a little off, maybe, with the changing names and locations, but my father and my mother loved me. And my brother was the only good friend I ever had. The impact was beyond contemplation, Tucker. There aren't even words."

"God, I'm sorry," he said, reaching out to cover her hands with his. "I didn't mean it like that. Shit. I'm not always the most sensitive of guys. What I meant was that you didn't have to stay underground. That with the threat gone, there was no reason for anyone to come after a kid."

Alexis turned her hands palms up, reveling in the feel

of his skin against hers. It had been a long time since anyone had touched her. "I'm sorry too. Maybe I'm a little oversensitive."

"No," he said, shaking his head. "I should have thought about what I was saying—how I was saying it."

She blew out a breath and pulled her hands free, surprised at how much she instantly missed the contact. "George thought it was better if I stayed out of sight. I was young. And there were bound to be questions. And he was afraid that if the people after my father knew I was still alive, they'd feel obligated to come after me. Loose ends—that's the way he put it. I didn't have a life in Walsenburg anyway, not without my family. George was all I had left. It was easy just to do what he wanted."

"And you've lived off the radar ever since."

"Yes."

"Lonely way to go," he said, and she had the feeling he was speaking from personal experience, that he actually understood the box she'd been trapped inside for all of her life.

"It was easy at first, with George. But then I grew up, and he insisted I needed my own life. Separate from him. And so Alexis Markham was born. I've just been off the grid so long that I can't even begin to conceptualize what it would take to be legitimate. And even though the problems originated with my father, I'm still his daughter, and I'm not convinced there wouldn't be fallout if someone figures out who I am."

"Well, I think now you know."

"So you really think all this has to do with me?" She ran a hand through her hair, emotions running riot.

"I think it has to do with your father. And his relationship with George and whatever the hell someone thinks you have access to. So what happened with your father? What set all this in motion?"

"I wish I could tell you definitively," she said, pushing off the sofa and walking to the window. "Most of what I know comes from my father, but he was just talking about the general situation, not the specifics. Over the years I've tried to dig out more, but for the most part I've hit dead ends. And I didn't dare push too hard because I was afraid I'd accidentally out myself."

"Well, why don't you tell me what you do know."

She paused again, wondering how much she should tell him, and once again opted for the truth. "My dad was a chemist. And before I was born, he worked at the Department of Defense. Selected projects, from what I can tell. Maybe two or three over the course of his tenure there. But it was the last project he was working on that caused problems. As I said, he never discussed specifics. All I've been able to glean from my years of digging was that it was called Omega. And that it was super-top-secret stuff."

"I think most of what DOD does is top secret."

"Well, apparently Omega was as secret as it gets." She sighed, moving again to sit across from him in an armchair, leaning forward, her hands cupped beneath her chin. "My dad and his lab partner were the key players. And according to my father, they believed they were doing theoretical research. Just playing with equations and applying them to biochemistry. But somewhere along the way they realized that the work wasn't theoretical at all. That it was, in fact, being used to develop a biotoxic weapon."

"Sounds like pretty serious stuff."

"Yeah, and when they found out, they threatened to go public with it. As I said, it was a secret project. Anyway, shortly after that, my father's partner wound up dead. And Dad figured he was next."

"So he believed people within the government killed his partner?"

"Yeah. Which meant he didn't stand a chance on his own. So he took my mother and my brother and disappeared. He said the conspiracy, whatever it was, went to the top. That there wasn't anywhere legitimate he could turn."

"He told you all of this?"

"No." She shook her head and attempted a smile. "I overheard a lot of it. My mom and dad talking. She hated giving up her life. She was a college professor. English literature. I don't think she ever really got over losing it all. Although don't get me wrong—she made the best of it. Just like we all did. We loved my father. And we understood that it was the only way we could all be safe. But in the end it was all for nothing. They found him anyway."

"I'm sorry. I can't even imagine what it must have been like for you. I've lost people I love—some of them violently—but I never had to witness it firsthand." He leaned forward again but this time she shifted away, avoiding contact.

"I managed." She shrugged, the gesture forced as she pushed up to walk over to the window again. Below her, over the balcony, she could see the street and the restaurant on the other side. "I even thought I'd put it all behind me. Until someone took out George and tried to do the same to me."

"And you honestly have no idea what they want? Or who 'they' are—other than people who may have been connected with this Omega Project?"

"No. I've got nothing. And, believe me, I've been over and over it. But I just don't have the access to the information I need. To be honest, I'm not sure anyone does. It's been thirteen years since my father died, and almost thirty since he worked on Omega. That's a long time for someone to have to cover their tracks." She frowned as her gaze settled on a black car sitting just past the coffee shop.

"What is it?" Tucker asked as he came to stand behind her.

She frowned, eyes still on the car. "I think we're being watched."

CHAPTER **10**

There's a car down there. See?" Alexis pointed and Tucker shifted so he could follow her line of sight. "It was there when I looked out the window just a little while ago. But it's moved—maybe a parking place or so. I think there are people inside. It's probably nothing, but..."

"Better to be sure," he said, pulling a small scope from his pocket. He put it to his eye, adjusting it until the car swam into focus. "There's definitely someone inside. Two men. Can't make out who they are, but I think you're right. I think they're watching the apartment." He slid the scope back into his pocket. "Good catch."

Despite the seriousness of the situation, she smiled, clearly pleased with his words. He wondered, not for the first time, how often in her life someone had taken the time to give her praise. George Atterley and her father had clearly cared, but her father had died early and George had been in prison almost half the time since her dad's death. That meant she'd spent a lot of time on her own. And he knew better than most the loneliness that kind of existence created.

"So what do we do now?" Alexis was still looking up at him, a shadow of worry crossing her face.

"We get out of here." He smiled, reaching out to squeeze her hand. "You keep watch here at the window, and I'll give Harrison a call and check the fire escape." He hit speed dial and waited.

"Yo, what's up?" Harrison said, answering on the first ring.

"We've got company out front," Tucker said, striding over to the bedroom window and pulling the curtains back. "There's no one watching the fire escape, though. They must figure we'd have to spill onto the street if we try to get out."

"Any other option?" Harrison asked, the sound of tapping keys accompanying his words.

"Not that I can see. You got anything?"

"Yeah, maybe," he said. "There's a door at the end of the alley. Assuming you can make it, it'll take you through an absinthe shop and out onto Bourbon Street."

"Well, at least that gives us an option. There's no movement yet, so I can't be positive they're there for us. Got a license, though. Local. CZH 964."

"Tucker?" Alexis called from the other room. "I think they're coming up here."

He moved back into the other room, crossing over to the window, passing the phone to Alexis as he pulled the scope from his pocket. "Damn," he whispered as he gained focus. Two men in overcoats on a steamy Louisiana evening couldn't be a good thing. "Tell Harrison we're on the move. We'll go with his plan. They've just now entered the building, which means they're on the way up."

Alexis relayed the message, and again Tucker was struck by how calmly she handled crisis. "He said he's on his way. So you going to fill me in?"

"We'll go down the fire escape. But we need to move now," he said, already shepherding her into the bedroom toward the window. "You go first."

She nodded and was just about to throw her leg over the windowsill when she stopped, a line forming between her eyebrows as she frowned. "Wait. I need my things," she said.

He started to protest, then changed his mind. It would be faster just to give her the damn pack. He reached across the bed for the pink and purple strap, and then tossed it across the room to her just as the door to the apartment burst open, a barrage of bullets strafing the living room walls and bedroom door.

"Go," he said, stopping to grab his own pack, figuring the extra ammo and gun inside might come in handy. Pulling his gun, he fired through the door, then made his way to the window and out onto the fire escape. Alexis was already on her way down, and he followed suit, the alley only two floors below them now.

Behind him he could hear the intruders as they clamored out onto the fire escape. Alexis had reached the bottom floor, but the final ladder was rusted firmly in place. "What now?" she asked as he joined her and a bullet whizzed by.

"You're going to have to jump," he said, turning to shoot behind him, the men ducking back to avoid the gunfire.

She opened her mouth to argue, took a quick look at the men above them, and, without another word, jumped down into the alley. Tucker took another shot, satisfied to see that he'd clipped one, and then followed suit. The men above opened fire, but by sticking close to the wall Tucker managed to keep them out of range.

The alley was short, lined with trash bins and other refuse. Although they passed a cardboard box that clearly served as a home, thankfully the occupant was not in residence. Tucker turned to fire again. The two men had reached the bottom of the fire escape, one of them aiming to shoot while the other tried to push down the ladder.

"Keep going," Tucker said, pushing Alexis forward. In front of them the alley curved sharply to the right and dead-ended into a small courtyard overgrown with plants from what had once been a garden.

"Shit." Alexis slid to a stop, frustration cresting. "Is this your big plan?"

"There's a door on the back wall. Must be behind the vines. We've got to keep moving."

She sprinted forward, pushing aside the heavy tangle of ivy that covered the back of the building. "You're right," she called, "it's here."

She pulled on the old wooden door but it refused to budge. "Maybe it's locked."

"You better pray it's not," Tucker said, pushing her aside and yanking with all his might. The door groaned as it granted access. "Inside," he said, "quickly."

She dashed through the opening and he followed, pulling the door shut behind him. "Come on."

They were in some kind of storage room, shelves stocked with boxes and crates. Alexis followed as he moved forward, gun still drawn. It was unlikely that anyone dangerous was waiting, but he didn't want to take a chance. The storage room opened onto a brick-lined hallway, old wrought-iron brackets standing testimony to the age of the building. A locked door led off to one side and a swinging row of beads separated the back rooms from the front.

"Through there," he said, following her through the beads, lowering his hand to mask his gun.

"What the—" The startled woman behind the counter jumped to her feet, dreadlocks swinging, the tattoo of a monkey climbing up one of her arms.

"Sorry to pop in like this," Alexis said, giggling like a schoolgirl. Surrounding them were the glass fountain sets, brouilleurs, antique bottles, spoons, and other accoutrements that accompanied the reviving practice of drinking absinthe. "I'm afraid it's my fault." She giggled again, swaying slightly as she placed a hand on Tucker's arm. "We've been partying all afternoon and—well..." She smiled beguilingly. "We ducked into an alley to— well"—she giggled again—"you know. Anyway, then I dared him to come through here."

Tucker forced a crooked smile, slipping his gun into his pocket. "I told her we'd get in trouble."

"No way," the girl said with an answering smile. "I've used that alley myself on occasion."

"Thanks." Alexis grinned, slipping her hand through Tucker's, pulling him toward the front door. "Nice shop."

They slipped outside into the twilight and the gathering crowds of tourists on Bourbon Street. "Good work," Tucker said, picking up the pace as they made their way up the street. "That was quick thinking."

"A lifetime looking over your shoulder makes you pretty nimble on your feet." She shrugged. "So what now?"

"We blend into the crowd until we hook up with Harrison at the rendezvous point," Tucker said, pulling out his phone.

"You keep sounding like a spy movie." She shook her head, her hand tightening on his arm as they hurried down the street. "Or a government operative."

"I told you I have a military background. They drill the words into your head. Guess I've carried them over more than I realized. Anyway, we need to keep moving— one of our guys just rounded the corner."

Alexis slowed, shooting a look over her shoulder.

"Don't look. He hasn't made us yet. But if you keep checking him out he's going to see us."

"Right." She nodded, her eyes back on the crowds in front of them. "I'm sorry. I'm not as good at this as you are. Where are we meeting Harrison?"

"Intersection with Toulouse. If he turns onto Bourbon, we'll never get out of here." He indicated the tourists, many of them spilling out onto the street, most of them already inebriated. Behind them their pursuer was closing the distance.

"I thought there were two of them," Alexis whispered as they hurried forward.

"I clipped one. Maybe he wasn't up to the chase."

"A girl can dream." Alexis started to turn again but stopped, resisting the urge. "What if he catches us?"

"He won't." Tucker shook his head to underscore his words, hoping he was telling the truth. Odds were that the man wouldn't open fire on a crowded street, but anything was possible. "It's just another half-block or so."

Ahead of them a black sedan pulled into the street. Tucker reached back for his gun, careful to keep it out of sight. His finger tightened on the trigger, the pressure just short of firing. The car, a Toyota, honked at an errant pedestrian and then moved forward.

"Is that the same car?" Alexis asked, her fingers digging into his arm.

"I think so," he said. "But unless they open fire we've still got maneuvering room." They picked up the pace, dodging laughing patrons spilling out of a bar, the piano music adding a macabre sound track to the already tense situation. "When I say go, I want you to run for the corner. Harrison should be there. A blue Jeep. He'll be watching."

"What about you?" she asked, her gaze darting over to meet his.

"I'll be right behind you."

She nodded, and Tucker stepped back into the shadows of an alley, checking behind him again. The man was closing fast, maybe three yards back. He lifted his hand, talking into a mic, and the Toyota hit reverse and then swerved to block the entrance to Toulouse.

"Go. *Now.*" Tucker barked. "Cut to the right to stay away from the car."

She nodded once, then sprinted forward, knocking people aside in her haste. He waited a beat, then stepped deeper into the shadows as the man behind them broke into a run. As the guy moved past, Tucker grabbed him by the neck and with a quick twist rendered the bastard unconscious.

"One down," he said to no one in particular. "Now for the Toyota." Reaching into his bag, he grabbed a flare and dashed out into the street just as the driver started forward again, gun stuck through the window, the muzzle aimed at Alexis as she hit the corner frantically looking for Harrison. With a mumbled curse, Tucker ran up on the car from behind, triggered the flare, and lobbed it through the open window.

The car lit up like a Christmas tree and then filled with smoke. People screamed as the driver lost control and rammed into a utility pole. In front of Tucker the Jeep roared into view, slowing as it approached the corner where Alexis was standing.

Tucker gave the car a last look and then made for the Jeep, following Alexis through the open door almost before Harrison could bring it to a full stop. "Go," he yelled as Harrison floored the Jeep, the engine roaring to life as they sped up Toulouse away from the frantic scene.

"Well, you guys certainly can't be accused of making a boring exit," Harrison said as he turned, heading for the highway. "Where to next?"

"Colorado," Tucker answered, turning so that his gaze met Alexis's. "George's house. And, hopefully, some answers."

Governor Bastion Carmichael looked out across the expansive Sacramento skyline. Below him traffic moved at a snail's pace, the cars surrounded by the swaying palm trees that marked the gardens, their arching branches stark against the darkening sky. The city—hell, the whole fucking state—was his kingdom. A lot better than his meager start at DOD. He'd worked long and hard to earn his place here, and he wasn't about to let it go easily. Especially not because some twit of a girl suddenly decided to become a player.

"So explain to me exactly how it is that you've managed to let her get away—again."

Peter Dryker winced at the accusation, his face flooding with color, his hands tightening into fists. "I told you. She has help."

"Clearly." Bastion waved his hand, impatience biting at his gut. "But so did you. You assured me yourself that Jason Fogerty was one of the best."

"This guy with the girl—he's good too. He's got training. Maybe military. Maybe something more."

"So you're telling me this guy's one of ours?" Bastion frowned.

"I'm telling you he's got special training. I don't know if he's working inside or out. But he's definitely got the moves of an operative."

"Did you get a good look at him?"

"Just the photo I gave you. And it's not very clear. The guy moves like a ghost. Took out Fogerty, damn near got me when I opened fire trying to save him. And I just got word that he wounded a second man this evening when they managed to jump surveillance."

"Any idea where they've gone?" Bastion asked, closing his eyes in an effort to calm the churning in his gut.

"No. Not for certain." Dryker shook his head, not quite meeting Bastion's gaze. "But if you're right and the old guy is dead, then my guess is she's scrambling to get the deal done before any more hell breaks loose."

"Like maybe a bunch of half-assed old security geezers screwing up their orders to take her out?"

"You didn't want her dead in the beginning, remember?" Dryker said, a flash of anger in his eyes. "Fogerty would still be alive if he'd been allowed to kill her. It was trying to kidnap her after we'd searched the house that got him killed."

Bastion shrugged. "Probably a mistake on my part. I thought I'd be able to reason with her. But clearly she's called in reinforcements, so obviously we can't take a chance on keeping her alive."

"So you want me to track her down and kill her?"

"Third time is the charm?" His grin lacked humor, and Dryker at least had the good sense to look uncomfortable. "No. I don't want you to do anything to her until we find out who it is that's helping her. If you're right and he's a government operative, then he just might pose more of a danger than she does. The last thing we need is to turn his attention to us. That's exactly what we're trying to avoid."

"So how do you want to handle it?"

"I'll call in some favors." Bastion turned for a moment to look out at the city again. "Use the photo you got and see if we can ID this bastard. Make sure he's not connected to an investigation into Atterley's death."

"You're sure the guy's really dead? I mean, maybe he's the one pulling the strings. Maybe he was playing us from the beginning."

"It's possible, but if that were the case, he isn't playing anyone anymore. He's definitely dead. Died in an explosion right here in California. Redlands."

"So how long have you been sitting on this?" Dryker was back to being angry. Fogerty had been an old friend.

"Not long. I had to do some real arm twisting to get the truth. Someone's hushed the whole thing up. I still haven't been able to verify who. Or why."

"Maybe the deal's already gone down and the buyer is trying to tie up loose ends. It's what you'd do."

Bastion smiled. "Yes. It is. But I don't think the formula's surfaced. If it had, we'd have heard more chatter. My guess is that the deal is still in play. And my hunch is that Ms. Markham will make her move soon. Atterley was certain it was her."

"Like I said, it could have been a trick," Dryker reminded him.

Bastion resisted the urge to slam his hand on the desk, reaching instead for a ball he kept beside his in-basket. Squeezing it in the palm of his hand, he waited a moment as he regained his composure. "He was telling the truth. He was devastated by her betrayal. That's the kind of emotion a man can't fake. He said she was the only one who could possibly have it."

"So you think she's on to us?"

"I think whoever's helping her is going to start digging. And thanks to you and your team, there's probably a trail of evidence leading right to me."

"You know I'm always careful. Hell, Bastion, we've been in this together from the beginning. Since the day they shut down Omega and Baker stole the formula. I thought when he died it was all over."

"Yes, well, that's what we get for letting our guard down. But at least now, thanks to Atterley, we know she's out there. And once I verify who's helping her we'll be able to figure out our next move."

"And until then?" Dryker asked, a frown creasing his face.

"Until then, you go home and sit tight. I'll be in touch."

Dryker nodded and, still frowning, left the office.

Bastion sat down, his mind spinning as he considered his options. The girl had proved to be far more

resourceful than expected. And if Dryker was right and
the man helping her was with the government, it wouldn't
be long before he found Dryker. Bastion sighed, releasing
the ball to pick up the telephone. It was a shame, really.
Peter had been right. The two of them went back a long
way. But there really was no other choice. He couldn't
afford to leave loose ends, especially volatile ones like
Peter.

"Hello?" he spoke into the phone, his voice automatically lowering to a whisper. "The discussion we had the
other night?" He waited a beat, then continued. "I'm
afraid it's time." He swiveled around to stare out into the
fading twilight, wondering when the price for success
had gotten so fucking high.

CHAPTER 11

The cabin was nestled into a grove of aspen at the foot of a rocky precipice. A stream cut through the rocks below, the sound of rushing water filling the air. Lupines mixed with Indian paintbrushes, orange and purple rioting together to fill the meadow in front of the little house with color.

In her mind's eye, Alexis could see George and her father laughing over a beer after a day on the river. Waders on the porch, rods angled against the outside wall, and creels overflowing with trout. She could hear the porch floor squeak as George went inside, her mother's laughter floating through the screen door, her father's arm warm as he pulled her close, smelling of cedar, and river, and fish. It had been a wonderful trip. She and her brother, Frank, had actually gotten along. Which was huge, considering she was younger and usually a pest.

She sighed, letting the warmth of the memory soothe her. Her family was gone. But she'd always remember.

"You okay?" Tucker asked, his concerned voice cutting through her thoughts.

"Yeah, I'm fine. Just remembering. The time we spent here was special. We were complete here, if that makes any sense. It was almost as if the rest of it—the running, the lies—couldn't follow us here. We were happy."

"I know just what you mean," he said. "With us it was baseball games. My dad loved the Angels. You know, the devoted, throw-things-at-the-TV-when-we're-losing kind of fan. And so when things got rough, he'd take us to a game—our own private retreat."

"'Us'?" she questioned, knowing she shouldn't ask but craving more insight into her self-appointed protector.

"My brother," he said. "It was a long time ago."

Alexis nodded, picturing Tucker as a boy with a crooked grin and a baseball cap.

"You guys want to go down memory lane or maybe see if there's something in the house that can help us figure out what the hell this is all about?" Harrison asked, coming to a stop beside them.

Alexis shook her head, banishing the image of little Tucker. "There should be a key under the flowerpot by the railing." Again her mind presented a picture—her father laughing as her mother reached beneath the pot of geraniums for the key.

They walked up onto the porch, the floorboards still squeaking. Harrison lifted the empty pot, the flowers from her memory long faded. "There's nothing here." He ran his fingers along the floor underneath to be certain.

"Doesn't matter." Tucker frowned. "The door's already open." He nodded toward the screen door, which on closer examination was slightly askew, the door behind it ajar.

"They've already been here," Alexis whispered, reaching for the screen-door handle.

"Wait," Tucker said, moving to stop her, his hand gripping her upper arm. "It could be a trap."

Harrison agreed, and together the two of them searched the door frame and the surrounding wall. "I think we're clear," Harrison pronounced.

"Seems so," Tucker said, reaching out to pull open the screen.

Alexis flinched as he pushed open the door but nothing happened, the only sound the wind rustling the aspens.

"You ready for this?" he asked.

Alexis nodded and, after sucking in a deep breath, walked inside.

It was like stepping back in time. Nothing had changed. The linoleum floor. The yellow kitchen table. Even the old plaid sofa. It was almost as if they'd all just gone out for a walk or dinner in town.

"It's just like I remember," she said, pulling away from the past to face the present. "Well, maybe a little more run down. But, essentially, it's the same."

"Except that someone has been here," Harrison said, pointing at the footprints covering the dusty floor.

Tucker drew his gun. "And not too long ago at that."

"What makes you say that?" Alexis asked, her skin prickling at the thought that someone might still be here, watching.

"The dust hasn't had time to cover the tracks," Harrison said, squatting down to have a closer look. "I'm guessing it'd be a good idea to check the rest of this place."

Tucker nodded as Harrison pulled out his gun. Then, after motioning for Alexis to stay back, the two of them moved forward, quickly searching the cabin. It didn't take long. There was only the living area, bathroom, and two bedrooms.

"We're clear," Harrison said, holstering his weapon as he came out of the first bedroom.

"Good here too." Tucker emerged from the second bedroom, the one her parents had used, lowering his gun. "But we'd best keep our eyes open."

"Why don't you guys look around in here and I'll check outside," Harrison said, already headed out onto the porch, the screen door squeaking in protest as it closed behind him.

"Doesn't look like George has been here in ages," Alexis said, running a finger through the thick dust that had accumulated on the kitchen counter.

"And whoever was here didn't toss the place, so my guess is that it was either a vagrant or maybe someone who was looking for George and not the formula."

Alexis pulled open the kitchen cabinet to find only remnants of what had once been a full set of dishes. She remembered the pattern well. It had been a favorite of her mother's. Heavenly Daze. She closed the door on her memories and opened the next cabinet door, to find some old cans of beans and a stockpot. The rest of the cabinets were empty, and none seemed to have been disturbed before their arrival, supporting Tucker's assumption that the intruder hadn't been looking for anything.

"There's nothing in the living room or bedrooms," Tucker said, coming to stand beside her. "You're right. It doesn't look like anyone has lived here in a while. Maybe even longer than the six years George was in the pen."

"We never came after my mom and dad died. I always

figured it was because he wanted to spare me the memories. But maybe it was that way for him as well. They were all really close."

"Is there anywhere else? An outbuilding or a cellar or something?"

She started to say no, then stopped. "There is something, I remember. It's nothing really special—just a place in the back of one of the bedrooms. A space behind a loose log. A place for treasures, George called it. But I don't think he'd have kept anything in there that was important. It was more for us kids."

"Won't hurt to have a look, though, right?" Tucker asked. "Which bedroom?"

"The one on the right. That's the one George always slept in." She followed him through the door, stopping at the sight of the faded quilt on the bed. Like the rest of the cabin, it had seen better days, but Alexis smiled anyway.

"What?" Tucker prompted.

"My mother made that quilt. I'd forgotten it was up here. She used scraps from all the other sewing she'd done over the years. This was from my first party dress." Alexis touched the faded cotton. "I loved that dress. I wish I'd known the quilt was up here. I could have preserved it."

"Maybe George thought it was best to keep the past in the past."

"I suppose you're right. I doubt he even knew what the quilt represented." She smoothed the old quilt and then pointed to the far wall. "It's over there. Where the floor meets the wall, behind that nightstand."

She followed him over to the corner, feeling as if she were being followed by ghosts, a memory of a family that existed now only in her mind.

Outside, leaves crackled as someone moved beneath the window. Tucker spun around, gun in hand.

"Wait," Alexis said from her vantage point near the window. "It's only Harrison. "

Tucker relaxed, holstering the gun and then reaching out to move the nightstand out of the way. Alexis dropped down on her knees, feeling for the crevice that marked the loose wood. With a satisfying click, the molding pulled away. "It's here. Just as I remembered."

She reached inside, expecting to find nothing, but her hand closed around a metal padlocked box.

"Well, I'll be damned," Tucker said. "Maybe this is what everyone has been looking for."

Alexis picked up the box, cradling it as if it were precious. But then again, maybe it was. It belonged to George, after all.

"I should have something in the car to get that lock off," Tucker said, but Alexis was already turning the dial.

She moved it first left, then right, then left again, and the lock clicked open. "I've got it," she called.

"I thought you said you didn't know there was anything in there." His brows had drawn together, suspicion coloring his expression.

Alexis allowed herself a smile. "I didn't. It's just that George is a little predictable. He always used my birth date for combinations and passwords."

She laid the box carefully on the bed and lifted the lid. Inside, there were a couple of faded pictures, a dried Indian paintbrush, and a book of some kind.

"What have you got?" Tucker asked, coming back to stand beside her as she reached for the pictures.

"I'm not sure. But I'm thinking this isn't worth killing

over." She lifted the first photo. It was her, as a baby, in a playpen outside the front of the cabin. Her mother was also visible in the shot, wearing Bermuda shorts and sunglasses. She was holding a drink and laughing. "It's my mom," Alexis said, holding out the picture. Tucker took it from her and held it up to the light.

"Nothing but a photo, I'm afraid."

"It's a lot more than that," Alexis murmured. "I thought all the photos were gone. I've only got one of my family. And it was taken before I was born. Before my father was forced on the run. So this picture is worth a great deal to me, Tucker."

"I didn't mean..." he started but trailed off, looking decidedly uncomfortable.

Alexis reached over to touch his hand. "I know." She held the contact for a moment, her nerves all firing at once. Then she shook her head and pulled away, reaching instead for the next photo inside the box. In this one she was dressed for her first school play.

She'd been the moon. Not a particularly challenging role, but her father had said the moon was the most beautiful star in the sky. It hadn't been until she was older that she'd learned the moon wasn't a star at all. Not that it mattered. The only important thing was that her father had thought she was beautiful.

There were three more photographs, all of her at various key times in her young life. Testaments to the worth George had placed on her role in his life. She fought a surge of tears.

"What about the book?" Tucker asked, clearly impatient with her trip down memory lane but, to his credit, trying not to show it.

"I don't know," she said, picking it up. The cover was spotted with mildew, the spine starting to split. She flipped it open. "Looks like a journal. Only the handwriting isn't George's." She flipped through the pages, stopping as a familiar smell filled her nostrils—Chanel No 5. Her mother's scent. Suddenly the tears were impossible to hold back, the handwriting swimming in front of her as recognition dawned. "This was my mother's."

She sank down onto the bed, holding the journal as if it might suddenly take wings and fly away. "She must have left it here, and George kept it for me." She wiped away the tears, wondering why he'd never mentioned it. They'd talked about her family so often. Especially her mother. Having her journal would have meant everything. But it would have broken the code. Maybe that was why he'd kept it hidden away all these years.

She drew in a breath and started reading midpage.

I think Randolph knows. Though I can't imagine how. We've been so careful, stealing moments when we can, but only when it's safe—when Randolph's away or the children are there to keep him occupied.

Alexis frowned as she continued to read.

I never knew love could feel like this. That I could feel like this. It's amazing and frightening and so wonderful I can't even find words. I wish there were a way I could leave Randolph. But he'd never let the children go. And I couldn't bear life without them. So I pretend that there is nothing between us and live off of stolen moments. Kisses and touches and nights spent dreaming of George.

George.

Alexis whispered the name, anger and grief flooding through her.

George.

He'd betrayed her father. Seduced her mother. And all these years he'd lied to her. Pretended he'd been part of her family when, in truth, he'd been trying to destroy it. She threw the book across the room.

"What is it, Alexis?" Tucker asked, hovering so close that she could feel his breath on her skin and see the worry in the blue of his eyes.

"My mother was sleeping with George." She spat the words, the taste of them bitter against her tongue. "They were having an affair. She was cheating on my father." Suddenly all of the memories took on new meaning. Her mother's quilt on George's bed. The secret smiles. The photos. She grabbed the pictures again, realizing this time that every one of them had her mother in it. Usually in the background, but always visible. George hadn't kept the pictures because they reminded him of Alexis; he'd kept them to remember his lover.

Her mother.

"She says she thought my father knew. He must have been devastated. He loved her so much. How the hell could she have done something like that to him?" She threw the pictures in the same direction she'd thrown the journal. The photos twirled in invisible eddies as they drifted to the floor. "My dad was George's best friend. How could George have betrayed him like that?" She looked up as if expecting Tucker to answer, then realized she'd been so lost in the past she'd forgotten the present. "I'm sorry. I know none of this matters now. They're all dead. It's just that I didn't know. And now that I do... well, don't you see, it changes everything."

"It changes nothing," Tucker said, sitting down beside

her, the cadence of his breathing more soothing than she could possibly have imagined. "Whatever they were to each other, they all loved you. That much is abundantly clear just from what you've told me."

"But we were a family."

"And you still are. Look, Alexis," he said, tilting her chin so that he could see her face. "When I was young, my mother ran away. She just left my father and my brother and me. Without ever looking back. And my father was destroyed. But slowly, with a lot of help, we put our family back together again. We realized we didn't need her to go on."

"That's what all the baseball games were for," Alexis said, her voice coming out on a rasp.

"Exactly."

"But don't you hate her? Your mother, I mean? For leaving you?"

"I did," he said, wiping away her tears with one large finger. "But I finally realized that in hating her I was letting her win. So I just quit caring altogether."

"Well, right now I hate them for what they did to my dad. For what they might have done to me—if my mother hadn't died, that is."

"You have no way of knowing what she would have done. But one thing is perfectly clear: At least in that moment, she chose you and your brother. And later, when it really mattered, George chose you."

"Because of her."

"Maybe a little. But he loved you too."

"You can't know that," Alexis insisted, shaking her head. "And I don't know that I'll ever be able to forgive them."

"Well, in the meantime I think we should keep the photos and journal."

"Take them if you think it could help us." She shrugged. "But don't keep them for me. I don't want them. And I don't think anything will make me change my mind about that."

"Okay. But I'll still hang on to them," he said, his tone still soothing, as if he were talking to a child. It should have made her angry. But, oddly, all she felt was protected. Clearly she'd lost her mind.

"I've got something out here you need to see," Harrison said, stepping into the doorway, his eyebrow raised at the sight of the two of them huddled on the bed. "You finding anything interesting in here?"

"Just some old photos and a journal." Alexis pushed off the bed and away from Tucker. "My mother's."

"We haven't read the entire thing yet." Tucker stood up too, his expression guarded. "But so far there's nothing in it that sheds any light on our current situation."

"Except the fact that my mother was cheating on my father," Alexis said, the words coming before she could stop them.

"With George," Tucker added.

"God, I'm sorry," Harrison said. "What a lousy way to find out."

Alexis nodded. "I guess maybe he really did love her. If he kept her pictures and her journal all these years. I don't know. Maybe I shouldn't be so angry. It's not as if either of them betrayed me. But my father had been through so much. It just seems so horrible that they'd add adultery on top of everything else."

"Sometimes people can't control how they feel,"

Harrison observed with an apologetic smile. "You just love who you love."

"And damn the consequences?" It was a question, but she already knew the answer.

"Sometimes." This was from Tucker, whose smile was bittersweet. "If there's one thing I've learned over the years, it's that wishing things had been different is a wasted effort." He shrugged, then turned to Harrison. "You said you found something we need to see?"

"Yeah, right." Harrison nodded. "I found an old suitcase under the house. But it's wedged in pretty tightly, and the space is too narrow for me to be able to get at it. So I figured you guys could help."

CHAPTER **12**

Tucker knelt down beside Harrison to look underneath the pier-and-beam foundation of the cabin. There was only a couple of feet of space, the rocky terrain beneath the bottom of the house anything but inviting.

"You can see why I needed help," Harrison said. "I'm not even certain it's worth trying to get it. I mean, clearly it's been there awhile."

"Or someone wanted to make it look that way." Tucker said, frowning as he looked at the case.

"Alexis, do you remember seeing this before?"

She dropped down beside him, bending low so she could see underneath the house. "No. It definitely wasn't there when I was a kid. Frank and I used to crawl under here all the time. If you crawl past the porch, it's big enough to sit up. We called it our secret clubhouse. Anyway, there wasn't a suitcase."

"Okay, so we know it dates from after the time Alexis's family died. I'd say that makes it worth giving it a look-see."

"Any idea how you want to retrieve it? I tried crawling in, but it's pretty damn tight."

"I can do it," Alexis volunteered. "It's not like I haven't done it before."

"Fine," Tucker said, fighting against the instinct to say no. She'd already had one shock, and there was no telling what else George had squirreled away up here. "Just be careful, okay?"

She squeezed his arm, smiled, and then dropped to her stomach and began to crawl underneath the cabin. "It's not so bad," she called, still shimmying forward. "At least there's nothing dead under here."

"You know, for a girl, she's pretty damn game," Harrison said, barely hanging on to his laughter.

"I heard that."

"Good hearing as well." Tucker, too, was working not to chuckle.

"All right," Alexis said. "I'm here. What now?"

"See if you can jimmy it loose."

"Okay." She shifted slightly so they could see the bag. "Looks like an old satchel of some kind. Maybe George threw it out."

"Or a vagrant left it. Anything's possible."

With a quick intake of breath, she started to pull the suitcase forward. "It's stuck against something. But I can't see what."

"Hang on," Tucker said. "Let me give you some light." He flipped on the flashlight he'd pulled from the car and aimed the light at the case. "That better?"

"Yeah, much. Thank you. Looks like it's caught on the wooden beam." She shifted position again, this time with her body blocking their view of the case. There was a grunt and then a whoop of satisfaction as the case pulled free. "Got it," she called triumphantly, already pushing herself backward toward the edge of the porch.

"Almost there," Harrison called, shining a second flashlight to give her even more illumination. She nodded and then shifted slightly to the right as she tried to turn around. Something from deep underneath the house groaned, and the floor above Alexis came tumbling down, a cloud of dust obscuring Tucker's view.

"Shit." Alexis's voice was muffled by the dust.

"You all right?" Tucker called, already trying to push his way underneath the house over to Alexis.

"I'm okay, but I'm stuck. And we've got a serious problem."

"More serious than your being trapped?" Tucker asked, his back scraping against floorboards and joists.

"Yeah," she said, her voice losing some of its bravado. "The suitcase just started blinking."

"Fuck," Harrison said.

"My sentiments exactly," Alexis agreed, a tremor of fear underlying her attempted bravery. "Any chance you can get me out of here?"

"I'm trying but it's really tight," Tucker said, pushing himself forward with a burst of adrenaline. "Are you hurt?"

"I don't think so. But I'm caught on something and I can't get loose. And I'm having a hard time concentrating on anything but the damn blinking light."

"Any sign of a timer?" Harrison asked as he aimed the flashlight beam at the two of them. "It might help if we knew how much time."

"Hang on," she said, her voice muted as she struggled

to pull herself closer to the suitcase. "I'm not seeing anything. Should I try to open it?"

"No." Tucker and Harrison said almost in unison.

"Okay, no touching the suitcase." She held up her hands for a moment in mock surrender, then started to squirm again as she worked to pull herself free. "I think it's my shirt. Maybe it's hooked on a nail or something."

"Can you get it off?"

"Sure, leave it to you guys to rig a strip show." Her laugh was forced, but Tucker smiled anyway, impressed with her ability for humor under pressure. "Okay, I've almost got it." She blew out a big breath. "It's off. *Shit.*"

"What?" Again Tucker and Harrison spoke as one.

"I found the timer. Fifty-six seconds. I'll never make it."

"The hell you won't," Tucker growled, worry making him sound angry. "Just keep moving and don't bother turning around. When you get close enough, I'll grab your ankles and pull."

"Okay," she called as she scrambled back, her feet finally coming within reach.

"Got you," Tucker called. "How much time do we have left, Harrison?"

"Forty seconds."

"Okay, Alexis. I'm going to pull now. There's a lot of rocks and debris, so this could hurt."

"Beats the hell out of being blown to bits" came the reply.

Despite the gravity of the situation Harrison smiled, then mouthed the words "thirty-five."

Tucker pulled—hard—and Alexis flew out from under the house. "Come on. We've got to run. Now."

The three of them stumbled to their feet, heading

away from the cabin toward the road and the safety of the Jeep.

Behind them the cabin exploded, a roaring wind of fire and heat enveloping everything as it shot toward them. Grabbing Alexis by the hand, Tucker pulled her forward, following Harrison, to dive behind the relative safety of a tree. Tucker used his body to protect hers as the fire whooshed past, the tops of the trees swaying with the force of the blast, embers and ash raining down on their heads.

"Are you okay?" he asked, her skin warm against his.

"Yeah." She nodded, her breath grazing his ear. "Thanks to you."

"Harrison?" Tucker called as he—somewhat reluctantly—rolled off of Alexis.

"Present and accounted for. And more or less in one piece." Harrison pushed an ash-covered tree branch off of his chest and sat up. "You guys sure know how to throw a party. That was one hell of a blast."

"Yeah, and unless I miss my guess, the person behind it is somewhere close by." Tucker pushed to his feet, extending a hand to Alexis. As if to underscore the thought, a Mini Cooper roared out from the trees and down the road.

"Damn it," Tucker said, starting to give chase and then realizing the futility of the move.

"Where's the bionic man when you need him?" Harrison quipped as he used the sleeve of his shirt to wipe the blood off his face, a small cut above his eyebrow the culprit.

"Did anyone catch the license plate?" Tucker asked, cursing himself for not making note of it.

"I did." Alexis said, hands on hips, her sports bra making her look at once tough and sexy. "B56 BKG. Texas plates, I think."

"That's my girl," Tucker said with a smile, brushing the debris off his shirt. "At least it's something."

"Hope it pans out better than the one outside the apartment in New Orleans," Harrison said. "I checked it out and—big surprise—the plates were stolen."

"Well, sooner or later we're bound to catch a break. At least we got here before the place blew. Although I'm not sure Alexis's mother's journal has any real value as far as all this is concerned."

"Oh my God," Alexis said, her hands covering her mouth. "The journal...I..." She trailed off, her expression stricken.

"No worries," Harrison was quick to say. "Tucker put it in the Jeep before we went to check out the suitcase."

"I didn't think I cared," Alexis said as she lifted her gaze to meet Tucker's, "but I guess I do. Thanks."

"Not a problem. At least we got something out of the deal. I just wish to hell we'd managed to catch up to whoever set off the bomb."

"You think it was the same person who killed George?"

"I think it's likely. But in order to be sure we'll need a little expert help," Tucker said, shooting a look in Harrison's direction.

"Don't tell me you have a friend who knows about bombs?" Alexis asked, eyebrows raised in surprise.

Actually he did, but one A-Tac member in the mix was probably enough. "No." He shook his head. "But if I call it in, then the local police or maybe ATF will be all over it, and with a little luck—"

"I'll be able to tap into the investigation and find out what's what," Harrison said.

"Sounds like a convoluted way to deal with it, but I guess under the circumstances, we really don't have a choice."

"Unless you've changed your mind and want to take this whole thing to the authorities," Harrison said.

Alexis's shoulders tightened, and a small line formed between her eyebrows as she frowned. "Not a chance in hell. There's no way to know for sure who we can trust. Especially if you're right and the bomber is connected to my father and the Omega Project."

"She's right," Tucker affirmed, not sure at all that it was the right move but positive that if he revealed himself now, she'd run. "For all we know, it's someone pretty high up the food chain. Which means they're connected. And that means they'll be able to get to pretty much anyone."

"Okay," Harrison agreed. "We go it alone. But I like your plan to report the bombing. You want to use my phone? It's secure."

"Secure?" Alexis asked, again looking at them both with suspicion, reminding Tucker yet again that she was nobody's fool.

"I'm a hacker, remember?" Harrison reminded her with a grin. "I figure if I can get to someone else, they can get to me. So I added a few bells and whistles to my phone. Makes it impossible to trace."

"Right. Of course," she said, her eyes going to the smoldering remains of the cabin. "I'm sorry. This is all just a bit much, you know?"

"It's understandable," Tucker said, taking the phone from Harrison. "Why don't the two of you go on and get in the car. I'll make the phone call and then we'll get the hell out of here."

"So where are we with Atterley?" Michael Brecht asked as he took a sip of cognac. The lights of Montreal filled the window behind the table, the restaurant one of the finest and most discreet in all the city.

"Other than knowing he's not really Atterley?" Alain DuBois asked the question, which was, of course, rhetorical.

"Yes, well, that was a given from the start," Brecht said. "But now that we've got DNA we'll know the truth soon enough. And in the meantime at least we've ascertained that he's not a government plant—which was a long shot but nonetheless a worry."

"So you still want to wait it out?" Alain wasn't certain exactly why Brecht was willing to tolerate Atterley's games.

"I think the prize is worth the risk, yes. And to be honest, I'm a little curious as to what the man is truly up to."

"You think he's running a scam?"

Brecht paused a moment, sipping his drink. "No. Interestingly enough, I think that except for the name, he's shooting straight with us. Something just happened to blow his plan to hell."

"Something involving the real George Atterley?"

"Yes, that's where it really gets interesting. The real Atterley seems to have disappeared. I've had all my sources checking on him, and so far, nothing. The man was released from prison and apparently dropped off the face of the earth."

"What I don't understand," Alain said, leaning forward

to light a cigarette, "is why he thought we'd believe he was Atterley in the first place."

"I'm not sure he really cared. My take is that he thought he'd make the deal and be done with it before anyone had time to question who he really was. It just didn't happen that way." Brecht shrugged, his perfectly cut suit creasing slightly with the motion. "And in the meantime we've got another problem. Or at least a potential one."

Alain inhaled deeply, then released the smoke slowly. "You're talking about Bastion Carmichael."

"Yes. I've gotten confirmation that he's been on the move again. Some woman in New Orleans. Word on the street is that he hasn't been able to run her to ground, but the only time the governor gets antsy is when he believes information regarding Omega is about to surface."

"So he's aware that someone is trying to sell the formula."

"Apparently so. At least that would be my guess. He's been using Peter Dryker again. And that's usually a tell-tale sign."

"Any chance he's on to us?"

"No. But even if he were, it wouldn't matter. He's addicted to power. And it took him a long time to work his way back into the political mainstream. Which means he'll do anything to protect his turf. Case in point—the activities in New Orleans. Push comes to shove, we'll simply make it impossible for him to say no to our offer of protection. But for the time being I think it's easier to let it all ride."

"Do nothing?" It was Alain's turn to frown.

"I didn't say that. I said we'd wait on both Atterley, who-ever he really is, and Carmichael to make their moves. And then we'll deal accordingly. But in the meantime I want men following them both. I'll admit I'm curious about this woman and where she fits into all of this. The intel I received has her traveling with two men, both of whom seem to possess unusual agility when it comes to evading capture."

"A-Tac." The word came out a curse, and Brecht smiled.

"I've nothing to confirm that. Although two of the team apparently were in New Orleans recently. They're back in New York now, though, which makes their connection potentially a spurious one. Still, I think it bears further investigation." Brecht sat back, draining his glass and then gazing out at the illuminated skyline. "A-Tac is like a gnat in your ear. Just when you think it's gone, it comes back again, buzzing and buzzing until it drives you insane."

CHAPTER **13**

So you find anything at the site?" Tucker asked, his attention centered on the video image of his brother on Harrison's computer. He, Alexis, and Harrison were ensconced in a roadside hotel just outside Amarillo in order to put distance between them and whoever had set off the bomb. With Alexis in the shower he'd taken the opportunity to come to Harrison's room for a quick confab with Drake.

"Tyler's still there working," his brother said. "But so far she hasn't come up with anything we don't already know. You guys were really lucky."

"Yeah, well, all in a day's work." Tucker smiled. "But I'll admit surviving two blasts in less than a week is maybe a little more than I signed on for."

"I still think you should call this off. Just bring Alexis in. This thing has gotten way too dangerous. And we still have no idea where the threat is actually coming from."

"We actually talked about bringing her in," Harrison

said, shooting a look at Tucker for confirmation. "But she's really jumpy when it comes to any kind of government involvement. For good reason when you consider the situation with her father."

"Yes, but we have nothing to confirm her version of how things went down."

"We have nothing to contradict it, either."

"Whoa. I wasn't trying to throw stones," Drake said defensively. "But like it or not, we do have credible intel that someone is trying to sell the formula."

"Well, it's not Alexis," Tucker said, feeling a lot like a stubborn second-grader.

"Look," Harrison said, playing the mediator. "The point here is that, guilty or not, until we find something else to go on, Alexis is our best bet. And the only way she's going to cooperate is if she continues to believe we're on her side."

"Well, unless she's actually the one trying to sell the formula, we *are* on her side," Drake insisted.

"Maybe technically," Tucker said, "but you know as well as I do that, at the end of the day, A-Tac is all about the formula, not Alexis."

"Sounds to me like you've let this get personal." Drake's eyebrows raised in question.

"No, I haven't," Tucker was quick to respond. "It's just that she's been through a lot."

"Harrison?" Drake asked, turning to his friend for confirmation.

"I don't think she's our target either. But I do believe she's the fastest route to finding out who is. And as long as we're careful and keep our cover in place, I think she'll give us free access to anything she knows. The key is to keep her believing Tucker was a friend of George's."

"What about the journal?" Drake asked. Tucker had filled his brother in when he'd called the "police" before leaving the bomb site.

"I've skimmed it, and Harrison had a look, and we're in agreement that it's nothing. Just a woman writing about an illicit affair."

"Between Alexis's mother and George," Drake confirmed. "That can't have gone down well."

"Yeah, I think it hit her pretty hard, but she's quick to rebound. A lifetime of bad news will do that to you. So, did you get a hit off the license plate from the Mini Cooper?"

"Yeah, but it was a dead end. The owner of the car sold it two days ago. Cash purchase. So there's no record. He signed over the title but said the guy was in a hurry and didn't sign it himself."

"He didn't give a name at all?"

"Yeah, he gave one, but it's only helpful if you believe in the supernatural," Drake said. "The guy who bought the car identified himself as George Atterley."

"Great. We're after a poltergeist."

"Hey, you're the one who said you were up for anything." Drake grinned, and for a moment Tucker forgot about the woman in the next room, just reveling in the adrenaline rush of being back on the job. "Anyway," his brother said, sobering, "on the good-news side of the equation, Hannah finally managed to run an address to ground for Peter Dryker."

"Sounds to me like we need to pay the man a visit." Harrison leaned back, crossing his arms.

"Yeah, well, Avery thought maybe one of us should do it."

"No." Tucker shook his head. "No way. We're the ones

in the firing line. And if anyone is going to have the satisfaction of facing our tormentor, it's going to be me."

"I'm down with that," Harrison said. "We're more than capable of handling it."

"What about Alexis?" Drake asked, the mention of her name throwing cold water on their exuberance.

"We'll take her with us. Hell, this is her fight after all. And she's not exactly a liability in the field. You should have seen her with that suitcase. Most women would have gone into panic mode when the damn thing started blinking, but she took it all in stride."

"Again, I'm hearing more than professional involvement, bro."

"It is what it is, *bro*." Tucker said, trying to keep it light.

"Point taken. Just be careful, Tucker." Drake's teasing tone turned serious.

"I'll be fine. Hell, I've got Harrison here, riding shotgun."

"I'm going to take that as a compliment," Harrison said, shaking his head. "So where's Dryker live?"

"Just outside of Austin."

Alexis stood by the window looking out at the cars on the highway below. The West Texas plains stretched in either direction, seemingly endless. The night was clear, the stars taunting her, sleep impossible. So many things she'd believed about her life were a lie.

Her family hadn't been whole and loving. Her mother had been cheating on her father. And George, the man she'd always thought of as her savior, he'd been lying too, pretending to be her father's friend. In hindsight she recognized now the tense silences she'd interrupted between her parents. Had her mother already betrayed her father?

Part of her wanted to reject her mother's words, to pretend the journal didn't exist. But it did. It was there on the table, mocking her. Like the stars. She blew out a breath and ran a hand through her hair, wondering what the hell she was doing in a hotel in Amarillo with a man she barely knew. A man who killed without second thought and had friends who could infiltrate even the most closely guarded security systems.

And the worst part of it all was that, in some really perverse way, she was enjoying herself. Tucker Flynn didn't treat her like some hot-house flower that had to be pampered and protected. He didn't try to tell her how to think, how to live. And he didn't lie.

She perched herself on the windowsill, touching her head to the cool glass. When had her life become so complicated? From the beginning, a little voice whispered. Since the day she was born into her father's world. It wasn't his fault he'd landed a life on the run. But it had affected all of them just the same. Her brother had been withdrawn. Her mother had found love outside of their family. And Alexis wanted to escape so badly that she'd wound up living when everyone else had died.

She shivered, not sure if it was the early morning chill or the realization that life as she knew it would never be the same. So many times she'd tried to pretend that she could be normal. That there was a reality out there that didn't involve false names and doctored papers. But the truth was that the people she loved best had all lied to her in one way or another. Except maybe her father. He was the real innocent in all of this. Hunted by the government for trying to do the right thing, he hadn't deserved anything that had happened to him.

Even as she had the thought, she knew in her heart that nothing happened in a vacuum. If nothing else, he'd chosen to work for the Omega Project. And even though he'd believed his work was theoretical, he had to have known there was potential for it to be used in real-life applications. No one was that naïve. Especially her father.

She tilted her head back, closing her eyes, trying to find an answer amidst all the questions. Someone was trying to kill her and she had no idea why. It had something to do with her father or George, that much was clear. But that wasn't enough of an explanation, and it certainly wasn't going to help her find answers.

She'd been over it and over it with Tucker and Harrison, but she still hadn't a clue what this was all about. The only thing she knew for certain was that whoever had killed her family had probably killed George too. So there was a serial bomber out there, but nothing at all to link those bombings to her attempted kidnapping or to the men who'd tried to kill them.

None of it made any sense. Why, after all these years, would her father's killer surface again? And why had he targeted George and, by association, her?

It was enough to drive a girl crazy.

She smiled at the thought, grateful at least that she still had her sense of humor. George had always said that if you could find a way to laugh, anything was bearable.

Behind her, in the adjoining room, she heard Tucker talking in his sleep. It had been the same in the apartment in New Orleans. She'd been embarrassed then, feeling as if she were intruding on something private. But now that she knew the man a little better, her only thought was to help him. To release him from the torment of his dreams.

She pushed open the adjoining door, the light from her window spilling across the room. Tucker was thrashing in the bed, his face coated with a fine sheen of sweat. He was wearing sweatpants but no shirt, his torso laced with scars. Battle wounds, she supposed, although she had no idea what those battles might have been. His hands were fisted as he struggled against his demons.

"No," he cried, jerking to the left as if avoiding an unseen foe. "Hector, no."

She crossed to the bed, reaching out to wake him, but froze as he called another name.

"Lena. Oh my God, Lena..." The pain in his voice was almost beyond bearing. Tears filled her eyes. "No..."

She reached for his arm, surprised to find the skin there puckered and scarred as well. "Tucker," she whispered, her fingers kneading gently. "Tucker, wake up. It's just a dream."

For a moment he went still, then he grabbed her hand so tightly she was afraid her wrist would snap. "Tucker," she called again. "Let me go. *Tucker.*"

Without opening his eyes he growled, his grip tightening as he flipped her underneath him, pinning her with his body, her breath releasing on a whoosh, the pressure of his weight making it difficult to breathe. "Tucker, please. Wake up. You're hurting me."

Again he stilled, but this time his eyes opened, the haze of his dream lifting until she could tell he was truly awake, confused but no longer dangerous.

"Holy shit," he said, rolling off her to sit on the side of the bed. "What the hell happened?"

Alexis gulped in air, her breathing labored as she tried to regain some sense of equilibrium. "You were having a nightmare. I tried to wake you up, but—"

"I attacked you? Jesus, Alexis, I'm sorry."

"It's okay," she said, swinging her legs around so that she was sitting next to him on the side of the bed. "You didn't know what you were doing."

"Did I hurt you?"

"No, not really." She rubbed her wrist, pretty certain there would be bruises. "You just scared me a little, that's all."

"You have to believe I would never—"

She covered his lips with her finger. "I know. Honestly, I do. I'm just sorry you had such a horrible dream."

He reached up to cover her hand with his, their gazes locking as her heart suddenly started to pound. Slowly, he lowered her hand and then bent to kiss her palm, the heat from his touch spiraling through her with an intensity that belied the gentle touch of his lips against her skin.

"Tucker, I—" she started, but it was his turn to silence her, his mouth covering hers, taking possession with one powerful thrust of his tongue. She'd been kissed before, but never like this. Somewhere in the back of her mind she knew this wasn't a good idea. Knew that he wasn't the kind of guy to settle down and live a regular life. But then maybe she wasn't that kind of girl. She'd never really had the chance to find out for certain.

Until now.

They fell back onto the bed, his hands hot against her shoulders. The feel of his palms moving against her bare skin was intoxicating—sensual beyond belief. Heat seared through her as they moved together, his tongue thrusting deeper into her mouth, the sensation sending tremors of need wracking through her.

He stroked the curve of her breast, her flesh responding

beneath the thin cotton of her camisole. His thumb circled one nipple, his other hand stroking her back, the rhythm hypnotic—carnal.

She pushed against him, desire spiraling out of control, and his hand moved lower, caressing the skin of her abdomen, soothing and exciting her with one touch. His lips moved too, following the hollow of her cheek until he reached her ear, his tongue sending more fire rippling through her as he traced the curve of its shell, his mouth moist and hot against her skin.

His head dropped lower, his lips trailing along the line of her shoulder, his kisses teasing in their simplicity, his hand continuing to move across her skin. His mouth found the crest of her breast, the hot, sweet sensation tantalizing with its promise of things to come.

Urgency built within her. The need for something more. For connection, belonging. The part of her that she kept locked away clamored for release. She knew there was every possibility that she'd live to regret this, but the physical pull was so strong now. So essential. Like breathing.

With desire shimmering between them, Alexis pushed closer, grinding her hips against his. Her hands slid to his waist, slipping beneath the waistband of his sweats, her fingers brushing the velvety tip of his penis. With a groan he pulled off her camisole, and she returned the favor. Undressing becoming a game between them, one piece for another until they both were naked, desire exploding with a power she'd never experienced before. It was as if she stood on a precipice, some intrinsic force urging her onward with the promise that she could fly.

God, she wanted this man.

But he pulled away, pushing up so that he towered above her, his gaze locking on hers, desire etched across his face. "I want you, Alexis. But I need to know that you want me, too." The vulnerability in his eyes made her heart skip a beat.

She opened her mouth but she couldn't form the words, instead nodding, her heart pounding a rhythm in her head. For a moment cold air surrounded her and she felt a flicker of doubt, but then he was there, his heat consuming her, his mouth and hands worshipping her.

She closed her eyes and let sensation carry her away. Opening her mouth to his kiss, she drank him in, wanting nothing more than this moment, this man. Their fervor increased, each touch, each movement raising the stakes, heightening the pleasure.

His mouth was warm and his touch delicious. He moved from her mouth to her neck, his tongue tracing the line of her throat as he worked his way slowly downward, his mouth moving across the valley between her breasts, the action sending her writhing against the sheets. Then he pulled one nipple into his mouth, sucking deeply, the resulting sensation cresting between her legs.

Sensation robbed her of all cognizant thought. And just when she thought she couldn't possibly feel any more, he pushed her legs apart and slid lower, the soft silk of his hair teasing her breasts as he slowly licked and kissed the tender skin of her stomach.

Anticipation built inch by inch until she wanted to cry out, but she stayed silent, forcing herself to wait, knowing it would be worth it. Finally, finally, his hands moved between her legs, his mouth following the curve of her inner thigh, his hot breath teasing her with its nearness. She sucked in a breath, waiting... waiting, one minute praying for him to hurry and the next arching off the bed, his hands holding her hips in place as he licked and stroked her.

She cried out, the pleasure almost more than she could bear. Clasping the headboard behind her, she arched her back, urging him on, her need building with each stroke of his tongue. The fire inside her built higher and higher until finally she reached for his hands, screaming his name, the world splintering into glittering shards of light.

For a moment, she felt suspended above the world, and then with an intensity that surprised her, she realized she needed more. With unbridled passion, she began to taste him. All of him. The salty skin at the corners of his eyes. His beard-stubbled chin. The softer skin of his neck, the scars that covered his arm and chest. This man was a warrior. His strength pulsed through her, and *he* wanted her.

Her.

She took his nipples into her mouth, caressing first one then the other with her tongue, delighted when they responded to her touch. Moving lower, she sampled the taught skin of his belly.

And then finally her lips found the velvety heat of his penis. She ran her tongue along its length, pleased to feel him tense in pleasure, his hand stroking her hair, urging her onward. With a smile she took him into her mouth, feeling him grow harder even as her own desire burgeoned.

And then he was urging her upward again, his hands settling beneath her hips, lifting her until her legs circled him, their gazes locked. There would be no turning back. She was clear-headed enough to know that. She wasn't one to give herself lightly. And a part of her—the rational, sane side—was screaming a warning, but the rest of her embraced the moment. And the man.

He moved back slightly, still holding her in place, and with one long thrust was inside her, the pure pleasure of the movement threatening to shatter her into pieces. And together they began to move. In and out, in and out. Each stroke taking them higher until she could no longer tell where he ended and she began.

She closed her eyes, letting sensation carry her away. Aware of only the feel of him inside her, filling her, binding them together with every stroke. They moved together, the friction unbearable, her pleasure and his coming together into a heated crescendo. For a moment she was afraid again, frozen on the edge of nothingness.

And then she could feel his fingers linking with hers, and the world disappeared into the fury of their climax.

Then slowly she drifted back to earth, his body wrapped around hers like a cocoon. For minutes—or hours—they lay like that, satiated. And for the first time in her life Alexis felt safe. Truly and completely safe. It was an odd feeling. One she almost hadn't identified. But nevertheless there it was.

Tucker stirred and she almost cried out in protest. She knew the moment couldn't last, but still she hated to let it go.

"We shouldn't have done this," he said, running a hand through his hair, his voice unusually gruff.

Pain knifed through her, his words cutting more than she could have imagined, but she'd be damned if she'd let him see how much he'd hurt her. "I think maybe you need to work on your pillow talk." She tried for cheerful, but missed by a mile. So instead she tried to pull away.

"Oh God, Alexis, I'm sorry. I didn't mean that the way it sounded. I told you I'm not always good with words."

"It's okay. Our being together—it doesn't have to mean anything." She said, fighting to stay calm.

"Of course it meant something. It meant everything. It's just that it's complicated."

"Because of Lena?" she whispered, holding her breath, praying she hadn't gone too far.

Beside her she could feel his body tense, and for a moment she thought he wasn't going to answer, the silence stretching between them. But then he sighed. "Lena was my fiancée."

"Ah, well, I suppose that explains the complication."

"Not in the way you're thinking," Tucker said, absently twirling a strand of her hair around his finger. She could feel the rise and fall of his chest as his heart beat beneath her hand. "Lena is dead." Again they lay in silence. And she waited. "It's a long and complicated story. And not a very pretty one. And I don't like talking about it."

"I see," she said, rolling away from him.

"Look, it's nothing to do with you," he said, pulling her around to face him again. "And it's over. Part of my past."

"Only you can't really let it go, can you? That's why you have the dreams. You're afraid that if you move on, you'll be betraying her. That's something I do understand. You go over it and over it trying to figure out if there's something you could have done differently. Something that would have kept them alive." She clenched a fist, his pain suddenly hers. "And when you're not trying to rewrite history, you feel guilty because you're the one that's alive."

"Exactly." He sighed, reaching over to smooth the hair from her face. "That's why it's complicated."

"Well, I believe you have to take your pleasure where you find it. Life is too short to overthink things. So please don't regret tonight. It was beautiful. And even if we never do it again, if we decide it's just too much, I wouldn't trade tonight—being here with you—for anything."

"You're an amazing woman," he said, framing her face with his hands. "You know that, right?"

"I think maybe I could be convinced." She smiled, leaning in as he slanted his mouth over hers. As she opened her mouth to his kiss, she had the passing thought that she was lying. That tonight wasn't enough. That for the first time in her life, she wanted more. She wanted everything. And she wanted it with Tucker.

But she knew it was only a fantasy. Tucker was still in love with Lena. She could hear it in his voice and see it in his eyes. And how the hell was she supposed to compete with a ghost?

CHAPTER **14**

Tucker jerked awake, reaching automatically for the gun by the bed. Alexis was curled against him, still asleep. Harrison stood in the doorway, key card in hand, finger over his lips. "We've got company coming," he whispered. "They're in the lobby now. Which has slowed them up a little since they can't afford to raise suspicion. But it won't be long before they come up here."

"How the hell do you know that?" Tucker asked as he pulled on his pants and reached to wake Alexis.

"I spliced my computer into the hotel's security camera. Been watching most of the night. I just had a bad feeling. Anyway, we need to get out of here now."

Alexis sat up, eyes wide as she hugged the sheet to her state of undress. "What the..."

Tucker shook his head and motioned for silence. "How many are there?" he asked Harrison, who had averted his eyes so Alexis could dress.

"Three. Two of them are armed for sure, and I'm betting

the third is as well. I've booby-trapped my room, but if they've got some kind of a lock on our location, I'm betting it'll bring them here to this room." His gaze met Tucker's, and with a slight tilt of his head he indicated Alexis.

"You're saying I'm the source?" she asked as she pulled on her jeans. "But Tucker checked all my stuff. And it was clean."

"I'm not trying to accuse anyone. But there's got to be a bug somewhere. We've switched cars, employed diversionary tactics, and basically done everything we can to make it impossible to follow us. But they're still here."

"Which means we need to get out of here. Finding the bug will have to wait until we've put some distance between them and us."

"Roger that," Harrison said.

Tucker walked over to the door and, after opening it a crack, stared out into the hallway. It was L-shaped, with the elevator bank at the top of the "L." By design he'd requested a room at the far end, out of sight of the elevator but close to the stairs.

"Have you got a visual?" he asked Harrison, checking to make sure his gun was fully loaded.

"Yeah, transferred the feed to my handheld when I realized they were coming our way. No idea who they are, but looks to me like they mean business."

"So how much time do we have?"

"Not much. They're getting on the elevators now."

"Well, I'm ready," Alexis said, coming back into the room with her backpack and duffel. "What's the plan?"

"We'll head for the stairs," Tucker said, reaching to retrieve his own pack. "We should have time to make it there before they've rounded the corner from the elevators. Any chance that once we access the stairs, you can do something to buy us a little more time?"

"Already on it," Harrison said, pulling a roll of filament wire from a bag he had slung on his back. "As soon as we're safely inside the stairwell, I'll set up a little welcoming present.

"All right, then. We'd best get moving." Tucker pulled open the door and motioned Alexis and Harrison through, then pulled it shut and hung the DO NOT DISTURB sign just for good measure. "You never know." He shrugged. "Might buy us a little time."

"Yeah, polite killers. Works every time." Harrison laughed, and Alexis looked at them both as if they were crazy. "Gallows humor," Harrison said, still laughing.

The three of them headed down the hallway on a sprint. Tucker pulled open the door and all three of them slid inside. The stairwell was utilitarian at best. The cement steps had been painted gray, the walls a drab beige. The fluorescent lighting overhead buzzed as it flickered off and on, threatening to go out.

"You guys go," Harrison said. "I'll be right behind you."

Tucker nodded. "Don't stay up here too long. I don't want to have to come back up here and save your ass."

"No worries—I'll be faster than lightning." Harrison was already running the wire across the top of the door. "Just a little flash and awe," he said with a grin. "Hopefully it'll slow them down a little."

"All right," Tucker said. "We'll see you on the flip side." He pulled his gun and grabbed Alexis's hand, heading down the stairs. They passed the landing on the fourth floor with no problems, but as he neared the third floor he slowed a little.

Above them they heard footsteps, and then the pop of explosives, the bright white light reflected all the way down the stairwell.

"Harrison," they said, almost in unison. Alexis turned to look upward, but Tucker pulled her forward. "We've got to keep moving. He'll be okay."

They started to move again, passing the third-floor landing and heading down the stairs that led to the second floor. About halfway down, Tucker heard something and pulled up short, finger to lips.

"What did you hear?" Alexis whispered. "Someone coming from the other direction?"

Before Tucker could answer a metallic clank from below signaled a door opening. Above them, Harrison appeared at the top of the third-floor landing. "What's the problem?"

"Company down below," Tucker said as Harrison came to a stop beside him, pulling out his smart phone for a look.

"Definitely hostiles," he told them, sliding the phone back into his pocket. "Two of them. And they're armed."

"How were things up top?"

"I used magnesium in the blast. So they're going to be seeing stars for a few minutes, but it won't last long."

Tucker nodded. "Okay, then we'll have to take our chances on the second floor."

As if to underscore the idea, a bullet whizzed past them, embedding in the wall just above their heads.

"Let's move," Tucker called, heading down the remaining stairs, pulling Alexis close to protect her from shots being fired both from above and below now. Harrison brought up the rear, providing covering fire as they sprinted to the second-floor doorway and pushed through to the relative safety of the hallway.

Moving at full speed now, they ran down the corridor, rounding the corner to head for the elevators, but as soon as they were clear the elevator dinged and the door slid open, the men inside opening fire.

With seconds to spare, Tucker pulled Alexis behind a housekeeping cart, Harrison following suit. For a moment he thought they were trapped, the sound of the opening door from the stairwell serving to underscore the perception.

Then he saw a room across the way with the doorway ajar. Praying there was no maid inside, he motioned to Alexis and Harrison. On a silent count of three, the two of them dashed from behind the cart while Tucker provided covering fire. Then, as soon as they were safely inside, Harrison returned the favor, and Tucker dove across the hall into the empty room.

Once inside, he slammed the door and moved to the center of the hotel room, a momentary hush descending as they quickly tried to regroup. Both Harrison and Tucker searched the room to try to find another way out.

"We're trapped," Alexis whispered, her voice calm but her eyes huge. "So what the hell do we do now?"

"We go out the window," Tucker said, pulling back the curtains, the early morning light harsh after the gloom of the stairwell and hallway.

"But we're on the second floor." Alexis licked her lips, her gaze still locked on the door; the knob rattling as the first of their assailants tried to gain access.

"There's a canopy over the front drive. We can use it to bounce safely to the ground. Old circus trick," he added with a smile. For a moment she hesitated, and then with a shake of her head, all fear was banished, and Tucker marveled again at her strength.

"Okay," she said, coming to stand beside him. "What do I do?"

"Harrison will go first." He indicated his friend, who was already straddling the window sill. "As soon as he's safely on the ground, you're going to follow him. Think of it as a reverse swan dive. You want to land butt first. Okay? Then you'll crawl to the edge and flip down."

"Just like a high-wire performer." She nodded. "And you'll come after me?"

"Of course." He reached out to touch her cheek. "Two seconds behind you. Harrison's down. It's time."

Taking a deep breath, Alexis swung out onto the windowsill and then with a whoosh of breath pushed off, her lithe grace making it look easy. She bounced twice on the taut canvas and then, with the ease of a gymnast, flipped down into Harrison's waiting arms.

Behind him the door splintered open.

Tucker jumped, hitting the canopy below on a roll, using the momentum to fling himself off the edge just as the window above erupted with gunfire.

"Go," he called to the already moving Harrison and Alexis. Across the front drive, a delivery truck sat parked next to a service door. "Head for the van."

Harrison, clearly, had already had the same thought, as he and Alexis had already switched directions. They covered the ground just as a man emerged through the hotel's front doors. He leveled his gun but Tucker was faster, taking him out as he followed Harrison and Alexis into the van.

In less than a minute Harrison had hot-wired the truck and they were careening out of the parking lot and onto the highway.

"That was close," Harrison said, keeping the van floored. "But if we're going to avoid being followed, we're going to need to switch cars and figure out how they're tracking us."

"Agreed," Tucker said, his gaze moving to Alexis. "We're going to need to go through your things again."

She tensed, her eyes flashing. "Fine. I don't see how anything could possibly have changed from the last time you looked. It's not like I haven't been with you the whole time."

There was a definite subtext to her words, and as Tucker reached for her bag their gazes collided, and he was forced to acknowledge that the intimacy that had existed between them last night couldn't possibly withstand the tension created by their situation. Not to mention the fact that he was keeping a secret that would eventually destroy every ounce of trust he'd built with her.

"Okay, so we've gone over my stuff at least three times and there's nothing," Alexis said, trying to control her irritation as she sipped her iced tea. They'd stopped in Weatherford near the Oklahoma border to refuel and grab a bite to eat. The truck stop was teaming with people, but, fortunately, there was no sign of the men from the hotel. "There must be some other way they're tracking us."

"Well, it can't be the car," Harrison said, as usual multitasking, eating a burger and typing on his laptop. "Because we keep changing that."

They'd actually ditched the "borrowed" van almost

immediately and bartered for an SUV in a small town just east of Amarillo, the whole transaction happening in less time than it took most people to get a dealer's attention.

"So how is it exactly that the two of you always seem to be able to conjure new transportation no matter where we are?" She tried to keep her tone light, but she was beginning to feel that there was far more to Tucker Flynn than just a man helping a friend of a friend. And considering last night's activities, the importance of understanding exactly who he was had taken a decidedly more personal turn.

"It's just a matter of having the right contacts—and money to grease the wheels," Tucker said, taking a bite of his grilled cheese sandwich. "I've played fast and loose with the rules for a long time. And along the way I've acquired a number of business associates, to use a more civilized term."

"And that's how you've managed to keep us one step ahead of this thing?" she asked, certain he wasn't giving her the full story but equally sure that he was at least telling her some version of the truth.

"I'd say it was more about thinking on your feet," Harrison answered even though the question hadn't been directed his way. "And Tucker is better than most in that department. By the way, how did you know that canopy would hold our weight?"

"I didn't." Tucker shrugged a crooked smile. "I just figured if you went first I wasn't really risking all that much."

"Yeah, right, use the geek as the test dummy," Harrison said, returning the smile. "Anyway, I think I'm ready for the cell phone now."

"I'm sorry?" Alexis frowned. "I thought you'd already looked at it. Twice."

"It was just a cursory examination. You know—looking for something on the outside or in the battery compartment. But I didn't look at the software. And considering we've come up with nada, I figure it's worth a shot."

"Sure," Alexis said. It wasn't as if she had anything to hide. "But it's just a phone. A pretty plain-Jane one at that. I've always used cell phones that can't be traced back to me."

"Disposable ones?" Harrison asked as he hooked the phone to the computer.

"Yeah, exactly," she said, popping a french fry into her mouth.

"Then how come the change in MO?"

The question was from Tucker, and she almost choked on her fry. "I beg your pardon?"

"That phone's not exactly run-of-the-mill disposable."

"I'm not sure what you're implying," she said, irritation on the rise again. "I got it from Milo. Just after I got back from California. He told me it was untraceable, and I believed him. I've only used it twice. Once when I called him to ask that he check you out. And the other time when he called me to tell me what he'd found."

"You checked Tucker out?" Harrison asked without looking up from the diagnostics running on his laptop. "Pretty damn smart. I'm impressed."

"I was too," Tucker said, his expression unreadable.

"So who's Milo?" Harrison asked.

"I already told Tucker. He's a friend. George hooked us up."

Harrison's eyebrows rose, mouth twitching as he suppressed a laugh.

"Well, not like that, obviously," Alexis said, feeling the heat of a blush. "But over the years he's been a big help. And after I got back from California I was pretty shaken, and the first thing George instilled in me is to change everything when something goes wrong. So I threw out the phone I'd been using, and when Milo offered a new one, I took it. I trust him."

"Well, looks like you shouldn't have," Harrison said, looking up from his computer screen. "Someone's embedded a pretty sophisticated tracking program in the phone's software."

"Like GPS?" she asked, her gut clenching at the thought that she'd been played for a fool. "A lot of people have that, right?"

"Yeah, but this program is a different animal altogether. It's like the ones put in computers for anti-theft purposes. Or even some cars. Only this one was buried so deep in the software it's pretty damn certain it wasn't supposed to have been discovered."

"So you're saying Milo purposely gave me a phone that could be tracked. That he's the one responsible for these people finding us all the time?"

"Pretty much." Harrison shrugged, looking apologetic.

"Well, first thing we need to do is get rid of it," Tucker said.

"Easily done," Harrison said, "but I'm thinking if we really want to fuck with their heads, we'd be better off giving the phone a new itinerary." He nodded at the trucks lined up in the parking lot outside the restaurant's window.

"I like the way you think." Tucker leaned back with a smile. "And once we've relocated the phone, preferably to a truck heading due west, I'm thinking we need to head back to New Orleans and have a little chat with Milo Alozono."

"But what about Dryker?" Alexis asked, still not sure she believed her friend had betrayed her.

"Not a problem. We'll stop in Austin on the way. If we're right and he's been following us, he'll be occupied elsewhere, and we'll have easy access to his computers and files."

"Assuming there's something there to find." Alexis hadn't meant to sound so negative, but despite the fact that they kept eluding Dryker and his men, they were still nowhere closer to understanding what was really going on.

"Well, whatever we find or don't find at Dryker's, I'm thinking we're better off discussing it on the move. Because until we relocate this puppy"—Harrison patted the phone still linked to his computer—"we're sitting ducks."

CHAPTER 15

The house sat on the top of a hill, a field of wildflowers between it and the county road. A whitewashed gray with a limestone chimney, the structure looked at home amidst the twisted cedar and live oaks. The yard was overgrown, but at some point, someone had cared. A scrawny yellow rose twined around a stone column, tenaciously clinging to life. A black Lexus sat in the driveway, the fancy car looking out of place in the rural setting.

"You think someone's here?" Alexis asked. Tucker had tried to get her to wait in the car, but there was no reasoning with the woman. She definitely had a mind of her own, and if he were honest, although at times it drove him crazy, he had to admit it was one of the things that made her so appealing.

"Well, the house is certainly sending mixed messages." He indicated the newspapers on the lawn as well as fliers stuffed in a mailbox at the gate.

"Maybe Dryker's just not much on reading material,"

Harrison said, as they cautiously made their way up the drive, guns at the ready.

"I don't like the feel of this." Tucker stopped on the steps leading up to the front door. "If there's a car here, you'd think someone would have picked up the mail."

Motioning for Alexis to stay put, he and Harrison walked up the steps and onto the porch fronting the house.

"I feel like we've been here before," Harrison said, referring to the condition in which they'd found Atterley's cabin. "I'm not sure I'm up for another bombing."

"Well, there's definitely been someone here before us. The door's open. You want to go first or should I?"

"Age before beauty," Harrison quipped. "Seriously, I've got your back."

"Okay, we go on my count. Three…two…one…" Tucker pushed the door open and swung into the foyer, turning a full three hundred and sixty degrees to be sure there were no threats. "We're clear."

Harrison nodded but didn't lower his gun.

Tucker motioned to Alexis, who had followed them up onto the porch. She stepped inside, chewing the side of her lip. He'd noticed she did that whenever she was nervous. "Let's check the back."

He and Harrison moved forward again, this time down the small hall that led to a dining room and kitchen. Both were empty. Although, based on the dishes in the sink, someone had been here quite recently.

"I feel like we're in the middle of a scary movie," Alexis said, stepping into the kitchen. "Like any minute, the guy with the hatchet is going to jump out of the closet."

"You're just now getting that vibe?" Harrison asked.

"Not when we were being chased by gun-toting men through a hotel, or when we were counting down a bomb blast in Colorado?"

"Yeah, well—I don't know why, but this feels creepier."

"It's the unknown," Tucker said, heading for the stairs. "We need to check the upper floor. Alexis, why don't you stay down here until we're sure everything's clear?"

"No way. That's exactly how you wind up dead. Get separated from your friends and it's all over. I'm coming with you."

"Fine." He allowed himself a smile. "But stay between us."

She nodded, and they started up the stairs, Tucker in front, leading with his Sig Sauer, and Harrison in the rear, his attention on the rooms below them as he watched their backs.

The landing at the top opened into a square, with three rooms opening off the hallway. Moving slowly, back to the wall, Tucker swung into the first room. A bedroom. At first glance nothing seemed out of place, but as his gaze swept the room a second time, he saw a streak on the floor.

Harrison, who'd followed him into the room, knelt to run his finger across it. "Blood. Fairly fresh. It's still wet." He lifted his finger to show the tip stained red.

"I'm telling you this feels like Freddy Krueger," Alexis said, pressing close beside Tucker.

"Yeah, well, I'm starting to be a believer." Tucker frowned, trying to find a secondary stain or maybe some spatter. But there was no evidence of either. And nothing in the bedroom showed any sign of a struggle.

"Looks to me like whoever made this stain was heading that way," Harrison said, motioning behind them to the door. "See how it starts heavier and then trails out. As if someone was dragging a foot or maybe even a body."

"So let's check the other rooms. And just for the hell of it, let's all stay together. All right?"

"You'll get no argument from me." Alexis tried for a smile but missed, her eyes wide with anticipation.

They walked into the hall, and Tucker moved left, toward the second door. This one was a bathroom. And although it, too, lacked any signs of disturbance or struggle, a bloody handprint on the door frame and a second stain on the hallway floor indicated that the person who'd been bleeding had headed this way.

The last door opened out into an office. And this time there were multiple signs of a struggle or at least a search of some kind. Papers lay scattered around the floor and a filing cabinet had been upended on the far side of the room. A desk in the corner was covered with cables and cords, but the computer they'd been hooked to was missing.

"Someone's clearly been looking for something," Harrison said, stating the obvious. "But I don't see any sign of our blood trail."

"It's here," Alexis said, her voice a strangled whisper. "*He's* here."

She was standing in the doorway of the closet, her fingers splayed on the frame, her knuckles white as she braced herself against the wall.

Tucker rushed to her side, Harrison right behind him. Peter Dryker lay on the floor, a pool of muddied red spreading out beneath him.

"Is he dead?" Alexis murmured, her eyes still locked on the body.

Harrison knelt down beside the man, reaching over to feel for a pulse. "Definitely dead. But not too long. He's still warm. Looks like it was a gunshot. Through and through near his groin—which explains the blood on the floor. Dude probably crawled in here and bled out."

"I should be relieved, I suppose, but..." She shivered again, and Tucker slid an arm around her.

"Death is never a good thing. And a violent one is the worst of all. Even when it's an enemy."

She sucked in a breath. He could almost feel her struggling for control. "I'm sorry," she said, pulling free of his embrace. "I'm all right now. I just wasn't expecting to find him here—like this."

"Any chance that whoever did this is still around here somewhere?" Harrison asked, pushing back to his feet.

Tucker shook his head. "My guess is that if he or she were still here, we'd have already had a run-in."

"Well, that's something, at least." Alexis offered a weak smile. "I wasn't really relishing a run-in with a real-life Freddy Krueger."

"One thing bugs me," Harrison said, eyes narrowed as he studied the body.

"Just one?" Tucker lifted an eyebrow.

"Okay, one major thing. Why no bomb? We've got a guy that's killed Alexis's family, George, and potentially Duncan Wallace that way, not to mention damn near blowing us up at the cabin. Why not blow this guy up?"

"Maybe we're dealing with different entities. Makes sense when you consider the attacks at Alexis's house and later at the apartment and the hotel. No bombs involved then, but the shooters were definitely aiming to kill."

"Okay, if we are talking about two separate killers,

then that begs a second question," Harrison continued. "Why the hell are the bad guys killing each other? Not that I'm complaining, mind you. It just changes the complexion of things."

"So does Dryker being dead mean that I'm in the clear?" Alexis asked, her eyes still on the body.

"No," Tucker said. "I think it means that whoever was behind the attacks at your house knows you've got help. And that we were getting close to finding Dryker. That'd explain someone taking him out."

"So we couldn't talk to him."

"Seems likely," Harrison agreed. "There was definitely a computer—the cables are still here. And I'm guessing any files that might have helped will be missing as well."

"So what else do we know about Dryker other than the fact that he worked for DOD?" Tucker asked.

"Not much. DOD can be pretty dodgy about that sort of thing. I went back in to do some digging after my initial discovery, but his personnel file only had the basics, and all of that was dated."

"What about after DOD?"

"He worked security jobs at a couple of private companies. Most of them out west. And most defense related. Anyway, a couple of years ago he just fell off the grid. It took a hell of a lot of digging just to get a current address."

"Well, as soon as we land somewhere, seems like you should do a little more digging into Dryker's background. But right now we need to see if there's anything here that might give us an idea as to why specifically he's been after Alexis." Tucker turned to have another look at the room.

"Agreed." Harrison nodded. "Although I think we

have to accept that one or both of our assailants is connected in some way to Omega. And that at least one of them believes that Alexis is in possession of something tied to her father and his work."

"But I don't have anything," she protested.

"Unfortunately, someone out there isn't as sure of that fact as you are," Tucker said. "And it may all be a moot point anyway."

"Meaning?" she asked, her jumbled emotions playing across her face.

"Meaning that in the beginning they may have wanted to kidnap you, but now, I'm afraid, they want to kill you. And I'm afraid my involvement may be why their intent changed."

"Well, that doesn't make any sense." A small frown creased her brow. "If they believe I have something they want, why would they want to kill me and risk never finding it?"

"Law of diminishing returns," Harrison said. "Anything can lose value if the cost of retrieving it becomes too expensive. So maybe it's simply become easier to eliminate the threat than to try and get whatever it is they want from you."

"Well, I haven't any idea what it could be. I swear. I decided about three years ago to let the whole thing with my father go. I figured my obsession with finding his killers wasn't going anywhere, and the anger was eating me alive. My own diminishing returns. It just seemed better to find a way to move on." Her gaze met Tucker's and he knew the last was about more than just her father.

"It's not as easy as just making up your mind to do it," he said, wishing it weren't so.

"I know." Her smile was sad. "I don't know that I'll ever truly be able to let it go. But at least until George was killed, I had sort of figured out how to keep it compartmentalized. Which is a beginning, right?"

"Yeah," Tucker agreed, "it's definitely a start." He had tried to do that. To put Lena's memories firmly in the past. The violence associated with her death. The betrayal that had set everything in motion. All of it. But Alexis was right. It was hard. Damn near impossible, actually.

"Um, guys?" Harrison said, breaking into his musings. "Not that I don't approve of clearing out old baggage, but it seems like we'd be better served checking out the office and then getting the hell out of here before someone comes along and finds us here with Dryker. You can resume the conversation when we're safely back on the road."

Tucker pulled his gaze away from Alexis. "You're right. We need to move—quickly. And then find out what, if anything, Milo Alozono has to do with this. If someone believed Dryker was a dangerous loose end, they're probably going to have the same thought about Alexis's friend."

CHAPTER 16

Milo lived on a block of cookie-cutter houses in Algiers. The neighborhood had flourished recently, but there were still pockets of poverty and areas where urban crime was frequent. Milo had chosen to straddle the line, which considering that he also played fast and loose with the law, made complete and total sense to Alexis.

— "Whatever Milo's gotten himself involved in here, it's not your fault," Tucker said, uncannily reading her mind. "If we're right and he set you up, that means he's playing for the other team. Or at least taking money from them."

"It doesn't matter. If he hadn't been linked with me in the first place, they'd never have used him to get to me."

Harrison pulled their latest car, a Volvo, in front of the house, and the three of them got out, Tucker with his hand on the butt of his gun.

"Maybe I should go first so we don't spook him," Alexis suggested, already moving toward the front door.

"No way." Tucker shook his head. "This guy's already screwed you over once. We don't need to give him an opportunity to do it again."

"He'd never hurt me. No matter what he's done, I refuse to believe he'd intentionally put me in harm's way."

"Believe what you want," Harrison said, "but the guy gave the killers an easy way to find you. If that's not putting you in the middle of a firefight, I don't know what is."

"Okay, fine." She sighed. "We'll go together."

She wasn't about to admit it, but she actually felt better with the two of them on either side of her. She'd seen them both in action and knew firsthand what they were capable of. And although she was used to acting on her own, it was kind of nice to have friends.

She shot a sideways glance at Tucker as they walked up onto the front porch. If she were honest, she'd have to admit that she was starting to think of him as more than a friend. But, unlike her previous thoughts, this one didn't give her comfort. Truth was, it made her stomach feel like the entire cast of *Riverdance* had taken up residence there.

Harrison reached out to ring the bell and they waited, the humidity making the day feel hotter than it really was.

"No answer," Tucker said, reaching for the doorknob. "I guess we'll just have to invite ourselves in."

The door opened easily, and Alexis's stomach upped the tempo a notch, her fear morphing into worry for her friend. "Milo?" she called as they stepped inside.

The house was cool after the heat of the sun—and dark. It took a minute for her eyes to adjust. The living room looked exactly the same as the last time she'd seen it, except for the addition of a new plasma television.

"Clearly didn't do his research," Harrison said, indicating the TV. "LED is the only way to go."

"Milo?" Alexis called again, but there was no answer, just the sound of the back door opening.

"Shit," Tucker said, "he's trying to run. You take the front." He motioned to Harrison. "Alexis, you stay put." He sprinted toward the kitchen and the back door; Harrison was already out the front.

Alexis sucked in a breath and turned slowly to survey the room. She knew it was empty, but a part of her mind wasn't convinced. There was a take-out container on the coffee table. Gumbo, from the look of it. She remembered that Milo had a penchant for spicy food. They'd met at Tipitina's more than once for crawfish étouffée. She preferred her Cajun food on the milder side, a muffuletta from Central Grocery or maybe fish with crabmeat Yvonne from Galatoires.

Above her head something rattled across the floor upstairs. Her heart skittered to a stop, all thoughts of food vanishing in an instant. She held her breath as the seconds went by, waiting for another sound. But when it came her blood ran cold.

A moan. Somebody had moaned.

Without stopping to think she ran for the stairs, taking the steps two at a time, her only thought to get to her friend.

Milo's bedroom, like the room downstairs, was spotless, simplicity of design making the furnishings seem more expensive than they probably were.

"Milo?" she called again. Another moan came from the far side of the bed. She rushed around the end to find him sprawled on the floor, a spatter of blood on the wall above him, his shirt stained an ugly reddish brown. "Oh my God."

She dropped to her knees beside him, reaching over to prop him up, but he batted her hand away. "In...the... drawer..." he whispered, his voice raspy and threaded with pain.

"Milo, you need to get to a hospital. To a doctor."

He shook his head. "Too...late." The words came out even more strangled than before. "Sorry...I'm sorry," he said.

"It's okay. Whatever happened, it's okay," she said, tears springing to her eyes.

"I didn't...know...." He closed his eyes, and for a moment she thought he was gone, but then his fingers tightened around hers. "In the drawer...thumb drive...your... eyes only." He struggled for a breath. "Promise me... only...you." His fingers went slack, and his eyes closed.

"Milo?" she said, frantically searching for a pulse. *"Milo."*

"Drawer," he murmured on an exhale of breath, his head lolling to the side as his life slipped away.

Alexis fought a wave of panic. From down below she heard Tucker call her name. The sound of footsteps on the stairs spurring her on, she reached over to the bedside table, sliding the drawer open. Inside there was a jumble of things, a comb, a dog-eared thriller, some medicine bottles, the kind of junk that accumulates in drawers over the years, but there was no drive.

Hands shaking, she felt along the bottom of the drawer and then underneath the top of the table. There was something taped in place there. She fumbled to pull it free, her mind identifying the shape even before she saw it. The thumb drive. She slipped the drawer back into place, dropping the drive into her pocket just as Tucker came running into the room, gun drawn.

"Alexis?"

"I'm here," she said, lifting up from behind the bed so he could see her. "With Milo. He just...he just died." Saying the words made it seem all that much more real, and she fought the urge to give in to her tears.

"Did he say anything?" Tucker asked as he knelt beside her, moving to confirm her words by checking for a pulse.

"No. Nothing that would help, anyway."

"Did you ask who shot him?"

"There wasn't time. He was only with me for a few seconds. And all he wanted was to tell me he was sorry. He said 'He didn't know.' "

"Didn't know what?" Tucker asked, his impatience showing.

"He didn't say. I'm assuming it has to do with the tracker. But he never clarified it."

"And that's it? There's nothing else?"

She shook her head, then closed her eyes, hating herself for lying but wanting more than anything to honor Milo's last request. After she'd seen what was on the drive, she'd decide how to proceed, but for now, no matter how guilty she felt, she'd keep it to herself.

"Did you find anyone outside?" she asked, lifting her gaze to meet Tucker's.

"No. Harrison is checking the neighboring houses to be certain, but I'm guessing the killer is long gone by now."

As if to underscore the idea, Harrison walked into the room. "Nothing," he said. "Not even a footprint." He came to a stop, his eyes on Milo's body. "Shit. Is he dead?"

Alexis nodded, her gut still churning. "He was alive when I found him, but there wasn't time to call for help."

"Did he—"

"No." Tucker shook his head. "He was all about apologizing to Alexis. Looks like we were right about his tampering with the phone, though."

"I checked downstairs in his office, and the computer is missing. Just like Dryker's."

"Even more support for our theory that Milo was playing for the other team. Dryker's, or whoever the hell was pulling his strings."

"And now they're tying up loose ends," Harrison said, his expression grim.

"Any chance there's anything still here that could help us?" Tucker asked.

"I'm thinking not."

Alexis clenched her hands, trying to maintain her resolve. She'd come to trust the two of them, and that made it tougher to keep quiet.

"Why don't you get Alexis out of here. And I'll call this in. And then we can head to the house we rented."

"You rented a house?" Alexis's voice rose with her surprise. Their resourcefulness was seemingly endless.

"It's just a cottage, really," Harrison said. "Near the lake. A friend—"

"—of a friend. I know. Anyway, I would like to get out of here, if it's okay. I think I've had enough death for one day." The minute that she said the words she regretted them. "Oh God, I didn't mean…" she trailed off, staring down at her friend's body.

"He can't hear you, Alexis," Tucker said, ever practical. "And besides, you were here with him when he died. That's got to count for something. He knows you cared."

She shook her head, unable to put her thoughts into words. In just a few days her life had literally exploded. And now all she felt was fear and confusion, the only escape the hours she'd spent in Tucker Flynn's bed—which came with its own set of problems.

She blew out a breath, steeling her expression, Milo's drive burning a hole in her pocket.

"What's wrong?" Tucker asked, pulling her over to the corner of the room out of Harrison's earshot. "This is more than just Milo being dead, I can tell."

"It's just that I don't want more people to die." Her hand closed around the drive. "And I don't want others put at risk. Just being with me is dangerous, Tucker. This isn't what you signed on for."

Something flickered across his face—regret, maybe—but before she could identify it, it was gone. He reached out to pull her close. "I'm exactly where I want to be. So don't give it another thought. And so is Harrison. We'll figure this out." He leaned back, searching her face. "So no more worries. Okay? I'm not going anywhere."

The tears she'd been fighting finally won the day, and her heart twisted as she fought the instinct to confess all. There was no reason to feel guilty. It wasn't as if she was going to keep it from him forever. But she owed Milo. Even if he had betrayed her, she didn't believe for a minute that he would have wanted to hurt her. And the cold hard truth was that, because of her, he was dead.

And besides, what if there was something on the drive that incriminated her or George? No matter how strong her feelings for Tucker Flynn, she had to protect herself.

Her father had always said she led with her heart, which he'd warned was a dangerous proposition. She'd always thought his pronouncements were a bit overzealous. But now, in light of her mother and George's betrayal, she wondered if maybe he hadn't been right.

Head over heart.

Easier said than done.

"Good evening, Mr. Atterley," Alain DuBois said, looking across his desk at the man impersonating George Atterley.

Michael Brecht steepled his hands and adjusted the monitor so that he could better see both men. He would have preferred to have the conversation with Atterley himself rather than let his Number Two deal with the man. But no matter how much better he was at playing the game, he couldn't risk the exposure. Better to remain the unseen puppet master. He'd just have to be content with watching—and feeding Alain information if necessary.

"Dare I hope that you're here to conclude our business deal?" Alain asked.

"I wish that I was," the other man said, his gaze shifting around the room, his fingers drumming out a nervous rhythm on the arm of the chair. "I honestly do. But I'm afraid there's been another delay."

"Meaning you haven't got the formula." Alain frowned.

Brecht leaned back, waiting, watching. Over the years he'd learned how to read men, especially ones with something to hide, and this one, for understandable reasons, showed all the signs. Unfortunately, his bravado was wasted. As usual, Michael was several steps ahead in the game. Just the way he liked it. Predator and prey was always so much fun when the prey had no idea the role they were playing.

"I haven't got it because someone stole it from me," the man said. "But I'm working to retrieve it."

"By killing people?" Alain tilted his head and lifted his eyebrows, a practiced gesture that never failed to illicit a response. Michael smiled and moved closer to the monitor.

Atterley's drumming stilled. "I'm not sure what you're talking about."

"Oh, I think you know exactly what I'm saying. But for the moment I'm not interested in your antics. I'm only interested in the formula."

"I'm telling you, I'm going to get it for you. I just need a little more time."

"Offer your help," Michael prompted, bending to speak into the microphone. "Use Carmichael to lead to the photograph. "

Alain gave the briefest of nods and then smiled at Atterley. "What you need is assistance. And you're lucky because I really do want that formula. And so instead of removing you from the equation, as my associates requested, I'm going to offer you my help."

"Your help?" The man's eyes widened in surprise.

"Yes. You've heard of Bastion Carmichael?"

"The governor of California? I don't know him, of course. But I've heard of him." Again the man's hands gave him away, his fingers digging into the arms of the chair so forcefully his knuckles turned white.

"Yes, of course." Alain contained a smile. "Well, it seems that Mr. Carmichael has been trying his best to waylay and/or eliminate a woman from New Orleans.

The jury is still out on what exactly he's trying to accomplish. But I guarantee you that it has something to do with Omega. By the way, you never did say how it was that you came into possession of the formula in the first place."

Michael smiled at the monitor. Alain had always had a dramatic flair.

"No. I didn't." The man paused, his gaze steady. Point to fake Atterley.

"Well, it's of no matter, really," Alain said with a dismissing shrug. "After all, curiosity did kill the cat."

"Yes, and if we're playing with clichés, it's better not to look a gift horse in the mouth." The man's smile belied his death hold on the chair.

"The problem, of course, being that I haven't actually received the gift." Alain arched his eyebrow again. "Which brings us back to Alexis Markham."

"Who?" Atterley asked, his reaction genuine this time.

"The woman Carmichael is so interested in." Alain pushed a file and a photo across the desk. Atterley picked them up. "I don't know why, but she's definitely the epicenter of all of this." He waited while the other man studied the photo. "So, do you recognize her?"

Atterley's brows drew together as he continued to stare down at the picture. Finally he looked up, still frowning. "No. I've never seen her in my life. But if you think she's the key, then why don't you go after her yourself? Why keep me in the loop?"

"There are complications. She's got guard dogs. Serious gentlemen who I believe may be connected to an elite CIA unit."

"And you don't want to risk exposure," Atterley said, his gaze turning shrewd.

"Careful," Michael cautioned into the mic. They wanted Atterley to believe they were truly on his side. "Don't overplay your hand." Alain blinked, his mouth quirking slightly on one side. Michael resisted the urge to burst into the office from the adjoining room. He'd never been good at delegating.

"I think you can understand why we prefer to take a backseat in this kind of situation," Alain said, his attention back on Atterley. "And, besides, the point here is that you made a bargain—for which, I hasten to remind you, you've already been paid in part. And unless you've lost your taste for living, I suggest you find a way to fulfill your end of the bargain—starting with Ms. Markham."

Atterley's gaze dropped unbidden to the photo in his hands. And Michael felt the familiar thrill of a battle won. Atterley had lied when he said he didn't know Ms. Markham. It was there in his face.

Perfect. The endgame was within sight. He'd use Atterley to get to A-Tac and, if things went really well, gain control of the formula and destroy them both in the process. And—worst case—if things went south, all the suspicion would fall on Atterley. It was a win-win situation. Just the way he liked it.

CHAPTER 17

The moon slid from a cover of clouds, a beam of light coating the old oak flooring with silvery light. The cottage was located in the middle of a bayou, surrounded by cypress trees. It was probably quite pretty in the daylight, but in the dark it felt sinister somehow. And now, sitting here about to view the contents of Milo's drive, Alexis's stomach was knotted with anxiety.

She held her breath, listening for signs of life. Harrison and Tucker were upstairs sleeping. She'd checked on both of them before coming downstairs. The evening had been tense, death hanging in the air like a physical being, the images of Dryker's and Milo's bodies burned in their brains. Ultimately, Alexis had pleaded a headache, even though she'd wanted to be with Tucker more than she'd ever thought possible. But neither of them had mentioned the night before or suggested a return engagement. Whatever was between them would have to wait until the shadows had cleared.

And at the moment, Alexis wasn't sure if that would ever happen. She sighed and pushed the hair out of her face, then opened Harrison's laptop. Considering his agility with all things cyber related, she was half afraid the thing would belt out some kind of intruder alert. But it merely flashed to life, presenting the picture of a smiling young woman, her multi-colored eyes and wavy brown hair marking her as a relative of Harrison's. A sister, maybe.

Alexis waited a few seconds more, but the computer remained silent, a blinking box indicating the need for a password. Fortunately, she'd managed to see him type it in earlier.

Brianna. A beautiful name. She looked again at the woman in the photo, then pushed aside her rambling thoughts. With an intake of breath, she typed in the name and hit Enter. The machine offered no resistance and the box disappeared, leaving only the smiling photo. And then, biting the side of her lip in the vain hope of maintaining her courage, she slipped the thumb drive into the USB port.

The computer hummed as the drive whirred to life, the sound seeming overly loud in the quiet room. Alexis's heart rate ratcheted up as she waited, every muscle in her body tensing as she watched the screen.

Then, just as suddenly as it had appeared, the photo of Harrison's sister disappeared, a directory listing of the thumb drive appearing in its place. The list wasn't long. A couple of text files with numerical headings and a video file labeled FOR ALEXIS. Her heartbeat moved into double time, and, with a shaking finger, she used the touch pad to click on the video.

For a moment the screen went blank, and then it was

filled with Milo's familiar face. Tears pricked the back of her eyes and she dug her nails into her palms, the sharp pain helping her regain control.

"So," Milo began, the corner of his mouth lifting in what resembled a grimace more than a smile, "if you're viewing this, it means that I'm dead. Otherwise I'd be telling you in person." He stopped for a moment and then began again. "I think I've really made a mess of things. I let my bank account rule the day. Not surprising, but you have to know that I'd never do anything to hurt you."

Alexis leaned forward, her eyes on her friend, her thoughts tumbling as he continued.

"I bugged your phone. Embedded the software with a tracking device. It was easy enough, and I figured what you didn't know couldn't hurt you. I thought they were after George, but I was wrong. It's you they want. And I've given them easy access." He dipped his head, then lifted it again, his blue eyes reaching across the pixels. "I'm so fucking sorry. And, worst of all, I can't even tell you who 'they' are. The man I dealt with is dead. Which is why I figure someone will be after me as well."

Alexis swallowed her tears, anger swelling instead. Whoever was behind all of this had taken two of the people she cared about most. George and now Milo.

"I've done some digging, but, unfortunately, I've got nothing. Except for two things. The first is that I'm fairly confident the order for the bug came from somewhere inside the government. The man I referenced before. The dead one. His name is Peter Dryker, and he had a career in security, including some defense contractors. And I think DOD." He blew out a breath, and Alexis felt tears welling again.

"And I got the feeling from the get-go that something big was afoot. Not that I heeded the warning, mind you. But the point is that digging deeper has only reinforced the idea. As I said, I thought it had to do with George, but I'm thinking now it's you. And something in your past."

She hadn't shared that part of her life with Milo. They were friends, but George had been insistent that she never mention it to anyone. Tucker was the first person she'd ever willingly discussed her past with. The thought brought on a wave of guilt, but she quashed it, focusing on Milo's words instead.

"Anyway, I'm afraid the news only gets worse. I didn't listen to your advice concerning Tucker Flynn. I didn't quit digging. Call it a character flaw. Anyway, I found out something rather alarming." He paused for a moment, his expression reflecting his remorse.

"Tucker Flynn isn't a friend of George's. He's CIA."

Alexis gasped, her mind reeling as she struggled to breathe, one thought repeating itself over and over in her brain.

Tucker had been playing her. Everything he'd said— everything he'd done—it was all a lie.

"I haven't been able to connect him to Dryker," Milo was saying, "but that doesn't mean there isn't a connection somewhere along the line. I'm sorry," he said. And it took every bit of willpower she possessed to focus on his words. "I know you have feelings for him. I could tell from the way you reacted when I said he was telling the truth. But I was wrong. And you can't let him sucker you, Alexis. No matter how much you want to believe he's on your side, he isn't."

She nodded as if Milo could see her, shudders racking

her body, her hands shaking as she clasped them together in her lap.

"Okay," he said, releasing an audible breath, "so I've said my piece, and you can confirm it with the documents I've stored on the drive. Maybe the information I've included here will make more sense to you than it did to me. All that's left now is for me to say again how sorry I am." He swallowed, his regret clearly visible now. "You were my friend, and I abused that privilege. Hopefully, someday you'll be able to forgive me."

The feed went blank, snow filling the screen. Alexis closed her eyes, her brain screaming to run, her heart wanting to stay, to wake up and find all of this a bad dream. She lifted a trembling hand and forced it to click on one of the files. A dossier appeared. Tucker Flynn. Facts and figures. Everything confirming Milo's assertion that he was working for the CIA. Originally some kind of deep operative group. Division 5.

There was a picture too. A photograph of Tucker in camouflage gear at some remote airfield, a jungle in the background. She flipped forward. There were other pictures. Same jungle. Only this time Tucker was gaunt and clearly wounded. Another man was helping him from a helicopter.

She flipped back to the first picture and frowned, trying to figure out what it was that was teasing her brain. He was clearly healthier here, but something else was different. She toggled back to the other photo, narrowing her eyes as she searched the picture. And then it hit her. The gray streak in his hair was missing in the first photo. Whatever had happened in the jungle, it hadn't been pretty.

Her heart twisted for a moment, and then she remembered his lies. Closing the window with the picture, she read through the dossier. His affiliation now was with a group called A-Tac. Another shadow organization within the CIA.

A government man, paid to do the country's dirty work. Just like the people who killed her father. Whatever she thought she'd felt for this man, it was based on lies. His lies. The stories he'd told her were created to make her trust him. To believe in him. And she'd fallen for it so deeply that she'd slept with the enemy.

Her father's face flashed in her mind: "Trust no one."

George and Milo were dead. And someone out there wanted her dead too. And the only man she'd thought she could trust was a liar.

"Alexis?" Tucker's voice loomed out of the darkness, and she slammed the computer lid shut and crept toward the window, trying to stay low, using the back of the sofa for cover. The moon was shining brightly now, the clouds having dissipated with the hint of the coming dawn. Somewhere out in the bayou a crane called, the low whooping sound haunting as it floated across the water.

"Alexis? Are you here?" Tucker strode into the room, his upper body glistening with sweat. She wondered if it had been a nightmare that had awakened him, cursing herself for caring. He turned slowly in a circle, his ice blue eyes probing the darkness. "Alexis?" he called again, his expression unreadable.

She held her breath, her heart pounding so hard she was certain he would be able to hear it. But after what seemed an eternity he turned and left, his footsteps hollow as he climbed the stairs again.

Sucking in air, she pushed herself off the floor, careful to stay in the shadows as she crossed the rest of the distance to the window. Two more minutes and she'd be free. She inched the sash upward, moving only a little at a time, fearful that any kind of noise would bring discovery. The wind whistled through the open window, the curtains billowing in the hot, humid breeze. She swallowed a curse and boosted herself up onto the sill.

Then with a quick look back to be sure she wasn't being followed, she jumped, hitting the ground hard but holding on to her footing. Her first instinct was to run. But she knew she couldn't leave her backpack. It had money and identification. And she'd need both if she was going to disappear successfully. Fortunately, the bag was still in the car. She'd been so exhausted she hadn't bothered to carry it inside.

She slowed as she reached the corner of the cottage. The car was sitting out front. For the moment it was bathed in darkness, but there was a motion-sensitive light situated on the far corner of the house. If she walked across the drive to the car the light would be triggered and alert Tucker and Harrison that someone was outside.

So instead of taking the direct route, she moved away from the house, heading for the cover of the trees, circling around until the car was between her and the house. She waited a moment, her heart still beating staccato, listening for any sign of life inside the cottage. But she could hear nothing except for the crane and the wind in the cypresses. Moving slowly, almost in a full crouch, she edged toward the car, stopping every few feet to reassess whether she was still alone.

Finally, she reached the vehicle. Only a few inches separated her from the backpack now. But it meant opening the car door, which risked motion and noise, both her enemies. Slowly she pressed the door handle and, with equal care, pulled it open. Then, with trembling hands, she reached inside, her fingers closing around the backpack's straps.

"Alexis, what the hell are you doing?" Tucker's voice rang out from behind her and she almost knocked her head against the door frame as she twirled around to face him. *Lie*, a voice inside her begged. *Tell him anything. Just not the truth.*

She swallowed and lifted her gaze to meet his. "I forgot my backpack." It was the truth, more or less.

"Yes, I can see that," he said, his eyes narrowed, voice flat. "What I don't understand is why you decided to go after it by going through the window in the dark."

"I didn't want to wake anyone," she said, knowing he wouldn't believe her. Hell, she didn't even believe herself.

"Now why don't I believe that?" he asked.

"Believe what you want." She shrugged, pulling the backpack from the car.

"Tell me the truth, Alexis. Why are you out here? Are you meeting someone?"

The question was so ludicrous she wanted to laugh. And cry. "There's no one to meet," she said, her voice cracking on the last word. "They're all dead."

"So what? You decided to run?"

Lie, the little voice said again. But words failed her, and instead she averted her gaze, trying to assess the distance from the car to the trees. She could lose him in the bayou.

"Alexis, talk to me. You know you can trust me with anything."

Anger filled her with a fierceness that surprised her,

spilling out in rushed words. "Trust you?" It was a question, but she already knew the answer. "After all the lies you've told? You're not a friend of George's. You didn't even know him. You set me up, you bastard. You made me believe you cared for me. But it was all a game, wasn't it? Using me as a means to an end. You're no better than the people who killed my father. Or was it the CIA who killed him? Is that it, Tucker? Do you work for the men who murdered my family? Have you come to finish the job?"

"Alexis, this isn't the time or the place—" he started, taking a step toward her.

"Stay away from me," she warned, holding up the bag as if it could protect her. Why the hell hadn't she listened to George and included a gun with her other stuff in the safe deposit box?

"We can talk about this inside. I'll tell you everything you want to know."

"And then turn me over to some higher-up who'll hold me prisoner until I tell him everything I know?"

His lips quirked upward at one corner. "I think you've been watching too many spy movies."

"Are you kidding me?" she whispered, inching farther away from him. "Milo died in my arms today. That wasn't a movie. It was real, Tucker. My friend is dead."

"Your friend betrayed you."

"Yes. He did. And he also left me a flash drive asking me to forgive him. Along with files that prove you're working with the CIA." Her heart dropped as she realized she'd left the drive in the computer. But there was nothing she could do about it now. All she could do was figure out how to get away. She inched back a little more, but he closed the distance, stopping a few feet away from her, hands extended as if to placate her. She fought the desire to laugh, a bubble of hysteria rising in her throat.

"I said I'd explain."

"Explain what? Why you always seem to be able to come up with a car or a house or money or guns or whatever the hell it is we happen to need? Or why Harrison has the skills to hack into almost any computer using nothing but a laptop? Or maybe why you decided it was a great idea to bed the mark?"

"It wasn't like that, and you know it," he said, his eyes reflecting her anger.

"It was exactly that. You've been using me in every possible way. What I don't understand is what everyone is so convinced I have. But I'll tell you right now that if I were to figure it out, you'd be the last man on earth I'd share it with."

"Alexis, whatever else has happened, you have to believe that I care about you."

"Right. And you have such a lovely way of showing it. Lying to my face about who you are, and using your imaginary past to sucker me into believing in you. And to think I thought that I was…" She stopped, the thought almost too much to bear and certainly more than she was going to share with him.

"Come back inside and we'll sort through all of this," he said as he took another step toward her.

"What? So you can lie to me some more? I don't think so," she said, moving backward again. "I'm done with you and your CIA. So unless you're going to force me to stay, I'm out of here."

She took a step backward, dropping the backpack as he lunged forward. Then, moving on pure adrenaline, she bent to scoop a large rock from the ground, swinging her arm with all her might. The rock connected with the side of his head, and he groaned and fell to his knees. For one instant she considered going to help him, but self-preservation took over, and instead she dropped the rock and ran. Covering the distance to the cypresses in seconds, she sprinted into the undergrowth, the trees closing around her, their arching branches blocking the moonlight and clothing her in darkness.

On and on she ran, heedless of the tree trunks and branches looming out of the shadows. They cut into her skin and clawed at her hair, but she pressed onward, determined to put as much distance between herself and Tucker as she could. And yet, still some part of her mind revolted, wanting to go back and make sure he was okay. To beg him to tell her that Milo had lied. That he was exactly who he'd told her he was. Someone like her. Someone living on the edge of existence. A shadow person.

A soul mate.

Tears ran down her face, leaving the taste of salt at the corners of her mouth, and still she ran until her lungs burned and her body ached. And then, finally, she came to a small clearing, a pool of water in the center shimmering in the moonlight. She knelt and stared down at her reflection, hating the woman she saw. Hating the fact that he'd made her feel as if she'd belonged. As if they were a team.

It had all been a dream. A terrible lie.

There'd been no connection. It had all been manufactured, a trick to gain her confidence. And she—Alexis slapped her hand against the water, her image shattering into ripples of moonlight—she had been a fool.

CHAPTER **18**

There's no sign of her anywhere in the vicinity," Drake said as he walked into the cottage, Nash following on his heels. "We tracked her to the highway, and from there, there's nothing.

"Son of a bitch." Tucker wasn't sure if he was cursing their lack of success or Hannah's probing fingers as she checked out the bump on his head.

Once Tucker had come to, he'd made his way to the house and apprised Harrison of the situation, and they'd decided it was time for reinforcements. Hannah, Drake, and Nash had hopped the first plane. He and Harrison had done a cursory search but found nothing. And when his friends arrived, he'd grudgingly ceded the hunt to them when Hannah had insisted on examining his head.

"We're thinking she must have hitched a ride," Nash was saying. "That would explain why the trail goes cold."

"Or maybe someone took her," Hannah offered, still

moving her fingers over Tucker's temple, the swelling there beginning to throb.

"It's possible, but it seems unlikely that they could have already traced us here," Harrison said. "We took precautions. And this place is practically in the middle of nowhere."

"But they've found her before when it was against the odds." Drake shrugged, dropping down on the arm of the sofa.

"When they had a way to trace her," Tucker added, frustration making it hard to hold still. "But we got rid of the tracker, so I'm with Harrison. I don't think they could have found her this quickly. Catching a ride seems like the more logical conclusion. But it doesn't really matter, because either way we don't have a clue where to start looking." He leaned back as Hannah peeled off the back of a bandage and stuck it in place over the injury. "She could be anywhere."

"Well, in my opinion, you should be in bed." Hannah stepped back to check her handiwork. "For all you know, you've got a concussion."

"Oh, come on, it was just a rock. I've got a cut and a bruise. Believe me, I'll survive," Tucker said, waving off further ministrations. "What we need to do is try and figure out where she might be. Even if they haven't found her yet, you can bet they're going to be trying."

"Actually, I think they've already made their first move," Harrison said, looking up from his computer, where he'd been studying the files on Alexis's disk. "I've been looking at this documentation, and there's no way Milo Alozono got it on his own. He had to have had help."

"What you mean?" Drake asked, coming over to stand behind Harrison. "What kind of help?"

"Someone with access to government files," Harrison answered, tapping the computer screen. "Specifically, CIA. Look, everything in these files is highly protected information. To the point that there aren't any paper trails out there that could have led him into uncovering this level of data. And even if there were, he still wouldn't have been able to gain access."

"Couldn't it be that Milo is just one hell of a hacker?" Hannah asked, moving to sit next to Nash on the sofa. "I mean, you always say there's nothing you can't access."

"Well, I'm a special case," Harrison said with a smile. "But seriously, there are databases that are almost impossible to hack into. And the CIA's division files are pretty damn impenetrable. I could probably hack it if I really had to, but only because I already have access to certain levels within the CIA hierarchy. And Milo wouldn't have had that benefit." He frowned as he turned from the computer to face them again.

"So you're saying it would have to be someone with top-level clearance," Drake said, eyes narrowed as he considered the option. "But that wouldn't be limited to the CIA, right? I mean, there are other people with that kind of access. The head of the NSA. Some of the brass at DOD. Homeland Security—hell, even the Oval Office."

Harrison nodded. "Of course, it could also be someone with the leverage to access someone with clearance."

"Okay, so we're looking for a bigwig," Tucker said, impatience rising. None of this was getting them any closer to finding Alexis. "Either one directly involved or one who is open to a blackmail or bribe. So how are we supposed to narrow it down?"

"I say we start with the Omega Project," Hannah said. "Everything we do know keeps pointing us back in that direction. Even if there isn't any paperwork specific to the project, we should be able to access personnel files from DOD at the time. We can cross-check that against all government employees with the right security clearance. And see what—or who—pops."

"That could take days." Tucker pushed out of the chair to pace in front of the window. "We don't have that kind of time. We need to find Alexis now."

"I agree," Nash said. "So we'll come at the problem from two sides. Hannah and Harrison can gather the information and run the cross-check. And in the meantime we'll try and figure out where Alexis might be heading."

"My best guess is that she'll be heading home," Tucker said, shooting a look at the pink-and-purple backpack sitting on the table next to Harrison. "Her money and identification are in the bag. Without either one, she's not going to be able to get very far. And if they get to her before we do..."

The street was quiet, the early morning hours leaving the neighborhood still shrouded in shadows. Alexis crouched in the shrubbery between her house and the neighbor's, watching and waiting, wanting to be certain there was no one lying in wait. It had been a huge risk coming back here, but she didn't have a choice. She'd dropped the backpack when she'd grabbed the rock and brained Tucker. She sucked in a breath, fighting her guilt. She hadn't meant to hurt him. She'd only wanted to get away. But desperate times and all that.

She regretted the loss of her keepsakes, but they were only things. And now more than ever before she realized the importance of putting the past behind her. The only thing standing in her way was getting in and out of her house without running into the men chasing her.

She'd racked her brains for some other avenue to get money, but short of robbery, the house had presented the best option. George was a great believer in backup plans. That was why she'd kept money both in the safety deposit box and hidden beneath the window seat in the dining room. There was ID as well, prepared by Milo. Her "just in case," he'd called it. A swell of anger and grief threatened to swamp her, but she shook her head. Now wasn't the time for regret.

She could do that later. After she was safely out of the country.

Her gaze swept across the distance between the shrubbery and her house. There was nothing moving, no sign of life at all. With a sharp intake of breath she made her way across the yard to the side of the house. Her back pressed to the siding, she waited again, searching for anything that might signal danger. This wariness was beginning to feel like second nature, and the thought frightened her almost more than the threat from the unknown assailants.

All of her life she'd longed for normalcy. Craved the routines of everyday existence. And now, here she was, breaking into her own house. She'd never thought of herself as someone who ran away from a threat, but she'd never been hunted by killers before—or almost fallen for a liar.

So many firsts.

She swallowed a bitter laugh.

Across the street, a light flickered to life in the front window of a house. Morning was coming and, with it, activity that was sure to bring witnesses and questions. Best to go now and be gone before the first light of day.

She made her way to the back of the house, ducking under a small magnolia for shelter, the insistent drone of a cicada breaking the silence. Only a few feet more to the back door. She'd hidden a key under a loose brick in the patio. At the time she'd felt rebellious. Doing something that she knew George would have forbidden, telling her it would be too easy for an intruder to predict her lack of caution. Now it was a godsend.

She knelt and retrieved the key, checking first to make sure there was no sign of activity. The backyard was small, bordered by a battered hurricane fence and a row of live oaks stretching across the back of the property. A pecan tree arched over the patio, a cluster of cannas framing the door. Heart rate ratcheting, Alexis pushed back to her feet and climbed the steps. She pulled open the screen and started to insert the key, but the door swung open from the pressure.

For a second she froze, certain she'd been discovered. But almost as quickly her brain reminded her that the house had already been ransacked. She stepped inside and closed the door behind her, waiting a moment for her eyes to adjust to the gloom.

Everything was just as she'd left it, although she hadn't really remembered it being this bad. Broken dishes littered the kitchen floor, pots and pans strewn everywhere. The cabinets were all open with doors hanging at awkward angles. She covered her nose, the stench of rotting food from the refrigerator almost unbearable. Instinctively, she bent to pick up a piece of broken pottery but stopped half-way, realizing it was too late for cleaning up. Life for her here, in this house, was over. And the sooner she accepted the fact, the easier it would be to walk away.

Ignoring the mess, Alexis walked into the dining room, picking her way across broken glass and scattered lemons, to the bay window that fronted the house. The street outside was still quiet, the first hints of dawn lighting the horizon. She needed to hurry.

Moving aside the ripped cushions that lined the window seat, she reached into a small crevice between the painted siding underneath the seat, quietly thanking Victorian cynicism and doubt. She pressed her finger into the crevice, and after a soft click the board swung outward, revealing a cubby hole the size of a bread box. She reached inside and pulled out the moleskin-wrapped package that contained the money and ID—a passport and driver's license in the name of Lisa Bennet.

"So much for Alexis," she whispered, a wave of sadness washing through her. But determination won the day—or maybe self-preservation. Either way, she knew it was time. Rising, she stuffed the packet between the small of her back and her jeans and started across the room, pausing for a moment at the broken mirror.

The reflection shocked her. A woman with wild gray eyes and matted blonde hair tangled with a variety of leaves and twigs. A long angry scratch ran down the right side of her face. And the deep purple of a bruise was burgeoning just below her left ear. It was like looking at a stranger.

Tears threatened, and she turned away from the image. Alexis Markham was dead. No more meekly following behind George or her father. No more pretending she had a chance at normal. This was the life she'd been born into. There was no escaping. But she'd be damned if she'd let the bastards who'd taken her family win. Her father deserved better than that.

She turned back to the cubby hole, reaching into the far recesses, her hands closing around a second package. She laid it on the floor, hands shaking as she pulled the wrappings off. The gun looked harmless lying against the pockmarked floor. After she'd refused to keep one with her backpack, George had insisted on putting it in the hidden compartment. For emergencies, he'd said. She'd never pulled it out before, never thought she'd have any reason to use it. She hadn't lied when she'd told Tucker she hated guns. But now, faced with the possibility of handling danger on her own, she knew that a weapon had become a necessity.

Dropping the gun into her pocket, she crossed the room again, pausing at the french doors that looked out onto the backyard. Like the rest of the windows in the house, she'd had wrought iron installed for protection. But she could still see the patio and the yard beyond. The sky was a pale pink now. It was time to move.

It seemed strange to think that Tucker was now one of the hunters. She had no doubt that he and Harrison would be looking for her. As hard as it was to accept, they were playing on opposite sides now, his lies only serving to reinforce what her father had drilled into her head.

Never trust the government.

No matter how charming the representative might be.

She closed her eyes, allowing a second to remember the feel of Tucker's arms, the touch of his lips, the moment when they'd—She opened her eyes, reality coming in the form of a noise from the front of the house.

Adrenaline rushing, she sprinted into the kitchen, intent on the back door. Just a few more steps and she'd be safely away. She rounded the counter, reaching for the doorknob, but lost traction when her foot hit something slippery. She fought for balance and lost, landing hard on her knees, her hands in front of her to break her fall. She tried to scramble to her feet but had trouble finding purchase, something behind her impeding her progress.

Sucking in a breath, she fought against her panic and reached for the countertop to brace herself. She pulled herself upright and looked down, her stomach churning as she recognized what she'd slipped on.

Blood.

The floor was covered with blood.

Swallowing bile, she spun around, searching for danger but seeing instead the body of a man—facedown on the floor. The blood was his, a wicked-looking bullet hole in his head.

Hysteria threatening, Alexis turned again, this time determined to get out the door, but through the window she could see movement in the backyard. Behind her the floor creaked, the sound more terrifying than an unknown quantity in the yard.

With a mumbled prayer she pulled the gun from her pocket and headed back into the dining room, moving on silent feet, her attention focused on the french doors. Reaching into her pocket, she produced the key and fumbled to slide it into the wrought-iron lock.

Another board creaked, this one on the stairs, and adrenaline rushed in to replace fear. She had to get the hell out of here. Fast. The lock clicked, and she yanked open first the door and then the protective screening. The early morning air rushed in, heavy with the perfume of crape myrtles. She closed the door behind her and ducked down behind the biggest bush, searching the backyard for the source of the movement she'd seen before.

But instead she heard gunfire coming from the front of the house. Confused, she froze, her mind trying to make sense of the commotion. Someone was shooting, but not at her. Pushing aside her tumbling thoughts, she sprang to her feet and sprinted out onto the lawn, heading for the gate at the far end that led into her neighbor's yard. A remnant from days when there'd been an alley, she'd always meant to get rid of that gate. Now she blessed her luck.

She headed through her garden, mindless now of the vegetables and herbs growing there. It was only when she reached the tomatoes that she stopped, her jeans catching on the edge of one of the cages. She bent to free herself and something whizzed by her face, the sound of the gunshot registering only after the fact. Panicked, she turned to find Tucker, certain that he would know what to do.

But Tucker wasn't here. She had only herself to count on now.

She jerked herself free and ran for the gate. A second bullet caught her arm, the sharp, burning pain making her dizzy. And then anger took over and she whirled around, searching for the gunman.

He was there on the edge of the garden, by the pecan tree, and even in the shadow she could see him smile as he lifted his gun. She opened her mouth to scream and then remembered her weapon. Seconds stretched into hours as she forced herself to raise her hand and tighten her finger on the trigger. Then, self-preservation kicking in, she dove for the ground.

In front of her the man's hand suddenly jerked upward, the bullet going wide as he dropped the gun and fell to the ground. Alexis lay still in the mud of her garden, afraid to breathe, afraid that the man would come for her again, or that his friends would find her. She was incapable of moving. Of thinking. Of doing anything but concentrating on each and every breath.

And then he was there. *Tucker.* Reaching down to pull her up, holding her tightly in his arms. She could feel the heat of his breath, see the stubble of his beard and the worry in his eyes as he brushed the hair out of her face. "Are you hit?" he asked, blue eyes probing.

She nodded, still not quite believing he was there. "Just my arm. I don't think it's serious." She wanted to be mad—to remember the pain of his betrayal. And she knew that eventually, when the adrenaline subsided, the anger would return. But right in this moment, she wanted him to go on holding her forever.

He lifted her arm and with gentle fingers probed the wound. She winced once but held strong even though it hurt like all hell. "It's just a graze. It's going to hurt for a while, but you'll be okay."

"And how about you?" she asked, reaching out with shaking fingers to touch his bruised face. "I'm so sorry."

"I know," he said, his hand covering hers. "You did what you had to do. And at some point we need to talk it all through. But not now."

She nodded, her gaze still locked with his. There was so much to say—and yet all she could think about was the warmth of his fingers against her skin.

"Don't worry," he soothed, pulling her close again. "Everything is going to be okay."

She wished it were as simple as all that. That the world was divided into black and white. But she'd learned a long time ago that things were far more complicated, the world filled instead with muted shades of gray. Good and evil looking practically the same. The trick being to choose wisely.

CHAPTER 19

Here," Tucker said, kneeling beside Alexis as she huddled beneath a blanket in the shambles of her living room, "drink this. You're going into shock. You need liquid."

She nodded but didn't take the cup of water he offered.

"You've got to try," he urged, holding the cup to her lips. He'd seen this before, in Afghanistan and in Colombia both. Soldiers who acted with bravery in the moment and then fell apart after the crisis had passed.

She took a sip and then pushed his hand away. "I killed a man," she whispered, her eyes wide with a mixture of both fear and fading adrenaline.

"No, sweetheart, you didn't," he said, lifting her chin, forcing her gaze to meet his. "Your shot went wide. You didn't kill anyone. I did. I killed him."

"And the other man?" she questioned, her voice raspy. "Did you kill him too? The man in the kitchen?"

"No." He lifted the cup to her lips again. "He was already dead."

She swallowed some water and then, after considering his words, took the cup and drained it. "So I didn't kill him?"

"No. You didn't."

"Oh God," she said. "I thought I'd...I thought..."

"Drink more water," he urged again, filling the cup from a pitcher on the table.

She nodded again, her mind clearly still out in the garden. "I wanted you to come," she whispered. "Even though I was angry, I wanted you to be there. To help me."

"You were doing pretty well on your own," he said, wishing he could make it all better but knowing he couldn't. Every person had a breaking point. And clearly Alexis had reached hers. Now she just needed to regroup—to absorb everything that had happened. Unfortunately, they didn't have the luxury of time. There were still people out there who wanted her dead.

"Do we know who the man you shot is?" Alexis asked, beginning to sound more like her old self.

"We do," Drake answered, coming into the room and dropping down on the arm of the chair. All of the team had assembled, everyone but Avery, who was holding down the fort at Sunderland. And probably chomping at the bit to be here in the center of the action. "His name is William Thompson."

"And, like Dryker, he's got a history in security," Hannah said, entering the room, Harrison just behind her. "Most of it falling on the legitimate side of things. But he's also been connected to some shady operations over the years. Strictly low-level kinds of things. Nothing that would have put him on our radar."

"And the guy in the kitchen?" Tucker asked.

"That's another story altogether," Harrison said. "Cristo Ramos. He's a big-time player. Connected to arms trafficking in the Middle East as well as some of the major drug cartels in Central and South America. Basically, he's available for most anything if the price is right. The important thing here is that his presence changes the game, moving it to a new and more dangerous level."

"So did this Thompson guy kill Ramos?" Tucker asked.

"Not a chance," Nash Brennon said, striding into the room. "Unless he tossed a second weapon. His gun isn't the right caliber."

"It was weird," Alexis said, sounding calm now. "There was no one in the kitchen when I first came in. And I never heard Mr. Ramos or the shots that took him out. But I did hear someone in the house. That's what made me run back into the kitchen. I was trying to get out when I fell over—" she paused, closing her eyes, clearly gathering strength. "When I fell over Ramos," she said, opening her eyes, her gaze steady. "So it had to have happened in the interim between when I first came into the house and then tried to run back out again."

"How long would you say that took?" Nash asked, eyes narrowed as he considered the situation.

"I don't know." She shook her head, frowning. "Ten minutes. Maybe a little less? I was moving pretty slowly. I wanted to be careful. But once I was inside, it wasn't too much longer before I'd gotten what I came for." She paused again, this time looking guilty. "My money and a new ID."

"Exactly what I'd have done under the circumstances,"

Hannah said with a smile. "So we've got to figure there were at least two men in the house when Alexis came in the door."

"Actually, I'm thinking three," Nash interjected.

"Why would you say that?" Tucker asked.

"Because I saw something when you took off for the back. It might have just been a shadow, but I could have sworn there was someone else here. Someone who ran when he realized we had the numbers."

"You're not going to believe this," Tyler Hanson said, walking into the room holding a length of filament wire and what was clearly a pipe bomb.

"Jesus, Tyler," Drake said, "are you sure that thing is stable?"

"It is now that I've disarmed it." She waved it around to emphasize the point.

Alexis was wide-eyed again.

"She's always a little bit scary," Drake said with a grin. "But she's usually harmless."

Tyler frowned, then shrugged. "I found this under the front porch. It had a timer, but the thing hadn't been set. I'm guessing your shadow man was scared off before he could finish the job."

"Great—so now the bomber is here too," Harrison said. "Hell of a party. So we're talking three players here?"

"No," Tucker countered. "I'm thinking just two. Ramos and our bomber. And then the secondary shooters, including Thompson."

"So Group Two surprises Group One, and all hell breaks out," Hannah summarized.

"And I walked into the middle of all of it," Alexis said, her fingers digging into his palm.

"If we're right," Drake added, "and someone went to the trouble to feed Milo information about who Harrison and Tucker really were, then it isn't too far a reach to assume they did it in the hopes of flushing you out into the open."

"You're saying my running away from Tucker was exactly what they wanted me to do?"

"Yes," Nash affirmed, not pulling any punches. "But Hannah is right. If I'd been in your situation, I'd have done exactly the same thing." He turned to Tucker, his eyes on the purpling knot on the side of his head, a smile curling at the edges of his lips. "And, quite frankly, I don't think I could have done it any better."

Alexis ducked her head, clearly mortified.

"So was it different here?" Harrison asked. "From before, I mean."

Alexis frowned, chewing on the side of her lip as she considered the question. "There was more damage. Like maybe someone else had been here. The kitchen was messier, and some of the cabinet doors were off their hinges. And in the dining room—when I came home the first time, I distinctly remember that the bowl of lemons on the table was untouched. But tonight I was tripping on them."

"What about you guys?" Nash asked, his gaze moving to Drake and Hannah. "Are things different from when you were here?"

Alexis opened her mouth to question this revelation, but then closed it again, leaning back against the sofa's torn cushions, pulling her hand free from Tucker's.

"I don't remember the bottom of the chairs being ripped out," Drake said, noting the foam spilling out from beneath an armchair. "And the paintings—they've all been removed from the walls." Two of them had been slashed, corner to corner.

"But there isn't anything here for them to find," Alexis protested. "Except my money, and somehow they managed to miss that."

"Where was it hidden?" Tyler asked, placing the disabled bomb in a padded duffel.

"There's a secret compartment under the window seat in the living room. The previous tenant showed it to me when I took possession of the house. It seemed the obvious place for a backup stash. George was big on backup plans."

"Plan B," Drake said with a smile, "my favorite."

"So is there anything else in this hidey-hole?" Nash asked. "Anything that you might have hidden away and forgotten?"

"No. There was just the pouch with the money and Milo's IDs and the gun. That's it."

"Harrison, you and Tyler check it out anyway, okay? It might be the only place in the house the intruders didn't manage to tear apart."

"If the house was searched twice," Tyler said, "does that mean you think both groups made a search? Or that one of them just made a second attempt to find whatever they're all so desperately after?"

"No way to know for sure," Tucker said. "But if Ramos and the bomber were here first, I'm guessing they were the ones searching this time. And since they were clearly planning to destroy the place, that would seem to mean they were ultimately convinced there was nothing here to find."

"Or they found it. Whatever the hell 'it' is."

"It's possible," Nash said. "But based on Ramos's untimely demise, and the fact that our bomber fled under duress, I'm thinking it's pretty unlikely. Maybe the bomber's just trying to get rid of anything that might link back to Omega."

"Or maybe the guy just likes to see things go boom," Drake suggested.

"I'm thinking it's time to get Alexis out of here." Hannah shot her a sympathetic look. "She's had more than enough for one night."

"I can't go back to the cottage." Alexis shook her head.

"No one expects you to," Tucker said. "But you're going to have to stay with us. We can't be sure of your safety otherwise. We'll set you up in a hotel for tonight. Hannah or Tyler can stay with you, and the rest of us will be nearby."

She looked down at her hands, blew out a long breath, and then lifted her gaze to his. "If someone is going to watch over me, I'd just as soon it be you, if that's okay."

It wasn't a complete vote of confidence. But it was a start.

CHAPTER **20**

Steam from the shower filled the hotel bathroom.
The mirror had fogged over, rivulets running down
the glass reminding her of tears. She closed her eyes,
shivering, not so much from cold as from the memory of
everything she'd been through. Her clothes lay in a pile
on the floor, her jeans soaked with a stranger's blood, her
shirt stained with her own. The bullet wound on her arm
had been stitched closed, but the ache was a constant
reminder of that moment in the garden. It could all have
ended so differently. If Tucker hadn't been there.

She shivered again, this time with the memory of the
warmth of his hands, the conflicting thoughts threatening
to undo her. She was holding on by a thread. Intellectu-
ally, she knew she was a strong woman, but emotionally,
she wasn't sure how much longer she could hang on.

Case in point. She was standing in the bathroom of a
hotel, bruised and shaken, with an ex-lover just outside—
if you could count a one-night stand—who had lied

about his background to seduce her into admitting she
had something she didn't. And as much as she wanted to
wash it all way, she couldn't quite convince her fingers to
release their hold on the counter and step into the shower.

"Alexis?" Tucker's voice sounded frantic.

It was the second time he'd called to her. And to be
honest, a perverse little part of her thought he deserved
the worry, after everything he'd done. But the rational
side of her brain insisted that he'd saved her life on so
many occasions now it had to trump any lies he'd told.
And the reality was that she simply didn't know what to
think. Let alone feel.

Tucker had said this might happen, that shock was a
funny thing. But she'd handled the situation at her house
with clarity. She'd held it together and pushed her fear
into the background. She'd even accepted all of Tucker's
friends, government operatives no less. Opened up and
discussed events, even though what she really wanted
was to crawl under the covers and pretend this was a
really bad dream.

Only it wasn't.

"Alexis, if you don't answer me, I'm going to break
down the door," Tucker called. And Alexis knew it wasn't
an idle threat.

Sucking in a deep breath, she reached over to unlock
the door, but hesitated, not sure whether she'd been
locking him out or herself in. She knew that being with
Tucker was a bad idea. And yet her body craved the contact. Maybe it was just a reminder that there was something out there besides death and destruction.

But Tucker was a liar.

Or maybe she'd given him no other choice. If she'd

known the truth from the beginning, she'd have ditched him at the first opportunity. And she'd most likely be dead.

"Alexis." He shook the knob, anxiety mixing with the anger in his voice.

With a slow sigh she opened the door, and he stepped inside the bathroom.

For a moment, they just stood staring at each other, eyes locked in a duel that had no easy resolution. And then, with a sigh, she threw herself into his arms, her desire for him outweighing the need for caution.

With one finger under her chin, Tucker tipped her face so that he could see her. "Are you all right?"

She nodded, then shook her head, unable to speak, losing herself in the cool blue of his eyes. Where he was concerned, she wasn't sure she'd ever really be all right again. "I can't...I don't...I mean—oh, God, Tucker, everything is so confusing. I don't know who to trust. What to believe. I just—"

"You can trust me," he said, pressing a finger against her lips. "I know it's counterintuitive considering the lies I told, but it's still the truth. I only want to keep you safe and figure out how to put a stop to this. You've got to know that all I really want is for you to be okay."

"I don't know if that's ever going to be possible. I've been running my whole life, and I've never really known why. And now someone out there believes I've got something they want. Only I haven't got anything, and I don't know how to fight back. So I just keep running. And I'm so tired, Tucker. I can't even find the strength to take a shower."

He cupped her face in his hands. "Let me help you

forget, at least for a little while. Just the two of us. Here. Now. Tomorrow we'll figure out the rest of it."

She held his gaze for a moment, relishing the feel of his fingers against her skin and the heated mist from the shower as it enfolded them. "Yes," she whispered, not sure exactly what she was agreeing to, but certain it was more important than breathing.

He pulled off his shirt, his muscles tightening with the motion, the scars on his chest softened in the misty light. She traced a finger down one of them. A rough and jagged line that slid beneath the pectoral muscle on his left side. "Does it hurt?" she asked, her voice hushed as she laid her palm against his chest.

"Not anymore," he said, framing her face again as his mouth slanted down over hers. There was so much about this man she didn't know. Questions bubbled to the surface, but she forced them back, lifting her mouth to his instead. He was right. There'd be time for talking later.

His kiss was hard. His mouth demanding. And she tasted him in return, exploring his lips. Then she opened to him, her tongue meeting his. The kiss built in intensity, passion coiling deep within her, waiting—wanting. She pressed against him, satisfied to feel the hard heat of him against her stomach, relieved to know that he wanted her as badly as she wanted him.

He trailed kisses down her neck, caressing her ear with his tongue, sending a delicious warmth spiraling through her. God, she wanted him—wanted him with mounting urgency, some deep inner part of her driving her onward, oblivious to everything but him. She sucked in a breath, whimpering with need, as his hand found her breast, his palm kneading the tender flesh, his kiss an echo of things to come. His tongue thrust possessively, robbing her of all rational thought.

He pushed her backward until they'd reached the tub and, after stripping off the rest of his clothes, they stepped into the bathtub, the warm spray from the shower caressing their skin. She stood still in the circle of his arms, tilting her head up, letting the water stream down her face and throat.

Tucker took the bar of soap and slowly, gently began to wash her, starting with her shoulders and working down in slow soothing circles. She closed her eyes, letting sensation take over, her body tightening with need as he slid his hands around her, soaping her breasts and her stomach, suds sliding down between her thighs. Her nipples hardened as he ran his hand lower, her heart pounding so loudly she was certain he could hear it. And then with a little moan she leaned back against him, lifting her hands to stroke his face. Moving slowly against him, pushing closer into the curve of his body, the water forming a curtain around them.

For a moment, they stayed like that, his hands working their magic. Then she turned, and with a groan, he bent his head, taking possession of her mouth, his hands spreading across the small of her back as the water beat down on them.

She pressed against him, sensation overcoming everything else, reveling in the feel of his tongue against hers, his hands as they kneaded and circled, exploring, and the heat from the water as it swirled around them. Raising her arms, she threaded her fingers through his hair, her breasts pressed against his chest, the sensation of their bodies rubbing together intensified by the pulsing water.

With a slow smile he bent and took one of her breasts

into his mouth, circling it with his tongue, and she arched against him at the touch. Holding her with one hand, he moved the other in slow circles down her abdomen, sliding lower and then lower still, until he slid one finger inside. Swallowing a moan, she pushed against him, forcing the finger deeper, arching backward. As he gently bit her nipple, she closed her eyes, offering herself to him, the steam and the water only heightening the pleasure.

Gently, he pushed her backward until she felt the warm, wet tiles. The water cascaded between them now, the feeling beyond erotic, his kiss making her knees go weak. Then, with a crooked smile, he moved back, kneeling before her, lifting her leg so that her foot rested on the rim of the tub.

She sucked in a ragged breath as he bent low, his hands holding her steady as his tongue delved deep inside her. Grasping the towel rod behind her, she arched back, urging him on as he licked and tasted, thrusting with his tongue, the pressure ratcheting upwards until it was almost painful, her body writhing under his ministrations.

Then, just when she thought that she couldn't possibly take any more, he rose to his feet, the water behind them now, a fine mist caressing them both.

"Please, Tucker," she whispered, her body literally throbbing with need. "Please."

He cupped his hands under her hips, lifting her up as she twined a leg around him, his penis pulsing against her. With a moan, she felt him thrust inside her, and then slowly withdraw with a gentle rocking motion that teased her already heightened senses. In and out, in and out, slowing sliding until she thought she'd go insane.

"*Please,*" she cried again.

The word echoed around them, and with one long thrust, he filled her. With driving need, she begged for more, wrapping her arms around him, holding tightly as he held her pinned above the world, her entire being concentrated on the exquisite feel of his body as he pounded deeper and deeper, harder and harder, until there was nothing left except the two of them locked together— spiraling toward release.

Suddenly he cried her name, and the world spun out of control, pleasure exploding through her with a strength beyond anything she'd ever experienced. And as the powerful contractions consumed her, she realized that she could no longer tell where he ended and she began. Somehow, in joining, they'd become one.

There would be a price to pay, of that she was certain. But right now, in this moment, she didn't give a damn.

"I think you ought to know that just because we've been, well…you know," Alexis said, as she took a bite of her cheeseburger, "it doesn't mean that I've forgiven you for lying to me."

They were sitting on the hotel bed eating room service, Alexis still draped in a sheet. The room-service dude's eyes had bugged out of his sockets, and Tucker had to fight against the urge to clock the kid. He'd wanted to write his reaction off as being protective, but sitting here now, looking at her with ketchup on her chin, all he was feeling was possessive.

Which didn't bode well for the fragile bridge they were rebuilding. Alexis wasn't the kind of woman to appreciate a man who tried to hold on too tightly. And hell, truth be told, he hadn't realized he wanted to be that kind of man.

With Lena, it had been a partnership for so long that when they finally fell in love, the routines were already in place. She was already a defined part of his life and their relationship shifted the focus slightly, but it didn't really change the reality of who they already were. With Alexis, it was different.

He'd been telling himself it was because of his lies. But now here they were, truth on the table, and despite the wedge he'd jammed between them, she was still here in his bed. Or at least *a* bed. So either she was so spooked by the shooting at her house that she figured fraternizing with a friendly enemy beat the alternative, or maybe— just maybe—he still had a chance with her.

Although he wasn't sure exactly when he'd decided it mattered so damn much. Maybe after the third time they'd made love. On the chair by the desk, *ergonomic* taking on a completely new meaning.

He smiled.

"I'm not kidding. You're not off the hook just because you can"—she waved at the chair, wiping at the ketchup, her cheeks turning a corresponding red. "I'm serious, Tucker," she said, eyes flashing.

"I know. I was just remembering"—his gaze shot to the chair—"fondly."

She turned a deeper shade of red but she also smiled, and his heart did a little flip. Hell, she made him feel like a teenager.

They ate in silence, the normalcy of the scene comforting. But eventually, he knew, they needed to talk. There were things she needed to know. And, more importantly, he needed to try to reestablish some of the trust he'd lost, both professionally and

personally. Although instinct deemed the latter a dangerous game.

Alexis pushed away her plate, leaning back against
the pillows, the sheet slipping low on one side, her hair
falling across her shoulders to splay across her breasts.
He was reminded of the first night he'd spent with her, in
the apartment in New Orleans. She was still alluring, and
despite her blush, still totally unaware of the effect she
had on men. The dichotomy pulled at him. And again he
thought about his need to protect and possess her. Man's
most deeply ingrained instincts. And yet, something
about her made the need even more pressing.

"So," she said, her eyes darkening as her fingers fidg-
eted with the sheet, "the things you told me, I mean I
know the stuff about George was a lie, but the stuff about
your dad and baseball—and your fiancée..." She trailed
off, staring down at her hands, and he heard the vulnerability in her voice and hated himself for putting it there.
She squared her shoulders and lifted her gaze to meet
his. "Was any of that the truth? Or was that all a lie too?
Things you made up to make me believe in you?"

Tucker grabbed the room-service tray and carried it
over to the table, playing for time while he ordered his
thoughts. "What I told you about my mother. That was
the complete truth. She abandoned us and never looked
back. And we really did find solace in baseball. Some
families go to church. We went to Angels games."

"Sort of an odd symmetry there, I guess." She smiled,
then sobered. "And Lena? Is she really dead?"

"Yes," he confirmed, memory surfacing, and guilt—
along with the pain he'd come to know so well. "She was
my partner." He started to leave it there, then realized

Alexis would need more, something to assure her that he was finally telling the whole truth. "We worked for a black-ops division of the CIA."

"Division something or other?" she asked, her frown forming a line between her eyes.

"Right, D-5," he said. "We did a lot of undercover work. And our last assignment was in Colombia."

She waited, listening, her fingers still kneading the sheet.

"We infiltrated the resistance movement, with an eye toward gaining intel on certain drug cartels."

"That sounds dangerous," she said, her eyes widening.

"It was. But we were used to that kind of thing. Anyway, no one knew who we really were, and for the most part, we found that the guerrillas were as interested in eliminating the cartels as we were. In fact, we were closing in on one particular drug lord when someone blew our cover. We were blindsided. And most of my team was killed. Only three of us got away."

"You, Lena," Alexis said, her fingers stilling.

"Right. And Hector."

She nodded. "You called his name during the nightmare."

"Anyway, we were separated, and I was captured by government forces. I managed to keep my cover, but I was, of course, considered a political prisoner. And as such, I was shipped off to a prison in northwestern Colombia. A place called San Mateo."

"But couldn't you have told them who you were?"

"No." Tucker shook his head, memories swirling. "I believed Lena and Hector were still alive but I didn't know where they were, and I couldn't risk blowing their cover. Only Hector had betrayed us. And Lena was dead.

He hunted her down and killed her. Only I didn't know that until much later."

"And so you stayed in San Mateo."

"Yeah." He laughed, the sound lacking any humor. "I stayed. And if it hadn't been for my brother, I'd probably still be there. He found out I was still alive—"

"He thought you were dead?" Her hands were clenched so tightly now her knuckles had gone white.

"When the operation went bad, the CIA had to cover it up. Pretend we were never there. Political protocol. So they informed our loved ones that we'd all been killed in a training accident—in Nevada."

"Oh my God. But Drake found you anyway."

"Yes. A friend—his wife, actually—had been incarcerated with me. And she recognized me in one of Drake's photos. Anyway, long story short, they went off grid to rescue me and here I am."

"And Hector?"

"He's dead." As usual, saying the words brought no relief.

"I'm glad," she said, sounding as if she'd like to have done it herself. Then she sighed, her voice turning hesitant. "You loved her very much, didn't you?" It was a loaded question, but he answered honestly.

"Yes. I did."

"I see," she said, chewing the side of her lip as she considered his words. "I'm sorry. It must be hard...."

"It is what it is." He shrugged, hating how callous he sounded. "Just one more thing I have to live with."

"But it wasn't anything you did." She frowned, reaching over to cover his hand with hers. "I mean, you did everything you could to protect her."

"And it wasn't enough," he said, the words coming of their own accord.

"You told me once that I couldn't blame myself for George's death—or my father's—that if I'd been there, I'd have been killed too. And while I know that makes sense, it doesn't stop me from wishing it could have been different. That I could have done something to save their lives. But the truth is, you're right. I couldn't have changed the outcomes. And neither could you."

"You don't know that." He pulled away from her.

"No, I don't," she said, leaning forward to take his hand again, her gaze locking with his. "But I know you. And I know that if it had been in your power to save her, you would have found a way. But sometimes, Tucker, there's simply nothing we can do."

"I want to believe that, but it isn't easy to let go."

"Well, maybe I can help with that," she said, letting the sheet fall to her waist. "At least for tonight. And tomorrow"—she sighed as he pulled her into his arms—"well, tomorrow is another day."

CHAPTER 21

Sunderland College, New York

If there were a picture next to the definition of American colleges in the dictionary, the photo would be of Sunderland. Founded in 1823, it was a liberal arts college of the highest regard. The ivy-covered brick buildings were surrounded by curving sidewalks and enormous trees. All around Alexis, students scurried to classes. Others sprawled out on the green lawn that fronted the Aaron Thomas Academic Center.

The center served as the heart of both the campus and Tucker's brother's undercover CIA unit. She'd had a briefing on the plane. Hannah, the unit's intel expert, had brought her up to speed on A-Tac's existence and cover. Leading a double life as both professors and operatives, the CIA's best and brightest made the unit their home.

The whole thing had a surreal feeling, as though she'd landed in the middle of a Robert Ludlum or Ian Fleming novel. Which she supposed, in reality, she'd been living for the past week. She just hadn't been made aware of the spy component.

Still, the people she'd met—Drake, Hannah, Tyler, Nash, and Harrison—seemed to really care about each other and their missions—which at the moment included her. And even though there was still a great deal of distrust on her part, the idea of working with them wasn't as repugnant as she'd have thought it would be. Maybe because they'd saved her life. Or maybe because they were affiliated with Tucker.

He was walking beside her now, his mind clearly on the meeting ahead. The decision had been made this morning to bring her here to keep her apprised of their investigation and to make sure she was kept safe, the latter being a double-edged sword. But so far, at least, she hadn't been made to feel like a prisoner.

She and Tucker hadn't had much of a chance to discuss the night before. And in truth, she wasn't certain what she felt about the situation. She'd come to care deeply for the man—there was no denying the fact—but she was far less comfortable with his chosen profession. By definition, they were on opposite sides of the game. While she hadn't committed any overt crimes, a lifetime spent off the grid made her part of the shadow world that housed many of the people he'd spent his adult life trying to eliminate.

People like George.

She'd lived long enough to know that there was no such thing as simply black and white, but it wasn't always easy to sort through the gray, and long ago, with her father's persecution, she'd chosen her path.

And the funny thing was, that even in light of everything that had happened, she still preferred her world to

Tucker's. Although if she were honestly given a choice, she'd have chosen neither. There had to be a middle ground—where normal people lived. Like the students they were passing. And, push come to shove, that was the life she wanted. No shadows—on either side of the fence.

"It's beautiful here," she said, glancing over at Tucker. "I can see why your brother and his wife love it."

He'd told her last night not only about Lena, but about Drake and his wife, Madeline, and the hell they'd been through when they'd been forced on the run. Madeline came from her world. And she'd clearly made the transition to Drake's, but Alexis was certain their happiness was the exception, not the rule.

"It's a good place," Tucker said. "Although I'm more partial to California. Redlands, in particular. But this will do in a pinch. And it certainly beats some of the places I've been stationed."

"Like Colombia." She nodded, as they started up the steps to the center. Aaron Thomas had been a revolutionary war hero. A spy—for the American side—as well as a political philosopher. So it was fitting that the center was named for him. He'd have no doubt been pleased with both the intellects and the secrets it harbored.

They walked into the lobby to find Drake talking with a couple of students, the two girls hanging on every word with adoring eyes.

"Looks like Drake is a popular professor." Alexis smiled as he raised a hand in welcome.

"It's the Indiana Jones thing." Tucker laughed, waiting while his brother broke away from the conversation and strode over to join them. "Who knew archaeology was a turn-on?"

"He's making fun of me again, isn't he?" Drake said. "The Indiana Jones thing?"

"Sounds like a compliment to me," Alexis said. "I've always had a thing for Harrison Ford."

"Well, it's not as exciting as the movie makes it seem," he assured her. "Just a lot of careful digging in hot and dusty places."

"When you're not off chasing the bad guys," she said, still smiling.

"There is that." His eyes were twinkling and, for a moment, he looked so much like his brother it was uncanny.

Tucker cleared his throat, and Alexis had the distinct feeling that he was irked at the attention she was paying his brother, his jealousy more satisfying than she'd have cared to admit.

They stopped in front of an elevator bank, and Drake inserted a key into an elevator marked PROFESSORS ONLY. The doors slid silently open, and they stepped inside.

"This feels very clandestine," Alexis said, feeling even more like she'd stepped into a spy novel.

"Just wait." Tucker smiled as Drake inserted another key and pressed a button hidden behind an Otis elevator sign. "It gets better."

The elevator started downward and they rode in silence, watching the numbers as they decreased to just below the sub-basement level. "Definitely a secret lair," Alexis said as the doors slid open and they stepped into an austerely appointed reception area. "Like *Get Smart* or something. Do the students ever try to come down here?"

"If they make it past the first key," Drake said, walking

across the room to a bust of an elderly man, "they're sent to a professors' lounge on the top floor of the building. If they were to make it past that, they wind up here—still none the wiser, but ultimately having to deal with Avery."

Avery Solomon was A-Tac's commander. Alexis hadn't met him yet, but she'd heard enough to know he wasn't someone you wanted to anger. "I'm assuming at that point they're on the way to expulsion?"

"They would be, if they ever managed to get this far," Drake agreed. "But, fortunately, that hasn't happened. We're pretty careful to keep it under wraps. And so far so good."

"This is the best part," Tucker told her as his brother slapped his hand against the back of the bust, a panel in the far wall sliding open.

"Wow," Alexis said, suitably impressed. "And that would be?" She tilted her head toward the statue.

"Aaron Thomas, of course." Drake motioned them forward into the inner sanctum, the panel sliding silently shut behind them. Drake led them down the hall into a large room filled with the other A-Tac members.

"This is the war room," Tucker explained, "the real heart of A-Tac." With computer banks flanking the walls and LCD screens above and behind the oblong conference table, the oversized space served as the hub of all activity.

Hannah and Harrison sat at the far end of the table, computer consoles popped up, both of them typing as they compared notes on something. Nash and Tyler sat on the right side of the table, the two of them also huddled in conversation. And at the far end of the room stood two men, the younger waving his hands to emphasize his words, the other man so big he dwarfed even Tucker and Drake.

Drake cleared his throat and conversation stopped, attention turning to the three of them standing in the doorway. For the first time since all of this had begun, Alexis found herself feeling like an outsider.

"Alexis," Tucker said, "I think you've met most everyone here." Harrison shot her a comforting smile, and she felt herself begin to relax. "But you haven't met Avery."

Drake pulled her forward as the big man crossed the room, hand extended. "Avery Solomon," he said, his voice deep and commanding. "Welcome to A-Tac. I'm sorry it's had to come to this." She took his hand, his fingers engulfing hers, but even with his overwhelming strength there was a gentleness there, and his eyes were full of understanding.

"I'm just glad to finally meet you. Your team has told me a lot about you."

"All of it horrible, I'm certain." He smiled, his dark eyes full of genuine humor.

According to Hannah, Avery was an ex-marine with service in both the CIA and the Pentagon, who'd worked with three different administrations and made a lot of powerful friends along the way. It was because of him that A-Tac had maintained its autonomy in the face of a political elite critical of all things espionage and the stigma of having found a traitor in their midst. Just looking at him, Alexis could see why the team admired him so, and that the respect ran both ways.

"No," she said, smiling back at him, feeling the rest of her tension melt away. "It was all quite flattering. And now that I've met you, I can see they were telling the truth."

Avery was charming, as were the rest of Tucker's friends. There probably weren't too many people who didn't quickly fall under A-Tac's spell. Which made them a dangerous adversary. Or, conversely, a valuable ally. The billion-dollar question being which of the two they were when it came to her. Which meant she'd do well to remember to keep her guard up.

"Tucker, I don't think you've met our newest recruit," Avery was saying. "This is Simon Kincaid. He's going to be running communications and logistics."

Simon extended a hand. "I heard about your ordeal in Colombia. Sounds like a hell of a firefight getting out of that valley after escaping San Mateo."

Simon wasn't as tall as Tucker, but he was well built, with the hardened muscles of someone who'd had experience with battle. Maybe military. He certainly had the stance for it, but there was also a reckless glint in his eye that spoke of something more rough and tumble. Street smarts. Covered up now with a little spit and polish, but she suspected that Simon Kincaid had walked on the wild side more than not.

"It wasn't a picnic," Tucker responded, "but we made it out in one piece, and that's what counts."

"Well, I can't say I'd have turned down the chance at a little action like that. I've been stuck here for the last few weeks, learning the ropes, as it were."

"You'll be in the line of fire before you know it," Avery said, moving back to the front of the conference table as the rest of them took their seats. "If I were you, I'd enjoy the downtime."

There was a quiet rebuke there, but Simon didn't seem to notice. And Alexis wondered if Tucker and Drake had started their careers with the CIA feeling as gung ho. Probably so, she thought, smiling to herself. They were admitted adrenaline junkies, after all.

"Okay, people, let's get to work," Avery ordered, clicking a remote to pull down a screen on the wall behind him. "We've got at least two groups of people out there actively hunting Alexis. We need to identify them and figure out what they're looking for."

"I think the last bit is pretty obvious," Hannah said, pushing her glasses, which were green today, higher onto her nose. "They're looking for the formula."

"But there isn't a formula," Alexis objected, fighting to stay calm. "My father never had the damn thing. So there's no chance I'd have it."

"Alexis," Tucker said, his tone apologetic, "you don't know that for certain. You were a kid. And your father wouldn't have admitted to having the formula. It would only have made it more dangerous for you."

"But he was the one being persecuted, not the other way around," she insisted, knowing he was right but not able to let it go.

"Having the formula doesn't change the facts as he laid them out. If he did threaten to go public with the truth about Omega," Tucker said, "and if his partner was killed as a result, stealing the formula would have been insurance. A way to make sure that they wouldn't risk taking him out too."

"But they did kill him," she said, her frustration rising. "So why would they do that if they believed he had the formula? It's self-defeating."

"Maybe they didn't know," Nash inserted. "At least then. Maybe that's what started all of this. If the intel circulating is right and the formula has surfaced after all this time, that would send all kinds of players into action. People wanting to buy it. People wanting to make sure it never saw the light of day. Even us, trying to find out if the damn thing really exists and keep it from falling into the wrong hands."

"And all of that," Drake said, leaning back in his chair until it was balanced on two legs, "would center the focus on people who could have the formula. Which would have led them to George and then to you."

"Except that George is dead. Just like my father. So if he had the formula, that's it."

"Unless he left it with you," Tucker said.

"But I don't have it," Alexis repeated, raising her voice as anger surged through her. After all this time, she'd have thought he'd at least believe her.

"He's just saying that maybe you have something you don't know you have," Tyler said, her gaze sympathetic. "Maybe your father gave the formula to Atterley. And then maybe he hid it with you. Thinking it would be safe."

"He was trying to tell you something"—Tucker frowned—"just before he was killed. Right?"

Alexis nodded. "I left before I found out what it was."

"And avoided being blown to bits," Simon said, no doubt trying to make her feel better. But it didn't. Not by a long shot.

"Look," Tucker said, "the point here is that George must have known someone was after the formula. And if you were going to become a target, George would have wanted to warn you. And he'd have wanted to keep you as far away from him and suspicion as possible."

"And if the guy after the formula figured all of that

out," Nash continued, "then George was no longer a valuable part of the equation."

"Hence the bomb," Drake said.

"Hence?" Tyler asked, barely containing a laugh.

"It's a word," he shot back.

"Yeah, like in some other century," she said, fighting her smile.

"So"—Avery's voice held a note of authority that brought everyone's attention back to the matter at hand—"where does that leave us?"

"Back at square one?" Simon offered, Tucker and Drake both glaring at him. "Hey, I'm just calling it as I see it."

"Maybe we're trying to come at this the wrong way," Hannah said, steepling her fingers and resting her chin on them. "Maybe we need to focus on the Omega Project and who is left to want to prevent the formula from surfacing and shining new light on a project that wasn't supposed to have existed in the first place."

"I'm assuming you already have some suggestions?" Avery asked.

Hannah smiled. "I do. After Alexis disappeared, we realized that her friend Milo had to have had help obtaining the information he had concerning Tucker's identity."

"And the only way that could have happened," Harrison said, picking up Hannah's train of thought, the two of them, as usual, working in tandem, "was if someone with incredibly high security clearance helped him get in. Or maybe even handed over the information."

"Anyway, to come to the point," Hannah said with an apologetic smile, "we did a search for people working at DOD at the time Omega was supposedly in existence.

And then narrowed the list to people who c̶
the kind of security clearance that would ano̶
access to Tucker's division files."

"Initially we had eighteen names," Harrison said. "But two of them were dead. Natural causes. And both of them well before any of this broke."

"And a third retired six months ago. Security clearance would have been revoked." Hannah hit a button on her computer and a list of names appeared on the screen behind the table. "So we ended up with fifteen possible candidates."

"Holy shit," Drake said, dropping his chair back into its upright position. "Those are some heavy hitters. There's at least two five-star generals there."

"Not to mention a couple of directors," Tyler observed, "including Homeland Security."

"And there could be others. Connections my search wouldn't have turned up. Someone on the inside helping someone else, that kind of thing," Hannah said, the orange streaks in her spiky hair catching the light.

"To that end," Harrison continued, "we're trying to cross-check DOD employees from the time of Omega with the employee rosters from the contractors Dryker worked for after leaving Defense. But since the companies are private, it's taking a little time to track down their records."

"But in the meantime," Hannah said, moving the conversation back to the list, "the biggest issue here is that if we go public with this list, the culprit will find a way to cover his tracks before we can identify him. So we need to narrow the list down without raising a lot of suspicion."

"And in an effort to fast-forward that," Harrison broke in, "we've found someone who might be able to help. Her name is Molly James. She spent her entire career at DOD mainly with the administrative arm—assigned to various projects."

"Sounds good," Avery said. "If she comes through, we'll be able to avoid pissing off half the big brass in Washington with accusations of misconduct. But how do you know we can connect her to Omega?"

"We can't know for sure, but Harrison managed to access her HR record, and we've got project assignments throughout her career, including dates, except for a two-year gap about the time Omega was supposedly operational."

"So she was paid, but her job assignment kept out of the records," Tyler repeated. "Sounds to me like they were trying to hide something."

"Agreed." Hannah nodded. "Which is why she's our best bet. She's been retired for years. And remarried. Twice."

"Which means new names," Nash noted. "And I'm guessing relocation?"

"Got it in one," Harrison said. "She's almost as under the radar as Alexis."

"And in a lovely bit of serendipity," Hannah continued, "she's currently living in Brooklyn."

CHAPTER **22**

Sacramento, California

I appreciate you taking the time out of your busy day to meet with me," Alain DuBois said, looking out onto the park in front of the capitol building. A group of children played a makeshift soccer game. It was still cool out, although spring flowers were already beginning to fade.

"I don't see why we couldn't have had this conversation in my office," Bastion Carmichael said, eyes narrowed as a couple of laughing tourists made their way past the bench where they were sitting.

"It's a lovely day," he replied. "Seemed a shame to waste it spending time indoors." The location, though seemingly random, had been chosen carefully. Hiding in plain sight, as it were, making it less likely that the meeting would be recorded or even noticed.

"Well, I can't argue with that," Carmichael said, "and I'll admit I'm curious as to why you wanted to meet with me. According to my staff, you're involved in antiquities. In Montreal. An old family business?"

"Yes, we started out in import-export, in Normandy in the late seventeenth century. Then, after a rather trying time during the Second World War, my great-grandfather immigrated to Canada and brought the business with him."

"So you come from a family of smugglers?" Carmichael asked, his expression dismissive.

"No more so than your Kennedys." He gave his best Gallic shrug, swallowing his irritation. After all, holier-than-thou politicians were a dime a dozen. "Anyway, my business with you doesn't involve my family or our company. I'm here on another matter entirely."

"One related to me in some way, I assume?" Carmichael sat back, stretching one arm along the back of the bench. "So why don't you come to the point."

"Yes, of course," Alain said. "My business, as you can well imagine, takes me all over the world, and in those travels I've been fortunate enough to make alliances with some very powerful people. And stemming from that, I've become involved in several coalitions, for lack of a better word. It is on behalf of one of these organizations that I've requested this meeting."

"So are you going to tell me who you represent?"

"I'm afraid I can't be any more specific, but I can tell you that we're quite interested in the possibility of you joining our ranks."

"In an organization you can't tell me about," Carmichael said, his tone turning indignant. "I'm a very busy man, Mr. DuBois. And a powerful one to boot. I haven't got time to waste on you and your riddles."

"If I were you," Alain said, enjoying the game of cat and mouse, "I'd find the time. As I said, the group I

belong to is comprised of some the world's most powerful and wealthy men. All of us with common interests.
And, at the moment, our goals coincide with yours, which
means that we're in a position to offer you our help."

"For what?" Carmichael's irritation was clearly evident, but Alain also recognized a spark of curiosity.

"Your attempt to keep your past buried. Specifically
your role in the Omega Project."

"Who the hell are you?" Carmichael asked, his face
tightening with concern.

"I told you—"

"Yes, I heard—antiques and smuggling and all that.
That's not what I'm asking and you know it."

"I know you've been spending considerable time and
taxpayer money to capture and/or eliminate a woman
you believe has access to the formula for aerosolizing
biotoxins."

Carmichael's fists clenched, his face going white as he
considered Alain's pronouncement. "And…"

"As I said, there are a lot of wealthy people involved in
our consortium. People with access to all kinds of interesting information and the power to use it. "

Carmichael frowned, then nodded, comprehension
dawning. "You're the ones who have been trying to buy
the formula."

"And the deal would have been concluded by now if it
hadn't been for your interference. Thanks to your mud-
dling, we've not only lost access to the formula, but we've
got intelligence operatives breathing down our neck."

"A-Tac," Carmichael said, a slow smile of satisfaction
spreading across his face. "Nice to know I'm not the only
one. But I still don't see how I can help you."

"You can call off your rather inept efforts to keep things under control. Leave Alexis Markham to us."

"And why would I do that?"

"Because we're in a position to make certain that Omega is buried once and for all—after we've acquired the formula, of course."

"Just for the sake of argument," Carmichael said, a frown creasing his forehead, "how would you do that?"

Alain reached into his pocket and produced a photograph. "Recognize this man?"

Carmichael gave the picture a cursory glance and then froze, his gaze returning for a longer look. "You're sure?"

"Absolutely," Alain said. "And I'm happy to report that we've currently got the upper hand where he's concerned. But if you continue to intervene in our business by chasing after Ms. Markham, then I can't promise we'll be able to maintain that control."

"And all you want is for me to back off."

"It's as simple as that," Alain said, offering a coarse smile. "You back off, and we'll make certain your interests are protected."

"How do I know you'll follow through?" he asked, his gaze turning skeptical.

"You don't. You'll just have to take my word. But I promise you, the alternative is far more dangerous. Because if you don't stop, we'll have no recourse but to go public with proof of your activities of late. Including the death of your dear friend Peter Dryker."

Again Carmichael flinched, but managed to hold his gaze steady. "But you'd have to have more than just allegations. You'd have to have proof."

"And you believe you've been very careful. I told you we

have access to information at all levels. And that includes your private phone calls." He paused a moment and held out a small digital recorder, hitting Play, Carmichael's recorded voice discussing the particulars of Dryker's murder. "This is just a sample, Mr. Carmichael. We have much more. All of it damning. So can I count on your cooperation?"

The man's mouth moved as he fought against his anger. "I don't see that I have any other option. But I do have a question. What happens if I do my part but you still don't get the formula?"

"To you? Nothing. To him"—he nodded at the photo—"I'm afraid he'll meet a very untimely end. Along with Ms. Markham. But you needn't worry about any of that. We'll handle it all. You just pretend as if we never had this conversation. Are we agreed?" He held out his hand but Carmichael ignored it.

"I'll play it your way, but you'd better be damn sure my ass is covered. You're not the only one with powerful friends, Mr. DuBois."

Carroll Gardens in Brooklyn was a throwback to a more gentle time. Tree-lined streets with rows of brownstones, fronted by unusually large gardens, gave the neighborhood an old-fashioned feeling that was missing from most urban areas.

Molly Dormond lived on the parlor floor of a brownstone on First Place. The garden was full of rhododendrons, peonies, hydrangeas, roses, and a variety of annuals. Snapdragons lined the front walk. An old, iron post box stood at the foot of the front steps, its cheerful red color reminding Alexis of a poster of London she'd seen once.

Tucker walked beside her, as usual searching the area

for signs of danger, the beauty of the garden completely lost on him. The team hadn't been particularly keen on her accompanying Tucker. But she'd held firm, reminding them that she had more invested in this conversation than any one of them, and that she was better equipped to recognize subtle significance in anything Mrs. Dormond might have to say. She wasn't completely certain it was true, but it had seemed to do the trick. Avery had capitulated with the caveat that Drake accompany them to keep watch.

At the moment he was standing near the corner, his hand resting casually on the jacket that concealed his gun, his attention on passersby both pedestrian and vehicular. As she and Tucker walked up the steps, the door opened. Evidently Drake wasn't the only one keeping watch.

"Can I help you?" It was the voice of a New Yorker, cautious and polite all at the same time.

"We're sorry to intrude," Tucker said, obviously channeling his best *NYPD Blue*, "but we're with the government, and if you don't mind, we have a few questions."

"The government?" she asked, arching two perfectly plucked eyebrows. "Would you mind clarifying that?"

"Sorry," Tucker said, realizing his mistake. "Department of Defense." He flashed the ID Harrison had so painstakingly replicated.

"Ah," she said, not even pausing to think about it. "I wondered how long it would take. I'll admit I was off by about twenty years." She opened the storm door and gestured them inside. "It's been a long time to sit on a secret. I think there's a part of me that's actually relieved. Can I get you tea?" She waved a perfectly manicured hand to a velvet-covered sofa.

"No," Tucker started, but Alexis interrupted.

"Yes, please. It would be so nice. It's been a long day."

Mrs. Dormond smiled and nodded toward the sofa. "I won't be a minute."

"What the hell are you doing?" Tucker whispered as they sat down. "She'll probably make a run for it."

"She's seventy-five, Tucker. What's she going to do? Vault out the kitchen window?" As if in response a window scraped open, and Tucker sprang from the sofa, gun at the ready.

"Put that away," Alexis hissed, certain that Mrs. Dormond wasn't going anywhere.

"But she..." he trailed off as the woman in question came into the parlor with a tea tray.

"I'm sorry, it's just so abnormally hot for this time of year. I can't seem to get enough windows open." She smiled and set the tray on the table. "So," Mrs. Dormond said, offering Tucker a cup of tea, "you're here to talk about Omega."

Any levity Alexis had been feeling fled in a heartbeat. This was her father's life, this woman the only link she had to the real truth and the people who'd killed her father.

"We are," Tucker agreed, displaying his most charming smile. Mrs. Dormond hadn't a chance. "I'm afraid the formula has resurfaced, and we're trying to track it down before it can be sold to the highest bidder."

"Surely not Randolph after all this time," Mrs. Dormond said, her snowy white brows drawing together in consternation. "He disappeared, you know."

"Randolph Baker was my father, Mrs. Dormond," Alexis said, unable to stop herself. Tucker shot her an

angry look. They'd decided not to share that particular
piece of information, but Mrs. Dormond had clearly
known her father, and so the words had come.

"Call me Molly," Mrs. Dormond said, her eyes kind. "I
knew you weren't DOD. And I thought I saw the resem-
blance. You must have been born after he disappeared. I
knew your mother and your brother."

Tears pricked the back of Alexis's eyes. It had been a
long time since anyone had remembered her family.

"Your father was very proud of his family. He had pictures all over his office." She handed Alexis a cup of tea.

"He's dead," Alexis said, again unable to stop the words.
"My mother and brother as well. Someone in the government killed them."

Molly nodded, the reaction not at all what Alexis
expected. "It wasn't a good time to be involved with
special projects. They killed Duncan too, you know." She
sighed, her mind fading into the past. "I loved him." For
a moment, Alexis thought they'd lost her, but then she
shook her head, reaching for her own cup of tea. "As I
said, it was a difficult time. And I always thought sooner
or later someone would come. Someone would question
what happened."

"But they never did," Tucker replied.

"No." She shook her head, "they didn't. And life
moved on."

"You had a relationship with Duncan Wallace?"
Alexis asked. "I never knew him, but my father always
talked about him. And he made him sound so alive. So
involved."

"He always lived and breathed whatever project he
was working on," Molly responded, brightening. "And

I was assigned to most of them. That's how we met. But Omega was different. Most of the projects I worked with at DOD were top secret, so there were always layers of security, but this time it was totally off the books. Which didn't matter to Randolph and Duncan. For them it was all just an exercise. A theoretical manipulation of nature, chemistry and biology working in tandem."

"So they believed the research was strictly theoretical?" Tucker asked.

"It was," Molly said. "Completely. But then we found out there was a second phase planned. A stage intended to move their work from hypothetical to practical. They wanted Randolph and Duncan to use the formula to make a weapon. I don't pretend to understand any of it." She waved a hand in dismissal. "I'm not a scientist, but even I knew the danger a weapon like that posed."

"But my father and Duncan—they refused to go forward, right? They threatened to take the whole thing public."

"Duncan was horrified. We spent days trying to decide what to do. He wanted to quit. But they wouldn't let him. He had a contract, and they threatened legal action. So he responded by threatening to go public. I begged him not to do it. I was so afraid there'd be repercussions, and I was right. He was dead three days later."

"And no one questioned what happened?" Tucker set his cup back on the tray.

"As far as the DOD was concerned, nothing had happened. At least nothing questionable. The explosion was deemed an accident. And shortly after that, the entire project was dismantled. And we were told to pretend it never existed."

"But what about my father? Didn't anyone question his disappearance?"

"No." Molly shook her head. "The general word was that he'd just moved on. And if anyone dug too deeply, they were told he'd disappeared with the formula when he'd heard the project was being canceled."

"So they painted him as the bad guy," Alexis said, not even trying to keep the bitterness at bay. Her father had been used as a scapegoat.

"It was a really frightening time. I'd always known there was a dark side to our weapons program, but I'd never dreamed it would affect me personally."

"And yet you stayed with DOD? Why?"

"That's a question I've been asking myself for almost thirty years." She sighed. "And I still don't have a good answer. At first it was because I was afraid. And then I guess because it was easy. And then I discovered what they'd done to your family. Another explosion. Another 'accident.'"

"I don't understand how you made the connection," Alexis said. "We had a new name. And the explosion wasn't exactly national news."

"I still had security clearance, and I stumbled across a memo with the speculation that the man killed in the explosion had been Randolph. I've often wondered if someone arranged for me to find it, a reminder of what happened to people who couldn't keep their mouths shut. Anyway, accident or no, it worked. But this time I did leave. I just couldn't take it anymore. And I never stopped looking over my shoulder."

"Even after you married and moved on?" Tucker asked.

"Especially then. I was certain they'd come after me,

or that someone else would come along with questions. But they never did. Until now." She sat back, her keen gaze encompassing them both. "You said that the formula has resurfaced?"

"Word of it has." Tucker nodded his head. "There seems to be some question about the actual formula."

"That's not surprising. I mean, the most likely people to have had it are both dead. So who do you believe has it?" Molly asked.

"We don't know," Tucker told her. "But someone was definitely trying to sell it. And now someone, possibly the same person, is trying to find it. And for obvious reasons, the search seems to be centering around Alexis."

"They believe you have the formula," she said, her gaze speculative. "And do you?"

"No," Alexis replied. "I didn't even know it still existed. But someone is definitely after me, and people are dying left and right. And if it hadn't been for Tucker, I'm fairly certain I'd have been one of them."

"But isn't it counterproductive to kill you if they think you have the formula?" Molly asked, her gaze turning shrewd. "And furthermore, why would someone offer the formula for sale if they don't have it?"

"Welcome to our world." Tucker shrugged with a wry grin. "It seems like every time we think we have an answer to a question, ten more arise to take its place."

"You think there's more than one party involved."

"Yes," Tucker agreed. "And there's some evidence to suggest that possibly the two groups aren't after the same thing."

"You think someone is after the formula, and someone else is trying to keep it buried." Molly reached for the teapot to refill her cup.

"It would explain a lot. But we have no idea who either of these parties might be."

"And you're hoping I might be able to help."

"If someone is trying to bury this recent activity surrounding the formula, it'd likely be someone who was involved with Omega and would have something to lose if that involvement was revealed now. Connection to a project like that in this political climate would be disastrous."

"Indeed," Molly agreed. "But it would be almost impossible to identify everyone who had some kind of connection to the project. Even something buried as deeply as Omega has to be approved, funded, and staffed. Which means there were people in all branches of the government who would have had to sign off on it."

"Well, we know it has to be someone with high-ranking connections within the government," Tucker said. "Or someone still on the inside with a high-level security clearance."

"And we have a list of possibilities," Alexis continued. "We just have no way of knowing if any of these people might have had a connection to Omega."

"But I might." Molly reached for the glasses that were hanging around her neck. "Let me see the list."

Tucker dug it out of his pocket and passed it to her.

She studied it for a moment, then shook her head. "There are a couple of names here that might have had an indirect connection, but I wouldn't have thought it would put their careers in jeopardy."

"So we still have nothing," Alexis said, frustration cresting.

"You didn't let me finish, dear," Molly said, lifting her gaze to meet Alexis's. "There's no one on this list. But there is someone who'd have a great deal to lose if his involvement went public. He was the administrative director of the project. And definitely someone who'd want to protect his reputation."

"Who are we talking about?" Tucker asked.

"Bastion Carmichael," Molly said.

"The governor of California?" Tucker asked, his frown indicating his disbelief. The man was a left-leaning liberal. Anti-war. And certainly against anything that might have to do with weapons development.

"People change," Molly said. "At least if it serves their purposes. Even back then Carmichael was all about the power. And he was willing to do what it took to make certain he got it."

"Were you suspicious of him at the time?" Tucker asked.

"Not specifically, no."

"And if the formula were to be sold," Tucker speculated, "and he were connected to the original fiasco that allowed it to be out there in the first place, he'd stand to lose quite a bit."

"The government loves to create scapegoats," Molly agreed with a sigh, suddenly looking every bit her seventy-five years. "Maybe I was wrong. Maybe I should have come forward all those years ago. But I was so afraid. People I loved had been murdered. And so I dug a deep hole and hid in it."

"There's no shame in protecting yourself," Alexis said, meaning every word of it.

"Yes, but if I'd had more courage maybe your family would still be alive."

CHAPTER 23

Sacramento, California

He wasn't there," Avery said, dropping down into the booth of the coffee shop, his frustration barely concealed. They'd left for Sacramento almost immediately after the meeting with Molly Dormond, Avery using his connections to arrange an appointment through Carmichael's secretary.

Tucker frowned. "Do you think he knew why we were coming?" They'd decided to limit the initial contact to Avery, partially in an effort not to spook the man, but also to ascertain the lay of the land.

"I don't see how," Avery said. "I had Hannah arrange a cover concerning a problematic operation and the need for the state's cooperation. Everything should have checked out if he tried to verify."

"What did his assistant say?" Alexis asked, fidgeting with her straw, clearly disappointed with this latest development. Since arriving at Sunderland she'd been pulling away, the presence of Tucker's colleagues straining the intimacy they'd developed on the road. Or maybe it was because he'd turned out to be employed by the very people she distrusted the most. Despite the fact that they'd spent a second amazing night together, he knew she still had doubts about him. But he'd hoped, somewhat irrationally, that their lovemaking would have helped her get past it.

"She said he called in sick," Avery said, pulling Tucker from his thoughts. "Which could be the truth or a cover. Whichever it was, I don't think the assistant was in on it. She was suitably apologetic. But that doesn't change the fact that he wasn't there. And if I had to call it, I'd say he knew exactly why I was coming."

"Which means he knows the jig is up." Tucker sat back, turning over the possibilities in his mind. "Which in turn could mean that he's gone to ground. That's what I'd do in his position. I mean, he did know I was involved with Alexis." The words came out sounding more intimate than he'd meant them to. He stole a sideways glance at her. She was sitting next to him, but she hadn't seemed to notice his turn of phrase.

"Unfortunately, I think you're probably right. Between Molly identifying his involvement with Omega and Hannah connecting him to Dryker through the Nevada contractor they both worked for, I don't think there's any question about his guilt. It just surprises me. I've worked with the man a couple of times over the years, and although he was always a little too territorial for my liking, I'd never have figured him for a traitor."

"It's possible that, from his point of view, he believes he's being patriotic. After all, initially Omega was a fully funded government operation. Any breech of protocol, like the threat from Alexis's father, would have risked damaging the government's reputation."

Alexis sputtered as she took a sip of coffee. "What reputation? For years, the government has done exactly as it pleased, keeping its nasty little secrets from the very people it's supposed to be serving and protecting. I hardly think that's patriotic."

"I'm afraid we'll have to agree to disagree," Avery said, his dark gaze solemn. "While there's no question that there are people who use their positions in the government as a springboard for political gain, I genuinely believe they're in the minority. There are a lot of dedicated public servants who are genuinely committed to their country and the people they represent."

"Well, clearly Bastion Carmichael isn't one of them," Alexis said, crossing her arms over her chest, her expression mutinous. "And that goes for the rest of the people who were behind the Omega Project. If nothing else, the whole thing was hypocritical. I mean, don't we have treaties that are supposed to keep research like that from happening? How is what they were doing any different from Iran developing a nuclear bomb?"

"It isn't." Tucker shook his head. "And that's why it was shut down. But there are always going to be things the government has to do that the people as a whole would prefer not to know about. Things that keep us safe and guarantee our freedom. The methodology may sometimes seem questionable, but sometimes there simply isn't another way."

"Like Avery said"—she glared, her shoulders rigid—"this is an area where we're just going to have to disagree. My entire family was wiped out because some asshole somewhere decided it would be a good idea if we could eradicate our enemies with aerosolized biotoxins."

"Yes, but it was your father's research that made it possible in the first place." He wasn't sure exactly why he felt the need to press the issue.

"*Theoretical* research," she said, her eyes narrowed in anger.

"Well, it won't be theoretical if someone manages to sell the formula," Avery interjected, his tone both calm and resolute, serving to deflate the anger arcing between them.

Alexis sighed with a tight nod. "So what do we do now, Avery?"

"We try to intercept Carmichael before he can completely fall off the grid."

The more they attempted to find Carmichael, the more apparent it became that he was on the run. They'd tried the governor's mansion, the family retreat, and even a second office Carmichael kept for personal business. So far nothing.

And almost everyone they'd come in contact with had seemed determined to shield the man. Alexis understood loyalty to family, but in this case it wasn't working in her favor. Fortunately, a secretary—a clearly disgruntled one—had slipped out of the office to let them know that Carmichael had another house. One his wife wasn't aware of.

The house, a Victorian near the governor's mansion, was on H Street. The gracious white home sported a wraparound porch with curved staircases to either side and heavy garlands of ivy twining up supporting pillars.

Potted geraniums flanked the double doors, an old miller's bench sitting to one side, and Alexis wondered idly if it was real or only a reproduction.

While she and Avery approached the house from the front, Tucker had gone around back to make sure Carmichael, if he was indeed in residence, couldn't slip out that way. At the top of the stairs the two of them paused, and Alexis marveled at how easily she'd accepted Avery's presence.

The man, though formidable in size, had a quiet resolve that immediately set one at ease. She reminded herself that the last man she'd instinctively trusted had turned out to be a liar, but it didn't change the fact that she was absolutely certain Avery Solomon was one of the good guys.

The thought wasn't all that surprising, after all. Tucker had chosen to work with the man, but she was still having trouble getting her head around the idea that the very people she'd spent most of her life avoiding were now the ones trying to help her.

There was a lesson in there somewhere, but she wasn't ready to explore it. Better to focus on finding Carmichael and convincing him to admit to his role in her father's death. It had taken everything she had to convince Avery to bring her. This was most likely the man behind the attempts on her life, but she was her father's daughter, and she wanted the chance to face Carmichael. Fortunately, Avery had acquiesced.

She reached for the bell but Avery shook his head, lifting a finger to his lips. He turned the doorknob, both of them surprised when the door silently swung open.

Leading with his gun, Avery stepped inside and then

motioned for her to follow. She moved through the door into a foyer dominated by an ornately carved staircase. On the right side, the hallway opened out into a parlor, where the sun shone through the bay window, projecting a swath of light across the parquet floor. The house was quiet, the only sound the hushed ticking of the grandfather clock standing sentry at the foot of the stairs.

"Now what?" she mouthed almost at the same time as a noise emanated from upstairs.

"We go up," Avery whispered. "Stay behind me. Okay?"

She nodded, already following him as they made their way up the stairs. The landing at the top led to a hallway with three rooms opening off it. The closest was a bathroom. Skirting it, Avery inched forward, swung into the open doorway next to it, and, after assuring it was empty, motioned her forward, pointing ahead to the door at the end of the hall.

He paused for a moment, speaking quietly into his com unit, no doubt notifying Tucker as to their whereabouts. Ahead of her a floorboard squeaked, and Avery was instantly back on alert. He held up a hand, signaling for her to wait, and then inched slowly forward, swinging into the room, gun at the ready. "Hold it right there," Avery barked.

Alexis counted to three before springing into motion and then skidded to a stop in the open doorway, where Avery was holding an older man in khakis and a white button-down at gunpoint. The man was straddling the windowsill, half in and half out.

"It won't do you any good to jump, Bastion," Avery said, motioning with the gun for him to step back inside. "You're liable to break a leg, and if you don't, my man outside will still stop you. So better to just call it a day and come inside. We did have an appointment, after all."

Carmichael narrowed his eyes, clearly considering his options, and then, with a brief shrug, swung his leg back into the room. "I'd rather hoped to avoid this conversation."

"I would imagine so," Avery said, not lowering his weapon. "But some things are inevitable, and this time I think you have some explaining to do."

"There's nothing to explain, because no matter what you think you know, you haven't a shred of hard evidence."

"Actually, I may not have everything, but I have enough," Avery said as Tucker sprinted down the hall to stand beside Alexis. "I know that you have a long association with Peter Dryker. And I can confirm that you used an old contact within DOD to access CIA personnel files, allegedly on gubernatorial business. Interestingly, though, when I asked her, your secretary verified that the request was personal."

"Does it matter?" Carmichael asked, eyeing the three of them. "My position allows me to review whatever files I see fit."

"Perhaps, but it doesn't allow you to pass that information on to civilians. Or to use them in an attempt to draw an innocent out into the open."

"I don't see any innocent people here," Carmichael said, his speculative gaze falling on Alexis. "Do you know who she is?"

"I do," Avery affirmed. "She's Randolph Baker's daughter. But unless you have substantially different information than we do, you've been chasing the wrong rabbit."

"How do you know you're not the ones being played?"

Carmichael asked, his mouth twisting into a tight little smile. "I have it on good authority that she's the one who has been trying to sell the formula."

"I'm assuming you're speaking of George Atterley?"

Fear flickered through Carmichael's eyes, and Alexis counted one for the home team. In all probability, she was looking at the man who had murdered her family. Or at least the one who'd arranged for it. And now he was attempting to deflect their suspicions by accusing her.

"But I—" Carmichael started.

"Used an alias?" Avery finished for him. "I'm afraid my people are really good at sorting through the chaff. We know you visited George Atterley in prison—twice. And I'm close to being able to prove that you're responsible for his early release."

"Well, don't bother. I'll confirm it for you. I did talk to George. And, yes, I arranged for his release."

"George is dead," Alexis spit out, fury rising, the emotion making her reckless. "You killed him."

"I most certainly did not," Carmichael said, the shock in his voice sounding strangely believable. "Why would I do that? The man was helping me."

"When was the last time you saw him?" Avery asked, motioning for Carmichael to sit down.

The room clearly served as a library. Bookcases lined all four walls, most of them packed to overflowing. The smell of musty paper filled the room, reminding Alexis of the public libraries she'd visited as a child with her mother. The only clear space on the walls was the window Carmichael had been trying to escape through. A leather-topped table sat in the center of the room, four armchairs arranged carefully around it. A shelf under the table was stacked with charts and maps and oversized books.

After Carmichael was seated, his back to the window, Avery and Alexis sat across from him, Avery still holding his gun. Tucker stayed on his feet, moving so that he stood between Carmichael and the door. "So I'll repeat," Avery said, "when did you last go to see Atterley?"

"About a month ago," Carmichael replied, his gaze still locked on Alexis. He looked as if he'd like to pounce, and despite the fact that she had numbers, not to mention firepower, on her side, she shivered. "I'd heard that the Omega formula had surfaced. And that George's name was attached to it. I did a little research and established the connection between Atterley and Baker. With Randolph out of the picture, George could, in fact, have had access to it."

"My father was dead because you killed him," Alexis whispered, still feeling like a butterfly stuck under a pin.

"Again, your accusations are misplaced," Carmichael said, his eyes narrowing. "Your father was killed in an explosion. An accident, I'm told. I assure you I had nothing to do with it."

"And I suppose you'll deny almost killing me?" she said, her voice still low and trembling.

"That, I'm afraid, was a mistake. My men can be a bit overzealous. And when your knight-errant showed up, things went from bad to worse. I only wanted to talk with you."

"And trash my house."

"Again," he said, "my people may have been a little overly enthusiastic. But you killing Fogerty only made it worse."

"So you're admitting your involvement in trying to capture Alexis?" Avery asked.

"I'm admitting nothing officially. But even if I did, I doubt seriously, under the circumstances, that I'd be criticized for trying to stop the sale of a very dangerous formula that was stolen by Ms. Markham's father in the first place."

"If my father had the formula," Alexis said, anger making her overenunciate each word, "it would be because it belonged to him. He and Wallace created it in the first place."

"Except that he had a contract with the government, which makes any discoveries he made our property. I was only acting in the best interests of the Department of Defense and, by association, the American public it is sworn to protect."

"Except that you don't work for DOD anymore," Avery said.

"I'm still a public servant."

"There's no point in trying to hide behind the flag, Bastion," Avery said, "not when you've been running an operation off the books with a number of questionable deaths in its wake. Depending on when you start the clock, the body count ranges from five to nine."

"Two of which can be attributed to you." Carmichael pointed to Tucker. "And I already told you I'm not responsible for the explosion that killed Atterley. I told you, George was helping me. He's the one who told me Ms. Markham had the formula."

"I don't believe any of what you're saying." Alexis leaned forward, her gaze locking with Carmichael's. "I don't have it. And there's nothing I've said or done that would make George believe I did."

"I don't have an explanation," Carmichael said. "I only know that I'm certain George believed what he was telling me. He thought you'd betrayed him."

"How? It wasn't even his formula. And I was just a kid when my father died." Alexis shook her head, fighting confusion. None of this made any sense. But she could see Carmichael believed everything he was saying. Maybe that was what George had been trying to tell her. Maybe he'd used Carmichael to gain his freedom and wanted to warn her of the resulting danger.

"Look, even if we stipulate that you didn't kill Alexis's family or George Atterley," Avery said, lifting a hand to silence Alexis when she started to protest, "there's still the matter of Milo Alozono and Peter Dryker. As I said, we've got proof that Dryker was on your payroll, and we have documented evidence that he was involved in the break-in at Alexis's house, as well as an attempt to break into her bank box."

"None of that has anything to do with his regretful demise," Carmichael said. "The connection is completely circumstantial. And as far as I'm concerned, a tragedy. Peter, as you already know, was a longtime friend. And his death hit me hard."

"And Milo?" Alexis asked, her nails digging into the palms of her hands as she fought to maintain control. The bastard was far too good at explaining away his involvement. "What about him?"

"I afraid I've no idea who you're talking about," Carmichael said.

"He's the man you used to plant a tracking device in

my phone. And the one you gave the stolen information about Tucker. He was my friend, and you used him to get to me."

"Doesn't sound like he was much of a friend. But I'm afraid I still don't know who he is. Dryker handled all of that. As you already know, I did pull strings to access the information. But it was at Dryker's request. It was his idea to smoke you out."

"So you're seriously sitting here claiming that none of this is your fault?" Tucker sounded as indignant as she felt.

"No. I'm telling you that anything I did was done in the interest of national security. I'll admit Peter's methods could be a bit on the rough side of things. But he usually got the job done with a minimum of fuss. You, however"—he turned his full attention on Alexis—"turned out to be more than he'd bargained for. If anyone is responsible for his death, Ms. Markham, it's you."

Alexis popped up out of her seat, rage ripping through her with surprising force. "Me?" The word reverberated through the room, and she felt Tucker's hand on her shoulder, his touch soothing her in a way nothing else could.

She sank back into her chair, gripping the arms but back in control again.

"I'm sorry," Carmichael said. "I know this has been difficult for you. But I truly believed you were trying to sell the formula."

"And now?" Avery asked, his gaze appraising.

"Now"—Carmichael paused for a moment, as if considering his words, then continued. "Now I think there are other forces at work. Forces far more dangerous than any of us would have expected. We've danced all around the idea of who might be offering the formula for sale, but we haven't talked at all about who might be trying to buy it."

"And you think you know," Avery said, his words a statement rather than a question.

"I do. I was approached recently by a businessman out of Canada. His name is Alain DuBois."

Tucker shook his head. "Never heard of him."

"Nor had I," Carmichael said. "He's French Canadian. Head of a company that buys and resells antiquities. But he wasn't coming to me as the president of DuBois, Ltd. He was approaching me as a member of an international group interested in buying the formula. His request was that I back down from my investigation and leave the handling of Ms. Markham to them. They, like you, seemed to believe my interest in the formula was all about making certain it was covered up. And it was their assertion that if I backed off, they could satisfy both their desires and mine."

"And you agreed."

"Of course—it was the only prudent thing to do. This isn't the type of organization one plays games with." Carmichael spread his hands wide, waiting for Avery's response. It came immediately.

"The Consortium," he said, his voice laced with certainty. "Alain DuBois was speaking on their behalf."

"I don't understand," Alexis said, feeling as if the power in the room had shifted back in favor of Carmichael. "What is the Consortium?"

"We don't know anything definitely." Tucker shrugged. "In fact, if this Alain DuBois is truly on the inside, it might be the closest we've gotten to finding a way in. They've managed to infiltrate our government—"

"—including A-Tac," Carmichael inserted, his words goading.

"And they appear to be interested· in manipulating high-end arms deals—both legitimate and black market—on an international level," Avery continued. "We ran into them full force in Colombia. And then came home to discover that one of our own had been turned. So for us, identifying and capturing these people is personal. Like Bastion, we believed you were the one trying to sell the formula. First, because of your connection to George, and then later, because we realized who your father was."

Alexis nodded, feeling again that she was on the outside, that none of these people really had her best interests at heart. Tucker's hand still lay on her shoulder and, without stopping to think, she shook it off, wanting nothing more than to escape all of them.

"Speaking of which," Carmichael said, leaning forward, his gaze encompassing the three of them, "since we're sharing, there's one more thing you need to know." He opened his mouth and then closed it again, his eyes widening in surprise, the sharp crack of a gunshot echoed through the room.

"Get down," Tucker cried.

For a moment everything seemed to move in slow motion: Tucker throwing his body against hers as he dragged her to the floor. The open windowpane shattering as a second bullet found Carmichael. The older man gasping once and then falling forward onto the table as Avery dropped back behind a chair, firing at the window.

Then there was silence, the only noise the sound of her heart as it pounded a staccato warning against her chest.

"We clear?" Tucker called, waiting for Avery's affirmative response before rolling off her. "Are you all right?" He framed her face with his hands, searching for signs of injury, his eyes filled with worry.

"I'm okay," she whispered, knowing that, in fact, she was not. But she wasn't bleeding, and, for the moment, that was all he needed to know.

"Avery?"

"I'm fine too." The big man looked back from the shattered window. "Whoever was out there is gone. I don't think they were interested in us. Just Carmichael."

"Is he dead?" Alexis asked, wondering how many times in one life a person could ask that question. She sucked in a ragged breath, fighting to keep her panic at bay.

"Yes," Avery confirmed after checking for a pulse.

Tucker's arm closed around her shoulders, and even though a part of her wanted to shake free, she couldn't find the strength, every ounce of concentration going into keeping her fear from turning into a scream.

Carmichael was dead. And he'd wanted to tell her something. Just like George.

CHAPTER **24**

"Every time we move a step forward," Tucker said, reaching for his bottle of beer, "something happens to send us right back again."

They'd gathered at Drake's house, in part because they'd wanted to spare Alexis more of the war room and partly because they all needed a modicum of downtime even as they proceeded to move forward.

Madeline had whipped together a quick dinner of homemade macaroni and cheese and salad, the former being a family recipe that made Tucker damn glad he was now a member of said family. She was sitting on the sofa, next to Alexis, who, though quiet, seemed to be coping well enough. Still, he'd seen her face at the scene and known immediately that she was holding on by only a thread.

Avery was there along with Nash's wife, Annie. Like Madeline, Annie was intent on circling the wagons around Alexis, immediately accepting her as part of the unit, hovering like a mother hen, offering her empathy.

Lord knows, between the two of them, Annie and Madeline had been there and back again. If anyone could help Alexis through all of this, it was them.

Harrison sat at the table within easy reach of both his computer and the mac and cheese. He'd already finished two servings, but Tucker had a suspicion that given the opportunity, he'd go for a third. The man could put away food like nobody's business.

Tyler and Hannah were in the lab going over everything they had on the three bombings and the unexploded ordnance from Alexis's house.

Simon and Nash were in California finishing up work on the scene and searching Carmichael's effects for additional insight into his revelations about the Consortium. They were all reporting their findings via computer, but so far there hadn't been anything earth-shattering.

"The ballistics report didn't yield anything we didn't already know," Annie was saying. "Probably a sniper rifle. Definitely modified for distance shooting. But the striations on the bullet don't match with anything we've got in the system." Annie had spent her time with the CIA as a sharpshooter, which made her the resident expert in ballistics even though she was partially retired.

"They haven't been able to pull anything from the scene, either," Harrison said, picking up where Annie left off. "Most likely site for the shooter is either the rooftop of the town house behind Carmichael's, or possibly an attic window in the home beside it. The first house, predictably, is empty. But there were no prints and no trace on the roof."

"And the attic?" Avery asked.

"That house is occupied," Harrison said, consulting

his computer screen. "But the owners are out of town and the attic window was open. But there was nothing else to confirm that it was the point of origin. And, frankly, the angle wasn't as direct as the empty house."

"If we are dealing with a shooter hired by the Consortium," Annie mused, "I wouldn't have expected to find anything. They can afford the best. And people that good don't leave a trace."

"A lesson we had to learn the hard way," Avery said, referring to an attempt to frame Annie a while back for the murder of a diplomat.

"Well, these days it's harder to get by without leaving something behind," Annie acknowledged. "But these people are ghosts. Anything in the chatter to indicate one of the freelance operators has been sighted in the States?"

"Nothing that Hannah could find," Harrison said, looking up from his computer. "Which doesn't really mean anything, of course, because they're as good at getting in and out as they are at killing a target without leaving any evidence behind."

"But what I don't understand," Alexis said, running a hand through her hair, "is why they'd want to take out Carmichael but not me. Surely I'm more of a threat when it comes right down to it."

"It's possible they believe you're still the key to finding the formula," Avery said, pushing out of his chair to walk over to an ice bucket for another beer. "But I suspect it was more about what Carmichael knew. If they thought he was about to come clean with us, which he was, then he'd have been deemed a liability and dealt with accordingly."

"Or maybe they already had him targeted, and it was just coincidence that we happened to walk into it," Tucker said. "Either way, you can bet your ass they were already aware of our involvement, and I'm guessing not pleased about it."

"And with Carmichael out of the way," Drake added, "we're the only fly left in their ointment."

"So why not try and take you out when they had the chance?" Madeline asked.

"Maybe they figured taking us out would only have stirred up the hive."

"We tend to go into overdrive when one of our own is threatened," Annie said to Alexis. "But I guess you've already seen that firsthand."

Madeline reached over to cover Alexis's hand with hers. "We've got each other's backs. No matter what."

Alexis frowned but didn't pull away. Tucker recognized that expression. She was feeling isolated and overwhelmed. But she wouldn't give any other sign of her discomfort. It was one of the things he admired the most about her. And one of the reasons he wasn't sure she'd ever really let him in again.

"So what about this Alain DuBois?" Madeline asked. "Have you been able to track him down?"

"Not so far." Harrison shook his head. "He isn't registered in any hotel in Sacramento. And his airline ticket was open ended."

"Meaning he could still be in California," Alexis said, pulling free of Madeline to pick up her water glass.

"Yes," Tucker agreed. "It's a definite possibility. Or he could have made it home via some other form of transportation. We're checking out all the options."

"DuBois's company is based in Montreal, but he has homes in Paris and London and a chateau in the Loue

Valley." Harrison was typing as he talked, his fingers flying over the keyboard. "We've got operatives abroad checking them all out. But so far we haven't been able to confirm him leaving Sacramento."

"Any chance he has a place there too?" Drake asked.

"If he does, it's under an assumed name. Or he's borrowing it from a friend. I'll run a check on known associates. The man's got to be somewhere."

"We'll find him," Avery said. "And with any luck, he'll lead us straight to the Consortium, but we've still got another problem."

"The bomber," Alexis said, leaning forward. "Carmichael said it wasn't him."

"And unfortunately, I think he was telling the truth. Which plays into an idea we touched on the other night at Alexis's house." Tucker wished Carmichael had been the key. Alexis deserved answers. "That there were three players involved that night."

"Carmichael's men, the man in the kitchen—presumably hired by the Consortium—and whoever tried to set off the fifth bomb." Drake frowned as he considered the list.

"Fifth?" Madeline asked.

"Yeah. Duncan Wallace," Harrison said. "Between what Molly told us and Tyler's digging, it looks like it was definitely intentional. There were traces of an accelerant used. So even if the MO isn't exact, it fits the pattern. And it's not that big a jump from arson to bombs."

"But if it wasn't Carmichael, then who the hell wanted my family dead?" Alexis asked, slamming the glass down on the table with more force than intended. "Sorry. I'm just trying to wrap my head around all of this. After we talked to Molly, I was so sure it was Carmichael."

"We all were," Avery agreed. "What about the other fifteen on the list?"

"Molly did say there were a couple of indirect connections," Tucker said, feeling as if they were swimming in mud. "But then she gave us Carmichael."

"Well, at the time it was the best lead," Annie said, getting up to pour herself a second glass of wine. "But now it seems like maybe we should follow up on the other people on the list. Maybe recheck things with this Molly."

"Oh God," Alexis gasped, half rising from her seat, "has anyone checked on her? I mean, if these Consortium people are getting rid of loose ends..."

"Molly isn't a threat to them," Tucker soothed, taking Annie's seat on the sofa but fighting the urge to put his arm around Alexis. "She was connected to the project, sure. But she doesn't have the formula, and she doesn't know anything about the Consortium's involvement."

"But maybe they think we told her. I mean, you said that they've probably been watching us—watching me."

"We'll send someone to check on her," Avery said. "Harrison can arrange it now. And we'll make sure the New York office keeps an eye on her until this is all over."

"Thank you." Alexis lifted her gaze to Avery's. "I don't think I could handle it if I got anyone else killed."

"None of this is your fault, Alexis," Tucker said, wishing there was something more he could do to take away her pain.

"Doesn't matter, does it?" Madeline's voice was soft and comforting as she spoke to Alexis. And empathetic. "It still feels that way. I know. I've been there. But Tucker's right—you didn't cause any of this. And sooner or later that's going to sink in. And even though it won't change anything, it will make it easier."

Alexis shot Madeline a grateful look. Kindred spirits and all that. Tucker was grateful too, and jealous. Madeline had managed to reach Alexis, to find the right words, when he couldn't.

"Okay," Harrison said, "seems to me like we need to find the common thread in all the bombings. We know the MO is the same, but what's the motive? Why would someone want to take out Alexis's father and the rest of her family, and then, thirteen years down the road, take out George Atterley?"

"Not to mention the cabin and Alexis's house," Tucker added.

"So if you include Wallace"—Avery frowned—"we've got someone trying to eliminate people with either a direct connection to Omega or, through Randolph, people who are still linked in some way to the project."

"Yeah, but at least as far as we know," Annie countered, "the bomber never tried to take out Carmichael. Or Molly Dormond, for that matter. And they both obviously had a connection."

"Seems to me like that makes them candidates to be the bomber," Drake offered.

"Well, Carmichael categorically denied his involvement. And in light of everything else he told us, I'm inclined to believe him," Avery said.

"And Molly Dormond?"

"She can't be the bomber. That would mean she killed Wallace," Alexis said. "And you should have seen her talking about him. She was definitely in love. So it doesn't follow that she'd want him dead."

"Then maybe she's the one with the formula?" Madeline suggested.

"No. It doesn't make sense that she would have it." Tucker shook his head. "Wallace was killed before he had a chance to go public. And my guess is that he'd have trusted the formula with his partner, not his girlfriend. If for no other reason than because he loved her." Unbidden, he shot a glance at Alexis. "He wouldn't have wanted to put her in any more danger than necessary."

"And even if you discount that, I checked her out pretty thoroughly," Harrison said. "She hasn't had any contact with people outside of her normal circle of friends and relations in the past year. She's not filthy rich, but she's certainly comfortably well off. Enough so that money wouldn't be a motivating factor. And there's been no unusual activity in any of her bank accounts. I don't think she's got it."

"Then who the hell does?" Drake asked, his exasperation mirroring Tucker's.

"Maybe no one," Avery said. "Maybe the damn thing doesn't exist."

"And what—this whole thing is a game?" Annie frowned. "To what purpose? No, I think it's out there somewhere. The trick now is to find it before the Consortium can."

"So how are you really doing?" Tucker asked as he walked into the bedroom. Madeline had asked what Alexis wanted, a room on her own or one with Tucker. And despite all her insecurities and doubt, she'd automatically opted for sharing. It was almost as if he was a part of her now. To be honest, she wasn't sure how she'd go back to a life without him, should it come to that. But her father had always said she borrowed too many problems.

It was a bad habit. So she pushed her scattered thoughts aside and smiled up at him. "Better now that you're here."

"Are you sure I can't get you some brandy or maybe a glass of wine?" he asked. "It really does help to smooth out the edges."

"I've never been much of a drinker." She shrugged.

"I realize I'm not much of a nurturer. But I'm trying. Maybe a sandwich or a glass of water?"

"Tucker, I meant what I said. I'm good now that you're here."

"I want to believe you," he said, coming to sit beside her on the bed, "but you've been through so much, and at least some of that is my fault. I can't help it—I worry." He tried for a smile but didn't make it, and she reached up to smooth away his frown.

"I know." She slid her hand down to his chest, his heart beating beneath her fingers, allowing herself to get lost in the bright blue of his eyes. "And that means the world to me."

"I know we said we'd wait to talk," he started, and her heart twisted in anticipation, "but I need you to know how important you've become to me. I've been dead inside for so long, just going through the motions. You know? But now, with you, I feel"—he paused, his gaze locking with hers—"I feel alive."

It wasn't a declaration of love, but coming from Tucker, it was pretty damn close. She swallowed, gathering her courage. "I feel the same way. But I don't know how we can..."

He shook his head, framing her face with his hands. "My father always says that you shouldn't borrow problems. And if I've learned anything, it's that you have to live in the present. It's all you've got. So for tonight, at least, let's concentrate on what we have right here, right now. And tomorrow will take care of itself. Okay?"

She smiled, thinking that both of their fathers were very smart men. "Absolutely," she whispered, getting lost again in his eyes.

With a groan, he crushed his lips to hers, their shared passion igniting into full flame again. Whatever it was between them, it couldn't be stopped. And suddenly Alexis wasn't at all sure that she even wanted to. He pushed her back onto the bed, each of them struggling to remove clothing without breaking contact, the effort making them both laugh.

There was an ease present tonight that hadn't been there before. As if somehow they'd crossed a barrier, opening themselves to each other in ways neither would have thought possible.

Alexis pressed against him, reveling in the feel of his hard body next to hers, anxious to prove to them both that together they were better than apart. She fell back against the pillows, pulling him with her, their lips still joined in an endless kiss that seemed to take and give and fill her all at once.

She explored his body, memorizing every part of him. Again she traced the lines of his scars. They were everywhere. Symbols of who he was—how he lived. It should have frightened her, but instead it excited her, the need inside her building until she was writhing beneath his touch, all thought banished as she concentrated on the rising heat between her legs.

And then they were one again. Moving together, searching for release, craving it, yet cherishing the intensity of the ride. She bucked against him, wanting him deeper, wanting to lock them together, to savor the moment. This night. This man.

Pleasure and pain collided into a spasm of intense sensation, her body threatening to fly into pieces. She heard him call her name, his voice hoarse with his frenzy, his body slamming into hers, the rhythm almost desperate. And for the first time in her life, Alexis let go, surrendering herself completely.

CHAPTER **25**

Alexis rolled over, letting the rise from sleep come slowly. She hadn't been sleeping well of late, and she wanted to cherish every second. She opened her eyes and stretched lazily as sunshine streamed in through the window, dust motes dancing in the light. And, just for a moment, everything seemed right with the world.

Then reality came crashing in.

For a moment she considered burying her head under the pillow. But that wasn't the answer. So instead she sat up, enjoying the feel of the sun on her face. Tucker had been up and out at first light, and though she'd intended to follow suit, her body had clearly had other ideas.

With a fortifying breath Alexis hopped out of bed and pulled on Tucker's sweatpants, rolling the top down so they hung comfortably on her hips. It was a teenage thing to do, but it felt good, and at the moment it was just what she needed.

After slipping on a sports bra and tank, she headed

downstairs with the thought of making a cup of coffee. But of course this wasn't her house, and it took three tries to find the cabinet with the coffee, and another moment or two to figure out the machine. But soon enough she'd measured the granules and water and started the pot brewing, the rich smell of french roast filling the room. Next up, a mug. She opened another cabinet, pleased to see that she'd chosen correctly. But as she reached for a ceramic I-Heart-New-York cup, a noise behind her made her spin in fear, the cup flying through the air to crash against the tile floor.

She dropped to a crouch and then realized her mistake as Madeline stepped into the doorway, surveying the scene without judgment, her eyes kind.

"I still jump at even the smallest noise," she said, her voice matter of fact as she held out a hand to help Alexis up. "When you've lived most of your life looking over your shoulder, it's not that easy to convince yourself to stop."

"So it isn't just me?" Alexis asked, embarrassment pushed aside by curiosity as she knelt to clean up the mess she'd made.

"No." Madeline shook her head. "It's just part and parcel of living on the edge. Whatever the reason. Even Annie has bad days."

"But she's so..." Alexis trailed off, not knowing exactly what she wanted to say.

"Fearless?" Madeline finished for her. "She is. But so are you. And, for that matter, so am I, even if I don't always feel that way. We're survivors, and that's nothing to be ashamed of. You know?" She opened a lower cabinet and Alexis tossed the broken cup, surprised at how easy it was to talk to Madeline.

Drake's wife was tiny, with the kind of curly hair women with fine, straight hair always coveted. It almost seemed to have a life of its own, curling around her face and neck, the sunlight highlighting russet tones amidst dark brown. Her eyes held both wisdom and the strength she'd alluded to, her smile equally engaging. And her soft Louisiana drawl made Alexis think of home, the combination comforting on some deep intrinsic level. In short, Alexis felt that, given the chance, she and Madeline could become friends. If she didn't break all of her crockery first.

"I'm sorry about the cup," Alexis said. "I hope it wasn't a special one."

"No. It was just one Drake picked up somewhere. Nothing important." She reached for another cup and filled it with coffee. "Here you go. I'm never quite right without my morning caffeine."

"Me too," Alexis said, grateful that Madeline had moved on to more mundane topics. "Only it's not exactly morning anymore."

"Well, you've still got an hour or so," Madeline said with a smile as she poured herself a cup. "I'm actually surprised all the noise didn't wake you up."

"I didn't hear a thing. Was something wrong?"

"Hardly." Madeline laughed. "The guy was just here to install our new TV. I got it for Drake's birthday. It's huge. And HD. And apparently comes with an amazing sports package. One that includes—"

"The Angels," Alexis finished for her on a laugh. "Tucker says it was like their place of worship."

"And then some." Madeline nodded, leading the way as they walked into the living room. The television was definitely the focal point of the room, the sleek black screen hanging above the fireplace. "So what do you think?"

"It's huge. He'll feel like he's right there on the field. It is a field, right?"

"It is." Madeline nodded. "I actually bought a book. When I was living with the two of them, it was like a secret club, and I finally figured out that if I wanted in, I had to be able to tell ERAs from RBIs."

"If you can't beat 'em, join 'em?"

"Exactly." They stood for a moment in companionable silence, and then Madeline smiled. "I know things are really rough for you right now, but for what it's worth, I've never seen Tucker this happy."

"Wow, I hate to think of what that says about before." The quip was meant to deflect Madeline's comment. She wasn't sure she was ready to share her burgeoning feelings with anyone else yet. Even someone as caring as Madeline.

"He lost a lot, Alexis," Madeline said, her voice growing serious. "The prison where we were, it was pretty awful. When they didn't beat you, they threw you in solitary. If Tucker hadn't been there, I don't think I would have survived. And he was at San Mateo a lot longer than I was."

"He told me a little bit about it. And about Lena," she said. She'd never had a woman to talk to before. She'd never really had anyone, except George—and her family, but they'd died so long ago.

"That was rough too. I know he loved her a great deal. But I never really believed she was the one, if that makes any sense." She shrugged. "Anyway, I just wanted to tell you that I think you're good for him. And that's it." She held up her hands with a smile. "Drake says I meddle too much."

"Drake's a lucky man," Alexis said, returning the smile as she sipped her coffee. "And I hear there's going to be an addition soon."

"Well, not too soon," Madeline said, her hand moving protectively to her belly. "We've only just found out. But Drake wanted to tell Tucker, and you can't keep anything a secret around here, which I find hysterical when you consider what they all do for a living."

"Is it hard?" Alexis asked, dropping down to sit on the sofa. "Living in the middle of all of this, I mean?" She waved a hand at the room as if it symbolized A-Tac and the hidden compound beneath Sunderland's campus.

"Sometimes I worry, if that's what you're getting at. But mostly I just take it all in stride. I've never had an easy life. In fact, more times than not, it was pure hell. So for me, living here with Drake is an amazing stroke of luck. I love him. And I love our life here. And I love my friends—who also happen to be Drake's partners in crime—or anti-crime, as the case may be."

"But weren't you wanted by the government at one time? And wasn't that why A-Tac came to Colombia in the first place?"

"They came because Tucker gave me an out. But that's a long story. And yes, I was not exactly citizen of the year. But the truth is that I was also my own worst enemy. I didn't trust anyone, so I was determined to make things better for my sister and me on my own, but instead I just made it all worse. Jenny wound up dead, and I thought I was going to be trapped in Colombia forever."

"But you're here now," Alexis said, hope blossoming at the thought.

"I am. Because Drake burst into my life, and though he pissed me off more often than not in the beginning, he also taught me how to trust." She rubbed her abdomen again, a soft smile of contentment coloring her face. "I believe in playing the cards you're dealt—in my case, literally. But you have to take the time to recognize what you're actually holding in your hand. And then you have to have the faith to play it through."

"Easier said than done, I fear," Alexis said with a rueful grin.

"Amen, sister." Madeline laughed. "But enough about me and my choices. You must be hungry. You hardly ate anything at all last night."

Alexis had the feeling that Madeline was already well on her way toward motherhood, the nurturing gene already kicking into high gear. "I was too tired to eat, but the mac and cheese looked great. If there's some of that left…"

"There's some in the fridge." Madeline stood up to head for the kitchen. "Which isn't always the case when Harrison comes to dinner. The man always eats like there's no tomorrow."

"Maybe he has a point." She turned to follow Madeline, stopping when something caught the corner of her eye. With a frown, she searched the line of the TV and then the stereo components stacked neatly against the hearth. Two of them glowed green, and she blew out a breath, realizing that it was the lights that had grabbed her attention.

She moved forward, thinking that at some point there would never be any true dark, entire neighborhoods lit

with the eerie glimmer of the modern plethora of household LED lights.

"You coming?" Madeline called from the kitchen.

"Yeah," Alexis answered, shaking her head at the silly
train of her thoughts, and then she heard a click and a
whiz, and her brain registered the fact that one of the
lights was now flashing red.

Just like the one underneath George's cabin.

"Madeline." Alexis screamed, her only thought to find
her new friend and get her safely out of the house. "Run,"
she yelled, rounding the edge of the kitchen door frame
and grabbing Madeline, who was standing by the refrigerator. "There's a bomb."

Madeline followed without question, the two women
sprinting through the kitchen and into the laundry
room, heading for the door leading to the backyard.
They'd made it as far as the dryer when the bomb went
off, Alexis diving to cover Madeline as the ceiling col-
lapsed, household objects becoming shrapnel as the walls
imploded, and a gust of scorching air escorted a plume of
fire as it rose up into the bright blue sky.

"I'm looking for Alexis Markham," Tucker said as he
came to a stop at the nurses' station.

"Are you family?" the woman asked, looking up at
him over the tops of her glasses, her eyes full of doubt.

"Yes," he said, barely holding on to his temper, his
heart pounding as he looked around the waiting room for
someone he knew. He'd been off campus when the explosion happened, investigating information about Alain
DuBois. "Yes, I am. And if you don't tell me where she is
right now, I swear I will—"

"Tucker, over here," Annie's voice carried across the room, and he saw her standing on the far side near a hall-way leading to patient rooms. She waved, and he turned his back on the nurse, pushing his way past people blocking the hall.

"Where is she?" he asked, knowing he sounded half crazed. But he'd had time to imagine a hell of a lot, and no one seemed to have any solid information, except that both Madeline and Alexis were alive.

"She's with the doctor now," Annie said, laying a hand on his arm. "She's going to be fine. Just a couple of cuts and a bruised rib."

"And Madeline?"

"She's fine too. And the baby. They're going to keep her overnight to be sure. But there's nothing to worry about. Although if it hadn't been for Alexis..."

"What do you mean?" Tucker asked, pulling his gaze from the rooms down the hospital hallway.

"According to Madeline, Alexis is the one who realized there was a bomb. And it was her quick thinking that got them away from the main part of the blast. If they hadn't moved"—Annie sighed—"well, put it this way: the kitchen isn't there anymore."

"Oh my God." Tucker sucked in a breath, his lungs seemingly forgetting to do the job automatically. "I should have been there."

"Don't be silly," Annie said. "You were doing what needed to be done. Getting us closer to finding this bastard. And they're both fine."

"Is my brother here?" he asked, his stomach still roiling.

"Yeah, he's with Madeline now."

"I just heard," Hannah said, rushing through the waiting room, her hair even more rumpled than usual, Harrison right behind her.

"How are they?" he asked.

"I haven't seen them," Tucker said, "but Annie says they're going to be okay."

"The baby too?" Hannah asked, the color washing back into her face.

"Yes." Annie nodded, and the two women hugged.

"Have you seen the house?" Tucker asked Harrison. "I came straight here when I heard."

"I went by on my way over here," Harrison said, lowering his voice. "It's not good. The back half of the house is gone. If they hadn't made it into the laundry room—"

"I know," he cut Harrison off. "Annie told me how close it was. But I want to know if we've found anything to ID the bomb. Where it originated, how it cleared our security to get into Drake's house. Anything."

"Tyler and Avery are there now. Simon and Nash are still on their way in from California. Alexis says the blast came from one of the stereo components. A guy came early this morning to install a new HDTV. We figure that's got to be how they got access. I've been working the cable end of things but I wanted to come here first and make sure they were okay." Harrison ran a hand through his hair, looking apologetic.

"I'm glad you're here," Tucker said, surprised at how much he meant it. Harrison had been with them from the start of this thing, and as such, he felt like they were a team. "Once we see for ourselves that they're both okay, we'll head back and see what we can figure out together, okay?"

Harrison nodded, looking relieved, and Annie touched Tucker's elbow, nodding toward a man in scrubs coming down the hall. "You're here for Ms. Markham?" the doctor asked, his gaze encompassing them all.

"Yes, I am," Tucker said, taking a step toward the man. "Is she really going to be okay?"

"She's going to be sore," the doctor said, allowing a small smile. "I gave her a pain reliever so she's going to be a little groggy, but she should be fine."

"Can I see her?" Tucker asked.

"Are you family?"

"Yes, goddamn it," Tucker said, his voice rising in tandem with his frustration. "I'm her family. So can I please see her now?"

Hannah hid a smile, and Harrison cleared his throat, but the doctor didn't miss a beat. "She's just down the hall. Room 305."

Tucker set off at a sprint, not bothering to wait for further discussion. The door was open a crack, and he pushed it with more force than intended—the door swinging back and hitting the wall.

Alexis turned toward the commotion, looking beat up but, to his eyes, beautiful. She had a gash on her forehead that had been stitched closed, and the skin below her right eye was already beginning to purple. She sported an Ace bandage around her middle, and there was gauze wrapped around one wrist.

He shuddered, thinking how close he'd come to losing her. He stopped beside the bed, resisting the urge to touch her, afraid he'd only make the pain worse. "I came as soon as I heard."

"I'm so sorry," she said, her voice low and husky from

the smoke or maybe the medication. "This is all my fault. If you hadn't brought me here, none of this would have happened. They said Madeline's okay?" She shifted so that she could see him better, wincing with the motion.

"I haven't seen her, but Annie assured me that she's fine. The baby too. And none of this was your fault. Madeline told Annie you're the one that saved them both."

"But I couldn't get them out in time." She sucked in a ragged breath and closed her eyes. "I tried. I swear, Tucker, I tried."

"Alexis"—he reached out to gently take her hand, and her eyes fluttered open—"you did the best you could. And it was enough. They're both going to be all right."

"But their house," she whispered, tears filling her eyes, "their beautiful house, it's gone. Because of me."

"It's just a house, sweetheart," he said, pushing the hair from her face. "The only thing that matters is that you and Madeline and the baby are all right."

She shook her head, a tear sliding down one cheek. "It's still on me."

"No," Tucker said, squeezing her hand. "It's on the bastard who did this. Do you understand me? This isn't your fault." He'd been living in a shell for so long he'd forgotten what real rage felt like. As soon as he got his hands on the man behind this, he'd break his fucking neck.

"You're angry." She sighed. "I can see it in your face."

"Not at you, Alexis. I swear it. I just want to find the man who did this to you and make him pay."

The side of her lip curled into the semblance of a smile but disappeared almost before it had time to register. "I can't do this, Tucker," she said, turning her head away. "I thought I could, but I can't. Because of me, your family was almost killed today. I can't risk something like that happening again. I can't stay with you any longer."

"Alexis," he said, a tremor working its way through his voice, "you are my family too. And you aren't going anywhere. Do you understand me?"

"Yes, but..." she protested, her lower lip trembling, as the tears spilled over her lashes.

"No buts," Drake said, striding into the hospital room. "Tucker's right. You're family. And we Flynns are big on sticking together. Madeline would have my head if I let you go." He paused for a moment, his brows drawn together in a fearsome frown. "I could have lost my wife and my child today, Alexis. But because of you, I didn't. And I will never forget that. Ever. So no more talk of leaving. All right?"

She lifted her gaze to meet his brother's and nodded, her lower lip still quivering slightly.

"Besides," Tucker said, still holding her hand, "someone needs to stay here and watch over Madeline. She can be a little headstrong when things don't go her way."

"And then some," Drake said. "And she's not going to like being cooped up here. But the doctor wants to keep her under observation for a least a day. So you think you can keep her distracted? And let us work on finding the asshole who did this?"

This time the smile was genuine as Alexis stifled a yawn. "I'll stay with her. I promise."

"All right, then," Drake said, his eyes meeting Tucker's as he turned to go, the black anger there a reflection of the rage that had been building in Tucker. "When you've finished here, I'll meet you out front."

Tucker turned back to Alexis, who had fallen asleep.

He leaned over to kiss her forehead, and she shifted, mumbling something beneath her breath. He started to pull back, but her eyes flickered open, a soft smile forming as she looked up at him. "I love you," she said on an exhale of breath as she slipped back into sleep again.

Tucker watched for a few minutes longer, feeling like he'd been given the most precious of gifts, then turned to go find his brother. There was work to be done.

CHAPTER 26

W hat have we got?" Tucker asked as he and Drake walked into the war room.

Harrison looked up from the conference table where he was working at a computer console. "Most everyone is working at the bomb site or in the lab to try and sift through the wreckage and find something that might help us ID this bastard. Tyler's preliminary examination seems to confirm a similar MO to the other bombings, but she needs more time to be certain."

"Well, that's something we don't have," Drake said, his nervous energy ratcheting up the tension in the room. "The longer it takes us, the more time this guy has to cover his tracks."

"You said almost everyone." Like his brother, Tucker felt as if he were set to explode, and he knew that he had to maintain control if he was going to be of any value to their investigation.

"Yeah." Harrison acknowledged. "Simon's been working

with the superstore that arranged the installation. They found the real tech on old Route 22. He was dead. No surprise there."

"Well, I guess that explains how they got past our security," Drake said. "No one expects a van from Buy Mart to present a threat. I assume they asked for ID?"

Harrison nodded. "It passed muster. I'm going over our security tapes now. I've strung some stills together to give us a real-time look at what happened." He hit a button and the security booth at the front of the college filled the screen above the conference table. "Here's the truck passing through security." He zoomed in on the truck. "You can see the license. It matched the information provided by Buy Mart. And you can see from this close-up"—he zoomed in farther—"that the guy at the wheel was wearing a baseball cap, tipped down."

"So there's no way to ID him from this picture," Tucker said, sitting down in a chair across the table. "So what about after that? Any luck?"

"Unfortunately, this guy knows what he's doing. I've got clear shots of the van here"—he switched to a picture of the vehicle turning into the cul-de-sac that served as home for most of the unit—"and here." A new photo showed the van pulling up in front of Drake's house. "Even at the door the shot's no good." A last picture showed the man in profile as he talked with Madeline. But, even enlarged, the slant of his head and the hat effectively hid his face.

"What the hell?" Drake said, moving around the table to get a closer view of the photo projected onto the screen. "Look at the hat." He frowned, waving for Harrison to enlarge it. "That's a fucking Angels cap. This guy knows who we are."

"Could be a coincidence," Harrison suggested.

"Right, because there are so many Angels fans in New York," Tucker said, clenching a fist. "This guy is thumbing his nose at us. He knew he'd be on camera."

"It's possible. I mean, he's managed to stay off the radar this long—maybe he's getting cocky."

"Or maybe he's sending a message." Drake observed. "I don't know."

"Has anyone talked to Madeline about a description?" Harrison asked.

"No," Drake said. "She's still too out of it."

"They found the van?" Tucker asked.

"Yeah," Harrison said, "we got lucky there. The guy left it in the parking lot at the Buy Mart."

"Blinding glimpse of the obvious." Tucker frowned.

"Well, it gets better. I pulled the security footage from the store's cameras." Harrison hit another button and the parking lot appeared, cars coming and going as the time stamp advanced. He fast-forwarded a little bit, then hit Play again. "Here's the van coming in."

"Hell, he's acting like he's got all the time in the world," Drake said, his jaw set in anger. "When was this?"

"Less than thirty minutes after he left your house." Harrison froze the picture for a moment, pointing to the time stamp. "He parks the van in plain sight." The video started forward again. "But then makes sure to place it so that when he gets out, we can't get an ID."

"What happens next?" Tucker asked, leaning forward for a better view.

"He gets into a 2009 Nissan and drives away. We've got him turning north onto the highway, and that's it."

"Did you trace the plates?" Tucker asked, pushing away from the table to pace along the side of the room, nervous energy threatening to get the best of him. He needed something to do, sitting on his ass not being an option.

"Of course," Harrison said. "They were stolen. But not original to the car."

"So again the guy was prepared."

"Considering this is the first time in thirteen years we've even gotten a bead on the dude, I'm guessing it's safe to say he's pretty good at what he does."

Tucker blew out a breath, staring up at the screen. "What about satellite? Any chance we can find him that way?"

"I'm already on it," Harrison said. "That's what I was working on when you came in. So far, the program I'm running hasn't identified the Nissan, but it's still searching."

"It's like looking for a needle in a fucking haystack," Drake said.

"Only we've got technology on our side and access to damn near every satellite out there. I'll find the car. It's just going to take a little more time." Harrison's shrug was apologetic.

"What we need is a break." Drake dropped down to sit on the edge of the table, his eyes on Harrison's computer screen. "This guy has got to make a mistake eventually."

"I think maybe he already has," Tyler said, striding into the room, a piece of paper in her hand. "I found a fingerprint on one of the bomb fragments. And I ran it against our databases and got a hit." She held the paper out for Tucker to see.

"Son of a bitch." He reread the report, then lifted his gaze to meet Tyler's. "You sure?"

"Yeah." She nodded. "I've got two verified sources. It's a twelve-point match."

"Do you have any way of dating it?" Tucker asked, handing the report to Drake, whose eyes widened as he let loose an epithet.

"No. Latent prints in the right circumstances can remain for years. But the odds of a fingerprint on a piece of pipe bomb being thirteen years old aren't very likely."

"So what are you telling me?" Tucker asked, already pretty sure he knew the answer.

"Well, there's some chance that the print could have been purposely transferred. An attempt to throw us off. But there's no evidence to support the idea. Which means the fingerprint is recent. Bottom line"—she took a breath—"it looks like Randolph Baker is still very much alive."

Alexis shifted in her chair by Madeline's bed. She'd been sitting with her friend ever since the doctor had released her. Madeline was asleep but otherwise fine, and Alexis had been trying to kill time by going over her mother's journal again. Annie had brought it, along with the backpack, from where they'd been stored in A-Tac's underground compound, understanding Alexis's need to feel as if she were contributing something.

So far there'd been nothing new from anyone. She hadn't seen Tucker since he'd left her at the hospital. And she wasn't sure how he felt about the words she'd blurted out just before she'd fallen asleep. She hadn't meant to tell him. She hadn't even known for certain that was how she felt. But now that the words were out there, she knew they were true.

Alexis blew out a breath, wondering how everything had come to this. One moment she'd been living her life, and the next it had imploded into the chaos surrounding them now. And yet out of all of that had come Tucker. But he hadn't said a word. Just walked away. She told herself it was because she'd been falling asleep. Or maybe because he hadn't heard. But in her heart of hearts, she was scared to death that it was because he didn't feel the same way.

Not that any of it mattered. There could be no talk of a future until they put an end to all of this. And to do that, they needed to find the bomber and the formula. She glanced at the book in her lap, her mother's handwriting filling the pages. She was nearing the end, but nothing new had presented itself. Just the words of an unhappy woman living in impossible circumstances. She still hadn't forgiven her mother—or George—but after reading through her journal a second and now a third time, she could feel her mother's pain.

Things are growing more difficult with Randolph, her mother wrote. *He's moody and angry. He's become a different man, and it scares me. I don't know what to do. George is worried too, but I can't leave my babies. Especially Lexie. She's at an age where she needs her mother.*

Alexis leaned back, tears threatening. She'd loved her mother so much. And as crazy as it sounded, reading the journal was like losing her all over again. Across from her, Madeline shifted and sighed, still sleeping. Alexis turned the page, forcing her thoughts away from the past. She needed to concentrate on finding something in the journal that might help locate the formula.

Randolph hit me today. Reflexively, Alexis covered her cheek, long forgotten memories surfacing. Her parents yelling, her mother's tears. *It wasn't the first time. And maybe now I deserve it, I don't know. But I'm afraid. For myself and for the kids. I hate the idea that my transgressions could hurt them too.*

The journal went on for another couple of pages. She talked of more discord. But no more violence. Just of her growing love for George. And her shame at having broken her vows. Whatever had happened between her and George, her mother had regretted the inevitable fallout for the family.

She turned to the final entry.

Lexie and I had a good talk today. I think maybe she's becoming adjusted to this life. But as I listened to her talking about her hopes and dreams, I realized all over again how much Randolph has asked us to sacrifice. George still says we have to bide our time. And I guess I'll have to accept that. Although I can't help but feel that time is precious. And that we're wasting it.

Alexis closed her eyes, thinking that her mother's words had been prophetic. She'd died two days later. Her heart twisted as she considered all her mother had lost. She'd been unhappy—Alexis could see that now. And she could understand how hard it must have been to give up her life to go underground. But surely that wasn't an excuse for breaking her marriage vows.

With a sigh she opened her eyes again. Life was complicated. And no matter what had happened between her parents and George, Tucker had been right. Her mother had loved her and her brother. Enough to give up the chance at real happiness. And despite her anger over her mother's affair, there was comfort in that.

She reached down to close the book, her finger catching

on the bottom of the final page. Frowning, she bent down to examine it more closely, realizing that the page had been folded under, the corner stuck in the cover's lining. Over time the two had bonded together, so that they appeared to be one and the same. Using her finger, she carefully pried it free, and then straightened the page. There was another entry, the writing hidden by the fold.

There's hope, her mother wrote. *I hardly dare to write it. But George says he's found a way out. An insurance policy. Something to guarantee that Randolph will let us go—with the children.*

Alexis's hands were shaking, heart pounding. The insurance—it had to be the formula. It was the only thing that would have stopped her father cold. She smoothed the page, frowning down at the faded handwriting of the last sentence.

For safekeeping, he's left it with Mary. He knows she's my favorite. It won't be long now. Soon. Soon. I'll be free.

Mary? Alexis tried to think of someone they'd known by that name. But there was no one. At least not that she'd been aware of.

Mary.

She shook her head, trying to make sense of her mother's words. Then suddenly she knew.

The one place her father would never think to look. And by pure serendipity, one of the few things of her mother's that had survived the explosion. Grabbing her backpack, she checked for the Mary Stewart book, running her hand over its worn cover. *Mary.* Her mother's favorite.

With shaking hands, she opened the book.

CHAPTER 27

Y ou need to turn right on Old Bridge Road," Harrison said, his voice crackling into Tucker's headset.

Harrison had located the Nissan via satellite, and Tucker and Drake had decided to try to intercept. They'd been on the road for almost an hour now, so far with no results. But, at least according to Harrison and his celestial view, the car had finally come to a stop in the small town of Mill Valley. Once a thriving industrial hub, the village was now made up primarily of abandoned factories and warehouses.

They were currently driving along the river. Dilapidated red brick buildings lined the waterfront, their turn-of-the-century smokestacks long idle.

"You should be coming up on it now. Do you see it?"

"Roger that," Drake said, making the turn and leaving the river for a rutted road leading between two old factories. "How much farther?"

"Just another block or so. Looks like he's parked

behind a warehouse. According to the map, it should be marked Jackson Road. But there's no telling if there's still a sign. I've got you on-screen, though, so I'll tell you when you're there."

"Gotta love modern technology," Tucker said, his eyes peeled for a street sign indicating the turnoff. "Any word from the hospital?"

"Annie was in here a few minutes ago," his friend said. "When she left, Alexis was in Madeline's room reading her mother's journal. Madeline was sleeping."

"Is Annie heading back over there?" Drake asked, his voice laced with worry.

"No. She has to take Adam to baseball practice, but Hannah's there now. And the guards are still on duty. So don't worry, they're fine. Just concentrate on finding Baker."

"They really are going to be okay," Tucker said, his gaze meeting his brother's.

"I know." Drake nodded. "I just worry. This all seems a little too easy."

"Well, everyone makes mistakes sooner or later. So let's just hope this is Baker's turn."

"Should be there," Harrison's voice piped into his earpiece. "Can you see the turnoff?"

"There." Tucker pointed as Drake slowed the car.

"The Nissan's parked beside the warehouse, on the south side just inside a gated fence. Maybe a hundred yards," Harrison said. "There's a second entrance on the north side. Now remember, you're just there to scope things out. Please don't go all cowboy or Avery will have my head."

Drake and Tucker exchanged glances. "No worries, dude." Drake smiled across at his brother. "We'll take it slow."

"I'm not sure that's the assurance I was looking for, but I guess it'll have to do," Harrison groused.

"So, any other intel?" Tucker asked as they slowed to a roll, moving onto the outskirts of what had once been a parking lot.

"Couldn't get a blueprint of the place. It's been out of commission too long, but I've sent an annotated aerial shot to your phones so you can get an overview."

Tucker flipped on the phone to confirm that he had the picture. "Got it. What about infrared?"

"It's a no-go there, I'm afraid," Harrison told him. "I couldn't get a firm read. I don't know if it's the satellite or if it's the warehouse. Some of these old buildings are pretty good at shielding. But either way, I can't tell for sure whether he's inside. Or if he's got company. But from what I can see, there aren't any other cars. Which would tend to support his being in there on his own."

"All right, then. We'll take it from here."

"Stay on this channel," Harrison requested. "So at least I can monitor the situation."

"Quit worrying. Avery is going to be fine with us being here," Tucker said, not completely certain he was telling the truth. They hadn't wanted to waste time tracking Avery down to advise him of their plans and had convinced Harrison to go along with their solo mission, promising to wait for backup before taking any action.

Of course, some promises were meant to be broken.

"Well, I'm the new guy, remember? So it's better for me not to piss off the boss."

"Actually, Simon is the new guy," Drake corrected. "Which means you're off the hook. So chill."

"Good point," Harrison assented, his tone like an

audible shrug, "Okay, then. Off you go. Best we go radio silent in case they're scanning. But I'll be able to hear you if there's trouble."

"Copy that," Tucker acknowledged, flipping his earpiece to silent mode.

"I think I can see movement inside," Drake said, lowering the field glasses he'd been using to scope out the building. "But we're going to have to get closer to see for sure." He put down the binoculars, adjusted his own earpiece, and then picked up his gun, checking the magazine and loading extra ammo into the pocket of his Kevlar vest.

"Let's go." Tucker checked his weapon too and then got out of the car, careful to stay low to avoid any watchful eyes. Drake followed as they moved across the edge of the parking lot toward the warehouse, using trees for cover.

Once part of a grand complex, the warehouse had two stories. Large casement windows ran the length of the structure on the second floor, the glass long gone. An old, twisted oak at one end of the building had grown through the windows, a large branch emerging from what must have been a hole in the roof, making it look as though tree and building had merged into one entity. Ivy grew untended everywhere, so overgrown in places that it had begun to erode the walls, bits of masonry dotting the broken walkway that circled the warehouse.

"I think it'll be easier to check the place out if we split up," Drake said as they came to a stop under the shelter of the oak at the corner of the building. "You head for the door by the Nissan, and I'll circle around to the other entrance to the south. According to photos Harrison sent, there aren't any windows on the east side. So after scoping things out, we'll meet there to regroup."

"In what—fifteen minutes?" Tucker asked, looking down at his watch.

"Mark that." Drake nodded.

"All right, see you then," Tucker said. "But keep your com on the emergency channel."

"Will do," his brother agreed, tapping his ear. "Be careful out there. I'm kind of getting used to having you around."

"Roger that." Tucker grinned, then turned his attention to the far right side of the warehouse and the fence that enclosed the Nissan. Using the undergrowth to shield him, he made his way past the abandoned bay doors that had originally opened to train cars and then trucks to offload their cargo. Through years of disuse, most of them were rusted shut now and at least partially obliterated by the ropelike vines of ivy.

He approached the fence cautiously, the chain link about seven feet high and topped with a spiral of barbed wire. He could see the Nissan inside now, parked catty-corner in front of a short flight of steps that led to a wooden landing and an open door. There was still no sign of activity. And no additional cars. Which could mean that Baker, if it really was him, was on his own. But the whole thing could easily be a setup, too.

Ignoring the invitation of the open door at the top of the stairs, Tucker skirted the enclosure and the Nissan, choosing instead a regular-sized door cut into one of the bays just beyond it. There was a small window at the top, and after wiping it down with his sleeve, he took a quick look inside.

The warehouse was shadowed, the morning light penetrating only as scattered beams across the floor. The cavernous room was mostly empty, a few abandoned crates here and there, as well as piles of debris from the collapsing roof above. The second floor consisted of a balcony-like structure running around the room on three sides, the flooring there composed of rusted metal grating.

A staircase made of the same material ascended from the far corner. Two doorways opened off the east side of the room, probably leading to what had once been company offices. One door was rotted and hanging off its hinges. The second, however, was new—and padlocked.

Tucker started to pull his scope from his pocket for a closer look, but just as his fingers were circling it, something moved in his periphery vision. Something inside, at the other end of the warehouse. He shifted so that he was better concealed by a fall of ivy and waited, eyes narrowed as he peered through the window into the shadows.

For a moment he thought he'd made a mistake, and then a man stepped from behind a pillar into one of the beams of sunlight. Harrison had dug up an old employment photo of Baker, and Tucker had seen the childhood photo that Alexis carried in her backpack, not to mention the ones at George's cabin. And even though the man in the warehouse was older, there was no mistaking him. Hell, he'd have known the man even without the corroborating pictures. Alexis had inheirited his nose and eyes.

Tucker tapped his earpiece, whispering into the com. "Drake, are you there?" Static filled his ear. "Drake?" Frowning, he switched the channel, taking the risk of reception going wide. "Drake, are you there? Harrison, can you hear me?"

The static rose to an uncomfortable level and then stopped, the com going completely silent.

"Fuck," Tucker swore under his breath, pulling out the earpiece, his spidey-sense tingling—hell, screaming. He reached for his gun and started to turn back toward the safety of a clump of trees, but he hadn't made it two feet when something hit him hard upside the head. He swiveled and managed to get off a shot, but it was a Hail-Mary attempt, and as his brain spun into a black void, he had the thought that he'd been right.

The whole damn thing had been a setup.

"Shit," Harrison said, slamming his hand against the table. "The com's dead. I've lost them."

"Lost who?" Alexis asked as she walked into the war room, Annie right behind her.

Harrison and Avery turned toward the sound of her voice, Harrison avoiding her gaze.

"Who did you lose?" she repeated, fairly certain she already knew the answer. "Tucker?"

"And Drake." Avery nodded. "But don't jump to conclusions. It could just be a communications glitch." As if to confirm that fact, Harrison started typing furiously while continuing to call both Drake and Tucker's names.

"Where are they?" she asked, crossing over to them, setting the journal and the backpack on the table.

"Unbeknownst to me, following a lead," Avery said, shooting an angry glance in Harrison's direction.

Alexis clenched a fist, her gut roiling as she considered the possibility that something had happened to Drake—or Tucker. "You have to tell me what's going on. I have the right to know."

Annie stepped forward, her hand on Alexis's arm. "She's got a point, Avery. She's more than proved her loyalty to the team, and this is her fight, after all. Besides, Tucker would want her in the loop."

"Yes, but it's my call," Avery said, clearly trying to telegraph something to Annie, the action scaring Alexis more than his evasion.

"Come on, Avery," Alexis begged. "Tell me. Please."

Avery blew out a breath and opened his hands in surrender. "Fine. Harrison managed to get a lead on the man who we think is the bomber. And Drake and Tucker followed him to a warehouse in Mill Valley."

"And..." she urged.

"Harrison was monitoring their communication. They'd gone dark, but he could still track them, and, in an emergency, hear them. But now there's nothing."

"But you said it could be a communications glitch."

"It's not," Harrison said, swiveling around in his chair to face her. "Someone's either jammed the system or destroyed their earpieces. Or both."

Alexis fought against a wave of sheer terror. "So you think they're—"

"We don't know anything for sure," Avery said, his reassuring tone cutting into her rising fear. "We just know there's a problem. We need to get another team out there as fast as we can."

"I'm already working on it," Harrison told them. "Nash and Simon are on their way here now."

"I'm going with them," Alexis said, her fingers closing around the handle of her backpack. "I can help."

"You aren't trained for this kind of thing." Avery dismissed her offer. "I need you and Annie back at the hospital. If things have gone south, someone needs to be with Madeline."

"But Hannah's there"—Annie frowned—"and you might need my particular set of skills."

Avery considered the idea, then relented. "All right, fine. You can go. Why don't you start getting the gear together."

Annie squeezed Alexis's arm and then headed for the door and the storage locker beyond. Avery turned his attention back to Harrison, who was still trying to raise Drake and Tucker.

Alexis swallowed, still determined to convince Avery to take her with them. "If you don't let me go, I'll just follow you. Don't you understand? I can't just sit here and wait."

"Alexis, we know what we're doing," Avery said, his tone brooking no argument. "You're just going to have to trust me."

She opened her mouth to argue and then closed it again as Harrison raised his hand, signaling for silence.

"I'm getting something," he said.

"Put it on speaker," Avery responded.

Alexis held her breath, praying that the next voice she heard would be Tucker's.

"I have your people," a man said, and Alexis felt her body go cold and her knees threaten to buckle. She knew that voice. Knew it almost as well as her own. And she'd never thought to hear it again. And certainly not like this.

Avery was beside her in an instant, his big arms keeping her from falling.

"Daddy?" she whispered, her voice too soft to carry over the radio.

"And if you want to see them again," the voice continued, like a disembodied spirit from beyond the grave, "you'll do exactly as I tell you."

"I'm not in the habit of responding to threats," Avery said, his arm still around her, "Mr. Baker. It is you I'm talking to?"

"Very good," her father replied. "I wasn't certain you'd be able to follow the clues I'd left. But since we're all on the same page now, you'll have to admit I'm holding all the cards."

Alexis scrambled to make sense of what she was hearing. Her dead father was speaking to them, and he had apparently set Tucker up. Questions flooded through her mind, threatening to swamp her, the confusion so overwhelming she wasn't certain she could breathe.

"I wouldn't say that," Avery replied, his voice still calm and assuring as he signaled Harrison to try to triangulate the transmission. "But just for the sake of argument, what is it you want from us?"

"I want my daughter," he said. "And the formula. Bring them to me, and I'll let your people go free."

"I already told you we don't respond to threats."

"Bullshit," her father said. "You do it every damn day. And I can promise you this one isn't empty. I'll kill them both if you don't produce Lexie and the formula within the hour."

Lexie. Her head started to spin again. No one had called her that since the night her family—correction, her mother and brother—had died. "Dad?" she called, this time loud enough to be heard.

"Lexie? Is that you?"

"I'm here. And I'm asking you to let them go. Let

Tucker and Drake go. This isn't about them. They were only trying to help me."

"Help you betray me." His voice was sharp, his rebuke slamming her with physical pain.

Avery motioned for her to keep talking, and she fought to maintain control.

"I don't know what you're talking about."

"You took the formula. You stole it from me." There was an obsessive note in his voice she'd never heard before.

"I didn't. I was just a kid. How would I have even known it existed?"

"You were working with George and with her."

"Mother?" she asked as Avery circled his hand for more time.

"Yes. She betrayed me too, you know."

"I do. But *I* didn't, Daddy. I didn't even know I had the formula until today." The words came out before she had the chance to think about it, Avery and Harrison's heads whipping around in tandem, their eyes full of surprise. If everything hadn't been so horrifying it would have almost been funny.

"Prove that you're loyal, Lexie," her father urged, his voice softening. "Bring me the formula."

"And you'll let them go?"

"As easily as that, pumpkin." He sounded almost jovial now, her sensory reaction to his use of her pet name discordant with the chaos of her emotions. "Bring me the formula, and I'll let your boyfriend and his brother go."

The transmission clicked and went dead.

Alexis felt as if she'd been dropped into some kind of fractured fairy tale where the evil king captures the prince and demands the princess give him up in order that he could live.

Only this wasn't a story—this nightmare was real.

"That was really my father?" Alexis forced the words out, her hands shaking, her body threatening full revolt. "He's alive?"

"Yes," Avery confirmed, his hand still supporting her elbow. "Do you want to sit down?"

"No. I want to go to that warehouse. I want to save Tucker and Drake. I want to give him the stupid formula and be done with all of this."

"You know that's not possible," Avery said, his fatherly tone beginning to wear thin.

"Anything is possible, Avery. And I should know better than most. My father—my dead father—has just placed Tucker's life in my hands. So I'll be goddamned if I'm going to let you tell me what I can and can't do." Anger rushed through her, chasing away her doubts and her fear. Tucker needed her. He was depending on her. And she wasn't about to let him down. "Did you confirm where they are?" she asked, working to sort through the details of an idea forming in her mind.

"They're still at the warehouse," Harrison said. "But I've lost visual access. I did manage to confirm the location, though."

"How long will it take us to get there?" she asked.

"I told you it's better if you stay here. And even if I do let you go," Avery said, his tone still uncompromising but his expression wavering, "we're not going to give your father the formula."

"I wasn't thinking we would," she agreed, reaching into the backpack. "But he doesn't have to know that, does he?"

"You have a plan?" Avery asked, his eyes smiling, his capitulation complete.

Alexis squared her shoulders, her fingers closing around the journal as she drew strength from her mother's words. "Yes," she said. "I do."

CHAPTER 28

"You son of a bitch," Tucker said, struggling against his bonds.

He and Drake had been strung up by the arms, the ropes suspended from the metal grating that formed the second story's floor. His feet were bound, as were Drake's. And his brother, after a failed attempt to take out one of the guards, was out cold. At least said guard had a bloodied nose and a black eye, thanks to the toe of his brother's boot. He'd counted five men so far in addition to Baker. None that he recognized, and all of them carrying weapons.

He returned his attention to Baker, who had dropped the transmitter he'd been using to talk to Avery—and Alexis.

"Do you have any idea what you just did to her?" Tucker snarled, wishing he had a gun. Or a knife. Or just free hands. "She thought you were dead. She mourned you. Hell, she worshipped you. And then after everything you've already done to her, you just reappear and destroy her like that?"

"That's one way of looking at it. But isn't it also possible that I just gave her a gift? Her father resurrected. You're right, you know—she did worship me."

"So you blew her up."

Baker shrugged. "I'm a practical man. Her mother was threatening to leave me."

"So to prevent that, you faked your own death and killed your whole family? Seems like a little bit of an overreaction to an affair."

"George was my friend, so it was more than just an affair. It was full-fledged betrayal. But that wasn't why I blew up the house. Ginny was threatening to go public if I didn't let her go and take the children with her. I couldn't risk that. It was just easier if the whole thing died a natural death. Don't you see, it had to be the whole family. That way there wouldn't be anyone to question whether or not I might still be alive."

"But George wasn't there."

"No." Baker's eyes narrowed in anger. "He wasn't. Pity that. He was always a meddling fool. First taking my wife. And then my formula."

"But if he'd already taken the formula, I don't understand why it took you so long to exact your revenge."

"By revenge you mean blowing him to bits?" Baker asked, dropping the transmitter into a bag, his shoulders radiating anger. "I didn't kill him because he had the formula. Fool that I am, I didn't even realize he'd taken it until after the son of a bitch was dead."

"So what was the motive? His betrayal? Seems to me you could have taken care of that a long time ago."

"It had nothing to do with my wife," he said, waving his hand in dismissal. "George figured out I was alive. I couldn't risk him going public with that little tidbit. So I had to take care of him."

"Only then it turned out he'd taken the formula," Tucker mused. "I'll admit there's a certain irony to that. Must have really pissed you off to find out he'd played you for a fool."

"The joke was definitely on me. All this time I'd thought it was safe. And when I decided to sell it, I didn't even bother to look. Just made the deal and then discovered the microchip I'd been holding in my vault contained nothing but an old article I'd written about nuclear fission. It wasn't my finest hour. And I've been doing the quickstep ever since. But, thanks to my daughter, it looks like it's all going to work out anyway."

Tucker realized that Baker's admissions indicated he wasn't planning to let them go. But then Baker hadn't ever dealt with Avery. And so he'd keep Baker talking.

"Why the bombs? Seems there are easier ways to kill people."

"I've never been very good with firearms," Baker said. "But as a chemist I'm pretty good at making things go boom. The first time it wasn't really a full-fledged bomb, but after that, well, let's just say I upped the ante."

"The first time?" Tucker asked, still playing for time. "You're talking about Wallace, right? I still don't understand why you killed him."

"I seem to have surrounded myself with people of conscience. He also wanted to go public. And I felt like there were other, more lucrative options. I tried to reason with him, but Duncan was never really good at seeing the big picture."

"And the bomb at George's cabin," Tucker asked, still playing for time, "it wasn't meant for Alexis?"

"No. I didn't even know she was alive. I just wanted to get rid of the place. It was a symbol for everything George took from me. He and my wife met there, you know. To carry out their affair. So after I searched it, I destroyed it. I knew there was someone there—that's why I beat a hasty retreat—but it never occurred to me that it was Alexis."

"But you did try to kill her. What about the failed bomb at her house?"

"I wasn't trying to kill Lexie. I tried to destroy her house to keep Carmichael and his men from getting too close. To her and to me. I had no way of knowing if she had something that might link to me. So after making certain the formula wasn't there, I set the bomb to destroy the place."

"But she was there," Tucker said. "In New Orleans. In the house."

"I know that—now. And anyway, I never got the chance to set the thing off, so no harm, no foul." He held up a hand in halfhearted apology.

"And my brother's house?"

It was Baker's turn to frown. "I have no idea what you're talking about."

"The bomb you set off at Sunderland. You almost killed Alexis and my brother's wife. We found your fingerprint on the bomb."

Baker's jaw tightened, both anger and surprise reflected in his expression. "There must be some other explanation." He shot a look at the men standing guard, his fingers tightening into a fist. "It wasn't me."

"So who else could it have been?" Tucker asked, sensing an opening. "Carmichael is dead."

Again, surprise flashed across his face, but he covered it almost as quickly as it had surfaced. "Good riddance. The man has been a thorn in my side for over twenty years."

"What about the people you promised the formula? Maybe they're setting you up?"

Again he glanced over at the guards. "Impossible. They came to me and offered their help. Why would they want to set me up?"

"Maybe to tie up loose ends? We take you, and they walk away unscathed."

"Except that I'm holding you hostage, and in short order, will be in possession of the formula."

"These people—they're part of the Consortium, right?" Tucker asked, still trying to fit this latest piece of information into the puzzle. The Consortium certainly had an ax to grind with A-Tac. But setting up Baker didn't make sense. Unless all of this was meant to be a trap.

"I have no idea what they call themselves. I just know they were willing to pay me a hell of a lot of money for the formula. The only person I ever dealt with was a man named Alain DuBois."

Full circle stop. It seemed everything came back to DuBois.

"Well, I don't know what they told you, but according to the evidence, you're the man who set that bomb. You should just be thankful Madeline and your daughter survived."

"None of this matters," Baker said, almost to himself, clearly unmoved by his daughter's plight. "Whoever set this chain in motion, I have the upper hand now. I have you and your brother. And my daughter is on her way with the formula. And once I have it, then I can complete the bargain I made with DuBois. No need to sacrifice anyone. Except maybe the two of you."

"Not if I have a say in it," Drake said, sputtering with anger as he came to. "The minute I'm free, you're a dead man."

"Okay, Baker," Avery said into his com unit as he and Alexis stood outside the warehouse. "We're here. Now what?"

"Well, ideally you'll leave Lexie and all go home," her father said, his voice sounding tinny coming from the little receiver. "But I'm guessing that's not going to happen."

"Not until we have our people back—including Alexis."

"Actually, that wasn't part of the deal. But I'll take it under advisement." He sounded almost cheerful, and for a moment Alexis was transported back to the time when he was just her father, not a crazy, murdering bomber with a God complex. "Right now I want you and your people to stand down and then send Lexie in."

"Not by herself," Avery insisted, even as Alexis shook her head.

"Your call," her father said. "But I'm going to start counting. If she's not in here by the time I get to fifteen, Flynn dies. Oh, dear, should have clarified. *Tucker* Flynn dies. One . . . two . . ." The transmitter went dead.

Alexis reached out to grab his arm. "I can do it. Besides, you can't expect me to just stand here and let him kill Tucker."

"No," Avery conceded, "I suppose not. But I want you to keep to the script we agreed to. No deviations, okay?"

She nodded. "I promise. Trust me. I've got as much riding on this as anyone—except maybe Madeline. I'm not going to screw it up."

"If anything happens and you get hurt—"

"Nothing is going to happen. He's my father. I don't believe he'll let anything happen to me."

"But he's already tried to kill you."

"In absentia. Never face-to-face. And besides, you guys are going to have my back."

"Seven," the transmitter crackled to life. "Eight."

"I'm going in." She started forward, hands raised, not feeling particularly brave but determined to do everything in her power to rescue Drake and Tucker. Even if it meant facing her father.

The pertinent page from her mother's journal was folded and taped beneath her sports bra along with the microchip. Even with a pat-down no one would be able to feel it. Eventually she'd be forced to produce it, but in the meantime she'd use the actual journal, which she was holding in her hand, as a decoy. Sort of a double bait and switch—if everything went as planned.

At the top of the steps Alexis paused for a moment to suck in a fortifying breath, then stepped into the warehouse. She blinked, trying to focus, her eyes not adjusted to the dim light. But before she had the time to adapt, her father's goons were there, grabbing the journal and doing the rudimentary pat-down. No weapon. And no discovery.

So far, so good.

One of the men led her forward, his gun in her side, and as her vision adapted to the lower light, she saw Tucker and Drake strung up from the rafters. Anger lashed through her, her eyes flashing as she whirled around, looking for the man who had caused all of this. The man whom she'd once called "father."

"Lexie." It was almost as if no time had passed at all. And when he turned, her heart literally skipped a beat, and she wondered how it was possible to hate someone she had once loved so dearly.

He was her father. The man who'd held her when she'd had a bad dream. Comforted her after she'd had a fall. Kept her safe from monsters under the bed. He'd been her hero. And now she was being forced to face the reality that he'd been the monster all along.

"I told you never to trust them," he said, tipping his head toward Tucker, who was watching her intently, his eyes full of love.

She fought her fear. All she had to do was buy Avery time. "You were wrong about that. Turns out you were wrong about a lot of things."

"I didn't want you to die. You have to know that." For a moment she almost believed him—and then she saw his eyes. They were hollow. Cold. There was no sign of remorse. "It was your mother," he continued. "She gave me no choice."

"So you killed her and Frank and if it hadn't been for Mike Kennedy, you'd have killed me too." She clenched her fists, wishing she'd brought a gun even though she knew she'd never be able to use it.

"Who is Mike Kennedy?" Her father asked with a frown.

"Nobody, really. Just the boy I snuck out to see that night. If I hadn't taken the chance, I'd have died too. And you'd have won."

"But don't you see, darling? I've won anyway." He waved a hand toward Drake and Tucker. "So what have you brought me?" he asked, taking the journal the guard offered.

Alexis took the moment while he leafed through the book to glance surreptitiously around the warehouse, looking for signs that the team was in place. From the second floor she thought maybe she saw movement, but nothing definite. Nothing to confirm that it was time.

"What the hell is this?" her father asked, waving the journal through the air. "There's nothing here but Ginny's whining about her life and her precious George. Where's my formula?"

"You didn't think I'd just hand it over, did you?"

"Why wouldn't you?" he asked, clearly surprised at the question. "You're my daughter. My blood."

Tucker growled something, but one of the guards silenced him.

"I don't belong to anyone. And for the record, my father, the man I thought I knew—he died that night in Walsenburg. You may look and sound just like him, but you're not my father."

For a moment she thought her words had broken through. That there was still some kind of bond between them, but he shook it off with the ease of a duck shedding water, and she knew for certain that she'd spoken the truth.

Her father was dead.

"Where is the formula?" he repeated, nodding to one of his guards. Behind them, near the railing that bordered the second floor, Alexis saw Annie. Her friend tilted her head toward the adjacent side of the warehouse, and

Alexis shifted her gaze, glancing up quickly to see Nash standing behind a pillar in the shadows.

"I've got it," she said, working to sound resigned, as if she'd given in. "I just wanted to be sure you honored your end of the bargain." She nodded toward Tucker and Drake. "To set them free."

"I want the formula first."

"Fine," she said, reaching into her shirt to pull it from her bra. "Come and get it." She held the page up, her eyes meeting Tucker's over her father's shoulder.

"Is this another trick?" Her father frowned. "That looks like your mother's writing."

"It is," she said. "It's the last page from the journal. It's the clue to where George hid the formula. It was in Mother's book. You know, by Mary Stewart. *Airs Above the Ground.* It was her favorite."

"You're lying," he said. "The book was destroyed in the explosion. Everything was."

Off to the right, she could see Simon behind a stack of crates, and to the left, a little farther back, Avery.

"Except for me," she said, working to keep her father's attention on her. His men stood by idly, unaware that they were slowly being surrounded. "And the things I had with me. I had a book report due that day at school. And I'd forgotten to do it. So I grabbed Mom's book off the table and took it with me. I figured she'd read it to me so many times I could write a report in my sleep. And I kept it all these years because it reminded me of her. Of home. Of my family."

"I still don't see why you brought the page here."

Above her Annie nodded, leveling her sniper rifle.

"Because it proves I'm telling you the truth about this."

She reached into her bra again and produced the tiny chip, adding it to the journal sheet she had in her hand.

Her father took a step forward and all hell broke loose, gunshots flying. Alexis's gaze moved to Tucker and Drake, but before she could be sure they were okay, someone tackled her, driving her down to the floor. She slammed against the cement, white lightning flashing through her head, black velvet creeping into the edges of her vision as she struggled to maintain consciousness.

The man on top of her moved, and her father's face filled her fading vision. For a moment she actually believed he'd been trying to protect her from the still-flying bullets, but then he reached for her fingers, prying them apart as he freed the microchip, a smile of satisfaction on his face.

She tried to follow as he walked away, but nausea swelled, and she dropped back to the floor, a tear rolling down her cheek as the whole world tilted and then went black.

"Alexis," Tucker called, cradling her head in his lap, his heart twisting with relief when his finger found her pulse. "Come on, sweetheart, wake up." Across from him, Nash was unloading a weapon while talking with Avery and Tyler. Simon and Harrison were helping his brother with the ropes still binding his feet, while Annie was checking bodies.

Business as usual.

Alexis stirred, her eyes flickering open, her muscles tightening for a fight.

"It's okay," Tucker said. "Just relax. It's all over."

Comprehension dawned, and she reached up to cup his face in her hand. "You're all right? Everyone's all right?"

"We're all good. Nothing hurt except maybe my vanity. I hadn't really counted on you having to rescue me. I'd kind of figured it'd be the other way around, you know?"

"It doesn't matter as long as we both came out the other side." She moved to sit up, and he helped by supporting her with his arm. "You need to move slowly," he cautioned. "You hit your head pretty hard."

She winced but managed to stay upright, still holding on to his arm. "My father?" she asked, her eyes searching the warehouse.

Tucker shook his head. "He's gone. I'm sorry." He hesitated, hating to have to tell her but knowing there was no sense in postponing the inevitable. "It was me, Alexis. I killed him. I was just so afraid he'd hurt you."

"Then we're even because I was afraid he'd hurt you," she said, her gaze locking with his. "And if he'd tried, I'd have..."

"Don't," he said, shaking his head. "Don't say it."

"But it doesn't matter, Tucker. I meant what I said earlier. That man wasn't my father." She leaned against him and he pulled her close, grateful just to feel her heart beating against his. "What happened to the chip?" she asked.

Tucker blew out a breath. "It's gone. In my effort to get to you and to deal with your father, I didn't see the guy taking the formula until it was too late. I suspect Avery will have my head, but I don't care. I'd do it all again. When you hit the ground and I couldn't get to you, I thought I'd die."

"But you did get here," she said, her smile warming him in places he'd thought forever frozen. "You always get here." She shrugged. "I wasn't worried."

He leaned down to kiss her, offering her his soul. "I love you," he murmured against her lips.

"I know," she whispered back, pulling away just enough so that she could see his eyes. "And just so you won't worry, that wasn't the formula. It was a copy of the latest nuclear proliferation treaty. Harrison thought it was apropos." She frowned, wincing with the motion. "I guess it did the job."

"And the real formula?" he asked, his breath mingling with hers.

"I destroyed it." She pulled him close again, her lips moving against his, her kiss full of promise and endless tomorrows. And, suddenly, everything was right with the world.

EPILOGUE

"Come on, Adam, keep your eyes on the ball," Nash yelled as his son swung at a pitch well below his knees.

"Nash, don't yell at him," Annie scolded. "He's nervous enough as it is."

"I was just cheering him on," Nash said, folding his arms over his chest and shooting his wife an indignant look. "That's what fathers do."

Drake slid an arm around Madeline, who was blissfully eating a bag of potato chips, her eyes on the field. "I can't wait."

"Don't even think about it," Tyler said, shaking her finger at her husband, Owen, who was looking longingly at Madeline's swelling belly.

Alexis laughed, reveling in the camaraderie. Avery sat on her right and Tucker on her left, the two of them still a little overprotective. As if they thought she might break.

It was in turns charming and annoying, especially with Tucker, who followed her everywhere these days. But it was also pretty damn wonderful.

She leaned against him, nestling her head on his shoulder as Harrison, who was sitting in front of her, tweeted the entire game to the rest of the team back at headquarters.

It was a gorgeous spring day, the sky so blue it looked more like a painting than reality. The field was green, the boys decked out in opposing colors, their excitement more about the event than the game itself.

"Come on, Adam," Alexis yelled as he struck at another ball, just managing to tip it.

"Count is one and two," Drake said, playing the role of announcer.

It had been a month since her father had been killed in the warehouse. Alain DuBois, the only link A-Tac had to the Consortium, was still missing. Which meant that although A-Tac had won this battle, the war was ongoing. But at least the direct threat to her had ended when the Consortium had realized the formula they'd stolen was a fake, and that, thanks to some strategically placed intel, the real deal had been destroyed.

There had been some fallout over her having destroyed the formula, certain key players no doubt wanting the power possessing it would have given them. But, in the end, Avery and the team had stood beside her and the brass had backed off, accepting that, even without acquiring the formula, they'd won the day. And Alexis had no doubt that the world was a safer place without a way to aerosolize biotoxins. Someone else would most likely come along and figure it out again, but for now she would celebrate the victory. And her new life—with Tucker.

They hadn't talked about where they'd go from here, content for the moment just to be alive and together. But, sooner or later, Alexis knew they had to decide on the kind of life they wanted for themselves, and someday for their family.

"So," Avery was saying to Tucker as the pitcher threw Adam another ball, "have you given any thought to staying here permanently? Working with A-Tac full time?"

Alexis suppressed a smile. Okay, maybe they'd be discussing it sooner rather than later.

"Avery, you know I can't make a decision about something like that without talking to Alexis. And you know how she feels about government entities."

"*Most* government entities," she qualified, still smiling. "I think I can safely say that A-Tac is an exception. And if working with you guys is what Tucker wants, then it's what I want too."

"Seriously?" Tucker asked as Adam took another ball.

"Full count," Drake announced.

"Yes," she said, reaching up to touch his cheek. "I love you. And this"—she waved at the surrounding company, and the field, and the campus beyond—"is where you belong. Which means I do too. Besides, Madeline and I have plans for the new house, and it'd be really hard for me to commute from California."

"You're an amazing woman, Alexis Markham," Tucker said. "And I can't wait to make you Alexis Flynn."

"You're making me legitimate," she said, looking down at her engagement ring. "I'll probably have to get a driver's license, and a social security card, and a voter's registration card...."

"One step at a time," Tucker suggested.

"Okay," she said, reaching up to kiss him as the bleachers erupted, Nash screaming "That's my boy!" as Adam hit the ball straight and true, right past the center-fielder and over the fence.

Tucker pulled Alexis to her feet, the two of them joining the furor as Adam rounded third base, heading home.

Home.

She smiled.

In finding true love, she'd also found home.

Passions run high as a vicious
killer leads new partners Hannah
Marshall and Harrison
Blake in a...

DEADLY DANCE

Please turn this page for
a preview.

PROLOGUE

Sunderland College, New York

Sara Lauter looked up from the textbook she'd been reading. The English Industrial Revolution just wasn't holding her attention. Too many other things on her mind. She stretched and looked around the edge of her study carrel. The library was almost empty. Frowning, she checked her watch, surprised to see that it was so late. Almost midnight. The library would be closing in another couple of hours.

With a sigh she closed the book and gathered her things. She had an early class tomorrow and Professor Brennon wasn't one to tolerate tardiness. Not that Sara had any intention of being late. She'd just have to set an extra alarm. Her roommate was going to love her.

"Hey, babe? You ready to go?" she asked, smiling over at her boyfriend, Anthony Marcuso. He'd been buried in a midterm paper on Keynesian economics. Everyone said the new econ prof was a major hard-ass. And if this paper was evidence, Sara was inclined to believe it. Tony was spending every spare moment on the thing.

"I can't." He shook his head, his gaze apologetic. "I've still got three sources to verify. And I'm having trouble with the Internet in the dorm. So I'm afraid I'm here for the duration. Paper's due at three tomorrow."

"All right." Sara nodded, reaching out to squeeze his hand. "I won't waste any more time talking. But I'm beat and I've got an early class, so I'm heading out. Meet you for breakfast?"

"Definitely," he said. "And this weekend, we'll celebrate." He smiled up at her and, as usual, her heart melted. They hadn't been dating all that long, but somehow she knew this was different. Something worth hanging on to. "I'll call you."

"You can't, remember?" She'd lost her cell phone. Left it God knows where, and she hadn't had the chance to replace it yet. "How about we just meet in front of the cafeteria at eight?"

"Perfect," he said, his concentration still on his paper as she bent to drop a kiss on his tousled head and then swung her book bag over her shoulder.

"All right, then. I'll see you tomorrow."

She waved at a couple of friends as she headed upstairs to the library's entrance. Built into the side of a hill, most of the building was underground. Which was nice when it came to avoiding distractions. And also the terraced area outside the front doors was a favorite student hangout, with grass-covered hills on both sides making the perfect place to sit and watch passersby.

She and her friends had actually sledded down the taller hill once her freshman year, using lunch trays. The risk of wipe-out had been enormous, but with the right amount of dexterity it was possible to make it all the way from the chemistry building to the front doors of the library. It was a great memory.

Outside the night was crisp, the last remnants of autumn making her think of cider and pumpkins and flag football. Their dorm was currently in second place in the intercampus league. Not that anyone took it that seriously. She pulled her coat closer as she started up the stairs leading to the quad. Passing the Aaron Thomas Academic Center, she noted a light on in an upper-floor window, a professor or grad student working late, no doubt. Most students didn't have after-hours access.

Other than that, the campus was pretty deserted this time of night. Not that she minded. It was kind of nice to be alone with her thoughts. Although she wouldn't have minded if Tony had been along. She passed the Student Center, darkened like the rest of the buildings, and smiled as she thought about their first kiss. Right there under the hanging oak, so called because legend had it that some revolutionary figure or other had been executed there. But also because the arching branches were the perfect cover for a stolen kiss.

Despite the fact that most of the buildings were closed, the campus was still bathed in soft light, the fixtures mounted high in the trees. So the squirrels could study at night, was the standing joke, primarily an insult from the state school across town. But Sara had always found it funny.

She frowned as she passed the cafeteria. The central hub of campus, it always looked sort of sad at night. Beyond that she could just make out the gym. And the philosophy and religion building. The smallest on campus, it was also the best place for a seminar—intimate little rooms with gorgeous views looking across the intermural fields into the woods that surrounded the campus.

Behind her the bushes rattled, and despite the fact that she had made this trek almost every night since coming to Sunderland, she sped up the pace, suddenly fighting the feeling that someone was following her. She glanced over her shoulder, then sped up even more, her gaze moving automatically to the nearest blue light.

The security station was at the far end of the cafeteria building, the opposite direction from her dorm, but she knew there was another one at the edge of Regan Hall. And, besides, she was being silly. Nothing ever happened at Sunderland. It was one of the safest campuses in the state. Her mind was just playing tricks on her. As if to support the idea, the wind gusted, leaves swirling. She smiled to herself, turning the corner, the lights of Varsley Hall just ahead. There were three women's dorms: Varsley, Regan, and Gallant. It was kind of old-fashioned these days to have single-sex housing, but Sara had always liked it.

Besides, there were always ways of getting around the problem if the need arose. Again she smiled, her thoughts turning to Tony, and the endless possibilities their relationship presented. She'd even phoned her mother to tell her that she might have met "the one." A conversation that hadn't gone particularly well, her mother being convinced that marriage before thirty would be a mistake.

Anyway, Sara wasn't interested in marriage—but she was interested in Tony.

The sound of footsteps broke through her reverie, nervous energy pushing her to move even faster. It was probably just another student, but it was always best to be careful. Off to her left, she could see the shadowy outline of Regan and the faint glow of the blue light. Maybe a hundred feet.

She shot a glance behind her but there was no one there, the empty sidewalk only serving to ratchet up her worry. Still, there was no point in panicking. She tightened her hold on the book bag, thinking that as weapons went, it probably wasn't lethal, but her bio-chem book was at least three inches thick.

She reached into her pocket for her keys, wishing she'd not put off replacing the damn phone, but she hadn't wanted to tell her father. He sort of went ballistic when she lost things. Which, unfortunately, happened a lot. Anyway, she'd definitely take care of it tomorrow, first thing. The night had grown eerily quiet, but she was only a short distance from the back porch of Varsley now. Two minutes and she'd be safely inside.

She pulled out her keys, relaxing a little, and then something hit her. Hard. The keys went flying and a man's arm clamped around her shoulders, his gloved hand covering her mouth as she opened it to scream. Twisting and kicking, she tried to pull free, but he was strong, and a sickly sweet odor filled her nostrils, making her feel woozy.

Chloroform.

Panic crested, along with adrenaline, and she rammed her elbow into the side of her attacker, but he was too strong, and the drug was taking effect. She tried to hold her breath, but even that was too much effort. She felt her strength ebbing as her vision started to cloud, and her last thought was that she wished she'd told Tony she loved him.

CHAPTER 1

Northern Lake Champlain, Quebec

The scene seemed overly bright, despite the fact that it was nearly three in the morning. Local police cars were lined up in the rutted lane that fronted the old building, lights flashing a garish red. Harrison Blake killed the engine and was out of the car almost before it stopped, heart pounding as he made his way past the requisite crime-scene tape, a halfhearted effort to contain access to the site. In truth, there was nothing to contain. The out-of-the-way house was surrounded by the twisted cedars and rocky inclines that marked the Texas Hill Country.

He flashed his FBI badge at a uniform standing guard on the front walk, then stopped on the weather-beaten porch as his partner, Madison, emerged from inside. With an unbidden intake of breath, he waited.

"It's her," Madison said, her eyes dark with emotion.

"Is she..."

"Yeah. ME says maybe as long as twelve hours. They'll know more when they get the body back to the lab."

His stomach threatened revolt, but he started forward anyway, determined to get to her. It made no sense. He'd arrived too late to be of any help. Hell, even with all his training, all his connections, he hadn't been able to make the difference. He hadn't been able to find her in time. But he still needed to see her, if for no other reason than to prove that this was real.

Brianna was dead.

"No," Madison whispered, her hand on his arm preventing forward motion. "You don't want to go in there. You don't want your last memory to be…" She swallowed, a shudder rippling across her frame.

"She's my sister, Madison. I don't have a choice." He shook off her hand and stepped inside the little house. The living room looked almost quaint, but he ignored the homespun comfort and headed down the hall to the room in the back where the forensic techs were hard at work, their bright lights cutting across the shadowed hallway with a garish glow.

The harsh, metallic smell of blood filled the room. And even though the odor wasn't something new, it still made his skin crawl and his gut clench. There were blood stains on the bed, the spatter on the wall behind the headboard looking like some kind of macabre painting. A piece of rope had fallen to the floor, the hemp also stained with blood. But despite the signs of violence, there was no body.

"Where is she?" Harrison asked, his voice sounding harsh against the forced hush within the room.

Tracy Braxton, the ME, blinked once, her chocolate eyes taking a moment to focus as she pulled herself from her train of thought. "She's downstairs. In the basement.

But you don't want to go down there, Harrison." Like Madison, she was trying to protect him. He knew that. Knew also that she was probably right. But he didn't have a choice. Bree was a part of him. And he was supposed to have protected her.

Exactly two minutes older, he'd always been quick to remind people that he was the eldest sibling. But in truth, Bree had been the wise one, the calming influence that tamed his wilder instincts. He'd been the one who'd walked the razor's edge. And she'd always been there, waiting until he'd needed her to rescue him—mostly from himself.

And now, the one time she'd truly needed him...

With an apologetic shrug to Tracy, he turned and made his way back down the hallway to the cellar door. In his haste he'd missed it the first time—the faint light from below barely visible at the top of the stairs.

Like the bedroom, the first thing that hit him was the smell. And he stopped for a moment, reaching inside for strength. Then with a slow exhale he made his way to the bottom of the stairs, nodding at a uniform and again flashing his badge, before making his way to the back of the brick-lined room.

It was cold. Colder than he'd have thought, considering it was spring. Like a grave. He pushed aside the thought and turned the corner, walking into the little alcove that marked the center of activity, his mind revolting at the sight before him. She was naked, strung up by the arms, her position reminiscent of ancient crucifixion. The disrespect was evident not just in the horrific way she'd been left to die, but in the carvings on her skin. Each cut, surgically precise, was accentuated with a trail of dried blood, the garish result making her look more like a battered doll than than a human being.

His sister. Bree.

White-hot rage ripped through him, the pain doubled by the feeling of impotence. Nothing he'd done had mattered. He hadn't been fast enough. And now the bastard behind this—this carnage—was out there somewhere, waiting to do it all over again.

He reached up to touch her face, mindless of the tech trying to shoo him away, praying that somehow he'd wake up and find it all a dream. His fingers touched the cold flesh of her cheek and her eyes fluttered open, the condemnation there shattering his heart.

"Why didn't you come?" she asked, her brownish green eyes the exact mirror of his, the anguish reflected there sucking the breath from his body.

He opened his mouth but there were no words, and still she held his gaze, imploring him, condemning him. "I believed in you," she whispered, and then slowly the life began to fade. He screamed her name, trying to pull her back to him. To will her to life.

And then it hit him. As it had a thousand times before. This was a dream. Bree was dead and gone. He hadn't saved her then, and he couldn't save her now.

Drenched with sweat, he jerked awake, the first rays of sunlight slanting through the hotel-room window. He sat up, head in hands, still fighting the last remnants of the dream—the sensory memory as strong now as it had been all those years ago in Texas.

He frowned, trying to find logic where apparently there was none. At first the dream had been an almost nightly occurrence, the horror still so fresh that his mind

had needed the outlet. But with time the edges had softened, the dream coming less frequently, less violently.

And now its appearance usually signaled something
else wrong with his life, a ghoulish message from his sub-
conscious. But things were good. A-Tac was the right fit.
And he was happy. There was nothing in his life that should
have called forth the horror from all those years ago.

He pushed back his hair, fighting a wave of uncertainty.

If everything was so fucking great, why the hell was
he having the dream?

THE DISH

Where authors give you the inside scoop!

From the desk of Christie Craig

Dear Reader,

As an author of seven humorous suspense romance novels, I'm often asked how I come up with my characters. Since the truth isn't all that fun to describe—that I find these people in the cobwebs of my mind—I usually just tell folks that I post a want ad on Craigslist.

One of those folks replied that she'd be checking out my ad and applying for the position of romance heroine. Right then I wondered if she'd ever read a Christie Craig book. Well, it's not just my books—every good story is really a triumph over tragedy. (Of course, I have my own lighter spin of tragedy.) And by the ending of my books, my heroines have found a man who's smoking hot and deserving of their affection, and they've experienced a triumph that's sweeter than warm fudge. Friendships have been forged, and even the craziest of families have grown a whole lot closer. And I do love crazy families. Probably because I have one of my own. Hmm, maybe I get some of my characters from there, too.

Point is, my heroines had to earn their Happily Ever After. The job requires a lot of spunk.

Take poor Nikki Hunt in DON'T MESS WITH TEXAS, the first book in my Hotter in Texas series, for example. Her cheating ex ditches her at dinner and sticks her with the bill. She then finds his dead body stuffed in the trunk of her car, which makes her lose her two-hundred-dollar meal all over his three-thousand-dollar suit. Now, not only is Nikki nearly broke, she's been poisoned, she's barfing in public (now, *that's* a tragedy), and, worse still, she's a murder suspect. And that's only the first chapter. Nikki's fun is just beginning. You've hardly met Nikki's grandma, who epitomizes those family members who drive you bonkers, even though you know your life would be empty without them.

As we say in the south, Nikki's got a hard row to hoe. For certain, it takes a kick-ass woman to be a Christie Craig heroine. She's gotta be able to laugh, because sometimes that's all you can do. She's gotta be able to fight, because life is about battles. (I don't care if it's with an ex-husband, a plumber, or a new puppy unwilling to house-train.) And she's gotta be able to love, because honestly, love is really what my novels are about. Well, that and overcoming flaws, jumping over hurdles, and finding the occasional dead body.

So while in real life you may never want to undergo the misadventures of a Christie Craig heroine, I'm counting on the fact that you'll laugh with her, root for her, and fall in love alongside her. And here's hoping that when you close my book, you are happy you've met the characters who live in the cobwebs of my mind.

And remember my motto for life: Laugh, love, read.

Christie Craig

www.christie-craig.com

♥ ♥ ♥ ♥ ♥ ♥ ♥ ♥ ♥ ♥ ♥ ♥ ♥ ♥ ♥

From the desk of Isobel Carr

Dear Reader,

I've always loved the "Oh no, I'm in love with my best friend's sister!" trope. It doesn't matter what the genre or setting is, we all know sisters are forbidden fruit. This scenario is just so full of pitfalls and angst and opportunities for brothers to be protective and for men to have to really, really prove (and not just to the girl) that they love the girl. How can you not adore it?

Add in the complications of a younger son's lot in life—lack of social standing, lack of fortune, lack of prospects—and you've got quite the series of hurdles to overcome before the couple can attain their Happily Ever After (especially if the girl he loves is the daughter of a duke).

If you read the first book in the League of Second Sons series, you've already met the sister in question, Lady Boudicea "Beau" Vaughn. She's a bit of a tomboy and always seems to be on the verge of causing a scandal, but she means well, and she's got a fierce heart.

You will have also met the best friend, Gareth Sandison. He's a committed bachelor, unquestionably a rake, and he's about to have everything he's ever wanted—but knew he could never have—dangled in front of him... but he's going to have to risk friendship and honor to get it. And even then, things may not work out quite as he expected.

I hope you'll enjoy letting Gareth show you what it means to be RIPE FOR SCANDAL.

Isobel Carr

www.isobelcarr.com

♥ ♥ ♥ ♥ ♥ ♥ ♥ ♥ ♥ ♥ ♥ ♥ ♥ ♥ ♥ ♥

From the desk of Hope Ramsay

Dear Reader,

In late 2010, while I was writing HOME AT LAST CHANCE, something magical happened that changed the direction of the story.

A friend sent me an email with a missing pet poster attached. This particular poster had a banner headline that read "Missing Unicorn," over a black-and-white photograph of the most beautiful unicorn I have ever seen. The flyer said that the lost unicorn had last been seen entering Central Park and provided a 1-800 number for tips that would lead to the lost unicorn's safe return.

The unicorn poster made me smile.

A few days later, my friend sent me a news story about how hundreds of people in New York had seen this poster and had started calling in reports of unicorn sightings. Eventually, the unicorn sightings spread from Manhattan all the way to places in Australia and Europe.

At that point, the missing unicorn captured my imagination.

The worldwide unicorn sightings proved that if people take a moment to look hard, with an innocent heart, they can see unicorns and angels and a million miracles all around them. As we grow up, we forget how to look. We get caught up in the hustle and bustle of daily living, and unicorns become myths. But for a small time, in New York City, a bunch of "Missing Unicorn" posters made people stop, smile, and see miracles.

The missing unicorn and his message wormed its way right into my story and substantially changed the way I wrote the character of Hettie Marshall, Last Chance's Queen Bee. Sarah Murray, my heroine, tells Hettie to look at Golfing for God through the eyes of a child. When Hettie heeds this advice, she realizes that she's lost something important in her life. Her sudden desire to recapture a simple faith becomes a powerful agent of change for her and, ultimately, for Last Chance itself. And of course, little Haley Rhodes helps to seal the deal. Haley is a master at seeing what the adult world misses altogether.

I hope you keep your ability to wonder at the world around you—to see it like a child does. You might find a missing unicorn—or maybe a Sorrowful Angel.

Hope Ramsay

❤ ❤ ❤ ❤ ❤ ❤ ❤ ❤ ❤ ❤ ❤ ❤ ❤ ❤ ❤

From the desk of Dee Davis

Dear Reader,

Settings are a critical part of every book. They help establish the tone, give insight into characters, and act as the backdrop for the narrative that drives the story forward. Who can forget the first line of *Rebecca*—"Last night I dreamt I went to Manderley again." The brooding house in the middle of the English moors sets us up from the very beginning for the psychological drama that is the center of the book.

When I first conceptualize a novel, I often start with the settings. Where exactly will my characters feel most at home? What places evoke the rhythm and pacing of the book? Because my books tend to involve a lot of adventure, the settings often change with the flow of the story. And when it came time to find the settings for DEEP DISCLOSURE, I knew without a doubt that Alexis would be living in New Orleans.

One of my favorite cities, I love the quirky eccentricities of the Big Easy, and I wanted to share some of my favorites with readers, including the Garden District and the French Quarter. Of course, Alexis and Tucker don't stay in New Orleans long, and it isn't surprising that they wind up in Colorado.

We moved a lot when I was a kid, and one of the few stable things in my life was spending summers in Creede. But because I've used Creede already in so many books, I decided this time to use the neighboring town of South Fork as the place where George has his summer retreat. And Walsenburg—one of the places we often stopped for groceries on the way to Creede—as the scene of Alexis's family's disaster.

I confess that Redlands, Tucker and Drake's home, is a place I've never actually visited. But a dear friend lived there for several years and tells such wonderful stories about it that it seemed the perfect place for my boys to have grown up and developed their love of baseball.

And of course Sunderland College, while fictional, is indeed based on a real place: Hendrix College, my alma mater. I spent a wonderful four years there, and I hope you enjoy your time at Sunderland with A-Tac as much!

For insight into both Alexis and Tucker, here are some songs I listened to while writing DEEP DISCLOSURE:

The Kill, by Thirty Seconds to Mars
Breathe (2 am), by Anna Nalick
Need You Now, by Lady Antebellum

And as always, check out deedavis.com for more inside info about my writing and my books.

Happy Reading!

Trust is the ultimate weapon

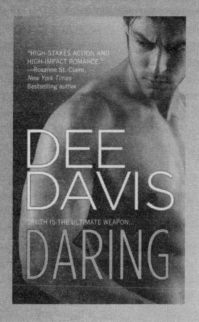

"HIGH-STAKES ACTION AND
HIGH-IMPACT ROMANCE."
—Roxanne St. Claire,
New York Times
Bestselling author

DEE
DAVIS

TRUTH IS THE ULTIMATE WEAPON...

DARING

Lara thought working a world away would heal
her. Yet volunteering to treat the sick and injured
in revolution-torn central Africa can't stop the
shattering memories of losing the man she loved.
A night with sexy security officer Rafe Winters
seems the perfect temporary escape until
insurgents attack her clinic and Rafe becomes
her only way to survive . . .

A novella available wherever ebooks are sold

Find out more about Forever Romance!

Visit us at
www.hachettebookgroup.com/publishing_forever.aspx

Find us on Facebook
http://www.facebook.com/ForeverRomance

Follow us on Twitter
http://twitter.com/ForeverRomance

NEW AND UPCOMING TITLES

Each month we feature our new titles
and reader favorites.

CONTESTS AND GIVEAWAYS

We give away galleys, autographed copies,
and all kinds of exclusive items.

AUTHOR INFO

You'll find bios, articles, and links to personal websites
for all your favorite authors—and so much more.

GET SOCIAL

Connect with your favorite authors, editors, and
other Forever fans, and share what's important to you.

THE BUZZ

Sign up
and be the first to read all about it.